The Realists

The Realists

EIGHT PORTRAITS BY
C. P. SNOW

✗ ✗ ✗ ✗ ✗ ✗ ✗ ✗ ✗

STENDHAL

BALZAC

DICKENS

DOSTOEVSKY

TOLSTOY

GALDÓS

HENRY JAMES

PROUST

✗ ✗ ✗ ✗ ✗ ✗ ✗ ✗ ✗

New York

CHARLES SCRIBNER'S SONS

Copyright © 1978 C. P. Snow

Library of Congress Cataloging in Publication Data

Snow, Charles Percy, Baron Snow, 1905-
   The realists.

     CONTENTS: Stendhal.—Balzac.—Dickens. [etc.]
     1. Fiction—19th century—History and criticism.
    2. Fiction—20th century—History and criticism.
    3. Realism in literature.   I. Title.
    PN3499.S6   809.3'83   78-14921
    ISBN 0-684-15872-8

1 3 5 7 9 11 13 15 17 19 V/C 20 18 16 14 12 10 8 6 4 2

PRINTED IN THE UNITED STATES OF AMERICA

TO MY BROTHER
PHILIP

CONTENTS

PREFACE

WHAT do we read novels for? One answer is supremely simple. For various kinds of pleasure; and this is true however sophisticated we like to think ourselves. Most of us want a kind of pleasure that human beings have enjoyed since they began to talk. We like to hear a story, and to be eager about what is going to happen next. To keep us eager in that fashion is an element in the greatest novels.

It scarcely needs saying nowadays, but we have seen attempts to throw this element overboard, and to regard novels, and to compose novels, as verbal puzzles to be worked out by persons cleverer than the original writers. Similar processes have happened before in literary history, and have always meant a period of decline, not only in the art itself, but also in the society from which it derives. If novels get too far from their primal impulse, then we can say good-bye to them, except as a private game. One can see the hunger for novels set in motion by the primal impulse in the public that rushes for, say, the books of John Fowles or John Le Carré.

Still, though the story element is necessary, it is not sufficient, at least when we are reading at the time our needs are freshest. Which for most of us is when we are fairly young and eager to pick up experience anywhere. Much experience we can learn only at first hand, but from the wisest art we can learn also. There are plenty of other rewards from art, but this is one: we discover something about other people and ourselves.

Some are too impatient, and sometimes too conceited, to give themselves to any such discovery. For these persons, art is too long—a psychological statement can be written on a postcard—one knows it all. Well, none of us understands much, but anyone as complacent as that isn't going to understand anything whatever. Our own natures, other people's natures, the societies in which those natures have their existence require all the humility we possess, as well as our small scraps of observation and experience, before we can hope to understand even a little. It is there that the greatest realistic novels can teach us. This book tries to say something about those novels, and those who wrote them, as some sort of primitive guide.

Anyone who reads it will find that I am suspicious of categories. The bold categories that attempt to define novels as "realist," "naturalist," "symbolist" are certainly oversimple, and can be deceptive. Most, though not quite all, of the great novels do not fit neatly into these compartments. In particular, the distinction between realism and naturalism has been argued about inconclusively for a hundred years. As a rule, it is sensible not to worry too much about definitions, but to proceed by what in England is called case law. That is, most people would agree that the writers discussed in this book—with one partial exception—produced realistic novels, as contrasted to the naturalistic work of, say, Zola, Arnold Bennett, James T. Farrell.

In the great realistic novels, there is a presiding, unconcealed, interpreting intelligence. They are all of them concerned with the actual social setting in which their personages exist. The concrete world, the world of physical fact, the shapes of society are essential to the art. The people have to be not only projected, as novelists, major and minor, have tried to project them, but also examined with the writer's psychological resources and with cognitive intelligence. Both those components are features of realism. It is interesting, and sometimes significant, to see how often intuitive wisdom and cognitive thought have converged, and have anticipated later discoveries brought about by more strictly rational processes. That needs some thorough exploration; one would like to see it done.

It is in those aspects—there are others, but these are the ones where controversy doesn't really enter—that the realistic novels have so much to teach anyone willing to learn. As for society, in the text (page 66) I have called in aid testimony to the value of Balzac's works. Engels wasn't the softest of touches, and wasn't naturally well disposed to a reactionary Catholic, such as Balzac was. Nevertheless, Engels said that Balzac told us more of the nature of French society in his time than all the sociologists, political thinkers, historical writers in the world. The same could be said of other realists as they dealt with their time and place—above all, perhaps, of Galdós, who was beyond compare in dealing with the society of nineteenth-century Spain.

Most of all, in these novels the lessons about individual human beings are some of the deepest, and the most complete, ever written. Owing to various trends in twentieth-century literature and thought, many of the realist's discoveries still haven't been accepted into the general consensus. All of them said things of startling originality. Some of those statements haven't proved valid; but a good many now seem incontestably true. In the midst of his fugues of psychological imagining, Dostoevsky shot out insights about multiple motives and hidden purposes that no one had thought of before or has been able to challenge since. Much earlier, Stendhal, with absolute lucidity, made findings about the intermittences of emotion, and about his famous "crystallizations," that should be part of anyone's psychological equipment.

About the choice of these eight writers. From the beginning I was clear about seven, but hesitated over Dickens. He is one of the greatest of English geniuses, but he is only realistic occasionally and, as it were, by courtesy. Still, with a little sleight of hand, one can bring some of his best work within the confines. He is obviously not a realist in the sense that Trollope, Jane Austen, George Eliot were. I have written a little about Trollope, and should like to do the same with the other two. But, against my own inclination, I can't pretend that any of them is of the same stature as the greatest realistic masters. Dickens is; and so, with a touch of chauvinism, I had to include him.

With at least six of my eight, their lives were as picturesque, complicated, and instructive as their work, and I wanted to write about those also. As the coolest-headed of them said himself, briskly dismissing the opinion of outsiders (meaning those who were not creative), a writer's life is not just connected with his work; it cannot be separated from it. I believe that to be utterly true. I have also to confess that I should in any case have enjoyed writing about those lives.

I have discussed all but one of my eight realists with friends, colleagues, acquaintances, since I was young. The number of people to whom I am indebted is so large that I can't write down the roll call of names here. But one I must mention. During a long friendship, I have had the privilege of talking to Jacques Barzun about many things, among them, and very often, novels and novelists. We have not always agreed, but these talks have been a part of my education. To give me even more reason for gratitude, Jacques Barzun has read through the first draft of this book with the scrupulous attention of which he is a master. He is not responsible for any of my opinions or mistakes; but he is responsible for the book being better than it otherwise would have been.

The same applies to two friends who have given me the most generous help about Galdós. I came to him, unlike all the others in the book, late in life. As soon as I read him, I had no doubt that he was one of the major realistic novelists. But I was very ignorant about him apart from the texts I was reading. Then I had the good fortune to get in touch with David Ley, now the London editor of the *Revista de Occidente* and for years the cultural attaché at the British embassy in Madrid. Through him I met Pedro Ortíz Armengol, at present minister-counsellor at the Spanish embassy in London, a devoted Galdós scholar who has remarkable knowledge, not only of Galdós's work, but of the history and geography of Galdós's life, including the streets he walked in nineteenth-century Madrid. Señor Ortíz is engaged himself in preparing a new edition of *Fortunata y Jacinta* and writing an introduction to that great work. Both of these friends have provided me with their own material, published and unpublished, answered questions, corrected blunders of fact and interpretation, and discussed matters of judgment. It was an unusual piece of luck to have come to know them, and I am more grateful than I can easily say.

December 1977   C. P. Snow

The Realists

STENDHAL

S TENDHAL was one of the most singular of men and
one of the most singular of writers. From his boyhood he set himself to acquire what he called a
knowledge of the human heart. In his own fashion he did
so, and made discoveries that were quite original. These
discoveries can still surprise us and teach us today.

By his knowledge of the human heart he didn't mean
the total comprehension that was the gift, as it were by
nature and not by conscious searching, of greater novelists
than himself or of his idol Shakespeare. He meant a knowledge of his own emotional states, above all of his emotional
vicissitudes in love, which he studied as coolly and clinically as any man has ever done. In that, as in many other
ways, he was much closer to egocentric writers of the
twentieth century than to his own contemporaries. For
better and for worse, he often speaks to us in the tone of a
modern Western man. You can meet him today at literary
parties in New York or London, aggressive, abrasive, amusing, rancorous because the great commercial break hasn't
yet come. It never came in his own lifetime. He had a

stronger will and more energy than is common among twentieth-century writers, but he was as ruthless, as much on his own, and as permanently young.

That last word may sound baffling. But somehow into late middle age Stendhal preserved a young man's hopes, restlessness, discontent, romantic dreams, isolation. In the company of other men of the same age he can't have seemed quite grown-up. Perhaps that is why he can have a special fascination or poignancy for young readers. The proper age to begin reading Stendhal is about twenty. You may, if you have already tasted Dostoevsky and Tolstoy, realize that Stendhal isn't of the same magnitude; but there is a good chance that you will identify yourself, according to sex, with Julien Sorel or Mathilde, and that in consequence he will have a claim on you always.

He was born in Grenoble in 1783. The date is significant. He was six when the French Revolution started, ten when Louis XVI was guillotined (an act of which in the midst of a stiff conventional royalist family he enthusiastically approved). He lived through the Consulate, Napoleon's military coup, the Empire. He was an official in the Imperial administration, got to Moscow with the army, took part in the retreat. He survived the Restoration, and finally got another official job in the reign of Louis Philippe.

All through his life, it was a time of constant change. For men like Stendhal there were periods of danger. It was also a time of opportunity. Under the Empire, very young men got dramatic promotion. This happened to relatives of his. We think that we have lived in a period of maximum instability, and that our nineteenth-century ancestors were luckier. That may have been true in America and England, but it wasn't true in France. Most of us, even in war, have lived a sheltered existence compared with Stendhal. Very few of us have been so much under the eye of intelligence services of a good many different countries. The police state is not a new invention, and the reports on Stendhal were often remarkably well informed.

His family came from the professional middle class. His father was a lawyer who attempted to increase a respectable fortune by speculating in land. Like so many of the early nineteenth-century bourgeoisie, he didn't understand money at all, and lost most of his. When he died, Stendhal, who had expected a comfortable income, received a pittance. Stendhal detested all of this—his origins, his father's incompetence, his father's obstinacy, his father himself, usually referred to in correspondence as "the Bastard." Stendhal detested being a bourgeois, a provincial, not well off (though he was never really poor). He wasn't overfond of his real name, which was Beyle. In due course he thought it could be improved by an insertion of a *de* to which he wasn't entitled. He also gave himself a whole collection of pseudonyms, partly for reasons of discretion but more because he wasn't satisfied to be plain Henri Beyle of Grenoble.

It is usually a fair guess that people who play about with their names would wish to have been born in more romantic and loftier circumstances. Henri Beyle would have liked to be an Italian aristocrat. In fact, he wished to have inscribed on his tomb "Arrigo Beyle, Milanese." Stendhal, though the best known of his disguises, is only one of them. It was taken from a German village that he passed through on one of his missions as an Imperial official. He happened to get the name of the village wrong. It is actually *Stendal,* without an *h.* But Stendhal, in spite of an intellect of beautiful lucidity, was a very bad linguist. He was devoted to English literature, and proudly scattered English phrases all through his diary. They are usually endearingly funny. He spent much of his life in Italy, and never spoke the language well.

Through all those early miseries about his family, his provincial awkwardness, his hatred of the Bastard, he was persevering with his researches into the human heart (he wrote in the language of his time, of course, and used words like *heart, soul, spirit,* where we should prefer others; it seems better not to tamper with his own). He kept a diary from the age of eighteen to thirty with regular analyses of his findings. For anyone unfamiliar with Stendhal this diary is a good start, if only to dip into and sample. It is supremely egocentric, as he was to remain all his life. It is also supremely honest. Here is a fairly typical example, written when he was no longer a boy. As so often, he had conceived a romantic infatuation for a woman utterly unattainable (and whom, since she was the wife of his only powerful patron, it would have been disastrous to attain). As so often, he had totally misjudged both her character and her feelings or, rather, absence of feelings, for him.

June 3rd, 1811. As I approached the Château, my heart beat with timidity.

I was greeted with eagerness, gaiety, and a shade of tenderness. . . .

As for myself, I had planned to say that I was in love. I reproached myself nightly for not having put my plan into execution, but it was decided that I should stay until Sunday. That gave my timidity a little respite. . . . This period was a happy isle for me. I was debonair, and then [she] was infinitely so with me.

On 31 May I wrote the following: The army I was commanding [that is, Stendhal himself] was full of terror and looked on the undertaking as beyond my capacity. That is what I told myself with rage on 30 May as I walked in the Park alone at a quarter past eleven after everyone else had retired. Heavy clouds were passing before the moon; I contemplated their flight and I thought of the tender mythology of Ossian in order to take my mind off my dissatisfaction with myself. Five or six obvious reasons showed me the advantage and necessity of engaging in battle, but all my courage vanished at the sight of the enemy. Another step, and I'd have blown my brains out rather than tell a woman who possibly loved me that I love her. And I'm twenty-eight years old and I've seen the world, and I've got some character!

His search for self-knowledge was unsparing, but it wasn't disinterested. It didn't give him any of the empathy with the other human beings that came so naturally to other writers, such as—to leave out the most powerful for the moment—Chekhov or Trollope. In fact, Stendhal showed little insight and foresight about other human beings, especially women, all his life. He was a classical psychologist of his own intermittences, to use the Proustian term. He wasn't a psychologist in the sense of understanding others' makeup or having perception about their purposes and their fates. He hadn't any such kind of detached curiosity. His intense curiosity about himself was for his own benefit. It was to help him toward his life's supreme aim, which was—it sounds faintly absurd to us nowadays—the pursuit of happiness (*la chasse au bonheur*).

Remember, he was a child of the Enlightenment. His romantic imagination didn't need much encouragement, but it had been supercharged by Rousseau. In all his activities, it struggled against his clear, skeptical, debunking mind, and usually prevailed. He tried to use the resources of that mind, his irony, his sardonic cynicism, his ability to see people as even more ridiculous than they were, in order to suppress his spontaneity and his hopes. He didn't succeed for long, but this conflict gave some of the puzzling flavor of both his personality and his art.

The pursuit of happiness, he decided when he was an adolescent, even more awkward and obstinate than other adolescents, could be fulfilled only by three kinds of success. He needed success with women. He needed glory. He needed to realize his ambition.

There is nothing strange in all that. It would be interesting to know how many young men haven't longed for something of the same. It has often seemed specially urgent in the blank periods of youth when there seems no future. The trouble with Stendhal was that, more than most young men of force and talent, he hadn't much instinct about how to achieve such desirable ends.

Glory should have been the easiest. In the very long run, years after his death, it actually arrived. But he didn't know what his real gifts were. He didn't begin to write the novels on which his glory now depends until he was well over forty. In the meantime he made plenty of bosh shots. He was a great star at his Grenoble school, as his father recognized (actually his family were nothing like so unperceptive about him as he insisted on believing). He showed unusual mathematical insight. Languages apart, he probably had the best academic mind (in the technical sense) of any eminent novelist, except maybe George Eliot. His mathematical ability was fully realized, and he was duly sent to Paris, before he was seventeen, to compete for entrance into the École Polytechnique. This had just been started, but was already the channel for almost any kind of career in Napoleonic France.

Stendhal liked mathematics, but he didn't like the prospect of a disciplined career. He deceived his father, and didn't sit the entrance examination. He wanted a greater glory. Unfortunately he wanted the kind of literary glory that was least accessible to him. He thought he ought to become the successor to Molière. For years, when he was hanging about Paris and afterward when he was attached to the French armies, he attended assiduously any play that he could get into. With his fine analytical intelligence he made notes and constructed theories. All he wrote made sense. He was a good critic of any form of literature (not so of visual art and music).

That devotion to the stage, though it produced incidental rewards in the company of actresses, didn't help him to write plays. Most of what he saw, as he knew clearly enough, was trash. Even if he had had the gift, there was no one to learn from—nor would there have been in England. But he had no semblance of the gift. Of all the major writers who tried to write plays in the nineteenth century—Hugo, Lamartine, Byron, Shelley, Dickens, Browning, Tennyson, almost anyone you can think of, all tried, and all their plays are dead beyond resurrection—he was about the least fitted to become the successor to Molière. The others' plays were pretty dreadful, but his were worse. He wrote them in alexandrines, but regrettably had no ear for verse. He was the briskest of sarcastic conversationalists, but had no comic sense. He had a strong internal imagination, but little invention. Above all, he had no sense of what would work on the stage. That is a rare gift, and has no relation to any verbal literary talent.

So he didn't become the successor to Molière—nor to Shakespeare, whom he admired much more. Sporadically, in an amateur fashion he attempted other forms of literature. He had a robust confidence in his own powers, but couldn't decide what they really were. He certainly knew that he was a formidable man, and one who deserved glory. Yet he was modest about his literary ability all his life, and about his literary achievements when he had anything to show.

He made literary forays that wouldn't have got into print in the twentieth century—*History of Painting in Italy* (an odd farrago, much of it pinched), *Life of Rossini* (which infuriated musicians), *Rome, Naples, Florence* (which, so far as it is about anything, is about Milan and Bologna). But the early nineteenth century was a very small world for educated people. Everyone seemed to hear about anyone who put opinions on paper. Stendhal couldn't be prevented from putting his—anti-Bourbon, anti-Austria, anticlerical, anti most established things. So those works of muddled journalism, lit up by odd original flashes, had two results that a modern writer would obtain only by miraculous intervention. He became intensely suspect to authorities all over Europe; and he won the respect of some of the most illustrious writers alive, including Goethe and Byron. It was a subdued sort of glory, but it was the beginning.

At the age of thirty-six, shortly after his father's death, maddened at finding that the Bastard hadn't been able to leave him comfortably provided for, he had what he called his "day of genius." It struck him that he had been examining his states of love for so many years. He had made original discoveries. Why not write them down? Thus he wrote *De l'Amour,* the first part of which is the first real appearance of the authentic Stendhal. There is more to say about that astonishing work later on.

It would be a mistake to imagine that he had become any kind of professional writer. He didn't write the novels until years in the future, and even then the glory—as he sometimes dared to think—was destined for the next century. He was never a professional writer in the sense his greatest contemporaries were. At some periods, he had dreams of entirely different roads to glory. In the high days of the Empire, soldiering was the quickest and most glamorous of those roads. As a youth, Stendhal reflected that many men not much older than he was became generals. One or two became kings. What about having a triumphant military life?

Well, he did get a commission in a regiment of dragoons. At that time he had had a year's experience as a civilian quartermaster but no army training whatsoever. The Napoleonic armies weren't rigidly professional. He liked the uniform. He was tough and courageous. But he found the military existence boring and, among all the many things he hated, he hated boredom most. So, casually, not yet twenty-one, in the middle of the occupation of Italy, he resigned his commission, to the not unreasonable irritation of his father and patrons.

Glory for Stendhal was one aim. Ambition was quite another. As he used the terms, glory, though it might bring material rewards, was something that could justify a life. It wasn't prosaic—one wanted to leave some kind of memorial behind one. This is true of a good many creative men and it has its characteristic tone, both pathetic and admirable. "And I may dine at journey's end with Landor and with Donne." In his last years Stendhal thought his dinner would come very late, perhaps fifty years on, perhaps a hundred—that is, in the 1930s. He wasn't far wrong.

Side by side with the attempt at glory, and often suppressing it for long periods, Stendhal did have what he called ambition. This was really prosaic ambition, the commonplace climbing of a middle-rank official. He wanted a nice comfortable bourgeois income. He also wanted some of the perks and decorations of office. Through highly effective relatives (whom he despised) he rose to be an Inspecteur Générale du Mobilier de la Couronne, which was a moderately well-paid job. Such civilians were utility men when the Imperial army needed them. Hence his attachment, as a kind of commissariat organizer, in the invasion of Russia and the retreat. His devotion to any kind of official duty was, by modern standards, remarkably perfunctory. He took weeks off when he felt the need, which was very often. In the retreat from Moscow, though, he couldn't take time off; and there, clear-headed, brave, more efficient than most when he gave his mind to the job in hand, he distinguished himself. With ruthless energy he organized a supply depot at Smolensk, having rushed ahead of the relics of the Grande Armée. He played his part in getting them out of Russia.

This made him enthusiastic about cozy down-to-earth ambitions. He decided that he ought to become a prefect, which was a big step upward. He expected the Légion d'honneur. If his father would only testify that he had a sufficient income, he could see himself as an Imperial baron. It would be nice to have a title.

None of these cheerful middle-class aspirations was to be realized. Later he told Byron that he had known Napoleon intimately during the Russian campaign and had been highly esteemed. This is more than doubtful. Stendhal, who told the unqualified truth about his innermost failures, wasn't above adorning his successes in the external world.

Patronage from Napoleon apart, many officials in Stendhal's place and with his opportunities would have gone much farther. The fact was, he hadn't the equipment. He hadn't the application, certainly not the steady application. Though the general climate seems to have been slapdash, his superiors must have noticed that he was too slapdash by half. Much more important, he wasn't worldly enough.

That sounds bizarre, for someone who prided himself on how much he knew about the world. But his interest was always fractionated. He couldn't interest the whole of his nature in the world of busy men. He was either above that world or below it. He wasn't humble enough to live with other men, even for a shortish period, on their own terms. In fact, he turned his contempt for the gritty commonplaces of existence into an outlook on life that he loved to hear people call *le beylisme*. A *beyliste* must ignore pedestrian obligations, workaday duties, bread-and-butter experience, and live only for the heights of love's rapture, sensuous delight, aesthetic joy. *Beylisme* was, of course, the expression of his romantic dreams, though it was half-mocked by his classical and disgruntled mind. Often his cynicism and outbursts of sarcasm tell their own story. They were the protests of the unworldly. Worldly men don't talk or even think like that. To operate in the practical world you have to feel as others do, and take it on trust.

There is the same climate around the political passages in his novels. Look at the palace intrigues in *La Chartreuse de Parme*. They are sometimes entertaining, but they might have been written by an intelligent stranger—or by a Martian, drawing a diagram of what he observed, and then letting the drawing-pin slip. Mosca off duty has sparkling internal life, but Mosca as a politician is something constructed by an alien.

Ambition—he couldn't give much of his nature there. Glory—not his whole nature, or at least not for long. Women—that was where he came home, or thought he wanted to. There he could give his whole nature, and more than that. But once more, as in his role as a man of ambition, he really wasn't made to be a triumphant lover.

This time he didn't suffer from a lack of enthusiasm. Women lived in his imagination from his adolescence until he died. But he had what, in a less resolute character, would have been a major deficiency. He had a profound lack of confidence.

An acquaintance by the name of Destouches, writing shortly after Stendhal's death, was certain that this was entirely due to his unprepossessing appearance. He was short and soon grew fat. He looked common and bourgeois, thick-necked, and legs not long enough. He was just plain, not impressively ugly. He had no distinction, except for bright and intelligent eyes, and even those were too small.

All accounts report a not dissimilar physical impression. He was not a man who at first sight would draw much attention from women. Balzac, in the famous review in *La Revue parisienne,* one of the most generous tributes ever paid by one major writer to another, and the only significant public recognition Stendhal received in his own lifetime, transcended this first impression. Balzac, more than anyone of his time, and as much as anyone of any time, understood the interdependence of temperament and physique. Balzac would have dismissed the romantic thought that a major novelist should look like, say, Shelley or Aldous Huxley (which, by the way, Huxley pointed out himself). Balzac would have been the last person to be disconcerted by the Stratford bust.

He wrote about Stendhal:

> I had met Monsieur Beyle twice in society, in twelve years, until the moment when I met him in the Boulevard des Italiens, and took the liberty of congratulating him on *La Chartreuse de Parme.* On no occasion did his conversation belie the impression which I had formed of him from his works. . . . At first his physique—he is very stout—conflicts with the delicacy and elegance of his manner, but he triumphs over that at once . . . he has a fine forehead, bright and piercing eyes, a sardonic mouth; in fact, he has exactly the physiognomy of his talent.

In any case, many men have had greater physical handicaps than Stendhal and not doubted for an instant their charm for women. Stendhal did, much more deeply than worrying about his face (of course, he would have liked to be extravagantly handsome, and he had great faith in the compensatory effect of dressing with dandiacal brilliance, which didn't suit him at all). To an abnormal extent, in spite of his perfervid amorous imagination, he was sexually diffident. That looms out from the diary entry already quoted, written when he was getting on thirty and, in the crude sense, "experienced"—that is, he had had several mistresses, with one of whom he had lived on and off for some years. This was the amiable Mélanie: Stendhal says—it was one of his crass imaginative fugues—that he had always longed for a dark, slender, melancholy woman who was an actress. He goes on to say that he found one in Mélanie, but wasn't happy.

Much earlier, as one would expect, the diffidence was acute and it never left him. Right on into late middle age, he suffered from unrequited love, as in the great love of his life. It takes two to make an unrequited love. It can be an escape—maybe unacknowledged or denied—for one who shirks the final commitment.

As a very young man, only eighteen, Stendhal walked blindly into the first of his unrequited loves. He had arrived in Milan, in the earliest of his civilian attachments to the Napoleonic army (not yet Imperial). Almost before he had looked around, Milan became, and remained, his favorite spot on earth. That still seems strange. Milan in 1801 may have had its attractions, but to some they wouldn't have been so overwhelming. Stendhal claimed that he found in Italians the energy and will that he admired most of all human qualities. One wouldn't have imagined that some of the Napoleonic French were short of them. It seems that he admired Italians because they could choose and act as though they had no past and no future—or, as Stendhal's existential successors were to say, a century and a half later, they acted "in their freedom."

It also appears certain that, in Stendhal's heated imagination, Milan shimmered and glowed as a Venusberg. But not, alas, a Venusberg for him. It is hard not to be sorry for the young man. There he was, awkward, oafish, poor, unused to any sort of company, male or female, longing for love. We have to remember that he and his contemporaries used the word *love* much more freely than we do and often when we should say brusquely *sex*. He was a hanger-on of young French officers, who behaved like an invading army, most of them, it is reasonable to presume, not in the least sexually diffident. The Milanese women were forthcoming. There seem to have been a remarkable number of complaisant husbands around. Stendhal heard the talk of the young officers boasting of their conquests. He thought they were boorish, of course, and envied them. He couldn't rest supine. He promptly fell in love.

Her name was Gina Pietragua. She was the wife of a civil servant, and presided over a drawing room attended by hopeful men, most of them French. She was in her mid-twenties, and had considerable opulent attractions. In his wonderment at the first stupefaction of love (which later he was to define as a "crystallization," one of his most original and truest discoveries in emotional analysis), Stendhal endowed her with ultimate nobility of soul. As usual, his knowledge of his own state was exact. As usual, his perception of another person wasn't. She was actually an extremely superior tart.

He was much too timid to speak to her alone. He couldn't give her any indication of the storms of love whirling inside him. If she noticed him at all, it must have been as a bashful youth, not one of the dashing young officers, clearly not well off (which mattered a lot to Gina), lingering on the fringes of her court.

Any young man might have felt humiliated, but with Stendhal this was a wound. It was the signal for a succession of unrequited loves, some for girls he had scarcely spoken to, the last and most protracted, nearly twenty years after his disaster with Gina, for a woman who had no use for him whatever and treated him with paralyzing chill.

Not a good record, one might think, for someone whose strongest desire—so far as conscious statements mean anything—was to be a lover of women. He might have given it up as a bad job. But Stendhal was not a coward. In his own bizarre fashion, he was something of a moral hero. He applied to having successes with women the conscientiousness, almost the sense of duty, that he dispensed with so insouciantly as a public servant. He was not disposed to resignation. Even at nineteen, having struck no response from Gina, he made resolves and took active steps.

He made resolves. Some day he would return to Milan, prosperous, no longer negligible, and Gina would fall into his arms. Incredibly, this actually happened—though it didn't live up to romantic expectations, and she extracted largish sums of money. Another resolve: it was time he lost his virginity. The likelihood is that he went off with some of the young military to a brothel. With the bad luck of which he had had more than his share, he promptly contracted a venereal disease. It may have been syphilis. As with Disraeli, a rather more unlikely sufferer, the medical treatment of the time was hit-and-miss, and some consequences pestered him for years. That didn't deter him. After looking longingly at a very young girl, he turned to her mother as his first mistress.

There were to be several more. The nicest and most intelligent was attached to him in his forties. She understood him better than the others and may have been the only one who truly loved him. As well as this succession of mistresses, there were pickups during his travels.

This amorous history led some acquaintances, and Stendhalian students afterward, to believe that he was a man possessed by sensuality. Many indications, however, suggest otherwise. He had his share, probably a modest share, but one's guess would be that he was less sensual, not more, than most of the novelists in this book. He may have been a little unlucky in his sexual temperament. He was devoted to his mother, who died when he was seven. This didn't direct him toward males, few men less so (though there have been enthusiastic attempts to enlist him so on the strength of a solitary demonstration of his cheerful introspective honesty, when he sat next to a handsome young Russian officer at the Scala, and reported thinking that if he, Stendhal, had been a woman he would have followed the young man to the ends of the earth).

He certainly expected the impossible from life. He got bored very easily with sexual intimacy, which usually isn't a token of sensuality. He liked women, especially mistresses after he had left them, more in absence than in presence. He had nothing of Dostoevsky's late-found sexual realism, of which more later. He loved women the more they inspired him to solitary melancholy reveries. He never seriously contemplated marriage and wouldn't have been amused by the adage "What are a bachelor's occasional nights out, compared with a married man's three hundred and sixty-five a year spent in sin?"

When he had finally gone to bed with Gina, after all the years of romantic reveries about her, he left next morning for a two-month exploration of Italy, and during this thought how pleasant it would be to see her again.

None of this seems to have revealed a ravening appetite. Nor perhaps does his obsessive absorption in the delicacies of the amorous emotions. Emotions, not sensations. Of course, he was no prude, but we know surprisingly little of his sexual pleasures. We do know, from a chapter in the second part of *De l'Amour* and from his first novel *Armance*, that he knew all about fits of impotence.

It is easy to rush to more foolish conclusions, as some have done. Stendhal was far from impotent. He may not have been especially sensual or as rooted in the "insect life" as the Karamazovs were, but he enjoyed himself heartily enough. If anyone ever doubted that, the evidence is incontrovertible. On the other hand, in the transports of one of his romantic passions, he did expect more of love—of the rapture of the first night of love—than love could possibly give. That wasn't a safe state for an imaginative, anxious, highly sensitive man.

It is also not unlikely that deep down he had once doubted not only his charm for women, but also his own powers. The shadow of that doubt could have lingered long after he had proved the contrary to his own satisfaction, and to that of a good many others. Anyway, there certainly occurred what in an offhand fashion he referred to as "fiascos."

There might have been a fiasco if he had been able to try with Métilde, in the greatest love of his life, the most wonderful. But he was never put to the test, and never came remotely near having the chance to try. For years, from the age of thirty-five to forty, he got exactly nowhere. Métilde was slightly younger than he was, a well-born Italian separated from her husband, who was a general of Polish origin. She treated Stendhal, by the standards of her own time and class or of any other, scarcely with ordinary politeness, with something nearer glacial frigidity. She wasn't a fool (she became the origin of Madame de Rênal and Madame de Chastell, who in fiction are much kinder), and she knew that he was besottedly in love. She forbade him to mention it, or else she would cut off the rare visits he was allowed.

She thus deprived herself of some of the most brilliant love letters that could have been written. After all those years, when Stendhal was leaving Milan and saying good-bye for good, she asked, "When are you coming back?" He showed one feeble glint of spirit. "Never, I hope." In his heart, though, he did go back for the rest of his life. It is possible to make some excuses for Métilde's behavior. She was an ardent Italian patriot, and aristocratic Italian patriots were beadily watched by Austrian authorities. Those same authorities never ceased watching Stendhal, whom they knew to be anticlerical and republican, and whom they suspected of being a French spy. Any association with him might make her appear more dangerous. This is a charitable view put forward by some French scholars.

We have almost no contemporary opinions of what

she was really like. It seems probable that she was faced by violent emotion with which she couldn't cope. It isn't an easy test of character, either for a woman or for a man, to be loved passionately and not to be able to feel the most vestigial response. Many normally kind people have in such a situation behaved with cruelty. Perhaps one can fairly say that Métilde behaved with more cruelty than most. She doesn't seem to have perceived that he was a man of great gifts. True, he was often inarticulate, maddening for him, when alone with her. Still, more stupid women would somehow have realized that they weren't going to meet anyone quite like this again.

The pursuit of happiness, up to its supreme object in Métilde, hadn't brought him much. It didn't, though he went on pursuing it, until he died. But it did bring him intense self-knowledge, and a kind of poetry of self-knowledge, or a blend of passionate reverie and abstract definition that is unique. *Unique* is a word one wouldn't apply to many writers, not even to those of overmastering genius. One can use it of Stendhal when reading *De l'Amour,* which was written in the middle of his unhappiness over Métilde.

Concealed in *De l'Amour,* but not really concealed, are the love letters to Métilde that she forbade him to write. So there is an element, touching and abject, of self-explanation and often of apology. How can a man passionately in love behave like himself? What does the word *natural* imply? He is saying, of course, that with Métilde he is at his most incompetent. She hasn't seen him as others do—"He [the man in love, Stendhal] will be perfectly natural only in the hours when he loves a little less madly."

Being Stendhal, he gives a beautiful analysis, suddenly see-ing himself as a specimen for dissection, of all the varieties of natural behavior and how helplessly they slip away. Just as elsewhere he analyzes the bliss that comes, for an hour, even for a whole day, to a man in love when suddenly he feels free of his passion. The liberty! And also the blank-ness! Then captivity returns again.

A good many of his analyses, and the well-known def-initions, do not sound as subjective as they really are. But his subjectivity is usually reaching toward some universal, or at any rate general, truths. Four kinds of love, he states in his neat categorizing fashion—*amour passion, amour goût, amour physique, amour de vanité.* The first part of *De l'Amour* is occupied entirely with *amour passion,* which to Stendhal means the total involvement in the emotions of love. *Amour physique* is relegated to the second part, which is a ragbag and much inferior. It is here that chapter 60, "Des Fiasco," puts in its discreet appearance.

In chapters on *amour passion* Stendhal produces his concept of crystallization. Crystallization One. Hope. He (that is, Stendhal, or in theory everyone else) believes him-self loved. Every attitude in his life is a reflection of the woman's perfection. Yet there is subliminal doubt. He has a premonition of some disastrous fate. Crystallization Two. Happiness and misery fight inside him. Only this woman can give him peace.

Some parts of those crystallizations were truer for Stendhal than for most of us. Yet we know what he means. The book is an examination of an unhappy love, but strangely it is not an unhappy book. He was receiving al-most nothing in the way of ordinary pleasure, and still there is pleasure, or something more exalted, an intimation of joy behind the cool classical sentences. The reason is that he had a delight, a delight that came somewhere near reverence, in the state of being in love—of being in love for its own sake. Whatever was happening to him, he felt lifted above the boredom of life. This was *beylisme* at its height. He was superior to the animal herds of other human beings who were not in love.

As with much of Stendhal, that exaltation, expressed when he was middle-aged, rings like the experience of a very young man. It is curiously pure. There is scarcely a tremor of *amour physique* all through his love passages. In actual fact, through his devastating years with Métilde, he consoled himself with one or two pickups on the side. As in the rapture of a first passionate love (passionate in his own sense), his thoughts of Métilde were worshipping and innocent.

No one can pretend that *De l'Amour* was a major commercial success. It sold twenty copies in twenty years. Stendhal always believed that it was his best work. As has been mentioned, he was modest about his novels and contented himself by saying that they were better than his detractors seemed to think. But he was certain that in *De l'Amour* he had written some things that no one else could have done.

It is interesting to wonder how it would strike intelligent young men and women today. As a result of our concentration on sex, we have ceased to be able to talk about the emotions of love as Stendhal did. Emotionally we have become much more inhibited than he was—as we are, incidentally, about grief and death. Would his language now embarrass the young? Probably the genuinely clever would still be moved by the depth of his feeling and the acuteness of his mind.

When Balzac wrote his tribute to Stendhal's writing, he made just one complaint. He didn't approve of the prose "style." It was jerky, irritating, inelegant. Stendhal thought highly of Balzac's novels, but returned the criticism. There was much wrong with the "style." It is impertinent for a foreigner to offer an opinion, but on grounds of general probability it seems as though both were wrong. "Style" has been put in quotes because more nonsense is talked about this literary subject than about almost any other, which is saying a lot.

Critics of style are usually thinking of how they would write themselves. But there is no hierarchy of excellence. Writers have had to find their own. To a foreigner Stendhal's seems admirably suited to his purpose. It doesn't convey sensuous experience, but he wasn't trying to do so, and wouldn't have been good at it if he had tried. Stendhal's prose has the unpretentiousness of the better eighteenth-century French philosophers. That isn't surprising, for after all he was French much as he would have liked to be something else. His language is sharper than most of theirs. It carried the mark of a powerful personality. It is arguable that, in the novels, this controlled classical language, with the writer's seething romantic emotions just beneath, can produce some of the most memorable effects.

Above all, Stendhal's style shines—coldly for some readers—with a respect for truth. By the side of that, all else was minor. As he said himself, when one is trying to tell the truth, both writer and reader are moved only by clarity. For his kind of truth, clarity was the supreme virtue. He wouldn't have apologized, and we needn't on his behalf.

After he had at last given up any hope with Métilde, he had for him a relatively tranquil period. During the 1820s he made a bare living from various kinds of journalism, some of it as French correspondent for liberal English journals. He found another mistress who for once was devoted to him. On his side, however, there was none of the stages of crystallization. He had an unusual capacity for discontent, and longed for her only when she was getting rid of him. He behaved to her without much more kindness than Métilde had given him. She was an intelligent and interesting woman, and to any outsider appears more suitable than Métilde. He would have been the first to explain that an outsider couldn't share the processes of crystallization, and love is not a matter of will. This affair—her name was Clémentine Curial—lasted, with breaks, sadness on her side, reproaches, for some years. Like Métilde she was the wife of a general (he seems to have been allured by the womenfolk of senior officers), but this general wasn't separated from her. He became jealous and gave trouble, distinctly rare among husbands in Stendhal's amorous history.

In 1827, at the age of forty-three, he wrote his first novel, *Armance*. Whatever being a born or natural novelist means, Stendhal wasn't one. He seems to have written his first novel almost by accident or caprice, like a man suddenly thinking that it might be a good idea to take up fly fishing. For any of his novels (there are only four, one of which was not finished, and the outline of a fifth) he required a stimulus from outside, someone else's book, or a *fait-divers,* or a real-life story.

The stimulus for *Armance* was somewhat odd. A couple of novels had recently been published in Paris on the theme of impotence. They were very bad novels. Stendhal thought he could do better. He wrote *Armance* very fast, as he did the later novels. This doesn't imply that he lacked artistic conscience. Most, though not quite all, of the world's great novels have been written fast, including those by writers of the most scrupulous literary sensibility. Flaubert's example to the contrary for a long time interfered with the true record of literary history.

Armance is nothing like a great novel, but it is interesting. It has all the defects of the major Stendhal novels, and has them without the strengths. But it does show at least a foreshadowing of those strengths. Stendhal as a writer and the founder of the *beyliste* creed—and, as his life demonstrates, as a man—couldn't immerse himself in an actual, living, realized world, either romantic or unromantic, the world of human beings of flesh and bone. He didn't breathe what a fellow countryman of his later called "the odor of man."

So the minor characters in *Armance* have no substance. Nor has the environment—that is, the rooms, the streets, the buildings—in which they live. Stendhal never developed an ability to suggest the physical world (the contrast with Balzac is as sharp as any two eminent contemporaries could make it). Although the period is clearly stated, one has to remind oneself that this really is the Bourbon Restoration, mean-spirited, with only envious memories of the Imperial risks and glories.

The action of Stendhal's incorporeal figures is as causeless as the actions in gothic romances, far more so than in

Scott, who was one of Stendhal's admirations. These episodes of random behavior, as though any choice or act was as probable or improbable as any other, have led some devotees to regard him as a precursor of existentialism. Such devotees can't have a notion of the plasma of experience on which he constantly drew.

The figure of Octave, the central personage, stands out of the book as something different in kind from all the rest. Not externally, but in his inner life. He is completely aware that he is impotent. The rough word is never uttered, nor any reason for the condition, but it is starkly there. Against all his resolves and high intentions, he falls in love. He examines his emotions with passionate, pertinacious suffering. One often wishes that he would give himself a rest. There is nothing he can do anyway. He is an aristocrat in a worthless universe. He has bitter contempt for himself, and even bitterer for everyone else except the woman he loves.

He is the first supreme Outsider in fiction. Or the first romantic antihero. He is, in spirit, a precursor of Julien Sorel, the most successful of Stendhal's antiheroes. Octave is, of course, Stendhal himself—but Stendhal deprived of the workaday flesh and appetites that made his life, as they do lives of people more ordinary than he was, endurable.

It was at this time that Stendhal, in his workaday flesh, was taking a vigorous part in the great Paris literary struggle between classics and romantics, Racine versus Shakespeare, Boileau and Malherbe versus free poetry, the displaced past versus the emerging young. In this struggle Stendhal was, so far as utterance went, vehemently on the romantic side. Witty and harsh in controversy, he was one of the most effective of their propagandists.

He was not as single-minded as his propaganda seemed. As so often, his emotionality wasn't at one with his skeptical intelligence. The emergent young never accepted him as part of their movement. He went to the first night of Victor Hugo's *Hernani,* which wasn't so much a first night as a demo for romantics. Unstoppable applause as from a modern football crowd, from all young Paris. Stendhal didn't think much of the play. He didn't think much of Victor Hugo and grossly underrated his poetry. Victor Hugo didn't think much of him.

In theory, Stendhal remained a romantic and, just before his practical luck changed and surprisingly for the better, he produced his finest statement of the romantic antihero. This is the reason for existence of *Le Rouge et le noir.* Owing almost entirely to the internal passion, which was his own and with which he infused Julien Sorel, and to the internal longing that gives charm to the heroine, Madame de Rênal, who is Métilde as sanctified by memory, *Le Rouge et le noir* is by a long way Stendhal's most hallucinating novel. It has at the same time consoled and inflamed many young men, disaffected, seeing the pettiness of all around them, feeling that they have the power to be both hero and antihero, eating their hearts out because the world doesn't give them their chance. Any day you can meet staid, smiling, senatorial elderly men who in their dissatisfied days thought of themselves as Julien Sorel. The total impact of the book is much more impressive and longer lasting than the effect of its parts. Some of those parts are splendid, though, in particular the emotional to-and-fro between Julien and Mathilde de la Mole. In those scenes are exhibited the amorous tactics of which, in theory, Stendhal was such a master. Mathilde hasn't had her due as a character. She is one of the most living and independent of Stendhal's women. It is an unsupported guess, but she may have been his picture of Métilde taken back to her youth and, against her pride and will, at last in love with the young Stendhal.

Le Rouge et le noir was prompted by an accidental stimulus, a crime report in a newspaper. The story of this crime was imitated in the book with Julien Sorel as the culprit. But, as with other writers, Stendhal must have been waiting for just that trigger. That particular petty history would have meant nothing to others. With him, his whole experience, and the core of his personality, had become ready to be let loose. Julien Sorel is the Stendhalian will set free. He is transcendent self-consciousness. He is humiliated victim and also superman. He makes *Le Rouge et le noir* as the pathetic Octave couldn't make *Armance*. In a fashion that is semirealistic and semiabstract (the most realistic part of Julien is the obsessive cerebration that Stendhal knew so well), he is one of the most dominant characters in fiction, though in technical realization and to some extent in essence unlike any other.

A generation later, Dostoevsky was to produce Raskolnikov, another figure out on his own, protesting against existence. Raskolnikov is deeper-minded, and much less of a romantic projection. There is another major difference. Raskolnikov hates the whole of God's world. Julien, with intense and personal feeling, hates the class structure that keeps him down. This doesn't flash out of the narrative with full violence until his outburst at the trial. It is tranquilized by the even flow of Stendhal's narrative. In fact, however, Julien is the first voice of ultimate class hatred in a major work of literature. The first voice who has his creator's sympathy, that is: Shakespeare didn't identify himself with Jack Cade. There is no question that Stendhal identified himself with Julien. And yet Stendhal himself was the most sardonic, opportunist, and skeptical of liberals. So far as he had a political faith, it was as a nostalgic Bonapartist.

Just after *Le Rouge et le noir* came out, Stendhal had one of his few pieces of good luck. The July days happened. Charles X was ejected from the throne, Louis Philippe put on it. Friends and admirers of Stendhal now had the patronage, and he was promptly given a job. It was not the lofty job he had pictured for himself, when he dreamed of worldly ambitions. It was actually the consulship at Trieste, which during the nineteenth century seems to have been thought of as a suitable final home for eccentric men of letters. The Trieste consulship carried a comfortable middle-class income, and not excessive work.

Stendhal arrived in the town, and was with some celerity asked to leave. The French government might change: the intelligence service of the Hapsburg Empire didn't. Stendhal's name was still on their files. He had to content himself—though he hadn't much talent for contenting himself anywhere—with another consulship, appreciably less well paid, in appreciably less cultivated company, at Civitavecchia.

Stendhal's friends were doing their best, but he wasn't appeased. He regarded having to live at Civitavecchia as another injustice. Civitavecchia was a hole. It was a squalid port (more detached observers tended to agree). There was no one to talk to. However, Stendhal didn't suffer, any more than in the past, from undue conscientiousness about official obligations. His superiors were indulgent. No one objected much when he proceeded to spend much of his time in Rome. Nor when he felt the need for extended sick leave, went off literally for years, and wrote travel books. He also wrote the greater part of a novel that he didn't complete. That was a pity. The book, *Lucien Leuwen,* is subtle and interesting and has become one of the texts for *beylistes.* Here is the firmest exposition of how obligations and duties destroy the beauty of any human relations, and here is a contemptuous view of middle-class France as presided over by Louis Philippe, Stendhal's scorn loftier and more dismissive than anything Flaubert was to exhibit a generation later.

The consul of Civitavecchia didn't have too bad a time. He had enough money to live on. He had picked up a very young mistress who soon got married. However, she found marriage no obstacle, when Stendhal could visit her in Florence, to maintaining their relation. He even thought without excessive enthusiasm of getting married himself. *Le Rouge et le noir* gained a trickle of sales. At last, after nagging at everyone he knew for years, he was given the Légion d'honneur.

At the age of fifty-five, not in Civitavecchia, which perhaps doesn't need saying, but in Paris, he sat down to write his second major work, *La Chartreuse de Parme.* The impulse behind this novel isn't so obvious as with *Le Rouge et le noir.* Somehow all the covert romantic urges of his nature seem to have broken through. He didn't have to sit down to it for long. The whole work, just as we have it, except for minor textual tidyings, was finished in five weeks, November to December 1838. It runs to three hundred thousand words. It was written at the rate of eight thousand to ten thousand words a day, which is the all-time speed record for a major novel.

The novel has nothing like the central emotion that gives *Le Rouge et le noir* its power. There is no Julien. Fabrice, the main character, is for half the book only a juvenile lead, handsome, brave, just knocked about by events for which he isn't responsible. He gets into trouble because at seventeen, as a passionate idealistic worshiper of Napoleon, he goes to fight for him during the Hundred Days and finds himself, in the most famous scene in the book, on the edge of the Battle of Waterloo. It is Fabrice's puzzled, detached observation there that, so Tolstoy was to say, made it possible to write the battle scenes in *War and Peace*.

Stendhal had witnessed a battle, at Bautzen, and there his realistic eye (not a satirical eye, which is to misread the Waterloo scene altogether) had its chance. But not much else of *La Chartreuse de Parme* is in its external events realistic, though much of the psychology of mood is, in the sharpest Stendhalian vein.

The story itself, underneath the beautifully calm tone of the text, shot with impassive sarcasm, is romantic in the extreme, as though the skeptical camp follower of the romantic movement at last couldn't keep himself in check any longer. For those who don't find belief easy, the happenings in *Le Rouge et le noir* get in the way of the emotional exploration; much more so in *La Chartreuse de Parme*. The story is like one by a far less disciplined and sensible Walter Scott. In fact, Stendhal was writing in a tradition of theatrical adventure, where ambushes, impenetrable disguises, climbing through windows were part of the exercise—as required by custom as, say, the obligatory sex scene was to become in the 1970s. Those conventions of his time did get in the way, not of Stendhal's psychological analysis, supreme in the most unlikely context, but of his psychological common sense.

Fabrice is put in jail by political enemies. Every day for months he, his friends, all informed persons in Parma, know that he may be executed. His food is being poisoned. But he has caught a glimpse of the daughter of the prison governor. He has spoken to her only once, face to face. They have fallen in love. He is able to watch her from his cell, high in the tower. After having many casual mistresses, he knows for the first time what love is.

He is ecstatically happy. His friends are making plans for his escape. He asks himself, do I by any chance want to escape? Execution may be fixed for tomorrow. Do I by any chance want to escape? This is the height of romantic expression. It might be sung in an opera. Stendhal has lost contact with any kind of realism—and yet this tenor solo is combined with the subtlest of explorations of a prisoner's swings of mood.

It is hard, even for the hard-boiled, to evade the book's magic. Fabrice isn't a success, nor is his patient love, Clélia. Nor, as has already been suggested, is the court of Parma. The period is the 1820s, and not even one of the tiny Italian states could have borne much resemblance to what we are shown. Stendhal's hard eye had seen a battle, but not a court. His intuition wasn't really working. Yet his abstract intelligence was. He makes some generalizations about the nature of despotic rule anywhere, which we can check from this century's experience; they show startling foresight. And, describing his old archbishop who, though a good man, is hypnotized into adoration by the spectacle of others' power, Stendhal says things about the deferential society, and its inevitable disappearance, that would have been quite beyond the conceptual range of men like Bagehot.

The most brilliantly realized person in the book, and, along with Mathilde in *Le Rouge et le noir,* the most living of Stendhal's women, is the Duchess of Sanseverina. She is the embodiment of female will, the woman counterpart to Julien Sorel. She is only fourteen years older than her nephew Fabrice, and loves him. The crystallization is etched with Stendhalian precision. She can't express it in the flesh, though she can enjoy other lovers, including the devoted Mosca, who in his conversation and in his mixture of emotional surrender and sardonic commentary has a relation to Stendhal himself, or what Stendhal would have liked to be.

Gina Sanseverina can be ruthless, despises remorse, trusts her impulses for good or bad. She is just a bit too vivid to be true, but as one reads, she is true enough.

After *La Chartreuse de Parme,* Stendhal didn't exert himself again. He had the one great pleasure of his literary life when he read Balzac's great review. He continued with his own interpretation of his consular duties. Physically, he was becoming decrepit, but he was young enough in spirit to fall in love again, apparently without return. In 1841, when he was fifty-eight, he had a paralytic stroke in Rome. He contemplated death with clinical interest and stark courage. He didn't like periods of aphasia. The stroke had happened while he was walking about, and he speculated whether it would be ridiculous to die in the street.

He decided not, provided that he hadn't done it on purpose.

He seemed to recover from his stroke, and he was cheerful. It gave him a good opportunity for some more sick leave. He went to Paris. There he had another stroke—again in the street, walking back from a dinner party. He died a few hours later, without fuss, and was buried also without fuss, three friends attending.

BALZAC

As soon as Balzac began to be known in literary Paris, people thought him preposterous, vulgar, boastful, pretentious, more than a little ridiculous; but at the same time he won much affection. You mustn't trust his tongue, they may have told one another, and don't have any business dealings with him. Still, he enhanced life, he made it seem brighter, more exciting, larger than it really was. He was a most engaging man.

He must have been a most engaging child, one would have thought. In historical fact, he had a curiously desolate childhood. This wasn't owing to poverty. In 1799, when Balzac was born, his father was deputy mayor of Tours, where he had recently arrived with a young wife. Tours was a pleasant provincial town; the countryside of Touraine was some of the gentlest in France. Balzac *père*'s job was an official one, and brought in a steady middle-class income. His wife had set him up with some good middle-class capital. Which, since the marriage was arranged when she was eighteen to his fifty, was presumably a strong argument for his taking her—though she was a good-looking girl.

So in Balzac's childhood money was no problem. The family was comfortably placed among the bourgeoisie of Tours. Both parents were intelligent, and the reverse of commonplace. The father was born in a peasant's family in Gascony. Their real name was Balssa, but later it was changed to something more genteel, and a *de* kept surreptitiously creeping in. Somehow as a boy Balzac senior had made his way to Paris with nothing but the clothes he was wearing. By a combination of shrewdness, ability, hard work, and an opportunist's eye, he had educated himself as a lawyer and obtained appointments under the monarchy. He was actually a fervent royalist, and in the Revolution he talked too loudly for safety, not being his son's father for nothing; but his opportunism rescued him, he learned to keep his head down, he wasn't too proud to secure the protection of useful friends. One such useful friend was a general who became the first consul's prefect in Touraine. It was he who installed Balzac *père* in his nice safe job. Anything could happen in Napoleonic France.

Balzac's father during his self-education had picked up all kinds of literary interests. He read history, he read Voltaire, Rabelais, and Sterne. He even had literary ambitions, and thought of writing pamphlets. He had also a cheerful appetite, which reinforced itself powerfully when he got older, for the local peasant girls.

Balzac's mother, too, had literary tastes. She was better educated, and had read more widely, than similar middle-class English women of the period. Balzac's sisters, younger than he was, shared the prevailing literary enthusiasm. When he began to publish books, all of them, father, mother, sisters, had strong views as to how he could improve them. When he was running short of time, against one of his frightening deadlines, they were willing to write chapters for him. It ought to have been a good family for an imaginative child—not too rich, not too poor, interested, lively. It wasn't a good family for young Balzac. Part of the trouble was that too much was happening. Another part of the trouble was that his mother didn't love him, or so he felt from an early age. This wasn't entirely illusion, although he magnified it later to arouse other women's sympathy and then their love.

When he was an infant, his mother couldn't feed him and he was dispatched to a wet nurse in a village outside Tours, where he stayed until he was four. The village wasn't far away, but apparently his mother didn't often trouble to visit him. Then at eight he was, suddenly and without explanation, sent away from home again, this time to an Oratorian school at Vendôme. He didn't know why. The reason would have been surprising in Jane Austen's society at the same date. The Balzac marriage didn't work. Balzac *père* didn't exert himself, except sometimes to read Rabelais aloud, which shocked his wife. She was pious, respectable, bourgeoise. She fell in love with a smart young man who owned a château in the countryside. She became pregnant. Hence the exile of the young Balzac.

Everyone else, including Balzac *père*, the father of the illegitimate child, and Madame Balzac, behaved with a cool common sense that would have done credit to the Whig aristocracy in a similar fix. The child was taken into the Balzac family. His actual father, Jean de Margonne (for once the *de* was genuine), stood as godfather at the christening. Margonne settled down as a cultivated country gentleman, remained on intimate terms with the Balzac family, and a support to them in trouble. Balzac *père* continued to read Rabelais, Rousseau, and accounts of China. Madame Balzac became even more punctilious in her churchgoing.

Meanwhile the young Balzac was having a miserable time at the Oratorian school. There are plenty of accounts of the wretched school days of illustrious writers, but for neglect his ranks high, at least as high as Trollope's, which is saying a good deal. Perhaps to encourage him in frugality (an end result that was not achieved), he was kept starvingly short of money, as a poor boy among rich ones. He didn't have enough to eat. The place was as hard and as unhealthy as a nineteenth-century English public school. He became ill. He was left there until he was fifteen, and he claimed later, though this may not have been true, that his mother did not once come to see him.

He was neither a good nor a successful student. This may have been partly on account of his misery but, though his mind proved itself to be both fluid and exceptionally powerful, it didn't have the exactness and precision of, say, Stendhal's, and in any schoolwork Stendhal would have beaten him out of the field. On the other hand, his one consolation at school was to read with passionate energy. He wanted to read everything and understand everything. He had a very good memory, and a particularly fine visual memory. People marveled later that he remembered not only whole passages of what he read, but also their position on the page. Actually, that is not so uncommon as they thought. A good many people with visual memories acquire the same trick.

At fifteen he was so sick and emaciated (startlingly unlike the famous Balzac whom the cartoonists liked to draw) that the Oratorian Fathers insisted that he must be removed from school. Back in Tours, his life began to have some pleasures. He was sent away again, but this time to an agreeable place. It might have seemed, in a more censorious climate, a rather unexpected place. He was sent to stay with Jean de Margonne, his mother's old lover, whose son Henri was very much her favorite member of the Balzac family. Parental affections seemed to have been oddly capricious among those families. Margonne loved the young Balzac much more than his own son (who incidentally turned out to be an unmitigated disaster).

Balzac basked in the relaxed existence of a country establishment. Margonne fed him with good Touraine food and wine. He reveled in the boy's conversation, which, now that he was liberated, may already have been the most remarkable that the older man had heard. Margonne, good-natured and idle, had a taste for intelligent company but didn't take active steps to get it.

That was Balzac's happiest time for some longish while to come. The fortunes of the Balzacs were on the slide. Napoleon had abdicated, his officials were being ejected from their jobs, old Balzac's protectors couldn't protect themselves. Old Balzac was entirely prepared to write pamphlets expressing perfervid devotion to the Bourbon monarchy (which, though others found him unconvincing, happened to be genuine). That didn't help. He ceased to be deputy mayor of Tours. They all moved to Paris, where he could still earn a living. For the moment, they weren't badly off. They would have been better off if he hadn't fancied himself as a financial wizard. By shrewd-looking investments he had run through a sizable part of his wife's inheritance. Soon she in her turn was also to fancy herself as a speculator, and steadily ran through the rest—except for considerable sums that the young Balzac disposed of.

That occurred a few years later. For the time being, he was sent to a respectable Catholic *lycée,* where again he didn't distinguish himself. Then he was put into a lawyer's chambers. He picked up a good deal of information. His novels were to be packed with legal detail. It is all authentic. But, even if he hadn't spent a couple of years in those chambers, he was capable of picking up authentic details of anything. He had the gift that other great writers have possessed—for instance, Shakespeare and Kipling—that of assimilating other men's activities and shop talk as it were out of the air. It is a journalist's gift, if you want to be pejorative, but a very valuable one, and has given substance to some major works of art.

Still, those years weren't wasted. At eighteen he had had enough. He had no intention of becoming a lawyer. He knew his vocation. He was going to be a writer. That had been the purpose he had concealed up to now. He wanted everything this world could offer. This was the way. What kind of writer? In his period there was only one answer for an ambitious young man. He was going to write verse dramas.

Rather surprisingly, the family accepted this as sensible. They hankered after the middle-class security that was slipping away, and they had begun to realize that he was their last hope. But they had their streak of eccentricity and generous aspirations. He was to be given two years to try his luck. His mother would provide just enough money to pay the rent of an attic flat in Paris. The family income going steadily downward, they were living in Villeparisis (note the word—Proust took a good deal from Balzac, including some of his most resonant names, Combray among them).

Balzac would be allowed the minimum of money to keep alive. They couldn't spare much, but his mother was anyway determined to give him, as at school, only enough for subsistence, apparently to save him from the dreadful dangers of debt—which he duly got into and stayed in until he died.

So Balzac was installed in a bare attic room, dilapidated, cold, water dripping from the roof on rainy days. From there he could look out over the roofs of Paris, and there like his young adventurer Rastignac, to be written about fifteen years later, he could challenge the town and dream of conquering it. It is more than likely that, as Rastignac did, he actually said aloud to Paris: *"à nous deux maintenant."* Balzac, young or old, was not the man to abstain from a heroic gesture.

He was not as glamorous as his fictional young men from the provinces, Rastignac and Rubempré. Let us have a look at him at nineteen, writing away at the first play, *Cromwell,* as confident about it as any young writer who has ever lived.

He was very short. The average height has gone up by inches in the past 150 years, and nearly all the writers in this book were short by our standards. Balzac wasn't much above five feet. Owing to lack of food, at nineteen he was still thin, with unusually small hands and feet. He didn't stay thin. As soon as he could get his hands on any money, he became remarkably fat. In the agreeable account of his meeting Stendhal in the boulevard, and congratulating him on *La Chartreuse de Parme,* he says rather disapprovingly that Stendhal was very stout. That really was a trifle cool. Balzac was stouter. It is a nice picture, the two men walking amiably down the street, both little, both fat, two of the finest writers on earth.

Balzac's face was so mobile that it was difficult to read. He had lustrous brown eyes, and observers commented on the "golden flecks" that glinted in them. His brow was impressive. His mouth was as sensuous as an infant's eager to suck. It was a physiognomy, as he said about others, that was fitted to his temperament. No one knew better than Balzac that the psyche and soma are one. He studied the first primitive attempts, as of Lavater, to correlate physique and temperament, but like other great novelists he already knew it by something like instinct. His own temperament was as mobile as his expression, as difficult to understand, and for himself as difficult to handle as it was to understand. It had less structure than most men's. It could flow into anyone else's life, man's or woman's. It could immerse itself in any occupation, activity, place, material object, as though he had no core of identity of his own. This gave him his winning charm, though *charm* is too weak a word. It was one of the secrets, as he grew a little older, of his success with women. There was probably another secret, connected but more basic still.

His was a dangerous temperament to possess, for himself and for anyone close to him. It might seem that he was a weak and pliable character. That has often been the impression that fluid personalities convey. In Balzac's case, nothing could be more deceptive. He was a man of ultimate resilience and force. He was the opposite of self-centered. Egocentric personalities like Stendhal could not immerse themselves in others. But Balzac was, in his own fashion, inordinately selfish, which is quite a different thing. The whole passion of that amorphous nature could be devoted to what he wanted to do. To a transcendental extent, he was on the make. He could and did forget himself in anyone or anything that came into his life. That is the wonder of his novels. But, at the same time, he could and did use that self-forgetfulness to help him conquer. He had an unsuppressible desire (he didn't suppress any of his desires) for what might be termed personal imperialism. Through all the welter, liquidlike changes, absence of order, in his personality, he was going to rule. It wasn't an accident that, some years after he had left his attic with its view of the Paris roofs, he announced: What Napoleon achieved by the sword, I shall achieve by the pen.

The first play, the verse tragedy that he was sure would bring him fame, was finished. He went off to the family home at Villeparisis to read it aloud. The whole family was collected, along with his brother-in-law and a shrewd local friend. Balzac began to read, with his own ebullience, with the pride and joy of a creative artist. He was magnificently happy. No one else was. Even among the devastatingly boring verse tragedies of the early nineteenth century, for boredom this appears to have ranked high. It isn't a good idea for aspiring writers to read their works aloud. Balzac was told the truth.

He was an indomitable young man. If he couldn't write plays, he could write something else.

But it wasn't as easy as that. Here his capacity to plunge into almost anything set him back for years. High art had absorbed him. So could earning some money absorb him. In Restoration Paris the condition of publishing was changing—much as it was in Dickens's London. There was a demand for popular literature. New ramshackle publishers were bringing out what the English called sensation novels. Hack writers, ghost writers, could make some sort of living. The young Balzac joined in. He became what, a hundred years later in America, would have made him a writer for pulp magazines—compare Dashiell Hammett. He used a battery of pseudonyms, liking disguise in all its forms. Some of his stories were more gothic than the gothic. He dashed them off with manic industry and speed, as in time he dashed off his great novels; but with the great novels he corrected on proofs to the extent of equally manic rewriting, while these potboilers he didn't look at twice.

He felt (rare for him) something like shame. Yet there are signs in them of great gifts. Occasionally, when he got tired of his extravaganza, some of the scenes and physical settings have the three-dimensional solidity of essential Balzac.

He was writing for money. He wasn't in the least ashamed of that. Money was as interesting as anything in the world. If you wanted to know how the world ticked, money was more interesting than anything else. His imagination immersed itself in money and never ceased to be immersed. In brutal fact, however, he wasn't making much out of his potboilers, much less than other trash writers of the day. It doesn't seem to have struck him that he had a knack for making bad bargains. It did strike him that he ought to be writing real books.

It also struck someone else. This was his first love. He was twenty-three. In Villeparisis there lived a woman more than twenty years older than himself. This was Madame de Berny, whom he called Laure (he had a sister Laure and another sister Laurence, and he liked giving the name to his mistresses). With teeming gratitude he also called Madame de Berny "La Dilecta." She was cultivated, kind, had literary taste, and had been brought up at the court of Louis XVI. All this brought the imagination of the young Balzac to fever point. She was married to an aristocratic husband much older than herself. She had had a large family by him. He appears to have been a disagreeable and tedious man. She had already had one love affair and an illegitimate child.

Out of her natural kindness, she had appointed Balzac as tutor to the children. She also had an eye for talent and divined that underneath the brashness this wasn't a negligible young man. She thought he might be a match for one of her daughters.

Balzac didn't think so. He fell passionately in love with the mother. Whether he had had other women before her isn't certain; but he was born to understand women. He made the kind of love to Madame de Berny that, though she tried to, she couldn't long resist. He involved himself in everything about her. He devoted himself to the children—not out of deliberate art, but because he sank himself in all that belonged to one he loved (that was first nature, and later became second nature as a seductive technique).

He knew she was unhappy, told her so, explored each emotion of a woman wasted and sad because her life was dribbling away. He had the sweetness of understanding and the urgency of desire. It didn't need overmuch of that kind of wooing to get her into bed. Once that was achieved, she became as passionately in love as he was, soon more so, and stayed as passionately in love, as totally devoted, until she died twenty years later. She called this young upstart her "master." She gave him money, told him about the manners of high society, encouraged him to make the most of his talents.

This story tells us something about his life with women. He would never permit any of the later ones to forget his gratitude to Madame de Berny. He didn't desert her, though he soon had others going in parallel. All his major affairs were with women socially elevated, some, like Madame Hanska, who married him in the last year of his life, very grand indeed. He received much love. When he was in earnest, he seems to have been turned down only once.

All that mobile nature was involved in understanding the life of any woman he loved. No one had more intuition about the varieties of the emotional existence. But also the story doesn't make sense unless he had the same intuition about the erotic existence. No one who went to bed with him wanted to lose him. He might be fat, dress absurdly, be a cartoonist's figure of fun, have no front teeth; but in the sexual life, as in the emotional life, he wanted to give pleasure, and had the gift of doing so.

If one reads his love letters, especially to Madame de

Berny (it is a pity that those to the Contessa Guidoboni-Visconti aren't extant; Fanny, the Contessa, who was a wild and cheerful Englishwoman, had had many men, but she clung to Balzac with maximum heartiness), one can feel that passion to give pleasure surging through. Read in the late twentieth century, the letters may seem rather less directly sexual than a man of similar temperament would write today, but the idiom is deceptive. It isn't difficult to interpret what, in physical fact, he is saying.

It sounds perverse, as a remark about one of the most fervent lovers of women, but often his physical raptures, and his recollection and anticipation of giving physical pleasure, suggest a special kind of woman. That is, the kind of woman, self-forgetting, who delights most in the ecstasy of someone she loves. To interpret this as an element of homosexuality would be fatuous, though in his multifarious fashion he knew all about it, as he demonstrated when he wrote about Vautrin. He just knew all about the erotic life, and there no writer has been more universal.

It is inexperienced to try to insert him into neat categories. For instance, knowing persons have pounced on the fact that his first two great loves were for women twenty years older than himself. He was looking for a mother, the knowing persons have said, remembering the textbooks. We have to keep our heads, and remember that his other major loves—several of them—were for women younger than himself. It is true that he doesn't seem to have had much predilection for young girls, but even that is not certain. Much of his life was tangled, secret, and hidden—with love affairs proceeding simultaneously, like those of a mythopoeic commercial traveler. Probably the detailed truth will never now be disinterred. It is not even known how many illegitimate children he had, though there were at least three.

Established with Madame de Berny in his mid-twenties, he thought fervently of making his fortune. By this time, he had once more obtained a room in Paris, financed once more by his mother, who had come into a legacy, soon, like all Balzac money, to be got rid of. Balzac's earnings from the trash writing hadn't increased. His strategy for coping with lack of money was, and remained, forceful. It was to have a bright idea, double his bets, get into more debt, and double his bets again. During this progression, he spent more lavishly, bought material objects that he loved as though they were women, became more grandiloquently extravagant. He was not out of debt again until he died.

His first bright idea was, like all the others, imperial. Clearly, writers didn't make money. Publishers did. Therefore he became a publisher. He would publish editions of the classics for the rising middle-class public. He raised money from his mother, Madame de Berny, his nearest and dearest. Then lost it. How to recoup? Simple. At one remove behind publishers were printers. They made money. He bought a printing firm, once more getting all around him to subscribe. He loved the craft of printing, the smells, the sights, the technique, part of the palpable, cherished material world. He understood printing as no creative writer has ever done. In *Les Illusions perdues* he was, a few years in the future, to write about printing as no other artist has written about a craft industry. No twentieth-century writer has been able to write with any such insight about mass-production industries. His grasp was marvelous. Once more he lost all the money.

The curious thing is that both these ideas and most of his later ones, including some that sound improbable, such as chestnut growing and the development of Sardinian mines, were realizable. Other people took them over and were successful. And it wasn't that Balzac was a fool or was above the vulgar traffic of the market. On the contrary, he was acquisitive, preposterously energetic, and none too scrupulous. He understood as much about the workings of money as he did about printing. The trouble seems to have been that he couldn't concentrate long enough to carry an idea through. He was enormously persuasive at the beginning, at the expense of others and himself, but then lost interest. He couldn't devote himself to two things at once. Very few men can. Really he was, sometimes without knowing it, thinking of his imaginary world. Someone one-tenth as clever, giving his full attention, would have been more able in those businesses than he was.

He owed money everywhere. Private creditors didn't matter. The public ones were more exigent. Balzac found it necessary to go into hiding. On and off, he stayed in hiding, for precisely the same reason, for a good many years. It was a singular kind of hiding. He furnished his secret apartment in his rococo taste. He soon picked up another mistress, not relinquishing Madame de Berny. This second one was a Napoleonic duchess, also writing for money and no more fastidious about financial transactions than he was.

At thirty he was becoming the Balzac of literary fame. He published the first novel under his own name, or rather the name he had escalated up the social ladder, Honoré de Balzac. The novel was *Les Chouans*, a violent adventure story of the royalist peasant rising in Brittany. It didn't sell but made his reputation. Reputations were not so difficult to make in the early nineteenth century as a hundred years later. Writers were thinner on the ground. Balzac was writing, almost in the same day, certainly in the same week, work of utterly discordant variety—*Louis Lambert* (high-minded idealistic speculation, very bad), *La Physiologie du mariage* (not so high-minded, but very sensible), *Contes drolatiques* (not high-minded at all), and some of his best stories, later collected when he had hit on the idea of his collective titles, in *Scènes de la vie privée*. Then in 1833 *Eugénie Grandet*, the first of the great novels. This was a success, not only of esteem but with a large public.

That was the arrival of the legendary Balzac. He made the legend, he was the legend in the flesh. His public face and his life were preposterous. Commercial success didn't reduce his debts but increased them. He might be escaping his creditors, but he didn't resist the lure of any furniture he could see and touch. Objets d'art, carpets, a marble bath—he bought and bought, but he usually didn't find it desirable to pay the bills. He behaved like a semideranged parvenu come to town—which, in one of the whirls in his formless nature, he was. Like Stendhal he had great faith in dazzling clothes, and went to an expensive tailor. The minor fact that a tiny little man, ludicrously fat, with very short legs, wasn't really equipped for the fashionable costume of the 1830s didn't strike him. He acquired an enormous cane with a jeweled knob, which was a gift to the cartoonists. He even acquired a fashionable conveyance, with a groom and his bogus arms on the doors. He was ridiculous. He was Balzac. He had proved that he was a great genius. He was.

No writer in literary history has written on so many different topics, in so many different veins, at the same time. It is useless to wish, as critics have often done, for some unifying principle that could make all his work cohere. There was no organization in his nature. He was not Stendhal with a consistent line of thought running through his life. He had a powerful mind and an abnormally energetic one. But he wasn't a rational intellectual. He had no conception of organizing his business affairs, or his relations with women, or his ambitions in politics or society or art. The critic who understood him best, and who was a writer of his own stature, Marcel Proust, marveled at his conception of the recurring characters—that is, characters reappearing, prominently or obscurely, throughout *La Comédie humaine*. But that, and the title itself under which they all could shelter, came, as it were, from an idea after the event, or partway through it. There was no system in that prodigious creativity. He could produce half a dozen different, and contradictory, views of the human condition in the same book. To Balzac all through his life, any generalization, including one he had just thought of, was better than none.

Friends protested about this welter and chaos, particularly when it made his practical life nonsensical. Why should one of the most successful writers in Europe (the young Dickens was rapidly passing him in that respect) always be in financial trouble? Why should it get steadily worse? Madame de Berny until she died not only went on lending money, but also tried to guide him. So did the most intelligent woman he ever met, Zulma Carraud. Zulma may have loved him as protectively as Madame de Berny did, but for once—the only time among the women close to him—he wasn't attracted, and she wasn't his mistress (she was lame, but to judge from the pictures her face had its own charm). But she was an even better judge of writing than Madame de Berny, was more outspoken, and became his literary conscience. He replied to her submissively, and didn't change his ways.

His ways, in the actual process of writing, were as bizarre as in finance or love, but more methodical. They had an overwhelming effect on some of his French successors, who decided that this must be the necessary routine for a great writer. A great writer could write only at night. Balzac got three or four hours' sleep between dinner and midnight. Then his alarm clock went off. He put on a white monastic robe, spotless (in spite of the messiness of his practical affairs, he was fastidiously clean, and an obsessive hand washer), and wrote at a great speed, at an immaculate desk with each implement in its appointed place, for six hours.

He kept himself alert by coffee drinking as excessive as all his other activities. He may have notched a world record in cups of coffee consumed per year. He had a long bath in the early morning, meditating, keeping clean. From nine in the morning till one, he corrected proofs, which we have to remember was in effect rewriting the novel. For many of his novels there were six drafts, all scrawled out on a series of proofs. Printing was very cheap in the nineteenth century. This process would be impossible today, ruining not only him (which might not have mattered) but his publisher (which might). He had an egg for lunch. Then some hours' more proofreading.

This meant a working day, a real working day, pen close to the paper, of about thirteen hours. No modern professional could endure anything like such labor, and it wouldn't be good for anyone to try. Of course, it wasn't good for Balzac. It may have shortened his life. When he was writing, and his output was as prodigious as anyone's could be (if one includes novellas, something like ninety-six novels), his existence was as monastic as his robe. There must have been intermissions. He had to find time for love affairs—though one or two of his mistresses found his devotion to work distinctly irksome, the grandest of them, Madame Hanska (to an outsider the least agreeable, though not to Balzac), vociferously so. There are accounts of Balzac, off duty for once, guzzling food like a gold miner returning from the diggings, and—with his integral belief that there is nothing like excess—putting away at one meal several birds, a hundred oysters, and, as a kind of appetizer in the midst of serious eating, just a dozen cutlets.

The details of his financial goings-on are now inextricable, but we know that they, and his obsessive writing, and his love affairs were all simultaneously coexisting. From the midst of this manic tumult, he produced, at the age of thirty-four, *Eugénie Grandet,* a work of serene wisdom. It was a major popular success, and established him among serious people as one of the first writers of the age. It didn't establish him with Sainte-Beuve, who was a very clever man and had a gift not uncommon among critics of being totally indifferent to any glimpse of contemporary genius. Proust in the essay "Sainte-Beuve and Balzac" deals with this phenomenon in a miniature masterpiece of controlled sarcasm. To anyone today, it seems stupefying that a literate man was capable of missing the splendor of *Eugénie Grandet*. It hasn't the prodigal richness of Balzac's greatest novels and it hasn't their defects, which became prodigal also. It makes most writing of our time look like the work of playful children.

Eugénie Grandet begins, like its greater successor, *Le Père Goriot,* with a physical setting as visible, as touchable, as a writer can make it. In *Eugénie Grandet* this is the main street of Saumur, the shops (unwindowed, much like Asian shops today), the bourgeois houses as they got farther up the hill, the unkempt house of old Grandet, winegrower, investor in land, accumulator of money. He is one of those major figures in Balzac's work who drives the narrative along by the force of a single passion. He is a miser. In detached reflection, it strikes one that these Balzac monomaniacs ought to seem more unreal than they are. In fact, they are more common than our present psychological conventions allow; and Balzac tells one so much about Grandet (the cumulative effect of that direct, powerful, hammering language is very strong, as Tolstoy took to heart) that it is only occasionally, for the present writer just three times in the novel, that one feels that this mania is being overdone.

The emotional center of the novel is Grandet's daughter Eugénie. She is not a young girl. She is a robust woman of twenty-three. She is entirely innocent, pious, brought up in this narrow, claustrally parsimonious home. She is potentially a considerable heiress. She hasn't known any intimation of love, until in scenes of piercing brilliance, covering a period of only a few days, she meets her cousin. His father, threatened with bankruptcy, has committed suicide in Paris. His father's brother, old Grandet, is neither going to provide for the young man nor discharge the family debts.

The young man goes to the West Indies to make a living. Before he leaves, he and Eugénie have become secretly engaged. Eugénie's first love (and the only one she will have) is made actual from the vague unspecific idealistic thoughts down to the beat of her pulse. The rest of the novel is very compressed, perhaps too much so. Years pass. The cousin returns to France. He has made money. He is immediately contracting a fashionable marriage in Paris. He writes to Eugénie, jilting her. She herself, coerced and persuaded by her confessor, marries a man who promises to let her keep her virginity. She is left a widow. She is rich, since her father has died. Apart from good works, she spends no more money than he did. She is alone, apart from a devoted servant in the old house in Saumur. The end of the novel is as relentless as that.

We might compare this love story with one almost identical in form, though written thirty years later—that of Trollope's Lily Dale, in *The Small House at Allington* and *The Last Chronicle of Barset*. Lily is brighter, better educated, more spirited, and much wittier than Eugénie. She is younger than Eugénie when she also, as Victorians would say, "gave her heart" to a man. They, too, became engaged. Her man, Crosbie, is examined in more depth than Eugénie's cousin. Trollope is more compassionate to the temptations of careerism. Crosbie jilts Lily for precisely the same reason as Eugénie is jilted. Lily will not look at another man. She remains quick-tongued and lively, there is none of the somber religiosity of Eugénie's faith, but Lily cherishes, out of what seems a perverse pride, her first and only love. We are meant to believe, in *The Last Chronicle of Barset,* that she will devote, rather than resign, herself to spinsterhood.

The resemblance is close. It must be accidental. There is no evidence that Trollope read Balzac, and it is unlikely. In any case, Trollope was as original and independent as Balzac. Which of the stories tells more of the truth? Well, *The Last Chronicle of Barset* is one of the best novels in English. Everything dealing with Mr. Crawley, the personality of Mr. Crawley himself, is done with a subtlety and percipience that Balzac couldn't have matched. But, when one reaches the end of the two love stories, with Eugénie Grandet one thinks: This is how it was. With Lily Dale one is doubtful: life isn't quite like that. As with almost all the English nineteenth-century novels, even the greatest, the truth seems to be tampered with—certainly by the side of Balzac's unsparing vision. If Lily had been as we understand her to be—and like nearly all Trollope's young women she is admirably realized—then of course she would have come to terms and found another man. Not Johnny Eames. Trollope was right there, and his critics wrong. But Lily wasn't weighed down by Eugénie's grim heritage and was made for some sort of happiness.

It was just before the appearance of *Eugénie Grandet* that Balzac first met Madame Hanska and just after its success that they became lovers. Before that, she had written him fan letters, and he had enthusiastically replied. Not surprisingly, he received plenty of fan letters from women. Rather more surprisingly, both he and Madame Hanska seemed to have been prepared to fall in love on paper. That has happened to others, of course, but this was precipitate. There isn't much doubt that Madame Hanska was ready to go to bed with him almost on sight, if she could get free from her entourage. Actually she couldn't get free, and she became irascible, which was one of her common states.

Madame Hanska was a great Polish aristocrat. Poland was then part of the Russian Empire and she, being a patriotic Pole and a devout Catholic, hated Russians. She was in turn distrusted by the Tsarist regime, which was later a nuisance to both her and Balzac. She lived in the Ukraine, west of Kiev. She was a landowner on a vast scale and owned thousands of serfs. The land was fertile, and Balzac in later years, true to form, had many schemes for making it more profitable. Without his help, she was rich, a good deal richer than those illustrious landowners Turgenev and Tolstoy. When she traveled to Neuchâtel, where Balzac first met her, she arrived *en princesse* with about a hundred subordinates, house servants, miscellaneous domestics, and relatives, including an elderly husband who was also aristocratic and as rich as she was.

During that preliminary encounter, this impeded the consummation of their epistolary love. They wanted to make it. They did fall in love. It didn't matter that she discovered he was a fat and toothless little man, pushful, not used to the manners of high society. It didn't matter that, having expected her, for some romantic reason, to be elegant, slender, languishing, he saw that, though she was distinctly good-looking, she was also distinctly well fleshed. Sexual ardor often has an instinct for detecting another sexual ardor. She possessed as much as he did, maybe more. On her side, that was the force that kept her attached to him, even through long absences and disputes, for the next seventeen years. Their next meeting, a few months later in Geneva, when they did manage to contrive hours in his bedroom with tumultuous satisfaction, they began to talk of marriage—marriage, that is, when her old husband, supposed to be infirm, had duly died. Away from Balzac during the years to come, queening it on the great Ukrainian estate, she often wondered whether that marriage would be a good idea. Like a good many rich persons, she was careful about money, and horrified by Balzac's financial maneuvers. When she was with him, marriage seemed a very good idea indeed.

As has been indicated before, to an outsider, so far removed in place and time, she does seem the least endearing of Balzac's women. She wasn't stupid and had had a good upper-class education. She had taste of a decorative, drawing-room kind; but she had nothing like the literary feeling of Madame de Berny, or Zulma Carraud, or Balzac's own sister. She could accept that he was a great writer, but she didn't understand his gifts as they did. She hadn't the animal good nature of Fanny Guidaboni-Visconti, that dashing daughter of the English country gentry, liking all she could get hold of in the way of men and liquor, not giving a rap for what Bally, as she called him, put on paper, but cherishing him as the best and most amusing of lovers.

Yet, through a good many years, passionate epistles were exchanged between Paris and the Ukraine, while Fanny was showing hilarious resource in hiding Bally from his creditors and, though she and her husband weren't well off, paying his debts when arrest was imminent. Incidentally, Fanny's husband was fond of Balzac, as the husbands of Balzac's mistresses nearly always were, including Madame Hanska's.

Madame Hanska had none of that knockabout self-abnegation. She was vain, tiresome, and demanding. She couldn't, or wouldn't, understand why Balzac wasn't able to leave a novel on one side and travel to meet her anywhere in Europe. She was also jealous. She didn't like the sound of Fanny Guidaboni-Visconti. She didn't like the news of various other women, brought to her by Polish informants. She didn't believe Balzac's protestations of chastity and fidelity. She wasn't far wrong.

Still, he was in love with Madame Hanska, and remained so. It was a curiously blended or muddled love—muddled just as his existence was, struggling on until he died, with his art standing majestically clear of the fracas. He loved Madame Hanska, of course, with physical passion, but that didn't distinguish her sharply from some of the others. He thought that in essence she was a pure and innocent soul. That seems strange, but we ought to trust his intuition. He knew her, and we don't. In all his great loves, however, there was that strain of romantic idealization. With Madame Hanska, there was another strain. Being Balzac, he saw great advantages in such a marriage. It would eliminate all the financial imbroglios of a lifetime. He could have a splendid house in Paris. It would be presided over by a hostess of the highest birth, who could dominate the Faubourg Saint-Germain. He would at last have conquered Paris. He would be elected to the Académie. Like his friend Hugo, he would become a peer of France.

Proust knew all about such aspirations, and wrote wisely and tenderly about the part they played in Balzac's love for Madame Hanska. They were materialistic, snobbish, above all vulgar. Yet, if Balzac hadn't been capable of such vulgarity, he wouldn't have been capable of some of the greatest of his works. Proust knew that Balzac's kind of art isn't written by people who have never in Proust's terms got their hands dirty.

From the time that Balzac met Madame Hanska—he was thirty-four, but we should think of him, physically and in all other ways, as much older—his literary achievement moved smoothly to its peak, though nothing else in his life moved smoothly. Two years after *Eugénie Grandet*, he published *Le Père Goriot*. This is one of the great novels of the world. It is also the best introduction to Balzac for those who have been frightened off by the volume of his gigantic corpus. With Père Goriot, he was just developing the device of characters walking in from book to book, which Proust considered such a stroke of genius (to us it seems more obvious).

This novel is the first of three closely linked books, organically connected by much more than recurring characters—*Le Père Goriot, Les Illusions perdues, Splendeurs et misères des courtisanes*. Anyone who isn't captured by these three isn't made to profit from Balzac. Anyone who is can pick up a handful out of the ninety-six novels, some of which are very short, and except to a devotee little known (a few titles—*Gobseck, L'Interdiction, Le Curé de Tours, Les Secrets de la princesse de Cadignan, La Vieille Fille*).

Le Père Goriot was conceived as a kind of lower-class

King Lear, and in its devastating end the conception doesn't seem vainglorious. The setting is as solid as in *Eugénie Grandet* (or as in almost any of Balzac's novels except when he is floating in Swedenborgian mysticism, which suited him as badly as it would suit any writer imaginable, cf. *Louis Lambert*). With some visits to the two great houses of the Goriot daughters, Lear-like daughters married to titled husbands, the book is rooted in the Maison Vauquer, the classical boardinghouse of all fiction, whose atmosphere we breathe and whose smells we cannot escape. It is an awful boardinghouse, much grimmer than Todger's (the equivalent establishment in *Martin Chuzzlewit*), and yet, so exhilarating is Balzac's zest for the actual, zest for whatever is, that one feels as excited as the young Rastignac in his first lodgings in Paris. Balzac knew each room in that boardinghouse and enjoys telling us about the patches of damp on the outer walls, the prices in descending order that the lodgers pay, the kind of provender in the squalid dining room, the dotty repetitive jokes of the nonresident students who come in for the evening meal. They have a fashion of adding *orama* to anything they can think of (as a final touch, "we are going to have a little deathorama up there, aren't we," says the art student). The young are lit up by the high spirits of their age, and often this gives the effect of comedy. But Balzac, though himself as high-spirited as any writer, was not a comic one. He was too immersed in the life of his books to stand a distance outside it, which is the necessity for comic writers. Sometimes there is the deadpan comedy of fact—as in the conversation of the duc de Grandlieu and the vidame de Paniers.

The comte de Montriveau is dead said the vidame: he was a stout man with an incredible passion for oysters. Why, how many did he eat? said the duc de Grandlieu. Ten dozen every day. And none the worse for it? Not in the least. Really! But that's extraordinary. Didn't all this oyster-eating bring on the stone? No, he was perfectly healthy, he died from an accident. From an accident!—his constitution must have told him to eat oysters, they were probably what he needed.

The essence of *Le Père Goriot* is tragic—that is, as tragic as is possible for a novel immersed in the welter of the contradictions of life to be. Much of it is seen through the eyes of Rastignac. He is a young law student just arrived in Paris from Angoulême, coming from an impoverished gentlemanly family, ambitious, attractive, expecting men and especially women to be good, but quick at being undeceived. He is very much a projection of what Balzac had once been or even more, particularly in his physical graces, of what he would have liked to be. He is soon interested in the butt of the boardinghouse, an old man called Goriot. Goriot has gradually moved down the social scale of the house, going from fairly comfortable rooms to the cheapest. He has made money, so the report goes, as a vermicelli manufacturer. He seems stupid, absentminded, dense. His clothes are worn out, and he looks like the workman he once was. The report goes further: he has squandered his money on women, and is still doing so with whatever he has left. He is said to be visited late at night by beautiful young women, expensively dressed. The knowing characters in the boardinghouse comment that Parisian women would do anything for money. Balzac throws in some of

his authorial generalizations—"this is why," "this is because." These are occasionally ludicrous, occasionally shattering in their truth.

Much of what the boardinghouse sees or guesses is
true—except that the women for whom the old man has
impoverished himself are his daughters.

He really had made a comfortable fortune. He loved
his daughters with total sacrificial passion, and still does.
He had lavished much of his money in providing their set-
tlements, so that they could make grand marriages—one,
Anastasie, to the comte de Restaud; the other, Delphine,
to the baron de Nucingen. Both these marriages are loveless. Both husbands get hold of the money. Goriot has to
scrape around for more. He is not welcome in either of the
two elegant houses, being too humble. All he asks is to get
a glimpse of his daughters as they go off sumptuously to
balls. Oh yes, he tells young Rastignac, they love him, they
love him dearly; he understands their position and they
understand his. Each has a lover, and their lovers are as
grasping as their husbands (in Balzac's novels many women,
even the most sophisticated and desirable women of the
beau monde, are constantly giving money to their lovers—
this was a subject on which he had unequaled firsthand
knowledge). Rastignac falls in love with Delphine. She is
ten years older than he is, and becomes enraptured (again,
Balzac's unequaled firsthand knowledge of the impassioned
growth of her emotion). Rastignac sees the culmination
from the inside.

Financial disasters increase. Goriot is now living in the
worst room of the boardinghouse. He has kept for himself
not enough money for the bleakest subsistence. Delphine

has rented a handsome apartment for Rastignac, Goriot paying for it. The daughters clamor for more. There is a furious scene between them in the presence of their father. He collapses with a stroke.

He is known to be dying. There is no one to look after him, and no one to pay for doctors. Rastignac and the tough, decent young medical student Bianchon (Balzac found virtue in him and sometimes in other professionals, never in the high world, however much he was beglamored by it) have to do what they can themselves. It takes Goriot, in his squalid room, days to die. This is one of the most painful death scenes in all literature. In his conscious moments, he shouts for his daughters. When will they come? He talks gently of his love for them, and of how they love him. Yet he knows. In one interval he says, "Neither of them! They are busy, they are sleeping, they will not come, I know it. You have to die to know what your children are. Ah, my friend, do not marry; do not have children. You give them life, they give you death in return. You bring them into the world, and they push you from it. No, they will not come! I have known that for the last ten years. I sometimes told myself so, but I did not dare believe it."

He has a pauper's funeral. Bianchon and Rastignac cannot afford to pay for a mass, but scrape together enough for vespers. Rastignac stays beside the grave. He is not yet hardened, but this is the end of his youth.

Balzac makes as few concessions to gentility as any writer, and yet even this harsh work isn't dispiriting, because it was written from the midst of life itself, and his own life. When the pretenses are stripped off, this life still has its own wonder: this is how it is. That is perhaps even more evident in the two subsequent volumes of the trilogy. *Les Illusions perdues* is not so economical as *Le Père Goriot*, but to many the most satisfying of all his books, though completed when his physical vitality was already in decline. In that book and in *Splendeurs et misères des courtisanes* time passes, and Rastignac emerges as a successful competitor in the high world, as callous as those against whom he once revolted.

Quantitatively, Balzac's creativity may have slackened a little after the period of *Le Père Goriot*. He was still more productive than most men. Even toward the end, when the heart attacks had set in, he produced work of the highest quality—witness *La Cousine Bette,* one of the greatest of his novels. Cousine Bette herself is one of his forbidding characters, loveless, pitiless, rancorous, seen without sentimentality, alive. Occasionally one wishes, in a stern and beautiful work of art, that she would absent herself a little, so that one could revel in Madame Marneffe. She is a supreme forerunner of Becky Sharp. It is likely that Thackeray had read *La Cousine Bette* before he set to work on *Vanity Fair*.

Some years before *La Cousine Belte,* when Balzac was nearly forty, in a preface to a new collected edition—published as one of his glorious ideas in search of becoming solvent at last—he christened the whole corpus *La Comédie humaine*. The title was suggested by someone else, who had been reading Dante. Balzac was entirely capable of thinking of it himself.

Such a prodigious work of art has proved difficult for orthodox critics to cope with. For a long time Flaubert, not an abundant writer, was held up as the master of the nineteenth-century French novel. Proust, at the beginning of our century, was saying sardonically that Balzac was read only by the people he wrote about—engineers, country priests, society women, civil servants, doctors, etc., etc., not at all by intellectual persons. But Proust was one of his most understanding admirers. So was Henry James. About the same time as Proust was writing *Contre Sainte-Beuve*, James published an article called "The Lesson of Balzac" (1905). In this piece James states, with unusual explicitness, that there is nothing to argue about. Simply, Balzac was the greatest of all novelists. All the roads lead back to him, said Henry James. Proust wouldn't have entirely agreed, but his own tribute and James's haven't been given to many writers. Also, in a different vein, the tribute of Friedrich Engels. He said that, though Balzac was a Catholic, a monarchist, a reactionary, he taught Engels more about nineteenth-century France than all the historians, sociologists, political analysts in the world. That opinion was echoed by Lenin. Balzac, who venerated ability, wherever it existed, would have liked praise from those two.

After *Le Père Goriot*, as Balzac passed into his early forties, the great work went on steadily as if accumulated by the best adjusted of men, three or four volumes a year. The muddle of his life also went on, not so steadily. Schemes for wiping out those debts! And then becoming rich! Propperty deals! A new magazine! Plays! New lawyers, new contracts with publishers! Letters to Madame Hanska, far away at Wierzchownia! New houses with back entrances so that he could slip away from the duns! The cheerful Fanny, trips abroad with other women!

He didn't get much peace. In truth he didn't want much. His natural medium was this continuous hubbub. He took time off for rest periods with good old Margonne or the wise and anxious Zulma. He felt extreme euphoria as he calculated how much his new financial schemes would bring in. Debts discharged, money showering down. It was the arithmetic of hope, it looked infallible on paper. He was so elated that he went off with seraphic content and bought on credit more expensive objets d'art. But Zulma and other protective friends were anxious. He was too old in body for a man around forty. He had fits of giddiness, breathlessness, chest and stomach pains. His singular regime wasn't much help for that physical condition. He continued to make do with a few hours' sleep and the lashings of black coffee. The disorder of his life, the escapes from his house, weren't what a sensible doctor would have liked to see. Probably though, as he himself would have been quick to diagnose, his whole physique and temperament, his abnormal prodigality in all senses, wasn't conducive to a long life.

Then, when he was forty-two, just as he was about to publish the resounding title of his *oeuvre,* there was a dazzling trick of fortune. He hadn't abandoned all his dreams of marriage to Madame Hanska, but the correspondence had at last, after ten years, dwindled off. One morning he received formal notice from the Ukraine. Her husband had died. Balzac was in ecstasy. Now everything was in his hands. He was in love as much as he had ever been. Sexual delight, emotional communion. He genuinely loved her, and her violent feelings must have met a need of his. Not only prosperity, the solution of all his money troubles, but also luxury and grandeur. He had no conceivable shame about that component of his hopes. He wrote about it to his sister and confidante. He took it as natural, as he did the rest of the human condition.

However, it didn't work out like that. Madame Hanska hung back, and hung back for eight more years. There were some practical reasons for this. As an aristocratic subject of the Tsar, she would have to get permission for the marriage. The Tsar was impressed by Balzac's writing (like Stalin, Nicholas I had literary taste and often thought highly of Russian works that he wouldn't allow to be published), but his advisers disapproved of the marriage. So, much more strongly, did the Hanskis, and the Rzewuskis, the widow's own family. They had no use for the vulgar little Frenchman. They exerted themselves to get the land and the money out of his control.

This was a situation for which Balzac was magnificently equipped. By letter, and in his jaunts around Europe with Madame Hanska, he deployed all his psychological skills, which were great, and his command of worldly knowledge, also great, particularly in theory, to bring her to the crunch. He invented strategies with the families, he produced appropriate language for the Tsar, stressing Balzac's devout veneration for monarchy. He dwelt on plans for the splendid house they would build in Paris and the glory of their life together.

When she was with him, she succumbed. The erotic bond was as strong as at the beginning. People made fun of the couple, both middle-aged, both corpulent, he grossly so. Never mind. On their trips around Germany and Italy, along with Madame Hanska's daughter and her fiancé,

Balzac and his Rubens-style beloved were rapt in sustained carnal bliss. The young people adored him, and called him "Bilboquet," which became a family joke, teasing him about his rotundity. Bilboquet is a French children's game, in which a pierced ball is to be caught on a spike—something like cup-and-ball, but more appropriate to Balzac's physique.

Away from him, safe in the Ukraine, Madame Hanska's doubts returned. That was probably not only through her family. She didn't trust him. She thought he frequently deceived her; and that was not entirely unreasonable. She also thought increasingly that, despite his Napoleonic mastery of financial tactics, which in his presence overwhelmed her, he was not trustworthy with money; and that was not entirely unreasonable either. Certainly he had wheedled from her fairly sizable sums from her private fortune, which was separate from the Hanski estate. With sublime confidence, Balzac invested most of this in French railway stock. As usual with Balzacian projects he had made a good long-term judgment. As usual with such projects, he had forgotten short-term factors, such as political disturbances. As the stock exchange quotation collapsed, Madame Hanska was not pleased to be called on for more sizable sums.

Also with her money, he bought, and reconstructed, a house in Paris suitable to their future grandeur. Proudly he showed it to her on her clandestine visit to Paris. She thought it was dreadful.

Balzac visited her in the Ukraine and they had another of their high times. But by now the years had gone by. For once the teeming creativity had left him, and in her house he wrote nothing for months. He believed he had no future to look forward to, except the unobtainable marriage. They must all have realized that he was a sick man.

On Balzac's second visit to Wierzchownia, when he was fifty, he was taken ill. It was a heart seizure. The Polish doctors took a grave view. It was then that the Tsar, after one refusal, gave his consent to the marriage. Then either Madame Hanska felt she had no pretext for delaying any longer, or else she loved him in some fashion, or else she was moved by pity, or perhaps all those emotions came together. Anyway, she didn't hesitate, and they were married in a Polish church. That journey to the church was a long one over the steppes, and affected his heart. The journey to Paris, much of it through a Polish March, did worse. It took over a fortnight. They arrived home, the home he had built for her and which she detested. He was dying. He survived three months, and then consciousness left him. Mercifully for him, not for those who had to watch him die. His friend Victor Hugo, the other monstrous genius of contemporary France, came in on the last evening, and found him hard to recognize.

At the very last everything that Balzac craved had accrued to him, but he didn't have it for long. Victor Hugo pronounced the funeral oration on the hillside of the Père Lachaise cemetery, where Rastignac had once thrown down his challenge to Paris. The funeral was not a great assembly of national mourning, as Victor Hugo's own was to be. In the sunset, though, Hugo delivered some of his most rolling and generous rhetoric: "Monsieur de Balzac was one of the first among the greatest, one of the highest among the best. . . . On one and the same day, he enters glory and the tomb. Henceforth he will shine above the clouds that hide our heads, among the brightest stars in our country's sky."

DICKENS

I N their youth, Stendhal and Balzac wanted to write
plays. In his youth, Dickens wanted to act in plays.
Of all the great geniuses in literature, he was the born
actor. This may be partly responsible for the singular history of his literary reputation. From his own time until recently, sober critics have never known quite what to make
of him. That he was a great genius no one in his senses
would now be prepared publicly to deny. It is possible to
argue that, in the English language, he is the most marvelous writer after Shakespeare. Yet it has needed a new
kind of sensibility to begin to come to terms with him—as
one can see in the work of Geoffrey Thurley (1976).

It is dead wrong to try to ignore his histrionic necessities. If one isolates the "dark" Dickens, or regards him
only as a social evangelist, one ignores the complexities and
contradictions, and finally the hypermanic power, which
are inherent both in the man and in his art.

The story of his life is by now well known, thanks to
the biography by Edgar Johnson, one of the best of all
biographies of writers, which, by the way, are nearly al-

ways more intimate and deeper than the biographies of public figures. A new edition of Johnson's work was published in 1978, and there appears to be not much fresh information discovered in the last twenty years. More likely than not, modern scholarship has done its work, and we have as much hard information as we ever shall. One submerged fact has been dug up by Johnson. Dickens's father was not merely on the edge of bankruptcy, but actually went bankrupt. Most, perhaps all, of the other novelists in this volume would as grown men have laughed this off; but Dickens, with his own vulnerability and living in the regulated commercial civilization of nineteenth-century England, concealed it and must have felt it as a special shame.

He was born in 1812, into a family in the lowest fringe of the English lower middle class. His Dickens grandparents had been superior domestic servants in a noble house. One or two of their relatives had made a small step upward socially, and become minor civil servants in the ramshackle but growing national administration. At least one of them got into financial trouble: there was plenty of corruption in the England of Dickens's youth. Through some of those relatives, Dickens's father, John, also became a minor civil servant. He had, as we know both from the biographical facts and from the use that his son made of him in novels (compare Mr. Micawber and Mr. Dorrit), pretensions to gentility—the pretensions of the petty bourgeoisie, determined to be distinguished from the working class just below them. To Mr. Micawber, and no doubt to Dickens's father, the working class was different in kind from their own. We also know that Dickens senior was improvident, endearing but not unduly scrupulous about money, frequently and disastrously in debt, and, according to the law of the period, imprisoned for it.

It was a heritage for the youthful Dickens at the same time humbler and more precarious than that of any of the other great novelists. It was curiously similar to that of H. G. Wells half a century later. It couldn't have been more designed to produce extreme class sensitivity. In fact, Dickens was more profoundly wounded by class than any other major English writer. No one wrote with more passion, indignation, and concern about the sufferings of the poor; but the last thing he wanted was to be identified with them.

He could express, with eloquence and power, the class hatred of Bradley Headstone and Charlie Hexam; but he couldn't possibly express it as though he had that hatred himself, as Stendhal did in Julien Sorel.

He was wounded for life, as many men would not have been, by being set to work at twelve in the blacking factory near Blackfriars. This was because of his father's usual incompetence, and more than incompetence, with money. To the young Dickens it meant being treated like a common boy, working alongside common boys, deprived of the education that he felt should have been his by right. He never forgave the insult, and couldn't speak of it.

The same insistence on his status stands out of his novels whenever there is a boy who, however vestigially, reflects part of himself. Oliver Twist—workhouse, no proper education, but still immediately recognized by slum boys as someone superior to themselves and inexplicably, after the facts of his upbringing, speaking standard English. What did Dickens speak himself, when at nineteen he was courting Maria Beadnell? To anyone with an English ear, there must have been a trace of the sub-cockney of the Medway towns. He had a fine English ear himself, and by the time of his first success those cockney sounds would have been eliminated. Pip in *Great Expectations*—the most perfect of the novels of maturity. It is a sophisticated and beautiful examination of social climbing, but even there the wound, the unhealed wound of Pip's childhood, is more naked than the moral message.

The wound was unhealed in Dickens himself. Edmund Wilson was right; but not so right in making that somber resentment obscure so much else in a personality highly charged beyond any kind of human norm, just as the genius was. As a very young man, just growing out of boyhood, he was a dazzling figure. He had immense charm. He was a dandy and a show-off. He was unusually good-looking, in a curiously girlish way. The pictorial, and later the photographic, record of Dickens's face is the most puzzling of any writer's. The pictures in early middle age might belong to a different man from the soft-looking youth of twenty. But those soft looks didn't deceive anyone around him. His child's experiences had left their mark, and no young man ever had a harder will—though even with the easiest of upbringings it is impossible to imagine that his will would have been much less inexorable. He was determined to be what he always called "a distinguished man." His self-confidence was limitless. There aren't many great writers who have been lacking in self-confidence, but Dickens lacked it less than any other. It is difficult to think of any other writer who would, right at the start of his career, have christened himself the Inimitable—and meant it.

He had all the reasons in the world for self-confidence.

As well as being supremely gifted as a writer, which he must have known as soon as he wrote the first of his impressionist sketches (collected as *Sketches by Boz*), and which he probably guessed before that, he was both very clever and very able—which not all great writers are. He could have been successful at almost anything. He probably could have been a star actor, one of his first choices. He could have made a name as a radical politician. He proved himself to be, commercially as in all other ways, one of the best of editors.

In fact, beginning with no advantages at all except the considerable one of being himself, he showed himself efficient, as well as talented, at all he touched. He reported on cases in the courts (and, like Balzac, though not so professionally, picked up something of the law, which came in useful later on). He trained himself to become a first-class parliamentary recorder, a kind of private precursor of the present Hansard staff. As a journalist he followed elections all over the country (see the Eatonswill contest in *The Pickwick Papers*). He had insensate physical energy. He earned money on the side from free-lance articles. In his early twenties, even before the sunburst of *Pickwick,* his income was comfortable enough and safe enough for marriage.

About marriage he had his only reverse in those brilliant years. He had fallen in love, at the age of nineteen, with a girl called Maria Beadnell. He was not only handsome, but must also have had the attraction of a sexually vigorous man. He was inordinately high-spirited. He was fun. To an extent, she seems to have loved him in return. But she was a brainless and silly girl, as the distant future pathetically proved. She didn't see all the possibilities in Dickens. What was more decisive, nor did her family. Her father was a bank manager. They were prosperous middle class, and here was a young man without a penny. They may have also thought him vulgar and cocky. She let herself be persuaded to get rid of him.

Quite soon he consoled himself with another girl, Kate Hogarth, daughter of a journalist, socially nearer his own circle. He duly captivated her, and was already masterful and willful before the marriage. He remained masterful and willful during a marriage that lasted twenty years, until he broke it up. He was almost certainly, so far as we can judge from indirect evidence, a physically passionate man, but he had remarkably little intuition about women. This is evident in his novels, and in that respect they don't stand the remotest comparison with Balzac's.

With almost everything in his favor—primal attractiveness, glamor, early and continuing fame, plenty of money from twenty-five onward, everything that the other great novelists might have envied—he was a worse chooser of women than any of them. Maria, Kate, and much later his final choice in middle age—they were all disasters.

His fame came earlier and more completely than that of any other of the great novelists. By twenty-five he was a national figure and from then on never ceased to be one. This began because of *The Pickwick Papers*. No first novel in any language has made such a stir.

The story of how it happened is well known. An up-and-coming publisher had commissioned Robert Seymour, who had a reputation as an illustrator, to produce a series of drawings. The idea was to jeer at the adventures of a group of comic sporting men (in the 1830s, it was a standard joke that people not used to field sports liked setting out to imitate country gentlemen). The drawings would need some sort of textual accompaniment. They looked around for a writer, not too expensive. There was a young cockney journalist who might do. He would be told to follow instructions about what Seymour wanted. Dickens took the job. He also took charge. At twenty-four, almost unknown, he was the last man in London to do what anyone else wanted. This was the first demonstration in a publishing house of that demonic will.

He was going to transmogrify the original banal, uninspired idea. He couldn't escape a flat-footed beginning. He would improvise as he went along. Anything that interested him could be packed into this portmanteau of a book. The unfortunate Robert Seymour blew out his brains. Never mind. Dickens demanded a new illustrator of his own choice.

The story was issued in monthly parts, price one shilling. The first numbers didn't sell. Dickens introduced a comic, clever, witty servant, one of the oldest devices of knockabout art, and one that he may have had in mind all along. From that number he was home. The country went mad on *Pickwick*. It was something like the reception today of a supreme hit record. The publishers were made, and so was he.

It is a profound lack of literary—and of human—insight that leads solemn persons today to try to ignore *Pickwick*. It contains a great deal of Dickens. It foreshadows even more. It flashes and glitters with his hilarious high spirits—yes, disquieting and manic sometimes, but beyond anyone else's power, and part of him until life, his own life, darkened them, and capable of bursting out even then. In *Pickwick,* the young Dickens had gusto for nearly anything—the roads of southern England, very pretty in the 1830s (unless you looked into the rural hovels behind, which Dickens never explored), the great coarse lavish meals, the English weather, snow, ice, sunshine, the joys of physical endurance, the idiocies of parliamentary elections and the law. He had the gusto of simple appetite and also the gusto of disrespect—disrespect for all that a modern journalist in the Dickens style would call "the Establishment." He had gusto for his own conception of innocent sexless goodness, represented by Pickwick himself. This didn't leave him for a long time after, and often strikes false—until subtilized in a different and more deeply felt fashion, steeped in Russian tradition, as in Dostoevsky's Myshkin.

The manic spirits in *Pickwick* already showed their depressive complement. The gothic blacknesses entered there, in the totally irrelevant short stories, interposed presumably to fill up space. Serial publication allowed for self-indulgence in that side of his temperament. It is interesting to reflect that in his last book, *Edwin Drood,* that side is given full expression; but it is present in this first book too.

Further, he never could escape the shadows of the prison. They lurked over him not only through temperament but also through experience. It must have startled the original readers that in *Pickwick,* on the surface a jocular entertainment, the amiable gentleman has to go to prison.

Yet we, knowing more about Dickens than the original readers, go quite wrong if now we miss the jocular entertainment. *Pickwick* is a funny book. It was, and rightly, the source of Dickens's reputation as a humorist. In his own time, the Victorians read him for a good many reasons, but certainly, and perhaps most of all, for his humor. Nowadays we see it with different eyes from theirs; but we have to see it.

Dickens's humor has nothing in common with that of other nineteenth-century English writers. It isn't the understated witty comment of Jane Austen. It isn't the quiet, experienced, acceptant smile of Trollope. There is nothing understated about Dickensian humor. A lot of it is a mimic's humor. And at the same time it is a young man's humor, full of blissful confidence that he can tell all the foolish persons around him what the answers are. In these explosions of humor he sounds more benevolent than he really is, because of his violent delight in human absurdity. Often the laughter is discomforting. There is revenge hidden—or not so hidden—in the gibes of all of us. There was much revenge in Dickens's. Flora Finching is a mildly funny literary creation. But when we know the circumstances in life from which she was taken, the aftertaste is harsh. Dickens with romantic enthusiasm had encouraged the middle-aged Maria Beadnell to meet him, after twenty years. He found that she was a silly, gushing, loquacious, affected woman. It wasn't in Dickens's savagely disappointed heart to reflect that the scene viewed from her eyes, or from God's, had a touch of quivering pathos.

The mimic's, young man's, humor of Dickens is made wonderful by his speed of association and transference, between words or visual objects or anything else in the world of sense. Books can become human beings, human beings can turn into doorknobs. The mimicry vibrates with a great performer's mastery.

By and large, though, Dickens soon became tired of that mimicry. At thirty he could still write *Martin Chuzzlewit,* which has strong claims to be the best sustained comic novel in English. Pecksniff is the supreme example of Dickens's savage humor (just as Jonas Chuzzlewit is the supreme example of Dickens's gothic vision, and some of the criminal psychology there anticipates Dostoevsky). After *Martin Chuzzlewit,* there was an outburst of the sunniest Dickens in *David Copperfield* (published when Dickens was thirty-seven), where the young man's gibing can coexist with all his other kinds of humor.

From then on, presumably out of habit and, since Dickens was the last author to forget his audience, because they expected it, he did some mechanical mimicry and dutifully introduced comic characters. They are nearly all dead on the page—Captain Cuttle, Venus, and the whole fabricated troupe. It is rather like seeing an aging variety artist going through his old routine, sick and tired of it, wondering when someone will let him play a straight part.

He was one of the most complex writers, and his forms of humor are as complex, and sometimes as dissociated, as the rest of it. The mimic's humor hasn't worn well with late twentieth-century readers, but a quite different sort of playfulness—which we might call excursions into the surrealistic, though that is not entirely accurate—is far more difficult to resist. Sarah Gamp is an utterly unanalyzable feat of comic genius at its height. Could any other writer, Shakespeare included, have conceived such a char-

acter, and, apparently out of caprice, suddenly inserted her
in such a book? Another master feat of creative prodigality
occurs later in Dickens's career, in *Little Dorrit*. By that
time, the comic vein was running very thin and yet, in the
scene that contains the ill-natured jeering at Flora Finching, there is the splendid invention, grotesque and inexplicable, of Mrs. F.'s Aunt.

Little of Dickens's humor is gentle, less perhaps, under the high jinks, than that of any other of the great novelists, though he was more exuberantly funny than all the
rest put together, if we forget Proust. There is one glowing exception in Dickens's work. In *David Copperfield* his
deepest affections were engaged. Those deep affections were
more concentrated than the radiant spread of his creation
might suggest. With *David Copperfield* he was, in a literal
sense, on his home ground. He is far gentler to Mr. Micawber than to any other of his full-dress comic characters.
This is obvious not only in the treatment, but in the language. He is also far gentler to David Copperfield himself. David Copperfield is, of course, in essence Charles
Dickens; and it wasn't in Dickens's temperament to apply
savage fun to that tender and valuable being. But he does
apply some of the most delectable cheerful fun found anywhere in all his writing.

For instance, when David gives his first party. They
have had dinner, at which David has provided plenty to
drink, and has drunk, what he is not used to, plenty himself. They are leaving for the theater, which is a mile or
two away from David's rooms. "Owing to some confusion
in the dark, the door was gone. I was feeling for it in the
window curtains, when Steerforth, laughing, took me by

the arm and led me out. Near the bottom, somebody fell, and rolled down. Somebody else said it was Copperfield. I was angry at this false report, until, finding myself on my back in the passage, I began to think there might be some foundation for it." (There follows a scene at the theater, where he meets Agnes, who thinks sensibly that his friends ought to take him home. He makes an attempt to say good night, gets up, and goes away.) "They [the friends] followed, and I stepped at once out of the box door into my bedroom where only Steerforth was with me, helping me to undress, and where I was by turns telling him that Agnes was my sister, and adjuring him to bring the corkscrew that I might open another bottle of wine."

If there is a better, or better-natured, description of a young man's first drunk, it ought to be produced. Notice— "I stepped at once out of the box door into my bedroom." Dickens was a master of all the verbal arts, including, as here, economy.

While *Pickwick* was still in progress, and Dickens having to meet the monthly deadline, he was already building on the success, using energies that would make most men seem weaklings. Plans for new novels! *Oliver Twist, Nicholas Nickleby, Barnaby Rudge* beginning to take shape in his imagination! Contracts for the new novels! Contract to edit a miscellany for Bentley! Work, riches, fame! As for the books themselves, he wasn't yet the conscious artist that he was to become—losing something in the process, including the wildest of his spontaneity, gaining more. None of his novels before *Martin Chuzzlewit* has a coherent theme. They started off with the random eye-flash of a brilliant journalist—the Poor Law workhouses, juvenile crime in

London, the schools in the north for bastards whom no one wanted. Everyone knew about these miseries; Dickens knew he could light them up with his spectacular vision. But the artistic wonders of these early novels, and there are many, lie not in their apparent core, but out on the periphery. In one of them, *The Old Curiosity Shop*, Quilp glints on the edge of the scene as an extraordinary excrescence of genius. He must have come out of the blue; or, rather, out of the devil in Dickens's own nature. Some of his appearances in the Hogarth home had a distinctly Quilpish tinge, somewhat diluted for domestic consumption.

Though as a writer he hadn't become his full self, as a man of power, businessman, incarnation of will, he was already formed by the age of twenty-five, and didn't alter until he died. The moment he had his first intimation of moneymaking success, he was determined to get what he wanted. Nothing should stop him. He was ruthless with publishers. If he had to break contracts, contracts were broken. All the hardship of his youth had tempered his will. Resentment at petty slights made it more steely. He didn't forgive easily. He had all the bargaining weapons, since, as he knew with absolute confidence, he was the source of money on whom these publishers lived. But it was also the invulnerable edge of his personality that helped him to win.

In effect, he was not scrupulous. He had the gift, possessed also by George Eliot, of being convinced of his own rectitude in any business transaction. It didn't look like that to some of his publishers. It doesn't look like that today. One has to remember that publishing in the mid-nineteenth century was still an amateur, small-scale business, without much in the way of recognized practices. In his private dealings, Dickens was strictly honest. He soon began to live in a style appropriate for a distinguished man, and he took responsibility for a ragtag and bobtail of shifty and feckless relatives and in due course for disappointing sons. Despite all that, he handled his finances with his usual efficiency, and died leaving about £93,000, a substantial sum for a writer in 1870.

There is a diverting difference between the fortunes of the major writers in Victorian England and their contemporaries elsewhere. The English were all competent at literary business and effective with their money—Dickens, Trollope (straightforward, but driving hard bargains), Thackeray (after youthful extravagances, just as prudent), George Eliot (with Lewes beside her, the sharpest operator of the lot), Hardy (careful to the point of miserliness). Their French colleagues, Hugo apart, were usually in financial trouble, and Stendhal and Balzac never got out of it. The Russians were either well-to-do landowners (Tolstoy, Turgenev) who made unnecessary fortunes out of books, or penurious men (Dostoevsky) who made much less. There was a second diverting difference between the English and French life-styles, to be mentioned later. This one wasn't to the English advantage.

At the age of thirty Dickens was at his peak as a marvelous young man. Perhaps, to judge by our contemporary standards, he was not as young as all that, despite his still-juvenile appearance. His character was formed, more formed than most men's ever are. He may have had intimations that life, any life, even a life as externally glorious as his, was in an inadmissible fashion a dark and disappointing business. His greatest art was still to come, but the writing itself had already become more of a strain. It was no longer the sheer joyous spree when, in the exuberance of confidence, success, and the expectation of certain happiness, it had come as naturally as breathing. It might have astonished those who saw the public performances in which he came to find fulfillment or self-forgetfulness, but from thirty onward he knew little serenity and less happiness. He had bouts of hyperhilarious spirits. He expressed happiness, but he often, and increasingly, felt cheated of it.

Even in the supreme buoyancy of his youth he had been indignant about the social evils he saw around him. This was a generous indignation, and became more intense as his buoyancy lessened and the inner disquiet grew. It cried out in his Christmas stories and then became realized in *Bleak House, Little Dorrit, Our Mutual Friend,* the somber novels in which his social anguish is most naked. It isn't so naked when he is writing from other sides of his nature, as in *David Copperfield* and *Great Expectations.*

He was, and didn't stop being, in some sense a radical. It is necessary, though, to make some qualifications. He wasn't a political thinker. He hated a great deal of the society he was living in. His criticisms were savage, sometimes ill-informed, often just. The outburst in *A Christmas Carol*—after Scrooge has suggested that a system of what we might now call triage should be applied and cripples such as Tiny Tim allowed to die, so as to cut down the surplus population—is a splendid shout of passionate goodwill:

> Man, said the Ghost, if Man you be in heart, not adamant. Forbear that wicked cant until you have discovered What the surplus is and Where it is. It may be, that in the sight of heaven, you are more worthless and less fit to live than

millions like this poor man's child. Oh God! to hear the insect on the leaf pronouncing on the too much life among his hungry brothers in the dust!

Incidentally, only a writer of the greatest gifts could have produced *A Christmas Carol*. It was written in absolute internal freedom, whereas the dark novels of his middle age, structured and considered, were written under constraints.

He perceived wrongs, suffering, follies with all the acuteness of his eye and the passionate immediacy of his temperament. But he let fly with too much facility—Parliament was nonsense, administration was fatuous or corrupt, the English society was rotten. He didn't see that many of these evils were inherent in any conceivable society, and that societies are no more perfectible than individual men. Since his time the world has learned a lot about almost every kind of social management. Some of the wrongs on which he used his tremendous rhetoric have been put right, but not by his easy remedies. He desperately believed, or tried to believe, that men would become better, and that human goodness would remake the world as he decided it should be.

Well, it hasn't gone like that. A hundred years after his death he would see the grossest suffering diminishing, but through harsher means than any he could have imagined.

His immediate vision was brilliant. Like others with brilliant immediate vision, he hadn't much sense of the future. There was a characteristic example in his famous first trip to America—at the age of thirty, just as restlessness, impatience, disquiet were beginning to gnaw at his life. He went to America thinking that in that new society, free from tradition, with none of the legacies he detested in England, he would find something near his social dream. He didn't. No writer had ever been so feted. No writer can ever be so feted again. But he got attacked in the press when he raised the topic of international copyright (he would have made a fortune in America if he had been paid for his books). He didn't like being attacked. As usual his will hardened, and his protest became fiercer. He was soon loathing America more than England. The interesting thing was, he appears not to have envisaged for a second what the country would and could become.

That episode tells us something about Dickens. It is remarkably like the experience of the Utopian radicals, in spirit much like himself, who went to the Soviet Union in the 1930s, expecting heaven and not finding it. They, too, suffered negative conversion. In Dickens's time it was only more skeptical and reflective men such as Anthony Trollope who could imagine the future of America.

In his early thirties, Dickens still looked preternaturally young. Tom Trollope, Anthony's elder brother, later became a close friend of Dickens, but at their first meeting described him as "a dandified pretty-boy-looking sort of figure, singularly young looking . . . with a slight flavour of the whipper snapper."

Little they all knew. Dickens was no longer young. He had entered a phase, which he lived in until he died, of unappeasable restlessness. With strain and effort, great books came. With strain and effort, little Christmas books came, tawdry self-parodies after the first miraculous one, but very profitable. But the strain of writing made him invent strategies to delay getting down to it. Travel. Amateur theatricals, which took up a disproportionate amount of his frantic energy. Plans for editing newspapers. Plans, which in due course matured, for running a periodical. Then plans, ominous plans which also in due course matured, for public readings.

It isn't certain, but it is possible that for years he couldn't or wouldn't recognize why this restlessness was driving him out of control. He had on the surface everything that a man could wish for. Why was he dissatisfied?

There is an answer, and in time he accepted it; but it wasn't as simple as it may have seemed. His marriage had gone wrong; or, it came to appear to him, it had been wrong from the beginning. His wife Kate had borne ten children in fifteen years, often with the minimum of delay between childbirth and the next pregnancy. She had also had several miscarriages. But he had been bored and irritated by her very early—and Dickens wasn't the man to accept that some of the trouble was on his side. She wasn't especially bright, and gave him no sort of companionship. She was low-spirited and couldn't share his frantic energy. She wasn't any good in company, and as he rose to eminence he was invited out alone. Poor dear Mrs. Dickens, said the benevolent millionairess Angela Burdett-Coutts. At the heart of the domestic life of the greatest apostle of glowing family well-being there was a falsity and a fraud. Dickens felt that he hadn't received what he deserved and what he must have. The present life was intolerable.

There is no evidence that he asked himself whether something like this wouldn't have happened with any wife—though some of his intimates tried to suggest it. With his passionate romantic imagination, he felt that there might always have been the perfect love the other side of the hill. If he had been given to detached self-examination, he could have remembered that it was very odd, and not what other men would have done, to make a cult of his wife's sixteen-year-old sister in the first year of the marriage, and when the girl died to continue with a cult of her memory.

He had little insight about women, and less about what a woman might give him. In his rigid self-will and self-concern, it was his love, what he was expending on a woman, that mattered, not what she could return. The description of David's utter abandonment to Dora is one of the best descriptions of young love in any literature— but it is all on David's side. It seems irrelevant what, if anything, Dora is capable of feeling. We now know that something like this was true in life. Maria Beadnell's response to the young Dickens remains a mystery, simply because he never understood it. He understood her response to the old Dickens, and his own first intoxicated hope of recapturing his primal rapture. He was merciless about it and her in *Little Dorrit*.

In his relations with women, both in life and in art, Dickens was unlucky in his time. All the English Victorian novelists were handicapped by comparison with their European colleagues, he more than any. The English shone in their business deals—but, when one thinks of them alongside Balzac, Stendhal, Hugo, Tolstoy, Dostoevsky, they hadn't much knowledge of adult women in their flesh and bone. Some, notably Trollope and Hardy, had great natural insight into women, understood them as individual persons and not just as objects of love, and compensated for lack of Balzacian experience just by that kind of intuition.

Dickens didn't possess that intuition. His ego was too strong. He thought he knew what he wanted. What he wanted, in every aspect of life but this, he had every confidence that he could obtain. This led him to the bitter disappointment of his later years (compare Dostoevsky, who had something in common with Dickens, but who, contrary to all conventional expectations, showed much more acceptant wisdom; this made him, as will be mentioned in the next chapter, increasingly happy at the age when Dickens became increasingly distraught). This lack of detached intuition is also responsible for the greatest deficiency in Dickens's novels. There is scarcely one deep relation between man and woman in the whole corpus—that is, a relation where each is taking part, not necessarily with joy or love or desire, but a part as full human beings, as with Grushenka-Mitya, Natasha-Pierre, César Birotteau–Constance, Balthasar Claes–Joséphine.

Living with his wife had, after a marriage of more than twenty years, become intolerable to Dickens. He was not the man to tolerate the intolerable. Somehow or other, there would have to be a separation. The separation came, but in a manner of bizarre harshness. He had fallen in love with a girl of eighteen. Her name was Ellen Ternan, and she was a member of an acting family in which the women were intelligent and gifted, though not as actresses. His love was ecstatic and, so far as he admitted it, pure—another of his raptures for a youthful Spirit (which is what he called her in letters to incredulous friends). He gave her a piece of jewelry, and by a clerical gaffe the bill went to his wife.

She was desolated, upbraiding, given over to mourning. Of course she had known before this that they were near a crisis. Her family, to whom Dickens had been lavishly generous and who as a consequence disliked him, had also known, and had decided that it was for her to insist on a separation. To them, he was responsible for all her miseries. He had treated her, not only without love, but also without even common kindness. She must go at once, and he must provide for her.

Dickens was outraged. Not at the plan for a separation, but at being confronted by abuse and blame. He wasn't given to hearing doubts of his own rectitude, and when he did hear them he had an extraordinary gift for utterly impenetrable moral indignation. Then the Hogarths let slip the accusation that Ellen Ternan was his mistress. At that Dickens's indignation became something like deranged. All his furious and implacable will went into action. He wouldn't provide a penny for his wife, much less for any of the rest of them, unless that slander was withdrawn, formally, on paper, available for publication, with the statement that his wife without qualification joined in the withdrawal. There were negotiations that went on for some weeks. Dickens, as always in conflicts of will, prevailed. The Hogarths and Kate Dickens testified to Ellen's purity and to the innocence of her relations with Dickens. They didn't believe a word of it, though at the time it was true.

Dickens went on acting like a man deranged. He insisted on issuing statements to the press, saying that the separation was inevitable but friendly. He seemed to lose his judgment altogether. He was determined to assure his beloved public that he was as they knew him, without any trace of discredit attached. He received some bad advice, and, though he didn't usually take advice, this he did. The editor of *The Times* said that these public statements would minimize gossip. They multiplied it.

Dickens found his release, the only release he ever found, in frenzied activity. More theatricals. More public readings. Those last were the test of how his public were responding. Would they turn away from him now? He went on the stage at the St. Martin's Hall with absolute self-command. He was, after all, a supreme public performer. The audience rose to him with adulation and love, as great as it had ever been, or greater. This was repeated all over the country. Like some actors, he called on emotional support from his public much as, if he had been luckier or different, he might have received it from a woman. The love of his public he could rely on, as long as he lived.

So far as can be inferred (the evidence is fragmentary but cumulative) he didn't receive much support from Ellen Ternan. On his side, it was a rhapsodic love, a young man's love, recapturing some of the exhilaration he had felt at twenty with Maria Beadnell. He was drunk with that rapture, but he knew more now. It can't have taken him long to discover that this wasn't one of his adored childlike pets. In due course, she did become his mistress— apparently worn down by the pressure of his will (and perhaps not immune to certain worldly advantages). But a man who had more perception about women, like his friend Wilkie Collins, who had led him on women-chasing expeditions to Paris, quite unsatisfactory to the less light-hearted Dickens, might have told him, and perhaps did hint at it, that someone obtained by the pressure of will isn't likely to return much love. It looks as though she gave him little. Certainly, though this is a speculation that can't be verified, it looks as though she had no physical love to respond to his.

He established her in various suburban hiding places, and they remained in that lanthanine relation for a decade—that is, until he died. So Dickens's hope of idyllic love turned as dark as other hopes, and he must have known that this was the last of them. As for Ellen, she appears in later years to have referred to their time together with distaste.

All that can be said about her for certain is that she left a mark upon his art. Before he had become enraptured with her, Dickens, it is true, was becoming for the first time engaged in psychological exploration in the sense defined in the preface.

But it was Ellen who deepened his psychological interest—at this, at least, she was a help. That will be mentioned again very soon. It is standard practice nowadays to praise *Little Dorrit* (1856) as his model of society. That depends on one's ultimate social judgment. Dickens was representing his contemporary England as one enormous prison. In that same symbolic language, any society, anywhere, of any conceivable political form, in his day or any day, can be regarded as a prison. The Circumlocution Office can be made more rational and workmanlike. Actually it was being made so in his own time, and his picture is a stereotype by a brilliant journalist. But in any articulated society, which means any society that men in the future will be able to construct, there is bound to be an administrative machine. To temperaments like that of Dickens, particularly that of Dickens in distress, such a machine, even made as competent as the human limits allow, is bound to make society seem more prisonlike. That is just a fact of the social and human condition. For the purposes of action, Dickens's social vision is no help.

The prisonlike pressures of society had been frequent enough earlier in Dickens's work. The splendid novelty of *Little Dorrit* is Dickens's major attempt to master the development of a personality. How does a man act, or fail to act, over a lifetime? What makes him choose or fail? William Dorrit is the fullest, most detailed, least distorted of Dickens's life-scale personalities, up to this point in his writing. He is surpassed only once afterward, by Pip in *Great Expectations*.

In *Little Dorrit* there is another example, and a singular one, of this new or latent interest of Dickens. That is an almost irrelevant chapter, called "The History of a Self Tormentor," thrown in as though to prove—what was true enough—that he could do almost everything. It might have been copied from a novel of Dostoevsky's, and if it occurred there we should take it as a specimen, and a good specimen, of Dostoevsky's paranormal insight. Actually, Dostoevsky, at that time serving his sentence as a private soldier in Siberia, had not written any of his major novels, and it is unlikely that Dickens before he died had so much as heard his name. Dickens's work had much effect, and some influence, on both Dostoevsky and Tolstoy. There was no influence the other way around.

Little Dorrit was written before Ellen Ternan entered Dickens's life. With her advent, this concentration on the psychology of personality (not the psychology of mood, but of choice, purpose, life direction) became intense. It is reasonable to infer that she was herself not a nobody, nothing like negligible. For the first time in his intimate life, he had to admit the presence of a woman who wasn't a doll in a doll's house. The phrase was Dickens's own but, maybe because he wrote so many quotable phrases, escaped notice and was not picked up until long after he was dead.

It is also reasonable to infer that Ellen was not an especially agreeable young woman. Estella in *Great Expectations* and Bella Wilfer in *Our Mutual Friend* are different in kind from any of the girls in Dickens's novels before Ellen's arrival. These are young women of flesh and bone, not childlike nor playthings. They are not angels. They have a tantalizing charm. Bella is capable of flashes of kindness. Both are brittle, hardened, frigid. They are cruel to men who love them. In addition, Bella, who is studied more realistically than Estella, is chillingly mercenary.

In the end, each is transformed by one of the old Dickensian redemptions. *Great Expectations* is formally the most perfect, and in its innermost expression the most deeply satisfying, of all Dickens's novels. The self-examination of Pip is Dickens's most searching piece of introspection. It is unsparing, as he could not have borne it at the time of *David Copperfield*. We are left with the certainty (rare in Dickens despite all the other wonders) that this is how life is, and not otherwise.

One other point about the book, minor but worth noting. It was common form in Dickens's time, and much later, to say that though he might be able to deal with characters of lowly origin he couldn't begin to portray a gentleman. In *Great Expectations*, Herbert Pocket is as sympathetic a study of unassuming gentility as anything in Victorian fiction.

Estella dominates all her exchanges with Pip like the breath from a refrigerator. Yet, though frightening, she is real, and so is his love for her. She even inspires him, in the midst of tormented love, to a kind of protectiveness, for she is her own prisoner. Then, at the end of the book, after she has been broken down by a marriage as cruel as her own chill required, Dickens changed the original draft. In the original draft she and Pip meet each other, recognize each other's resignation, and part for the last time. The revised draft, which is the one we know, was suggested by Bulwer Lytton: in this one they depart together for a gentle, loving marriage. Bulwer Lytton was a good and loyal friend to Dickens and several times gave him serious help. This was negative help. For Dickens, just as in the similar conversion of Bella Wilfer through the love of a good man, was glad to reflect not the truth about the woman in his book, but his own hopes.

Few men have had more brilliant hopes, or clung to them more rapaciously. But this, the most compulsive of all, the hope for love fulfilled, didn't come true. It is clear, it is written in his own text, that Ellen brought him no fulfillment and little happiness. He took refuge in his old distractions, and chased them more frantically than ever. He craved the flow-back of love from his audiences, the only kind of love he could be sure of. The detail of his life in its last years is harrowing even to imagine.

It seemed to some close to him that he was determined to kill himself. He was in bad health, and that is an understatement. His left leg gave him constant pain, and he limped along propped up by a stick. His left hand likewise was often swollen, and the arm now and then was carried in a sling. There was a further symptom. He pointed out one day to a friend that, rather surprisingly, he couldn't read the left-hand side of notices over shop windows. It is unthinkable that doctors a hundred years later wouldn't have stopped him from any violent activity. It is as well to remember, though, that with Dickens, even granted accurate diagnosis and the grimmest warning, stopping him would have been easier said than done.

He tried to persuade others, and perhaps at times himself, that these minor discomforts meant nothing at all—the bad foot wasn't even the result of gout; it had been caused by frostbite. As for the singular visual oddity, that was caused by the medicine he was taking to ease the other discomfort. Thus, there was nothing to prevent his second tour of America, in 1867–68, or more readings when he came back to England in the spring. These included a new addition to his program, the murder of Nancy by Bill Sikes, during which a number of any audience fainted as a matter of course and Dickens's left hand went black. As in all the other conflicts of his life, he was relying on his heroic will. It had conquered many times before, and could do so now.

Yet in his secret self he may have admitted that even that will of his wasn't enough. At intervals, with lucid courage, he faced the prospect of death. He started a new novel, *The Mystery of Edwin Drood,* and it may have supported his self-deception to find that his verbal and atmospheric mastery were as complete as ever. Nevertheless, in the contract, he made provisions in case he died before the last installment.

He also wanted to alter the distribution of his estate. Although he had lived more lavishly than any professional writer since Walter Scott, in rather more than upper-middle-class state, generous to friends, providing for his family and sponging relatives, this estate was large by Victorian standards. By comparison with his £93,000, George Eliot left something between £30,000 and £40,000, though her business affairs were tangled with Lewes's, which prevents a precise estimate. Trollope's estate was proved at just under £30,000.

Dickens's, however, is a little deceptive. Nearly half came from the recent American and English reading tours. They may have hastened his death, but they were markedly profitable. That cheered him up. It is all very well to talk knowingly about death wishes; but it is also justifiable to remember that Dickens had always liked money.

As another intimation that he accepted he hadn't long to live, he made a new will. He made it as though it were the last one. It contained a cold reference to his wife: he didn't forgive her, any more than he forgave his mother for the blacking factory. It also contained a bequest to Ellen Ternan, which no one has been able to interpret. He left her £1,000. He must have known that this would raise all the rumors about her and their relation. In his lifetime he had believed, or acted as though he believed, that no one knew anything—including her sister Frances Eleanor, married to Trollope's brother. Of course, those two knew, and so did many others. Now he was giving them all plenty to talk about. Yet, if so, why such a mysterious sum, not small enough to be laughed off, nothing like large enough to provide for her? Had he made that provision already? There is no evidence of it, and no one has ever known.

He gave his last readings in the winter of 1870. They took place in the St. James's Hall, and he accepted that he wouldn't appear in public again. His doctor attended each reading, and Dickens's eldest son was posted at the side of the platform, in order to catch him if he fell. The doctor measured his pulse rate after each reading. Toward the end Dickens couldn't manage to say familiar names. Pickwick emerged as "Picnic," "Peckwicks." Nothing broke his will to continue. It came to the day for the final performance. Then as he finished the last item (it was the trial in *Pickwick*) he heard the applause for the last time. The excitement, the flow-back, the frenzy of the audience were over. He cried.

He made a speech of love, and ended: "From these garish lights, I now vanish for evermore, with a heartfelt, grateful, respectful, affectionate farewell."

He limped from the stage. The tumult brought him back. He was crying again. He greeted his audience and then made his way off. That was the end.

His spirit was still strong. It didn't dismay him that the physical symptoms remained distressing and fateful. His left foot didn't leave him free from pain; he couldn't read the left-hand side of the signs above the shops. To everyone except perhaps to himself, he went on saying that these troubles meant nothing, his general health was fine.

He went on writing *Edwin Drood*, as masterful and as disciplined as in the past.

Through April and May he lived the London social life that he had never enjoyed but had become acclimatized to. He breakfasted with the Prime Minister and dined with the socially grand. He even produced a play by an amateur company, wanting to act himself but inhibited because he was too lame. That production was his terminal activity in London. On June 3, 1870, he returned to Gadshill. In the mornings he wrote according to the pattern of a lifetime. Later in the June afternoons he limped indomitably in attempts at his habitual walks. He talked to his trusted sister-in-law Georgina, who had kept house for him since the breakup of his marriage. He talked to his daughter Katey, who had sided with his wife and with whom his relation had been tense, since she knew him better than his other children did.

On June 8 he wrote away at *Drood* all day, contrary to any of his routines. The last passage is alive with well-being, even though we now read it as his good-bye to the Rochester Cathedral of his childhood. At dinner, face ravaged with pain, he told Georgina that he had been very ill. His speech became unintelligible. Georgina got him to the floor. It was a massive cerebral hemorrhage. He was not conscious again. He died the following evening.

DOSTOEVSKY

THE apartment in which Dostoevsky spent his childhood is preserved today with scrupulous veneration.
It is not a cheerful place. In Dostoevsky's time—he
was born in 1821, lived in that apartment in Moscow, and
had all his lessons there until he was thirteen—there were
four rooms, and one used as a kitchen. Two of those rooms
have since had the connecting wall knocked out for the
purposes of the museum. Until that happened, none of
the rooms was larger than about fourteen feet by twelve.
All are still dark. The walls press in and induce claustro-
phobia.

As the Dostoevsky family increased, father and mother
and five children lived in that apartment, together with, so
we are told, seven servants. Where the seven servants slept
it is impossible to guess, but no one seems to have worried
about domestic arrangements in nineteenth-century Russia. Even in a comparatively rich manor house like Tolstoy's,
the servants, multitudes of them, just slumped down in
what corners they could find.

Seven servants did not mean that the Dostoevskys

were well-off. Far from it, they were distinctly poor. The father was a doctor, attached to the charity hospital in the same building block. This apartment was a perk, and a very unextravagant perk, of his job. He had also a small private practice. His income, in English money of the same period, would have been about £150 a year.

It is usually difficult to translate Russian social differentiation in Tsarist times into anything like an English equivalent, but perhaps Dr. Dostoevsky's status is more understandable than most. There is a certain amount of mystery about his family origin, but at some period they had undoubtedly become noble. Nobility in that sense wasn't hard to achieve in eighteenth-century Russia, and could come, rather like an appearance in the British honors list, with promotion in the government service. The Dostoevskys, however, had gone downhill, and Dr. Dostoevsky's grandfather and father had become priests. That automatically meant that the family ceased to be noble.

Dr. Dostoevsky, once intended for the priesthood himself, had moved into the army medical service, and had had a respectable career. He had been awarded a couple of decorations, which in due course restored him, equally automatically, to the old family rank. When he left the army and became an ill-paid doctor in a hospital for the poor, he had the formal standing of a hereditary nobleman (*dvoryanin*). But we mustn't think that this would make him, or his sons, seem socially elevated in the eyes of land-owning aristocrats such as the Tolstoys, or much richer landowners, a shade less aristocratic, as Turgenev was. The writer Fyodor Dostoevsky never thought of himself as remotely aristocratic. It is true that in the Omsk prison the ordinary convicts regarded him as a gentleman, and hated him in consequence. In similar circumstances in England that would no doubt have happened to Trollope, similarly poor and unfortunate.

For us to understand Dostoevsky's father, it is sensible for us to compare him with an Englishman of Trollope's class, clinging desperately to his social position. He wouldn't let his children mix with common children, nor even to speak with the paupers, his own patients, in the hospital garden. Dr. Dostoevsky was a miserly man, but he stinted the family and skimped himself to send his sons to a superior (that is, socially smart) school. In the same spirit, and with the same sacrifices, he arranged for Mikhail, Fyodor's eldest brother, and Fyodor himself to join the army school for engineering officers. There was nothing more gentlemanly in their Russia than to be an officer in the army.

Dr. Dostoevsky was no more cheerful than the apartment they lived in. He made them all attend mass each day. He was devoutly, or obsessively, religious. He was morose, disappointed, pedantic, jealous of his wife, ferociously strict (though not physically punitive) with his children. It must have been one of the most depressing of childhoods. The doctor's wife was far more amiable and loving. She was a merchant's daughter who had brought a little money with her and had some prosperous relatives. Such liveliness as entered that apartment came through the mother and those family connections of hers. It is another of the mysteries about Dr. Dostoevsky and the paternal line that none of his relatives is known ever to have entered those rooms. Further, as we find over and over again in these Russian families, the mother was out of proportion more competent, businesslike, and effective than the father. So far as there was any order in their affairs, it was the mother's doing.

They borrowed money to buy a small estate and a hundred male serfs in the Tula region. Though Dostoevsky and Tolstoy did not once meet, this humble patch of land-owning was quite near the less humble Tolstoy estate at Yasnaya Polyana.

Acquiring those derelict villages, unproductive land, and a four-room thatched-roof family house may have made Dr. Dostoevsky feel that he was at last a country gentleman living up to his rank. But any light and warmth in the Dostoevsky household came only from his wife. She was tubercular, though, and died when Fyodor was fifteen and before the elder boys left home for their military education.

It had been a grim childhood. In a pedantic fashion Dr. Dostoevsky wasn't uncultivated. He taught the boys Latin himself, they had tutors to teach them French and Orthodox divinity, there were a good many books in the gloomy Moscow flat. But there was no external release for spirited boys. When there were youthful demonstrations, Fyodor was the leader. At that age, he was the least discouraged of the children; but that was not saying much.

It wasn't a childhood utterly deprived of parental love and care, as for years Balzac's and Trollope's were. There was some love, and only too much care. There was nothing like the wound of Dickens being sent to the blacking factory. Still, it was an oppressive home. In later life Dostoevsky thanked God for being brought up in a "Russian and pious" manner. It was certainly pious. To a foreigner in another century, it doesn't appear especially Russian. A fair number of English homes in the nineteenth century were just as restrictive, though the physical environment wouldn't normally have been quite as glum.

Whether those years of childhood left much of a mark on him is doubtful. Underneath all the forces that struggled unresolved in his nature, he had astonishing resilience, as much as any man. He was always suspicious and uneasy with people unless he knew them well, and there his childhood may not have helped. Certainly he did become reserved and taciturn in company, abnormally so among writers, and something of a surprise if one expects him to have talked like the characters in his books. With intimates, of whom he had only about four in his whole life, he was the reverse of reserved and taciturn, and then he did talk like the characters in his books.

At the college of military engineering in Petersburg there was some foreshadowing of his future. He didn't like the college. He didn't like his fellow students. There was a lot of what Americans would call hazing, brutal hazing, and he was knocked about. The others soon found that he could look after himself. He was silent, unconvivial, without money among youths most of whom were well-off. He was pallid and not prepossessing, with a great forehead, small sharp eyes, a flattish Slav nose. The standard pictures and photographs make him look darker than he was. His hair was actually light chestnut, and he looked like a northern Russian. He was middle height for his period, perhaps five feet five or six, about the same as Tolstoy, inches taller than Stendhal, Balzac, Dickens. He was wide-shouldered, wiry, and much stronger than he appeared, as would-be persecutors discovered. It wasn't an elegant or graceful physique. He had unusually large hands, with very long bony fingers.

He didn't enjoy his studies, but worked conscientiously at them. In everything but mathematics, which he didn't understand, and considered useless, he did well in examinations and finally passed high in his class. Giving practical bourgeois advice in his late fifties, writing answers to correspondents, rather like a premature Dear Abby, he told young men to follow his example, work hard at their studies, and do well in their examinations.

He read a great deal, anything that a Russian intellectual around 1840 could get hold of—Schiller, Hoffman, Balzac, Hugo, Corneille, Pushkin, and, most dominant of them all, Gogol. He began to write. He seems to have known intermittently that that was to be his life.

He also began to get into debt. That was also to be his life. The habit started very early. Later on, when he took on responsibilities that most men wouldn't, it is easier to understand. But as a young student money was already slipping out of his pockets without discernible results. He didn't show any conception of what money was. True, youths of that age do get into debt. True also, he was a poor boy among rich ones, and didn't want to appear so. But what did he spend money on? Not on drink, where he was always abstemious for a nineteenth-century Russian. Not on gambling, which he hadn't started. Not on women, where he had been too delicately conditioned and took a long time to become sensually released. Yet at seventeen and eighteen he was constantly borrowing small sums,

20 rubles (perhaps equivalent to £3), 10 rubles, 5 rubles, and having dunning persons invading his room and demanding to be repaid. It was like a chronic ailment, and it didn't leave him until he was getting on toward sixty and alongside Tolstoy the supreme writer of Russia.

In his first days at college, his father, miserly and himself badgered for similar small sums, managed to help him out when despairing, begging letters arrived. But his father died in Fyodor's second year. The circumstances of the death are still not cleared up. Fyodor's life became ravaged by a series of dramatic, or, his enemies said, as though he were doing it on purpose, melodramatic, episodes, unique in any great writer's history, or almost anyone else's. The death of his father has for a good many years been regarded as the first of the series. Dr. Dostoevsky, after his wife died, had given up his job at the charity hospital and retired to his run-down estate. There he became more morose than ever, drank himself to stupefaction, took a serf woman to live with him. His temper, so the gossip ran, grew even more violent, and the serfs loathed him. One day in 1838, so the gossip also ran, some of his serfs murdered him on his own land. The police were persuaded to believe that he had died of an apoplectic stroke, having had frequent seizures before. The true cause of his death was concealed except from his family for many years.

When the news was finally released, everyone believed it. It was already in the spirit of the whole Dostoevsky life story and of Dostoevsky himself. Didn't Ivan Karamazov say, "Who has not desired his father's death?"

It is possible, though not certain, that Fyodor believed in the story of the murder. There is no clinching evidence for that, and some indirect evidence against it. In his late fifties he revisited the old estate, wrote cheerful domestic letters about the occasion to his wife, and strongly urged that she take their children there as soon as she had the chance. Dostoevsky took great precautions to shield his children from unpleasant literature or scenes, and it takes some swallowing that he could let them go there if he believed that his father had been murdered on the site.

His second wife, Anna Grigoryevna, a singularly truthful witness writing a generation after Dostoevsky's death, makes no mention of the murder story. She loved him devotedly, and she must have heard the truth, or what she thought to be the truth. There is no obvious reason why, after all that time, she should have concealed it.

There are many high-class Dostoevsky scholars in the Soviet Union today. The general consensus appears to be that the murder story is unproven. Some recent scholars come firmly down on the side of the prosaic police verdict, death from apoplexy, and that seems, though it is anticlimactic, more likely to be the truth. (Joseph Frank, who has just published the first volume of a scholarly biography, comes to the same conclusion. Frank also points out that Freud based a long analysis on the old, now discredited, story.)

At the end of Dostoevsky's training, he duly became a commissioned officer (an ensign) in the Russian army—a rank he was to reattain, by a somewhat less conventional procedure, nearly twenty years later. He was appointed to the Petersburg engineering corps, and set to work in the drawing office. What he was supposed to do on the drawing board is lost to history, but it may have been some plan of military fortification. The drawing office didn't appeal to him as a feature of a desirable life. It meant a small regular income, but he promptly resigned his commission. As he had long intended, he turned to writing. He had already received a few rubles from a translation of *Eugène Sue*. When his resignation was accepted, he was exactly twenty-three.

He was writing a novel. On this, he was sure, all his future depended. It is important to remember that underneath his nerves, his morbid suspiciousness, his inability to cope in the day-by-day exchanges of living, he had as a young man, and continued to have, during all that was to happen to him, a reserve of illimitable hope. He once said of himself that he was like a cat with nine lives. One of those lives, and the deepest, did not fail him.

Writing his novel during the winter of 1844–45, he was of course in debt. He was sharing a bleak apartment with a former classmate called Grigorovich. They had little to eat. The novel had to be a success, then such petty troubles would be over. He wrote and revised for about six months. This was not one of the massive lengthy novels that his contemporaries in England were writing. It was what we should now term a novella. We know it as *Poor Folk*.

Dostoevsky was made to have drama collect round him. Some of the stories can be doubted, but not the one about the reception of *Poor Folk*. The manuscript had somehow been passed to Nikolai Nekrasov. Nekrasov, not so much older than Dostoevsky, was not then the fine poet that he developed into, but he was already a literary figure, and was trying to collect material for, as it were, a trial shot at his famous liberal magazine *The Contemporary* (*Sovremennik*). All Dostoevsky knew was that Nekrasov might be considering the novel. Dostoevsky was restless, and one night didn't go to bed until nearly dawn, the early dawn, since it was June, of a white night in Petersburg. It must have been as light as day.

His door burst open. Nekrasov and Grigorovich rushed in together. They had been reading *Poor Folk* all night, and were overcome. Embraces, tears, congratulations, talk of Gogol, talk of the great future of Russian literature, talk of Dostoevsky, of the wonders of his novel. Nekrasov strode across the room, many times to and fro, and shouted that Belinsky, the great Belinsky, should be made to read the manuscript that day.

Belinsky was the most influential critic that any literature has had. He affected Russian writing profoundly in his own time, and to this day. It was he who, so far as a critic can, helped to give Russian literature its rooted social concern. He was also a splendid wide-ranging critic, not a blinkered one. Probably he wouldn't have come to terms with art that had no roots at all or with pure verbal aestheticism. It is difficult to imagine him having any use for Nabokov. Yet, maybe despite himself, he would have found Bulgakov's *Master and Margarita* hard to resist. His sympathies often stretched wider than his conscience. He was in his early thirties at the time of that white night in 1845, but he was tubercular and already seriously ill.

Actually, he didn't read the manuscript the day Nekrasov thrust it on him. He was a little tired of hearing about new Gogols, though he shared, or inspired, the passionate desire to create a great Russian literature. He waited two or three days. Then enthusiasm prevailed, and he, too, stayed up all night reading. He insisted, that same morning, that Dostoevsky must be brought to him at once. No delay. Dostoevsky was duly brought to Belinsky's ramshackle room. Whether Nekrasov or anyone else stayed with them isn't clear. Dostoevsky saw a man smaller than himself, and much more puny. But he heard a voice speaking with all the authority of Belinsky's nature. He heard what few writers, young or old, have heard: that he had written a great book, greater than Dostoevsky himself could understand.

Dostoevsky went out and looked over the river, elated and humble. It was the most joyful moment he had known, or was to know, for a long time to come.

To us, so far removed in time and conditions, it seems remarkable that Belinsky divined the genius underlying *Poor Folk*. Certainly he overpraised the book, judged just by itself. It has, needless to say, great qualities. It is one of the most untypical of first novels. It contains almost nothing of autobiographical experience except the knowledge of impoverished rooms, cheap eating places, the detail of how the Petersburg semigenteel poor (what we might now call lower middle class) lived. The social background of the clerk Makra and his pathetic girl wasn't anything like Dostoevsky's own, and must have come from observation. The pity, utterly unpatronizing, though sometimes sentimental, with which he watched them, and felt with them— that was Dostoevsky's own. So is the insight into the choices, or lack of choices, imposed by response to suffering. The tone of the whole novel is gentle, much more so than in the works of his maturity.

There is one oddity. On the whole, the language is less loose and slapdash than in most of Dostoevsky, possibly because he had time to revise. But it is difficult to imagine him writing elegantly or even economically. That excited, inflated journalistic idiom was the expression of a man in a hurry, who felt and said of his own books that he had conceptions that inspired him, but that he nearly always was dissatisfied with the result. Somehow his language works; Russian aesthetes have been known to say bleakly it doesn't suffer by translation. In his dialogue passages, however, he had the knack of throwing off phrases that are hard to forget. There the words stand out with startling impact, perhaps the more so because of the casualness of the narrative text.

Poor Folk was a major success. It was as much a success as Tolstoy's first publication, *Childhood,* ten years later, also brought out under Nekrasov's editorship. Neither was nor could be the gigantic popular success of *Pickwick* in England in the 1830s. In mid-century Russia there weren't the methods of publication and distribution to reach a wide public, nor was there so wide a public. Still, in intellectual Petersburg, Dostoevsky at twenty-five was one of the most famous young men, recognized, courted, invited out.

Within months all went wrong. The troubles were complex. Partly they were political and literary mixed, as literary affairs have been in Russia since Pushkin's time. Dostoevsky published *The Double,* a highly original book that foreshadowed some of his later work, though it was less embedded in solid flesh and bone. *The Double* had a glowing reception at the beginning, and then literary persons had second thoughts. Belinsky didn't like it, and wrote a review full of disappointment. It was too near the clinical fringe for him. Belinsky was the intellectual leader of progressive Russia, and this new direction of Dostoevsky's was disquieting.

Dostoevsky was being published in Nekrasov's magazine, which had become the chief progressive organ. Dostoevsky's friends and supporters were almost all on the progressive side, and regarded him as one of themselves. They may have detected ambiguities. However, it was with the Nekrasov circle that he still thought he belonged, as events were soon to show.

It looks as though a deeper trouble came from his own temperament. He was almost pathologically highly strung, morose, suspicious. When he could give his trust, he could also give total affection. When he could be protective, he was at ease. But when he believed that he was disliked, or—worse—when he thought he was being mocked, he was neither tolerant nor tolerable. For a newcomer on the literary scene, startlingly successful, he was a total loss in company. That didn't lessen the envy that a newcomer to the literary scene, startlingly successful, had to expect in Petersburg or anywhere else. He didn't mollify the envy. He made many enemies among writers, and did so until he died. He contrived to quarrel with Belinsky, who died soon afterward. He quarreled with Nekrasov, and they weren't reconciled for nearly thirty years, when it was Nekrasov who took the initiative. It seems likely that Dostoevsky grew up very late. In spite of the maturity of much of his literary art in *Poor Folk* and *The Double*, he was behaving like a lost young man. There is no evidence that he had a serious relation with a woman until he was thirty-four. He may have had girls as occasional pickups, and it is possible that he also picked up a venereal disease; in which case, among the early sexual attempts of diffident young novelists, he is in the rather improbable company of Disraeli and Stendhal.

He had, of course, acute psychological insight. Though not a common gift, there are other novelists who have possessed it, and used it as naturally as he did, Trollope and Jane Austen among English writers. In addition, Dostoevsky was endowed with extraordinary psychological imagination. That is a much rarer gift. It must have been innate. It can't be acquired, and it is difficult to control. As well as being a rare gift, it is also a dangerous one. It gave him the power to understand and participate in, not only double motives (as he called them) but also multiple motives, all carried in his own nature and his art at one and the same time. It didn't make for lucidity in cognitive thought, but did produce some of his most dazzling discoveries. It also led him into psychological inventions that weren't true, either in his own existence or in his writing. Tolstoy, who had a profound distrust of psychological imagination, distrusted Dostoevsky's work mainly, though not entirely, for this reason.

As a young man, after what should have been a triumphant beginning, Dostoevsky, in terms of intellect, his art, or his ordinary human living, couldn't come to any equilibrium with his imagination. There is an indication in the text of *Poor Folk* and the books that followed it. It is a negative indication. These books, wherever they are concerned with the relations of men and women, are abnormally devoid of sex or any tinge of sensuality. We know, as positively as we know of any writer, that Dostoevsky in later life demonstrated that he was an enthusiastically sensual man. He had his share, more than his share, of the insect life, to use his own phrase about the Karamazovs. His letters to his second wife, right up to the last months of his life, happily radiate his own kind of sensuality. He probably hadn't the animal prepotency of Tolstoy, but human beings are lucky who can enjoy themselves as much as Dostoevsky did.

It looks as though he learned to control or domesticate his imagination in that primal sense. Once his imagination was controlled, his art became more tied to the earth. *The Brothers Karamazov* is warmly sensual—not only in the relations of men and women—as the books of Dostoevsky's youth don't begin to be. So are *The Idiot, The Possessed, A Raw Youth*, all the novels of maturity.

It is true that Dostoevsky's enjoyment of the senses always had its limits. He had next to no feeling for nature. The streets of Petersburg moved him, the urban sights, a woman moving across a lighted window, the smell of a sleazy eating place, the unkempt court behind an apartment, the white nights beside the river, the clammy autumn fogs. At times he expressed the poetry of the city, as Dickens did of London or Galdós of Madrid. He could also become obsessed with objects, as though he wanted to touch them as possessively as he touched a woman's foot. He made hypnotic use of this fascination with objects in several of his most dramatic passages (compare the last two chapters of *The Idiot*). By and large, however, his sensibility was the sensibility of the erotic nerves.

In the very long run, that instinctive release, the de-

mands of the insect life, saved him—saved his own well-
being, saved him as an artist. But it took a very long time,
not helped by the most violent of the melodramas that he
had to survive.

In his middle twenties, he didn't know what he believed or where he stood. Just as his psychological imagination dazzled him with polymorphous motives, his own and
everyone else's, so did his political imagination. Often there
was no clear distinction between the two. He was a mid-
century Russian, pulled in all directions conceivable to a
man without constraint. Without constraint, because there
was none of the possibilities of rational action that imposed
their own restrictions—such as there would have been in an
organized bourgeois society like England. Very occasionally his instinct for reality broke in, but it was still too
much submerged to give him guidance. In his day-by-day
troubles he persisted in the chronic routine of borrowing
money. He was having his first attacks of epilepsy.

What his medical condition really was, and what caused
it, wasn't understood at the time, nor is it now. It harassed
his existence from about the age of twenty-five until his
death. It wasn't a mortal illness. He didn't die of it. It was
more of a frightening or shameful embarrassment than a
danger. It didn't start from any traumatic shock, contrary
to the usual legend. He gives a clinically detached account
in *The Idiot* of what the experience was like—the beatific
aura, the sense of transcendental bliss, before a seizure, and
the hopeless depression afterward (which in his own case
lasted for days). Suspicious, nerve ends hypersensitive, restless—other epileptics show parts of the same syndrome, and
there have been attempts to suggest that the condition was

at the root of his psychological gifts. Brutal sense has to reply that there have been a good many epileptics, and only this one who was a psychological genius.

So, in a state that even for the young Dostoevsky was one of maximum disquiet, spasmodically ill, continuously broke, he joined what would now be thought of as a dissident group, perhaps the most intellectual such group in Petersburg. The convener was a junior official in the Foreign Office, by name of Petrashevsky. There is nothing surprising in officials or army officers belonging to such a group; it happened throughout the Tsarist time. Some members of the group, though not a majority, were revolutionaries, though they hadn't a disciplined conception of what revolution meant. It is common form to say that the Petrashevsky group was nothing but a debating society. That may have been nearly true, but not quite. They read papers, discussed all kinds of plans for a better Russia. Most of it had no relation to action. A little of it, however, may have had. At one meeting, Dostoevsky himself read Belinsky's famous letter to Gogol. That doesn't sound excessively militant. But at the time it could have seemed so. Gogol had written an inflamed defense of Church and State, which denounced as ultimate evil even the possibility of change, either in the present or the future. Belinsky's answer, which was forbidden to be published or otherwise communicated, was a statement of the hopes of liberal Russia, asking the echoing question of the century—what is to be done?

It is possible that Dostoevsky was also involved in a project to set up a secret printing press, at that time a cardinal offense. It is true that Dostoevsky, with his capacity for being equally involved in both extremes at once, was introduced into a kind of conservative party within the Petrashevsky group—where there were passionate discussions of Russian messianism, the future of Russia as the savior of the world, under a benign autocracy and the Christ-bearing mission of the Orthodox Church. It is a fair guess that he was more deeply affected by that vision than by the prospects offered by the rational soul; but we ought to remember that the rational soul had its own appeal for him, and that the two messages seemed closer together than they would for us. He could coexist with faith and doubt both ways.

In the spirit of the 1840s, the Petrashevsky group was liberal. Any authoritarian government in the nineteenth century would have regarded it with suspicion. The Tsarist government wasn't a model of competence, but it had a remarkably effective intelligence service. They had filtered an agent inside the group. Memoranda went back, reporting talks of insurrection, peasant revolts, republican riots, socialism. In 1849 the Petrashevsky circle was arrested, and all of them, Dostoevsky and the rest, were taken to prison in the Peter and Paul fortress.

He was in his cell for months. It wasn't a cell anyone would choose to stay in for months, without intimation of how this was to end. He may have contemplated death; at times he must have done. He couldn't have imagined, no sane man could have imagined, the grotesque drama that was waiting for him. His nerves steadied. He could call on that ultimate vitality, the eighth and ninth of his catlike lives. He became more stable than he had been in those last years of freedom.

He stood the examination before investigating judges better than his colleagues. He probably didn't tell the entire truth, but he blamed no one else and didn't cower. He couldn't understand the judicial process, which was no fault of his, since it was a curious one. Unknown to the prisoners, the judges (acting like European examining magistrates) reported their findings to a military tribunal.

The verdict was death in front of a firing squad. That sentence was reviewed by the Auditoriat-General (Russian supreme court), who pointed out that all the Petrashevsky group were equally guilty, and that it would mean the execution of at least twenty men, most of them very young. They recommended terms of penal servitude—Petrashevsky for life, subsidiary figures such as Dostoevsky for eight years.

Finally, all sentences for political crime had to be decided personally by the Tsar. The number of decisions that in that autocracy had to go right to the top makes the mind boggle. The amount of sheer office work that the Tsar had to get through—and in due course Stalin also—would have caused an administrative revolt in England.

There was another unusual feature that Western persons, reading *Crime and Punishment* or *The Brothers Karamazov,* often miss. The Petrashevsky group had been sentenced to death. That was because theirs was a political crime. For any other kind of crime, including murder, there was no capital punishment in Russia, and hadn't been since the reign of Catherine the Great. Raskolnikov and Dmitri Karamazov were in no danger of their lives. If a soldier either killed or even assaulted an officer, there were ways around these sanctions, which for civil crimes were often merciful in comparison with Western Europe. *The House of the Dead* tells how a culprit who had struck an officer would be lucky to get out of prison alive.

The Tsar duly considered the sentence. Nicholas I was by a long way the most displeasing of the nineteenth-century Tsars. Cold-hearted, gloating over punishments, externally cultivated. This time he was disposed to accept that long terms in Siberian prisons were perhaps adequate. He altered Dostoevsky's sentence to four years as a common prisoner and then service as a private soldier. Then the Tsar devoted himself to a more interesting concern. He was devising a ghoulish practical joke.

The prisoners had no intimation whatever of their sentences or their fate. Three days before the Christmas of 1849 they were awakened, and made to dress in their civilian clothes—too thin for the December weather. They were driven in coaches to a familiar parade ground. Troops were lined up. The prisoners followed a priest to a raised platform, draped in black. A clerk stood among them and read out the verdicts. Petrashevsky. Condemned to capital punishment by shooting. More names. Then Fyodor Mikhailovich Dostoevsky. Condemned to capital punishment by shooting.

Address by the priest. The text: The wages of sin is death. They kissed the cross. Swords were broken over the heads of those who had noble rank, Dostoevsky among them, to signify that they had lost it. They were told to take off their jackets and put on white shirts, which were their shrouds. Petrashevsky and two other men were taken away and tied to posts, facing a firing squad.

Dostoevsky was number six among the sentenced. His

turn would come with the next three. The emotions of a man within minutes of such a death are expressed with searing truth in the famous passage in *The Idiot,* recounted at second hand by Prince Myshkin. A man of Dostoevsky's psychological imagination could have produced, and did produce, many experiences he hadn't known. This he couldn't have done. There are some experiences like this phantasmagoria, including some quite ordinary ones, that are beyond the imagination.

Dostoevsky was becoming drained of feeling. Commands were ringing out. "Ready, aim!" Rifles leveled. Drums rolled. A government messenger jumped from his carriage. He was carrying a paper. This was the reprieve. Here were the real sentences.

One man had become deranged. Some cheered. Some were savagely angry. Dostoevsky still felt nothing. Not until he was returned to his cell. Then there was a rush of joy.

It has been thought that this exercise of the Tsar's humor was the cause or trigger of Dostoevsky's epilepsy. That isn't true. It had started years before. In a life so ravaged by drama, and so full of what appeared like mental changes, it is a temptation to pick on simple causes. Why did he become devoted to the Tsarist regime? Why did he become the most fervent of Christian spokesmen? There is more to be said about that later. But the short answer here is that Dostoevsky had a mentality, as well as a temperament, of wonderful ambiguousness. It would be possible, if one selected quotations from his work or letters, to prove that he believed almost anything, or alternatively nothing.

Sometimes the reasons for his attitudes were more

prosaic than it is customary to think. Often the roots of the Dostoevsky of his last decade, the Dostoevsky of *The Diary of a Writer,* when his opinions ran flat in the face of all gentle liberal opinion, can be seen in the Dostoevsky of his first writings.

As a rule, convicts had to walk to Siberia, their fetters clanking. Dostoevsky was put into fetters, twelve pounds or so dragging on each leg, not to be removed, either on his prison planks, or in hospital, until release or death; but he wasn't made to walk. He was transported across the Urals by sledge, in temperatures going down to minus forty degrees Fahrenheit.

That was a fair start to his four years in the Omsk prison. It was an appalling time. Convicts herded together in a log hut, filthy food (literally filthy), stench, cold. The commandant was a repulsive brute. His first greeting to Dostoevsky and another of the Petrashevsky group was that the slightest infringement of the rules would mean immediate flogging. As noblemen, they had had the privilege of immunity from corporal punishment—not so insignificant a privilege in the Russia of Nicholas I. Now their rank had been stripped away, and they had the immunity no longer. One of the Tsar's thoughtful acts was to give explicit orders that they were to be treated in all respects like other common criminals.

It was a time of animal hardship, tempered by carelessness and corruption among the warders, and spasms of random Russian kindness. The prison doctors let Dostoevsky spend periods in hospital on bogus excuses, which made a change. He wasn't allowed any books by right, except the New Testament, which he came to know as well as Father

Zossima must have done; but somehow kind women from the town managed occasionally to smuggle books into the hospital. Eatable food and vodka, also strictly forbidden, got into the prison. Also money. In some inexplicable fashion, Dostoevsky contrived to borrow money, with the talent of someone who would borrow money at the North Pole. The commandant was replaced halfway through Dostoevsky's sentence, and some of the cruelty was softened. Despite threats, Dostoevsky and the other politicals escaped flogging, though on many days he saw sufferers dragged in.

Those convict years were an experience that no other great writer has had to endure. Later he wrote an account of it, only slightly transmuted, in *The House of the Dead*, clear-eyed, utterly without rancor, as though this had been a singular act of God that had happened to someone else. Tolstoy thought it was one of the most truthful studies of human suffering ever written, unsentimental in its fellow feeling, which is true. It was the only book of Dostoevsky's for which Tolstoy expressed any praise.

The clinical fact is that Dostoevsky became much better in health during that time in prison. His nerves settled down. His hypochondria decreased. When his nerves were stable, he was a very hardy man. He enjoyed doing manual labor in the Siberian air. He had only clandestine hours in the hospital when he could read and he couldn't write a word. That may have been a creative relief, such as some writers have found in wartime. He may have known that, when at last he was free to write again, the books would flow, and with more confidence than in the past. He believed that he was learning a lot.

He announced much later that it was in prison that

he came to understand and love the real Russian people, the lowest of the low. He was letting his memory be warmed and softened by a kind of nostalgia. His letters from prison do not suggest such a beautiful human exchange. Whether he loved the lowest criminals or not, it is certain that they didn't love him. He wasn't a convivial character even with his own kind; with illiterate convicts, he couldn't find a word to say, and didn't choose to.

The House of the Dead, though edited so as to make him a shade less morose than he was, is good evidence as to what really happened. He may have been liked by one or two, when he let his empathy show through. Then he had great and genuine charm. Most of them, though, just jeered at him as a gentleman and were glad that he was as degraded as they were. This gentleman was more wretched in prison than anyone used to their harsh life. Serve him right. He was below them now, at the bottom of the heap.

He also believed that he had learned to understand not only the Russian masses, but also the Russian mission in the world. This led him to some of his complex to-and-fro switches of thinking. At times he was certain that his sojourns among the liberal intellectuals had been wrong, that that was no home for him. He switched back to his old, and continuing, quarrels with the regime. There was great wrong being done by the regime. It denied human hopes and love. But it couldn't be set right by Westernized liberals, who didn't know anything of the evil in human beings. Those liberals made their hygienic program. It took for granted that all could be set right, neatly and simply, by changing the social setting. The liberals didn't require men to change themselves. No good. In those Petrashevsky meetings Dostoevsky had come to hate liberals more than he recognized. In the future he was going to let that hatred rip, the more so because there was experience behind it. Only the Russian masses could save Russia. He would go humbly along with them. That meant being loyal to the regime and the Tsar.

It is standard form to assume that Dostoevsky embraced suffering and subjugated himself to authority. Maybe. But it is just as well to remember that he could embrace a good many feelings at the same time. There was even a certain prudence in the way his thought was tending. His instinct for reality was beginning to intrude on his imagination. In practical terms, he had lost any faith he may once have had in the rebels, even the brightest and best rebels like Belinsky. Theirs was not the mainstream. If he was going to write his books, and say effective words in his own lifetime, he had to find his way into the mainstream.

In prison, he struggled with what to him was the ultimate question, with which he had to go on struggling until he died. Did he believe in God? He was to say it all in the Shatov-Stavrogin dialogue that he wrote twenty years later. But it was part of him always.

> *Stavrogin:* Do you believe in God?
> *Shatov:*   I believe in Russia—I believe in her Orthodoxy—I believe in the body of Christ—I believe that the advent will take place in Russia— I believe. . . .
> *Stavrogin:* And in God?
> *Shatov:*   I—I will believe in God.

It is easy to disinter from Dostoevsky most shades of belief and unbelief, social hope and social negation, conformism and rebellion. It is easy, but not conclusive. He didn't discover an organized cosmos. He talked, as Russians liked to talk, of their broad nature (*shirokaya natura,* which also includes wide-mindedness as a virtue). Whether it is a virtue or not, no one could have had more of it than he did.

Out of prison, his sentence served to the exact day, legs unfettered after four years, Dostoevsky was sent to serve as a private soldier in a Siberian battalion. He didn't know, nor presumably did anyone else, how long he would be kept in the army. It might be for many years. Still, he was partially free. He was made to tramp to Semipalatinsk, down in the wilds of the Kirghiz country. Semipalatinsk was a comatose garrison town, with nothing for the soldiers to do but drill, drink, and gamble. Dostoevsky did the first, and made himself an efficient private soldier. He didn't do either of the other things; gambling had no allure for him yet. Instead he wrote imploringly to his beloved brother Mikhail for books and money. Owing to cautiousness and timidity, Mikhail had not written to him while he was in prison. The brotherly love was real between them, but more intense on Fyodor's side.

In due course books and money arrived. Dostoevsky also managed to borrow from others. Debts mounted. It must have taken unusual energy to get into debt as a private soldier in Semipalatinsk. One has to remember, though, that a writer has always had a special distinction in Russia from Pushkin down to today, utterly unlike anything in the West. He won friends and supporters because people hadn't forgotten that he was a writer. He won an exceptionally loyal and valuable friend, a very young official, Baron Wrangel, who lent him money, put him up in his *dacha,* and used influence in Petersburg. A new Tsar came to the throne soon after Dostoevsky arrived in Semipalatinsk. This Tsar, Alexander II, in contrast to his father had benevolent intentions. The climate was relaxing. Dostoevsky wrote patriotic and sycophantic odes. He soon began to write serious novellas. While still a private soldier, he was allowed to publish one of them, though the name of the author was not to be revealed—which, since Dostoevsky's idiom was unmistakable to any literate person in Petersburg, seems a singular piece of official wisdom.

Semipalatinsk might be a comatose garrison town, but Dostoevsky's existence wasn't capable of remaining comatose for long. Within months of coming to the place, he had fallen in love. He was just thirty-four, and there is no evidence that he had been in love before. If he hadn't, it takes some explaining. Of course, the four years in prison had been cut out of his life. Nevertheless, his later life proved that he was a man of much ardor in all respects, soul, feelings, body. It seems too schematic to say that, as a young man, his emotions and, above all, his imagination had somehow censored or suppressed his senses. Yet that is how the actual record appears to read.

When he did at last fall in love, it was tumultuous, as whirling, pathetic, packed with contradictory emotions and affection as in *Poor Folk* or *Netochka Nezvanova,* written before he had had the experience at all.

Impressions of Marya Isayeva, the woman he loved,

are not sharp. She was about thirty, and in delicate health. She had a young son Pavel, known by the diminutive Pasha, who was later to be an incubus in Dostoevsky's home. The indications suggest that Marya was painfully sensitive, educated, and aspiring, nerves quivering with dissatisfaction at not being placed in circumstances more glamorous than hers. Think of *The Three Sisters,* and reduce them to poverty and social obscurity, and perhaps you get something of the conditions of Marya's discontent. None of the photographs of Dostoevsky's women is close to verbal descriptions given by acquaintances, but Marya's pictures make her look pretty in an oversensitive, apprehensive fashion.

Her husband was a minor official, left in Semipalatinsk without a job. He was drinking heavily when Dostoevsky came to know them. He was an overburdened, affectionate, ineffective man. Like Marya, he was ailing, and the obsessive drinking didn't help.

To begin with, Dostoevsky gave love to the whole family. This was before young Wrangel took up his post in the town, and Dostoevsky was starved for company. He hadn't had a friend for years, at least not one he could talk to. Marya had read books, and before Isayev became destitute they had bought the literary monthlies. The level of literary interests in educated Russia was much higher than among their counterparts in England, though the material standard of the English would be many times as high.

It was nice and companionable with the Isayevs. Suddenly Isayev himself was offered a job hundreds of miles away, at Kuzletsk. Kuzletsk was a place even less glittering than Semipalatinsk, but it was a job that as an official he couldn't refuse. Anyway, he and his family were living on scraps. Off they went. Dostoevsky realized, with a Stendhalian crystallization, that he was in love.

He wrote passionate love letters. She wrote back in kind. A few months after the move to Kuzletsk, Isayev died. They knew that he was ill, but perhaps his death was something of a surprise.

What to do? Dostoevsky wanted to marry Marya; they exchanged promises of marriage. But how? His debts were climbing. He might be given a commission, but a junior officer in the Tsarist army wasn't paid enough to live on. His fits were becoming more frequent, and some more violent. He couldn't make much money out of writing, away in Siberia. In the hateful Kuzletsk, five hundred miles between them, Marya was penniless, not knowing how to feed Pasha and herself. It was only too much like the helpless clerk in *Poor Folk,* not able to help the girl he loved.

Those problems were coped with, though it took some time, and there was a complication in which life appeared to be imitating art. Young Wrangel, kind, patient, and brave—though the new regime looked promising, he was taking risks in being intimate with a political convict, who was in fact under security surveillance for another twenty years. He lent Dostoevsky money to keep Marya alive, and went on lending money. Wrangel didn't exhibit fluctuations of temperament, and is one of the most generous characters in the whole story.

Marya did exhibit fluctuations of temperament. Just as the obstacles were being pushed away one by one, she fell in love with another man, a schoolteacher much younger than she was. There followed passages grotesquely, pathetically, at times beautifully like some in Dostoevsky's early novels. Storms of jealousy. Rages. Tears of repentance. Remorse. Dostoevsky befriending the young man, trying to get him a better job, defending him, and praising him to Marya. He was ready to sacrifice any claim he had, and would do anything for the two of them. That was true, and she knew it. She was so much moved by this kind of goodness that she decided it was Dostoevsky after all that she truly loved.

So, after all, they got married. Dostoevsky had by this time been given his commission. He had been restored to his rank in the nobility. That was surprisingly important to him, for one so fundamentally free from human superficialities, far freer than Dickens, Tolstoy, Balzac; but here as always he wasn't all of a piece.

He was then allowed to resign his commission. The excuse was medical, but the authorities were prepared to let him resume his literary career. He could leave Siberia, but not live in either of the capitals. For a short time, he and Marya took up residence in Tver (now Kalinin). At last he was allowed back in Petersburg, almost exactly ten years after he had been put, legs in chains, onto the sledge for Siberia.

Immediately he made plans with brother Mikhail, splendid plans as optimistic as Balzac's. Dostoevsky had sold a full-length novel, *The Friend of the Family,* and his debts were a trifle reduced. Mikhail was running a modestly prosperous business as a cigarette manufacturer, but he had always wanted to be somewhere close to the literary world. They decided to start a grand new magazine. Not a magazine for the smart liberals. Fyodor had

moved too far away from that. Too far from Western unbelief. In Siberia he had written to a woman benefactor:
"If anyone had written to me that the truth was outside of
Christ, I would rather remain with Christ than with the
truth." Such gnomic remarks would muddle and confuse
liberal Petersburg; they were the first sounding notes of
the ambiguities of the next twenty years.

On the other hand, he couldn't quite immerse himself
with the Slavophiles. Nationalism, yes; worship of the
Russian people, yes; but not every reactionary cause under
heaven. In some ways he was, and steadily remained, a
nineteenth-century intellectual, holding onto the residue of
Enlightenment values, radically unlike Tolstoy. For instance, unlike Tolstoy, Dostoevsky supported the emancipation of women. No orthodox Slavophile could do that.

So the new magazine had to tread delicately between
the right and the left. In nineteenth-century Russia this
was usually a recipe for disaster. In fact, the magazine,
Vremya (Time), made a reputation and looked as though
it might in a couple of years pay off the money they had
borrowed. Mikhail handled the business; Fyodor was editor,
as active as Dickens, interested in everything, as good a
journalist as Dickens, and with as sharp a nose. For a while,
many things were going well for him. His piece of classical
reportage about the convict prison, *The House of the
Dead,* was being a major success. That is, it had increased
his reputation. Great enthusiasm didn't mean more money,
for the magazines bought books outright. He was even
carefree enough to take a trip to Western Europe, which
like a good Russian born and bred he found detestable.
He went to Germany, France, England, Switzerland, and

then to Italy with Strakhov, a colleague on the magazine, and incidentally one of the few men of whom his judgment wasn't suspicious enough. The chief problem for Dostoevsky was which of those countries he disliked most; probably England, since it was the richest and represented commercial civilization at its height. Dostoevsky must have been the only traveler in the nineteenth century or since who discovered that Switzerland was excessively dirty.

He got back to Russia, became comfortable again, and wrote a travelogue, *Winter Thoughts on Summer Impressions,* which won more esteem. The pages on the glaring luxuries of London and the child prostitutes in the Haymarket burned with indignation. It was good to be back in a good country. Except for his marriage.

The marriage had gone wrong from the beginning. Or before. Many men, simpler men, would have known what to expect. A man with less contradictory intuitions, or one who had even a trace of Balzac's realism about women, wouldn't have considered taking on Marya. But once again, though he was nearly forty, Dostoevsky's imagination had been too strong for his sense of fact—or, if you like, too strong for his submerged vitality, his share of the "insect life."

Very few men have been driven by stronger or more widely ranging emotional forces. Very few men have lived closer to the deepest of experiences. He is the supreme exponent of what no one else has been able to reach or say. But in our own minds it is necessary not to make him too transcendental. After all, he was a man in some respects like the rest of us, a man of flesh and bone. The truth was —and, though there is no written proof, one needn't make a qualification—he hadn't found with Marya much, or any, sexual satisfaction. It doesn't matter whose fault it was, or if it was either of their faults at all. He had been searching for his erotic home, and it wasn't here. He was being very slow to find it. His imagination had been, and continued to be, a poor guide. Yet he wasn't defeated; in middle age he was as hopeful as a young man.

Heaven knows, he needed to be hopeful. Suddenly all fell apart. He had a disastrous love affair with a girl twenty years younger than he was, who had a temperament wilder than his own, more willing to rush regardless toward anything she thought she desired, whoever was going to be destroyed in the chase. She was Polina Suslova, a liberated product of the 1860s, daughter of an ex-serf, herself educated and fiercely free. Free in the exercise of a will that didn't recognize any laws. She had written a story for *Vremya*. She admired Dostoevsky as a writer. She was a very handsome girl. She was emancipated sexually as in all matters, though this was her first affair. It is likely that, in effect, she did the seduction.

It is also likely that she was sexually cold. Later on, rumors spread that she was perverse, and went in for sado-masochistic performances. It is possible that she thought she wanted violent stimuli, and was not going to be deterred. It is possible that Dostoevsky, his imagination racing away with him, thought he wanted the same. No one can know. What is certain is that she was emotionally cruel.

Once she had Dostoevsky in her power, she played with him. They arranged a meeting in Paris. He was doing his best to conceal the affair from Marya, whose health, frail all through the marriage, was getting worse. Polina had been demanding that Dostoevsky should divorce her, but there for once he resisted. He couldn't harm Marya now, in her present state. He and Polina had been sleeping together in Petersburg only a fortnight before he was able to get away to Paris. Polina greeted him with the cool, friendly announcement that she had found another lover, was totally absorbed, and unfortunately not his anymore.

The lover, a Spanish student, promptly left her. Dostoevsky had to comfort her like a brother, not a lover. He was helplessly enraptured. She could exercise her power again. It was arranged that they should travel through Europe together, as brother and sister, no lovemaking. He had to acquiesce. It was better to be with her on any terms. He had begun to gamble. Furtive attempts to have her again met with icy, inimical rebuffs. So it went on. He got back to Petersburg alone, penniless, desolate.

The affair with Polina left a ghost intruding into his life long afterward, and more than a ghost in some of his women characters. It was the most violent love of his life. He may have thought, at its most perverted point, that it was what he needed. In the light of what happened in the future, it was precisely what he didn't need.

It is worth noting that up to and beyond this period, all through his marriage and the havoc of Polina Suslova, the books he was writing are abnormally free from physical sex. It may as well be mentioned again that, if anyone ever suspected it, Dostoevsky was not prudish. If one reads his letters to his second wife, one cannot miss—despite her cautious censorship—his cheerful sexuality, as uninhibited as it could reasonably be. But in *The Friend of the Family* or *The Insulted and Injured* there is scarcely a vestigial glimpse of this, far less than in the novels of such a correct Victorian Englishman as Trollope. Dostoevsky's libido, which when released was persistent and pervading, is nowhere present. All the characters in *The Friend of the Family* and *The Insulted and Injured* exist in their emotion, very little in their physical selves. The emotions are reached, understood, depicted with all his conjuring-trick mastery, and the novels are much more interesting than is usually allowed. Foma Fomich in *The Friend of the Family* is from the inside totally realized. It is useful to compare him with William Dorrit, Dickens's most thorough effort in a not dissimilar direction. Dorrit is by far the more brilliant picture, but Foma exists with the effortless truth of a psychological genius.

Both the nonsacrificial personages in *The Insulted and Injured*, Valdovsky and Alyosha, carry the same internal truth. But none of these people stands out in his objective existence. It is difficult to see them. During those frantic years, Dostoevsky's total awareness of other people, visual, intuitive, objective, is shown only in his nonfictional record, *The House of the Dead*. There the men he watched in prison are seen as well as understood, the senses are active along with the emotions, the psyche and the soma are one.

Back in Petersburg, Polina lost, all other things fell apart too. *Vremya,* still existing on borrowed money but promising to be a success, was suppressed. This was 1863, and Russian opinion had consolidated around the government in its putting down the Polish rebellion. In *Vremya* the ineffable Strakhov wrote an article that was interpreted as pro-Polish. Strakhov was actually a time-serving conservative philosopher, and the article was misunderstood. After Dostoevsky's death, Strakhov, who professed intimate friendship, did the writer's reputation a startlingly bad turn, but here he was just inept. Nevertheless, passions were running high, Dostoevsky was still suspect, the journal was stopped. They were allowed to originate another one, *Epokha,* soon afterward, but the impetus, and the money, had dwindled away.

Meanwhile Marya was dying. She was tubercular and for a time had been living in Moscow, which was supposed, with the nineteenth-century faith in the effects of "air," to be for consumptives a therapeutic place. The disease rapidly gained on her, and Dostoevsky was with her when she died. Beside her body, he went through self-recriminations of guilt, remorse, and puzzled grief. He wondered if it were possible to love another like oneself.

A few months later his brother Mikhail also died, quite suddenly. This was another grief, more passionate and unmixed. It also meant a responsibility that not many men would have taken on. All Mikhail's money had been sunk in the journal. He left just enough to pay for his funeral. In addition he left a widow and children, a mistress and another child, and all the debts, large by their standards, something like several thousand 1864 English pounds, contracted by the two magazines. Dostoevsky at once undertook to provide for everything—families, debts, and of course his dead wife's son Pasha.

It isn't given to a man to be more incompetent in financial matters than Dostoevsky was. He didn't struggle out of these commitments until the last year of his life. No writer of consequence and not many writers without consequence, either, have had to work under the threat of such anxieties.

Families, debts—they were his fate. He may have been

incompetent at business, but he was more than competent about human responses. He didn't expect gratitude, and didn't get it. He just had, however ineffectual he was, to look after them all. It was noble. Many would have thought it exaggerated. Why he did it, with such ultimate expansiveness, none of his friends knew. He doesn't seem to have considered doing anything else. It probably didn't come from an extreme sense of financial rectitude or even of family duty. He had loved his brother deeply, and perhaps that motive was stronger than duty.

So, pressed by creditors, threatened with the debtors' prison, he sat down unflaggingly to write. The second journal folded. More debts. He borrowed more money. He had a legacy from a rich aunt; that soon melted away. The outgoings and the incomings of the Dostoevsky money would be an accountant's nightmare. He had more epileptic seizures, becoming more frequent and severe. He went on writing. It was a novel that came to be well known. English-speaking readers call it *Crime and Punishment*.

As with *Le Rouge et le noir, Anna Karenina,* and Dostoevsky's own *The Possessed,* the trigger for this book was a real-life case. But, as with Stendhal, a trigger does not operate unless there is a condition, up to that time unorganized or even unrealized, brooding below a writer's mind. Dostoevsky had, like Dickens, felt the fierce urgencies of crime. He might have accepted the need for authority and for behavior according to the rules of society; but he knew, maybe disconcertingly well, about getting outside society and cursing at it with contempt.

Thus his imagination was immersed in Raskolnikov,

with an insistence and power that obliterate the awkwardnesses of the story. The power takes over. The dialectic between the decencies of social behavior and the free and
dissident soul had not been done like this, as it were from
the inside, in fiction before. It hasn't been done like this
again. As happened once more with Dostoevsky and embarrassed him, the free soul listens to the decencies and
then tends to have the better of the argument.

The novel was written, like all but one of his, for
serial publication. It was written under barrages of inter-
ruption, creditors intruding, creditors threatening. He had
no kind of peace, and he hadn't time to revise. The total
impact hasn't been affected.

In a book so overpowering, points of technical interest
are liable to get neglected, but *Crime and Punishment* has
at least one. It is the first work of Dostoevsky's where he
developed, almost without thinking about it, a method of
representing states of the inner consciousness. *The Idiot*
and *The Brothers Karamazov,* as will be mentioned later,
give clearer examples of how he did it.

As the installments came out month by month in
Russky Vestnik (a journal that didn't often appear on
the date announced), Dostoevsky became established as
one of the three great contemporary masters in Russia.
Tolstoy was just beginning to publish *War and Peace.* Turgenev had been established for a long time, and was a
writer's writer, as Dostoevsky never was. Esoteric literary
opinion was cold to him, and remained so. But esoteric
literary opinion couldn't brush off what the rest of intellectual Russia took for granted—that here was something
like a force of nature.

He wrote on, chronically desperate about money. It seems strange to us that a writer so famous—his name, alongside those of Turgenev and Tolstoy, was already appearing in English guides to Russia—should be so destitute. This was due partly to his chivalry over Mikhail's debts and dependents, partly to his own incompetence, and partly because, having for those two reasons become so needy, he couldn't make bargains with the magazines. Book publishing brought in only a trickle, until firmer hands than his took over. The magazines paid according to a Russian system that still partially survives, an amount per *signature,* a signature usually meaning sixteen sheets. Hence the longer the book, the more profitable. The amount per signature depended on what the journals could get the author to accept. Turgenev, a very rich man, could insist on 500 rubles per signature. Tolstoy, a moderately rich man, at the beginning got rather less. Dostoevsky, an indigent man, got 150. With a feeling all writers will recognize, he cried: "I am prepared to admit that Turgenev is a better writer than I am" (he didn't think that for a single instant). "But I am not prepared to admit that he is *four times* better." Just to complete this story, he didn't get paid on the Tolstoy-Turgenev scale even when he reached the height of fame. For *The Brothers Karamazov* he got 300 rubles per signature.

It was in these circumstances that he signed the most foolish and most dangerous contract in recorded literary history. He was frightened, whether realistically or not, by the prospect of the debtors' prison. He came into contact with Stellovsky, who deserves remembering as the most consummate exploiter in all publishing. The contract was this: Stellovsky to have the right to republish all Dostoevsky's previous work. Further, Dostoevsky to guarantee to submit a new novel, not yet written, and not *Crime and Punishment,* by November 1866. If Dostoevsky failed to submit this novel, all rights in all subsequent writings for a period of the next nine years to belong to Stellovsky, without further payment. On his side of the contract, Dostoevsky to receive 3,000 rubles (roughly equivalent to £500 in English currency of the time). More than half this sum had to go to discharge promissory notes—which, though Dostoevsky didn't realize it, were already held by Stellovsky himself.

Only a man driven half-deranged by debts could have signed that contract. Even half-deranged, a more competent man still wouldn't have done so. Dostoevsky did.

He didn't promptly set to work to meet Stellovsky's deadline. Whatever he wasn't, he was a real writer. He knew that *Crime and Punishment* was a major work of art. As a major work of art, it obsessed him. He couldn't get his creative energy free for anything else. That probably would have been true, though maybe not so suicidally true, for any writer at the height of his power in the middle of a masterpiece.

Dostoevsky did have the energy free to pursue a delightful young woman, Anna Korvin-Krukovskaya, daughter of a general, only twenty-three, pretty, gifted, much impressed by the well-known writer, enough impressed to be a little in love with him. Another man in that slough in his fortunes, apparently irremediable, wouldn't have thought of marriage. Dostoevsky's teeming vigor wasn't so easily put off. He wanted to marry her. He pressed her. The general didn't approve, but that was a point in Dostoevsky's favor. The girl, like other well-born Russian women of the period, believed in feminine independence. Her mother had some sympathy.

Finally the girl refused him. She didn't love him enough, she seems to have told her young sister, to sink her life in his, as he would need her to.

It is pleasant to note that, though her own life turned out ill-fated, she remained on affectionate terms with Dostoevsky. It is also pleasant to note that that family, apart from the general, must have had an eye for genius. The mother thought that Dostoevsky was pretty marvelous. And the young sister was utterly in love with him. She consoled herself by marrying one of the greatest Russian mathematicians, thus fulfilling her desire to cherish genius.

Even a man with his capacity for hope might have felt some despondency. Hopelessly beset by money problems, turned down by one of the nicest of young women. By the end of September 1866, not a word written of the novel guaranteed in the Stellovsky contract. Appeal to Stellovsky to allow him more grace. A flat no. As anyone could have warned him, no hope there. Stellovsky was going to insist on the letter of the bond.

One month to go. Thirty days to write that novel. No one could have said, no one could say today, that Dostoevsky had had much luck in his life. Now he had his one major piece of luck. His literary friends knew of the Stellovsky crisis. They suggested farming out a novel for each of them to write a section, so as to cobble together a script that Stellovsky would have to accept. In a slightly less crucial situation, Dickens offered a similar service to Wilkie Collins. Dostoevsky refused. His artistic pride and conscience were stronger than those of many writers. Then one of the party had an idea. The Western technique of stenography had recently been reaching Russia. Stenographers were being trained. Why not get hold of one? They had all heard Dostoevsky, usually so silent, talk about a future project, soft-voiced, intense, hypnotic, sometimes unstoppable. Why not try it? If he got going, he could dictate a novel by October 30.

There seemed nothing else to try. On October 4 a girl of twenty, Anna Grigoryevna Snitkina, came into his apartment. She said later that she was overawed. He was a literary hero of hers, and she was ready to worship. He looked ill. He was irritable, nervous, restless, unable to start work that morning. He couldn't remember her name, and went on forgetting it for a fortnight. At night he did manage to dictate some pages. With a spontaneity that astonished her he told her about some of his sufferings, including the scene of the fake execution.

In her memoirs, Anna describes her own looks. She may not have been conventionally pretty, but the photographs show her as having fine eyes and a sensitive face. From the photographs, she looks in a quiet way more attractive than Polina. Anna was a good, efficient, bright-witted girl. Her father had recently died, and so she came to Dostoevsky in mourning, which suited the unobtrusive fashion in which she set about her work. There was no practical reason why she should have gone to work at all. Her father had been a middle-rank civil servant, and left his family in decent comfort. Anna could go on living with her mother, who was a Russified Swede. But Anna, though a devout Orthodox believer and no sort of liberal, was also one of the young women of the sixties. It was part of their creed that women should be independent. So here she was with Dostoevsky, in her very first stenographer's job.

She did it with competence, and devotion on top of competence. She went home with each day's dictation, transcribed it at night, and brought it to him next day. The pile of pages became satisfactorily thick. She kept encouraging him: of course they were going to meet the date. She was unassuming, didn't obtrude herself, but having her sit calmly beside him soothed him. He kept telling her stories of his life. She did presume to ask him why they were all so unhappy. He said, truly enough, that he hadn't had much happiness but still hoped for it. She went on worshiping, and she wanted to care for him.

They finished the dictation on October 29. The book was *The Gambler*. Polina Suslova had left a lightning flash across the story, but Anna appears not to have noticed it at the time. On the other hand, she did, in her sensible, responsible fashion, feel that the hero was too weak-willed. Surely he could have broken off this craze for gambling? She couldn't respect him. Dostoevsky told her that it wasn't so easy. Addictions could be hard to throw off, he assured her.

The Stellovsky contract stipulated that the manuscript should be delivered on October 30. Otherwise Dostoevsky paid the penalty. Both he and Anna, who already had a clear business head, realized that Stellovsky was intending to cheat. On October 30 he was not at his office, and Dostoevsky was told that he had gone away for several days. The office was forbidden to accept this manuscript or any other. However, by now Dostoevsky and Anna were forewarned. He had taken legal advice. If the manuscript were deposited at a main police station, and a receipt obtained from an officer of senior rank, then the contract would have been fulfilled. Even then, bureaucratic casualness caused them some heartburn. Senior officers took the afternoon off. It was not until 10:30 P.M. on October 30 that Dostoevsky obtained his receipt.

Anna's job was over. They needed a pretext to meet again. He got her to invite him to meet her mother. He called on them twice and asked Anna to help him with the last part of *Crime and Punishment.*

They arranged a day, only a fortnight after their last dictating session. When she arrived, he told her that he had been thinking, not of *Crime and Punishment,* but of a new novel. It had been suggested by the trouble of a friend of his, a man of his own age, a man who was ill, unprepossessing, laden with debts and responsibilities. He had fallen in love with a young girl.

Anna, not being a fool, had on the instant realized that he was talking of himself.

Dostoevsky went on; he would call the girl Anna, which was a good name. Anna, although no fool, had no confidence in her own charm. She leaped at the thought that he must be hoping again about Anna Korvin-Krukovskaya. That story, this other Anna had heard before.

Dostoevsky went on to ask her feminine advice, for the sake of the putative novel. Did she think it psychologically possible that such a girl could return the love of such a man?

By this time Anna had seen the truth. She said forcibly that of course it was possible.

Then Dostoevsky told her to imagine that she was that

girl and Dostoevsky himself the man, and that he was asking her to be his wife. What would she say?

This is what Anna remembered herself as saying: "I should answer that I loved you and would love you all my life."

So she did. But there was much to go through yet. They had fourteen years of married life before he died. On her side, there stayed absolute devotion and the certainty that he was the most wonderful man alive. It took him longer to become irretrievably in love (letters from Polina still devastated him), but as the years went on he became enraptured, wanted nothing and no one else and, as literally as one can describe his kind of rapturous love, adored every inch of her body.

In Anna's memoirs, straightforward and honest, she says that from the beginning she loved him with her whole heart and soul, but that at the beginning there was nothing physical about her love. She also hints that her love was always more spiritual admiration than anything nearer to earth. She certainly thought that was true, for no one tried harder to be candid. It is possible that she found action about physical love easier than admitting it in words.

Dostoevsky wasn't impeded by any constraints about either. Step by step his commitment to Anna became all-possessing. Maybe with incredulity he discovered that this was what he had needed all the time. None of Polina's torments to provoke him to desperate passion. None of the weathervane changes of his first wife. He was just presented with self-surrendering love. Which released like a flood the domestic sensuality that was his true home. Now he could let himself go and lead the insect life. When

Dostoevsky let himself go, he went a very long way. He was often remorseful about his sins, ready to atone for many guilts. But there were two domains in which he had less guilt than most men. He wasn't guilty, or even much embarrassed, about any of his shifts in raising a few rubles. He wasn't guilty about anything that he found agreeable in the way of sex, least of all in the sex of a happy marriage.

He became more immersed in love, more rapturous about their bodily love together, as the years passed. When sometimes he had to go to Moscow and leave her in Petersburg with the children, he wrote to her most days, sometimes several times a day. The letters were long, fervent, and naked to the carnal life, as naked as the times together that he was celebrating or telling her that they would soon have again. Before she published his letters, of which she was not unreasonably proud, Anna did some careful editorial pruning. She was perhaps a little prudish, or pleasurably shocked, at seeing what they had done described ecstatically on paper. She was sufficiently relaxed to tease him: he had better remember that the official censor might open his letters. Let him, wrote Dostoevsky robustly, and let him envy us. This passage occurs in a spirited letter in 1879 and goes on: "How many people enjoy themselves as we do after twelve years of marriage and enjoy themselves more than they did when they started?"

He sometimes scolded her for untidiness, but his one real reproach to her was that she was not sufficiently candid, meaning candid about their sexual pleasures. She was too modest to write (or in intimacy talk?) as he wrote and presumably talked. He wrote to her, in that same letter of 1879, as part of an exposition on marital sex: "You will say that this is only one side, and that the grossest. No, it is not gross. And besides, at bottom, everything else depends on it."

That was a simple statement, for a man not overgiven to simplicities. It had taken him a long time to let that instinctive realism show through. But now at last it was just that realism that had come to guide or even control his imagination. That is why the major novels of those last fourteen years are sensually much richer, and much more balanced between mind and body, than anything he had written before. There is nothing disembodied about the women in *The Idiot, The Possessed, The Brothers Karamazov*.

Anna did many things for him. One was to save him from his own imagination.

Even with her prudent crossings out, which concealed a lot of their erotic play, the letters are still paeans of cheerful unrestraint. He will take off all her clothes, and kiss her all the way down, front and back, from head to feet. He will linger over her beloved flesh, he tells her often. He seems to have been as multifarious about sexual activities as he was about emotional ones. Different thoughts about her body could excite him. Her exquisite feet. Feet were a specific attraction. Rather tedious for the young woman, one would have thought, but she was patient and adoring. Rather curiously, she never censored any of the passage about feet kissing, feet fondling, feet worshiping, as though she hadn't realized that her feet were a fetish stimulus. Yet she must have noticed and known. She did censor all the passages that, from the context, almost certainly contained threats of amorous chastisement. She does leave in a reference to a bruise from the last pinch he gave her before he went away; he replied cheerfully that he would go on pinching her until he ceased to love her, which would be never.

There are more explicit references, of uncertain authenticity. But the indications are clear enough. One would bet that there were some domestic spankings in the Dostoevsky bedroom.

Her own records should be read with a mildly suspicious eye. She talks about his passions of jealousy. At the beginning, they must have been wild and genuine. He was a middle-aged man married to a very young wife. He became distracted when she let anyone so much as kiss her hand. But later on—after all, he didn't lack perception, and it is absurd to think that he didn't know she loved him as deeply and faithfully as a woman could love a man. The habit of jealousy can of course live on, but one gets a feeling that some of those jealous scenes were contrived, and didn't proceed with quite the rageful dignity that Anna describes. She was anxious in all ways to preserve his metaphysical loftiness. We are under no necessity to do that. He was a great man, no one doubts it, but he may have been capable, like other men, of a little erotic calculation or forward planning. So may she. She confesses to what she calls an occasional prank, designed to test whether he was still jealous. In her account, he became furious, distrustful, repentant for having been distrustful, accepting the proofs of her innocence, full of contrition, and both shedding gentle delectable tears, utterly at one. Another scenario might be written in which both had been working toward a somewhat less dignified row, in which the deep-minded religious thinker was thoroughly enjoying a bit of make-believe vengeance.

Anyway, it became a supremely happy marriage, one

of the very few enjoyed by major figures in literature. And one that no one knowing the young Dostoevsky and his life history could have conceivably predicted. Who would have given him a chance of happiness—compared with the glamorous Dickens, and the massively prepotent Tolstoy? But it was Dostoevsky, not they, who became happy.

Not that the worries and frets subsided altogether until a couple of years before his death. It took Anna all that time to carve for him some sort of peace.

She was something of a heroine. She had remarkable stoicism and a great fund of resilience. She needed all of it. First she had to deploy her will against the tribe of Dostoevsky's dependents. *Dependents,* however, was not the term they would have used themselves. They acted as though convinced of their own obvious moral righteousness. They opposed the marriage. He should not think of such a marriage at his age. An even graver fault was for Dostoevsky to conceive that the money he earned was his own to dispose of. He belonged, and must continue to belong, to them all. That proposition was advanced, imperiously, rudely, by Pasha, who has claims to be the most impudent and importunate stepson so far known.

They couldn't stop the marriage, but Anna accepted that Fyodor wasn't capable of escaping from the net of obligations. It would have been wrong to press him. This wasn't cowardice on her side, but a kind of precocious wisdom. She could, however, get him away from them all. She had the excuses she needed. Mikhail's widow, the ineffable Pasha, the whole troupe who cluttered up the flat, in the weeks after the marriage, were making her life miserable. It was hard to gain any privacy with her husband. They

brought in young acquaintances, and treated her like a
silly girl not fit to talk to Dostoevsky. She was upset, but
she made a plan of action. When he next found her crying,
she told him that this enmity around her was going to
ruin their marriage. She and he must have a chance to
"know one another."

They agreed to travel in the West. As usual, they had
no money. But Anna's mother, who was a faithful friend,
had given them some handsome silver and a dinner service
for a future abode of their own, if and when they ever
lived on their own. They pawned these possessions and set
off. They expected to stay away from Russia for four
months. They stayed away four years.

It wasn't that they didn't wish to return. Often they
had the homesickness that so many Russians knew, like a
physical hunger. But now they were again afraid that, once
back, he would be imprisoned for debt. The pile of debts
was not being paid off. In fact, it was soon increased, since
his sister's husband had died, and this husband had stood
as a guarantor for Mikhail's journal. That meant another
promise from Dostoevsky of more thousands of rubles. Not
much money was coming in. When they arrived in Dresden,
he hadn't yet started a new novel. He could and did obtain small advances from Katkov, the editor and owner
of *Russky Vestnik,* another steady and sensible supporter.
Much of those remittances had to go back to Petersburg,
for Mikhail's family and for Pasha. Mikhail's widow pointed
out helpfully that it was most unsatisfactory to have these
payments at irregular intervals and that she would have to
insist on a quarterly allowance.

What little money they were left with seemed as usual

to slip through his hands. Without fuss, Anna took charge. All spending money was deposited with her. It didn't take long for her to know that she would have to be the practical partner.

So the two of them lived, for the next few years, what at their most prosperous was an indigent student life, often more harassed than that. They had a child who died in infancy and another daughter, Lyubov, who flourished. Dostoevsky borrowed money, as he did once from Turgenev, whom he disliked. To Turgenev, Dostoevsky behaved badly. To beg a favor from such a man—that brought out all the suspiciousness and rancor that Dostoevsky was capable of, which was considerable. He repaid that favor in the bitter, unfair, unfunny, satirical picture of Karmazinov in *The Possessed*. Turgenev stirred all the worst and most xenophobic in both Dostoevsky and Tolstoy. Turgenev, they both felt, might as well have been a Frenchman. He was too Westernized. He didn't love Russia, whatever he pretended. He was insincere. He was patronizing. They had no use for his kind of civilization.

Anna's mother sometimes helped them out, in a practical, tactful Scandinavian fashion. That was all right. Dostoevsky only bit one hand, Turgenev's. Anna's mother loved her daughter and was fond of Dostoevsky. He seems to have got on surprisingly well with mothers-in-law, actual or potential. When Anna and Dostoevsky had a few coins to spare, they stood themselves small student treats—a bottle of wine, fruit, pastries from the confectioners. Each of them had a childishly sweet tooth.

They moved from town to town, and from one rundown lodging house to another. Dresden—Baden—Geneva

—Milan—Florence—Wiesbaden. Sometimes there were Russian colonies, as in Dresden or Geneva. That made the places slightly less intolerable. They both spoke workman-like German, but disliked nearly all Germans and nearly all Swiss. Italians were more human, and Italian peasants reminded them of home.

Baden and Wiesbaden were casino towns. That meant danger. Dostoevsky, who had been seized with a gambling addiction when traveling with Polina, an addiction as mechanical as reaching for the next cigarette and as compulsive as needing the next fix, succumbed to it again. When he had talked to Anna about *The Gambler,* he wasn't speaking with lofty detachment. He had, like other gamblers, a rationalization that cheered him up. This was the way to restore their fortunes. All the debts could be swept away in a couple of weeks! Twenty-five thousand rubles—that was nothing with a winning run! All this penny-pinching, all the worry about poor Anna not having decent clothes—that was unendurable, and this was the way not to endure it! Besides, he had a system. All he needed was a cool head.

He didn't have a cool head. Also he didn't have any grasp of the laws of statistical chance. He seems to have thought that a cold-blooded Englishman would have played the system to perfection. He certainly did think that, if he had been an Englishman, he would have had a cooler head. He would have remembered his system. He would have known when to stop.

Constantly he lost every pathetic scrap of money Anna could give him. She did not once reproach him. This was another test of her wisdom. She understood that it would be like reproaching someone in the grip of insatiable love. Somehow she had to take it. She went to the pawnbroker with his overcoat or her last dress. She gave him the money. He blessed her passionately, went back to the tables, and lost it all.

That happened many times. Visits to pawnshops became part of their way of life. They had to conceal these visits from suspicious landladies. For themselves, they don't seem to have felt especially embarrassed, as a Western couple might have done. In Florence, where they had run out of money altogether, Anna pawned some of her underclothes.

She had more to endure than most young women. Within a month of their marriage, he had one of his violent seizures, and she had to look after him. Epileptic fits aren't pretty to nurse, but she knew that this would be the first of many, as it was. Other loving young women would have coped with that. In their exile, his nerves got more strained, and his restlessness and irritability became morbid. Other young women might have coped with that, or the sheer hardship he had brought her into. Many would have kicked at the gambling, which made the hardship more extreme and, except to the eye of love, more ridiculous. What nearly any girl but she would have struck against was at the demands and voracities of those parasites back in Petersburg. That called for every atom of her devotion, and many years later, when he was dead, it was that memory that drew out her one complaint.

She had been right to make him leave them. She had paid many kinds of price, and so had he. Subsistence poverty, and often below the level of ordinary subsistence. The gambling mania. Illness, death of the first child. His uncontrollable nerves; the strain of two people, living as they were, alone in exile. Yet, transcending all that, she had had him to herself. Now he was bound to her, unbreakably, until death parted them. This was marriage as she had craved for it, and worked for it. The single boast she allowed herself as an old woman was that, however incredible it seemed, her mind being so far below his (she was excessively diffident about that), he had truly and passionately loved her. Anyone who doubts it ought to read his letters, meaning the expurgated version she had published—so she wrote, with unashamed pride.

In the midst of her day-by-day trials in the foreign towns they detested, going to the post office hoping for a remittance, and then, receiving no letter, back to the pawnshop once more, she wrote in her diary that none of this mattered, perhaps this is what we pay for our happiness, with him I am ecstatically happy, I know that he is happy, I know now that he loves me.

There was no one to interrupt. In Florence there were no Russians to talk to. This had a good practical consequence. It was easier for him to write than it had ever been in Petersburg. He had carried his writing habits with him. The room might be a shambles, but his desk had to be in order, pens, ink, paper in their sacramental places. Efficient as she was, Anna wasn't so obsessively tidy, and got into trouble.

She had to fit into another of his routines. Like Balzac, but unlike most of the others, Dostoevsky wrote at night. Anna went to bed while he wrote for five or six hours, usually at great speed. Then he woke Anna, at four or five in the morning, and gave her what one of the best biographies describes modestly as a long and lingering good night.

It was in that manner, during their years in the West,

that he produced *The Idiot* and most of *The Possessed*. He was a good and severe critic of his own work, and he was accustomed to make, looking back at them, two comments. First, if he had been freer of anxiety, and had a modicum of leisure and not such need of money, he could have got rid of some of their awkwardnesses and muddle. He might even have made them nearly as polished as the books of the abominated Turgenev, and then they would have stood a chance of surviving as long.

Dostoevsky didn't know it, but his books have already lasted as long as any work of his century, and will continue to do so. There may, however, be a little in what he says. His initial plans, his sketches of his people, many of the originals of whom are suggested in his jottings, were as a rule considered and careful. Some of the improbabilities entered during the actual writing. It may be excessively romantic to ask whether Dostoevsky wouldn't have been less Dostoevsky if those improbabilities had been scrupulously trimmed. Maybe it is. It does still seem, though, that the blinding insight wouldn't have been altered by a flicker if the architectonics of the novels had been as perfectly composed as that of, say, Ibsen's plays.

The second self-criticism is more interesting. It is that the conception with which he began a novel was often splendid. He wasn't foolishly modest about his gifts, and he believed that no one else could have had such conceptions. But he accused himself of never carrying them to their proper fulfillment. Most writers have felt something of the same, but he meant it in a specific sense. He seems to have thought, though he didn't use our modern terms, that he often lacked the technical power. He can't have thought that he lacked the psychological power to make his impact. But it comes nearer the bone if he suspected that he didn't have the range of technical resources that Dickens or Tolstoy had.

He wasn't specially interested in finding a mode to express the movements of the inner consciousness. We have to come to Proust and Henry James before a major novelist wondered whether that might be something to try, though even they, for good reasons, didn't tackle it head on. Both Dickens and Tolstoy had casual shots at it. And, since they had resources for anything, they would have made more shots if they had thought it worthwhile. Whereas Dostoevsky had really only one resource that he used for every effect in his novels, which was the dramatic dialogue, heightened beyond the limits of any dialogues that could be spoken, yet miraculously suggesting not only actual emotion but also the intermittencies and purposes of the mind and soul.

In fact, drawing on Dostoevsky's psychological depths, this single technique often tells us as much as any writer could about many kinds of consciousness. Yet, when he was exploring Prince Myshkin in *The Idiot,* he seems to have been disappointed with the result. He had set out to tell us more than had been said before about a really good man. He hadn't brought it off.

That now appears to have been setting his expectations about as high as Shakespeare deciding that *King Lear* didn't really work. For many, the present writer among them, *The Idiot* ranks at the peak of Dostoevsky's art, second only to *The Brothers Karamazov.* Some put it higher. It was, despite his dissatisfaction, Dostoevsky's own favorite.

Aglaya Ivanovna, Nastasya Filippovna, Rogozhin would be enough to make the best of writers feel that his life was justified. But has anyone ever even tried to suggest goodness as in Prince Myshkin? It is a feat without a parallel. Perhaps it is more incapable of being paralleled because of the double-minded tact, or complexity, with which Dostoevsky leaves the Prince at the end. This doesn't mean the fact that the Prince goes mad. That is not intended to be a symbolic defeat of goodness. Dostoevsky, not intoxicated by his own great conception, isn't using Myshkin as any kind of symbol but as a fragile human being, just as much an individual as the rest of us, who would be diminished if he merely existed as the personification of the concept. No, the ambiguity strikes home before the Prince goes mad. He is talking to Radovsky, begging him to believe that Aglaya will understand why he, Myshkin, has to marry Nastasya Filippovna. Radovsky is not an admirable character, but like other Dostoevsky characters is possessed of unusual insight. The abnormal proportion of people with insight gives the novels, of course, some of their brilliant shimmer.

"I've always believed that she would understand," Myshkin says.

Radovsky tells him flatly that she won't. "She loved you like a woman, like a human being, not like an abstract spirit."

Then the knife thrust—"The most likely thing is that you've never loved either of them."

Once for all he is telling Myshkin that despite his universal kindness, his total absence of self, he is incapable of love. Love as human beings feel it. Is that where goodness takes you? *Is that what goodness means?*

Like most of Dostoevsky's deepest questions, this is left without an answer.

After four years of exile, Dostoevsky and Anna decided that they could bear it no longer. There was only one home for them. They must go back, though they knew the risk. *The Idiot* had been published in Katkov's magazine, *The Possessed* was coming out month by month, but they still had no money and a mass of debts. Never mind. Dostoevsky was capable of saying better a debtors' prison than living in the West. They pawned a few more possessions and raised enough for the fares to Petersburg.

They raised enough for the fares, but Dostoevsky begged it back from Anna. He had to go to Wiesbaden for another fling. He lost everything. He was in despair. He confessed to a priest. He promised Anna that he would never gamble again. She didn't believe him. She had heard those promises before.

As it turned out, this was the promise he kept. The gambling obsession had left him as suddenly as it had come. He didn't play the tables again for the rest of his life, nor, so far as Anna could observe, even want to. She didn't understand; nor has anyone else. How can one give up a mania overnight? The explanation may be simpler than we think of applying to any of Dostoevsky's actions. In the midst of all the tumults, there was a sharp calculating intelligence at work somewhere in his mind. Multiple motives, contradictory urges—and the capacity to reflect about himself. He may just have concluded that his system didn't work.

Somehow Anna raised more money for their fares. Katkov sent some to pay bills and redeem a few possessions. No writer has had a more long-suffering publisher.

It wasn't sheer benevolence, of course. Dostoevsky might be an intolerable nuisance about money, but he was one of the two great stars on Katkov's list. They arrived back in Petersburg with the equivalent of about a hundred of to-day's dollars, a couple of trunks, and utter, grateful, tear-stained joy.

They also arrived back to the old troubles. The house-hold goods they had left behind had been dispersed by the crowds of Mikhail's relatives. Pasha had sold Dostoevsky's library. He now proposed to live with them and bring his wife. Thanks to Katkov, they did manage to rent a two-and-a-half-room flat and acquire a minimum of furniture on credit. Creditors began to push into the flat, threatening Dostoevsky with their promissory notes. Very much like creditors in the novels of Dickens or Trollope brandishing their "bills."

Dostoevsky was now fifty, and they seemed to be start-ing again. Yet, almost without their knowing it, they were through the worst. They had precisely two assets. Anna had emerged from exile not as a girl but as a confident young woman, totally happy about their marriage, certain that she was able to take his affairs in her own firm charge. She was eight months pregnant when they returned home, but as soon as the child, young Fyodor, was born, she acted like someone of character and experience, and often like a more than promising business executive. She dealt with Pasha, whom she hadn't forgiven. She would no more have him and his wife to live with them than a couple off the streets. She wouldn't permit Dostoevsky to distress himself about the creditors, or meet them. Those also she dealt with herself. She could be a remarkably cool opponent. Yes, if they chose, they could put Fyodor Mikhailovich in the debtors' prison. If so, they would have to pay for his up-keep themselves. That was contemporary Russian law, which she had mastered. It would cost them quite a lot. They could keep him in prison for a fixed term, and then, again by Russian law, the debts would be regarded as discharged. So they would be out of pocket, and had better accept agreements to pay by installments. As for seizing the Dostoevskys' bits of furniture, that was not on; it didn't belong to them, but to the shops from which they hired it. They had nothing for any creditor to seize.

For the first time in Dostoevsky's fifty years, someone was making sense of his financial position. Very soon she thought it necessary to become his hardback publisher. Neither *The Idiot* nor *The Possessed*, after being serialized, had been bought by a book publisher. Why not issue it herself? She applied herself to visiting bookshops, learning about discounts, striking bargains. Hardback publishing was not yet much of a business in Russia, but she managed to bring in a steady flow of income. Immediately after Dostoevsky's death, she was visited by Countess Tolstoya, who had also decided to be her husband's publisher and who asked Anna to teach her about the business. The two became friends. In due course, a very large number of rubles passed into both literary estates.

The second asset of the Dostoevskys was that, during the years abroad, his literary fame had mounted, though it was a baffling and controversial fame. The critics in Petersburg and Moscow hadn't known what to make of *The Idiot,* and had solved their problem by writing about it as little as they could. They did know what to make of *The*

Possessed, which was to repudiate and denounce it. Literary opinion was, in the customary Russian style, divided on party lines. The liberals dominated most of the journals, though Katkov's was on the conservative wing. Whatever Dostoevsky's message in *The Possessed* really was, about which there was considerable dispute, it was certainly not liberal. Most progressive intellectuals became convinced that Dostoevsky had turned into a committed reactionary, and had denied with the most rending savagery the whole package of progressive hopes. That reading has been accepted with enthusiasm by Western opinion, and helped to make *The Possessed* in America and England his most influential book.

If one reads the book in cool blood, nearly everything said about it seems too simple. As a work of art, it is more muddled and confused than any of his other novels. It has marvelous things in it. Stefan Trofimovich is a creation that no Western writer has brought off, though we have had plenty of Stefan Trofimoviches all around us. No Western writer has produced such masterly pictures of men at the extreme of their mental tether, such as Kirillov and Shatov. But the book was written in a mood, long sustained, of passionate disgust, which makes one forget that there are many different, and irreconcilable, messages embedded there.

It had been suggested by a conspiracy in real life, a curiously bogus but lethal conspiracy, led by a man called Nechaev, a young colleague of Bakunin's, more steely-hearted and less agreeable. It reminded Dostoevsky of the conspiracies of which he had had a taste himself. Like many who have seen conspiratorial planning from the inside, he had come to hate it. In Geneva he had attended liberal conferences, and he had come to hate those, too.

He didn't find hate difficult. Above all, he had come to hate liberals. By liberals here is meant progressive persons in the middle of the road. Their bland, soft-minded views of human possibility repelled him. For him, crime existed, evil existed, each man was responsible for his actions. These complacent fools blandly pronouncing that it all depended on environment were making a farce of life. There is a great deal of his fierce insight into the liberal optimism that strikes dead true today.

It is important to read all the text, not two-thirds of it. He believed just as vehemently in his own vision of human possibility. If people think he would have seen any virtue in modern Western society, they are reading with their eyes half-shut. Dostoevsky's beliefs flew to the limits, wherever the limits were. He would have approved of the old theological statement of Charles Simeon—the truth lies at both extremes, never in the middle. Many of today's Russians, supporters of the party regime, understand him better than Westerners who think he speaks for them. In Moscow a venerated senior poet recently said that Dostoevsky fostered the Russian sense of responsibility for the fate of the whole world.

The immediate effect of *The Possessed,* however, was to lose Dostoevsky what little literary support he had held onto. He said himself, with the sardonic humor that Russians say foreigners somehow miss, that he had had only two literary backers in his career (Belinsky and Nekrasov, ironically both liberals) ; as for other literary persons, he didn't want to be buried near them—they had caused him enough irritation while he was alive.

The writers would have liked to pretend that he didn't exist. But he had a public; he spoke to them more immediately than anyone else in the country. After *The Possessed*, he was taken up by powerful conservatives. That was natural enough. Whatever his ambiguities were—and some conservatives had the shrewdness to notice them—many of his messages were theirs. Russia. Orthodox Russia. The horrors of Western materialism. The cataclysm for the world that he kept predicting. He was the only writer of high stature anywhere near the Orthodox side. They used him. He was made editor of the reactionary journal *Grazhdanin,* which was in reality controlled by an arch-reactionary, Prince Meshchersky. They paid him a modest salary, the only steady money he received in his life. But Meshchersky acted as a kind of supereditor, and Dostoevsky didn't like it. Further, he didn't like being used. He was unhappy in the job, and stood it for less than a year. He had his own pride. But he was no more immune to the charm of the powerful than other men are. There is no doubt that the patronage of Pobednostsev made his head swim. Pobednostsev was the most intelligent of high Tsarist functionaries. He had been tutor to the Tsarevich, became Procurator of the Holy Synod, and was known to be the supreme gray eminence. He had a view of human nature entirely pessimistic, both contemptuous and jet black, from which base he rigidly opposed the most gentle inclination to anything that men called progress. He read and admired Dostoevsky. All these highly placed Russians read a good deal, and were expected to. Dostoevsky was shocked to discover that the Tsar, Alexander II, had read only two or three of his novels.

Pobednostsev was an illustrious patron. He didn't think of wiping off Dostoevsky's debts. No one contemplated that. But Pobednostsev did in time remove the police surveillance that continued long after Dostoevsky was the favorite writer of the court. Pobednostsev privately influenced Dostoevsky's political statements—that is, his statements as a publicist, not as a novelist. In his miserable year on *Grazhdanin,* Dostoevsky had started a feature known as *The Diary of a Writer,* where he dilated on anything that occurred to him. Later he published the *Diary* monthly on his own account. It increased his rapport with the public. He took the most considerate trouble with his answers to correspondents, giving sensible fatherly advice, steady with sanity and caution, as though he had lived the most orderly and prudent life imaginable. In his political articles, he followed the Pobednostsev party line, though he may not have needed much guidance. He was also devoutly orthodox about the Church.

When it came to altering or bending a religious passage in a novel, though, he couldn't do it. Once he seems to have tried. He sent the proofs of *The Brothers Karamazov* to Pobednostsev installment by installment. Pobednostsev judiciously approved. When "The Dream of the Holy Inquisitor" went to Pobednostsev, it arrived back with a note expressing literary admiration, but saying sternly that in the next installment this must be conclusively demolished according to true religion. Dostoevsky said fervently that he would do just that. He may have tried. He didn't succeed.

In the years before he started writing *The Brothers Karamazov* (which was in 1878, when he was fifty-seven), practical living was becoming smoother for Dostoevsky. With Anna in control, the debts were being paid off, and by 1878 they were almost free. Pasha, who now had a large family, still made demands. Dostoevsky must have had a liking for that layabout. *The Diary of a Writer* brought in some money, Anna's publishing enterprises rather more. She was contemplating a mail-order business for books, not only Dostoevsky's, which she made into another success. In the middle 1870s Dostoevsky had published *A Raw Youth,* a novel with which he was bitterly disappointed, and for once with reason. It led, however, to a reconciliation between him and his old liberal colleague Nikolai Nekrasov. Nekrasov made the approach. He said that he would again like to publish Dostoevsky in his journal. He would pay twice as much as Katkov. Dostoevsky felt committed to Katkov, but discovered that *Russky Vestnik* was preempted for months by Tolstoy's new book, *Anna Karenina.* So Dostoevsky with genuine pleasure gave *A Raw Youth* to the man who had once launched him.

It had, for Dostoevsky, an unusually good press, out of comparison better than that for *The Idiot* or *The Possessed.* That now appears as though they had all gone mad. The explanation is simple. Nekrasov's journal was the favorite liberal organ, Katkov's the unfavorite conservative one. Not long afterward, Nekrasov died a lingering and agonizing death from cancer. He was a fine poet and a generous man.

Though the pawning days were over, the Dostoevskys had to move from apartment to apartment in Petersburg,

all of them dark, constricted, the kinds of places that a
minor civil servant or a junior academic might have rented.
Dostoevsky was pleased when his study wasn't overrun by
beetles. Up to the end, they didn't aspire in the capital to
anything better than the simplest comfort. They had
heavy medical expenses still. Dostoevsky's fits, when anxieties had been pushed some distance away, ravaged him
less; but he had developed a lung condition which, with
the nineteenth-century faith in geographical therapy, led
the doctors to insist that he should take the cure at Ems.
That he did several years running. It was too expensive for
Anna and the children to go with him. He was miserable
in Ems, even by the high standards of Dostoevskian misery.
It was from there that he wrote most of the letters that
have already been mentioned, in which he told Anna that
he loved her more each day, each month, each year, letters
that were wild, increasingly rhapsodic, increasingly adoring, and increasingly erotic.

His respiratory trouble was diagnosed, correctly, as
emphysema, but it was not disabling and not regarded as
especially ominous. The doctors told him that, in spite of
all his ailments, he had abnormal resilience and strength.

Pushed for money as they still were, the Dostoevskys
allowed themselves one small escape. Not long after they
had returned to Russia, they had rented for three months a
house in a country town, the house being a distinctly un-
luxurious wooden *dacha*. They got what was for them so
much tranquility that they went back to the little town
each year, managing to hire rather better *dachas*, and
finally buying one. Even when they were out of debt, they
had to scrape to raise the purchase price, which was 1,000

rubles (say, £200 in English money, period 1878). The little town was in the Novgorod district, where Russians had built some of the first of their Christian churches (in Novgorod, Rostov the Great, Pskov). The name of the town was, and is, Staraya Russa. It was about two hundred kilometers from Petersburg, and just south of Lake Ilmen. In summer it was used as a simple freshwater holiday resort, where people from the capital went to bathe and get the benefit of a primitive spa. Otherwise it was quite undistinguished.

It didn't remain undistinguished, for this became the town of *The Brothers Karamazov*, through most of the novel referred to as "our town," though in one of his sly asides Dostoevsky remarks: "The name of our town, I can conceal it no longer, is Skotoprigonyevsk!" Skotoprigonyevsk is an actual place not far away, but there is no question that Staraya Russa is the physical home of *The Brothers Karamazov*. This sometimes comes as a mild surprise to Western readers, who have usually imagined those dramas happening somewhere much more remote, perhaps in central Russia, on the steppes, in a ramshackle town miles from nowhere. Russians have always known that "our town" must be Staraya Russa. You can trace the streets, the river, the bridge, and many of the individual sites. In a brilliant novella, Daniil Granin has methodically revealed how much of the Dostoevskian town is still preserved.

You can trace so much because Dostoevsky took loving care with his geographical setting, as much as Balzac writing about the high street of Saumur. Maybe, in controlling his imagination, Dostoevsky needed the guidelines of concrete realistic fact. From the first pages of *The Brothers Karamazov*, he seems to have been certain that he must bring the physical world alive, as though he had to live with the flesh, mind, spirit, all in one. That is the explicit meaning of the book, and gives it a richness he had not achieved before, and somehow an extraordinary joy. Dostoevsky had often paid attention to houses in his art, even when the people within them might have seemed disembodied, whirls of multiple emotion and divided spirit, but he hadn't cast much of an eye on anything we call nature. In *The Brothers Karamazov*, Alyosha leaves the body of his beloved teacher, Father Zossima, goes out into the monastery garden, looks with exaltation at the night sky, kisses the earth, and vows to love it forever. There is no other passage like that in the whole of Dostoevsky's writing.

It was a book that any writer, even the greatest, is lucky to have once in a lifetime—that is, one where everything went right from the start. He seems to have been confident of that—unlike his usual state—when he gave up *The Diary of a Writer* and, early in 1878, began the novel. For some time previously, he had thought of a first-rate plot. Again, any writer, even the greatest, is lucky to have one first-rate plot in a lifetime. Hundreds of writers can invent good mechanical plots, but one that is organically mated to the theme—that is a grace. Such a plot is, of course, different in kind from ordinary narrative, of which Dostoevsky had always been a master. Narrative is essential for any novel that is not a plaything, but a natural, or nonartificial, plot hasn't occurred often in major novels, and the occasions can be counted on the fingers of two hands.

Dostoevsky's plot is that of a good detective story, and worked out with consummate skill. Who had killed Father Karamazov? To deal with this story he had all the technical resources that he needed. And now, and perhaps for the first time, he had all the technical resources for the profound explorations that are the marvels of the novel. It is possible that he was helped by the neat construction of the story—that is, the requirements of the plot. It may have been a case where the form, or the novel's architectonics, gave him the proper chances, no less, no more (in other books he had had excessive chances), for the deep things he wanted to say.

In his theme, as distinct from the narrative and plot, he had taken a risk, though it was a smaller risk for him than for most writers. The theme might have been too schematic. It was suggested by Gogol's famous Troika, the wild vehicle that was careening uncontrollably across Russia, taking the Russians only God knew where. In Dostoevsky's development, one of the Troika horses was to represent flesh, one mind, one spirit. The father of the Karamazovs, a debased, cunning, corrupt old man, sometimes lit up by the flashes of insight, humor, and wisdom that Dostoevsky often saw in such characters, had bequeathed his unresting sensuality, the insect life that Dostoevsky had come to know so deeply in himself, to his three sons.

In the eldest son, Dmitri, the sensuality expresses itself in violent physical passion; in Ivan, it is suppressed beneath the skeptical intellect; in the youngest, Alyosha, it is sublimated into religious feeling. Those are the three horses of the Troika. As has just been said, that could easily have been too schematic, and the people could have faded away into stereotypes. With Dostoevsky's vision the reverse happened. He uses all his emotional versatility to show three instinctive young men as divided as he was himself and as fully human and actual as fictional personages can be. Not many young men can have read the book without imagining that he is one or the other. Most intellectuals tend to fancy themselves as Ivan, clever, tentative, not even certain of his unbelief, not yet released in physical love but as drawn to it as the others. At the Moscow Art dramatization of the novel in the early 1960s, young men could be heard crying to each other in the corridors, "We are all the heirs of Ivan Karamazov." Another shout: "Don't forget. We are all the heirs of Alyosha, too."

Ivan is usually thought of as the nearest approach to Dostoevsky's picture of himself. There is something in that. Some of Ivan must be close to Dostoevsky in his youth. Perhaps one has to grow older to realize that Dmitri is an even more marvelous creation. He has some stronger qualities that Ivan has not yet found in himself. Dmitri does bad things, he is more than a bit of a cheat, and yet he wants to be good. He is a dangerous and violent man, but he can love, not only with his body. Dostoevsky was drawing on a lifetime's experience and the experience of his own life. To some, particularly as they become old, Dmitri seems the greatest triumph in the book.

The greatest triumph as a person made completely actual, that is. The greatest triumph as a dramatic scene, and much more than a dramatic scene, is the conversation between Ivan and Alyosha in what is sometimes called a restaurant, though it is really more like a saloon bar, as noisy, tawdry, and unrestful as a modern-style London pub. It is characteristic of Dostoevsky's art that he sets his deepest revelation in such a place, and lingers on it with a kind of affection, so that we can't miss the smells or the hubbub.

Few people who have read that conversation—one-sided, nearly all of it passionate, articulate outbursts from Ivan that elicit tormented replies from Alyosha, clinging desperately to his faith—can forget it. It is one of the most memorable scenes in all literature. To some it seems above and beyond literature, and the impact has been so shattering that they can remember the precise place and time where they first read it. The subject of Ivan's protest against life is the suffering of the innocent. He tells Alyosha of the torturing of children. He is telling him of what, to reduce it to simple terms, is the problem of evil. But that is too simple for Dostoevsky and for this scene. Ivan is describing the existent world. At the end, he says that if this is God's world he contracts out of it; if there is God's heaven, he will not enter. In his self-destructive phrase, he returns his ticket.

Then Ivan goes on to recount his Dream of the Grand Inquisitor. Ivan's intense human indignation has been damped down, but the prophetic and spiritual rhetoric is at its highest. And yet that may not be the final wonder of the whole exchange. Maybe that wonder is that throughout, under the surface of a magnificent but ostensibly impersonal argument, Ivan and Alyosha are themselves, each with nerves tingling with excitement, darkened by the sensuality that provokes evils that they loathe, Ivan trying in this complex, brotherly semilove to beat down Alyosha's belief, Alyosha longing to say, "Help thou my unbelief."

From the first installment, *The Brothers Karamazov* had a reception such as Dostoevsky hadn't known since *Poor Folk* thirty-five years before. The reading public lapped it up, and increasingly so from issue to issue. The demand for Katkov's journal climbed each month through 1879 and 1880. Katkov was getting his reward. Dostoevsky's reputation climbed, too. Even his enemies were forced to a reluctant admission that this novel showed talent. Many of the young, including the progressive young, saw that it was wonderful. Some liberals forgave him for his reactionary statements. As for reactionaries, he was their hero who had written a great book. Pobednostsev regarded him with stern approval—and, with a pleasing touch of human weakness, decided that he himself was a part original of Father Zossima, which was totally untrue. The Tsar asked Dostoevsky to talk to some of his younger sons, as he would be the best possible influence. The Tsarevich, the future Alexander III, wasn't especially bright but read the book conscientiously and wrote to ask earnest questions about it.

Dostoevsky appeared to be in better health than usual. After his last visit to Ems his breathing had given him less trouble, though he was working frenziedly, getting off installment after installment to Katkov, working as in the past through the small hours, planning a new issue of *The Diary of a Writer* as soon as *The Brothers Karamazov* was finished. It is possible that he was thinking of a sequel. For many years past, he had been brooding over a novel to be

called "The Story of a Great Sinner." That might have
been realized by sending Alyosha into the world, as he had
hinted. It could have been written, though a fair number
of Dostoevsky's projects didn't crystallize. If he had done
it, it wouldn't have damaged the wonder of *The Brothers
Karamazov,* since the novel form is elastic enough to survive anything.

In the summer of 1880 there was a distraction. The
most reputable literary societies in Moscow had decided to
put up a monument to Pushkin. Partly as an attempt to
reconcile the literary factions, they invited both conservatives and liberals, in great numbers, as much of literary Russia as they could collect, Dostoevsky as the genius
of one side, Turgenev of the other. Tolstoy wouldn't attend,
dismissing the function with contempt. He may have had
a more private reason, since he would have been obliged to
make a speech in public, at which he was inept.

Dostoevsky and Turgenev did attend. Each gave readings from Pushkin, vehemently applauded by their respec-
tive supporters. There were days of talk, excitement,
literary argument, political argument. This had become a
highly charged national occasion.

On the third morning Dostoevsky had to give the
celebratory address. No speech, certainly no speech by a
writer on a literary occasion, has ever made such an effect.
Dostoevsky was not a practiced speaker as was Dickens,
who could compete with any orator in England. Dostoevsky's voice was low and strained, perhaps something like
an intense whisper. How it carried to a large audience is
one of the mysteries of that morning of the Pushkin
speech. But the Pushkin speech became part of Russian

cultural history. Dostoevsky's reputation, and his past suffering, may have helped hypnotize the audience. More so,
from the accounts on the spot, did his sheer intensity, the
depths of his being.

To read, as with most speeches, the Pushkin speech
isn't especially exciting. He had said most of it before.
Pushkin had the special Russian quality, Dostoevsky said,
of speaking to all men, feeling for and with all men. He
was the spokesman for the brotherhood of all mankind.
He was that spokesman because he was Russian. It was
Russia's mission to lead the world into a future where men
would live in one great community of love.

Ecstatic applause. In the audience, they wept, shouted,
hugged each other, called out for Dostoevsky, Pushkin,
Russia, the brotherhood of man. Crowds mounted the platform, and men and women took Dostoevsky into their
arms. Turgenev, overcome, in tears, kissed him and said
that he was more than a genius. The next speaker on the
program shouted that they had been present at a historic
event, now there was going to be goodwill everywhere, and
he could say no more. The audience shouted again, people
fainted. Many cried, "You are our prophet."

It wasn't in the nature of Dostoevsky's fortunes, or in
the temper of late-nineteenth-century Russia, for that fantastic acclaim to stay for long, unanimous and undisturbed.
Turgenev, who had a habit of changing his mind, decided
that he had been bemused by Dostoevsky's passion and that
he hated this inordinate Russian chauvinism. Other liberals,
and progressive papers, were as usual baffled. Some of Dostoevsky's faiths were compared and reexamined. They liked
his populism, his trust in the Russian masses—and yet he

wasn't a democrat, he didn't believe in parliamentary government (in which they were right, since there were few things in which he believed less).

Dostoevsky was hurt. He had been through much, and now had finally emerged to supreme recognition. It was bitter to be carped at. However, in spite of critics and his own nerves, he knew once for all that among Russian writers he could stand beside Tolstoy as a public figure. He may have known that, while Tolstoy attracted active disciples as he didn't, his own voice had reached farther into Russia and brought him more personal love.

That was a happiness. So, and perhaps a more radiant one, was the enthusiasm for *The Brothers Karamazov* as it reached its end. None of a writer's qualms, of which he had more than most, could make him doubt that. It was a climactic success.

At home with Anna there was undiminishing love. The Christmas of 1880 brought him all the causes for happiness he had wished for, and hadn't known. All the causes together in one great benefaction. The year 1881 began, and he entered his sixtieth year, with not many men having so many reasons for gratitude happening so late. In the last week of that January he had a lung hemorrhage. Others followed, and he died, peacefully, on February 9. It is estimated that twenty thousand people joined the funeral procession. Nothing like that had happened for a writer anywhere, though four years later as large a crowd in Paris followed Victor Hugo's coffin to the grave.

Fate, though, hadn't finished with Dostoevsky's memory. Scandalous rumors about his life were whispered in private. His books and his fame spread all over his own country and the reading world. As the Soviet Union moved into the hard climate of the 1930s, the books were disapproved of. Gorky thought, as he had thought for years, that Dostoevsky was an evil genius. Stalin thought that he was one of the most marvelous writers in the Russian language but a dangerous influence. Not many of the books were printed for a couple of decades.

Then the climate softened. Very large editions were printed. Works of rigorous scholarship appeared, collections of letters, textual emendations, biographies, scholarly industry like those with which we are familiar in the West. The public appetite for Dostoevsky was much hungrier than in his lifetime.

TOLSTOY

S OMEONE once said of *War and Peace* and *Anna Karenina,* Tolstoy's two great novels, that it was as though God Himself had taken up his pen and written. Proust made a similar remark, to the effect that in those books humanity was being judged by a serene god. Even in the backing and shifting of literary opinion there is no room for doubt about the supreme greatness of the Tolstoyan masterpieces; and there is not much room for doubt, either, about what makes the greatness.

It is permissible to argue, and many of us have done it, whether *War and Peace* or *The Brothers Karamazov* is the ultimate height of all novel writing. Crossing their hearts, some have to say that, though *War and Peace* may be more godlike, *The Brothers Karamazov* means more to them. Neither Tolstoy nor Dostoevsky would have considered any comparison reasonable. Dostoevsky, though he once tried to make amends in print, couldn't understand why all this fuss was made of Tolstoy. Tolstoy, as will be mentioned later, had even less use for the one contemporary of his own stature. He produced an adjective for Dostoevsky's work that few others would have thought of. It was *superficial*.

Anyway, there is no question about Tolstoy as a writer, and won't be while men are able to read. There is considerably more question about Tolstoy as a man. We can all accept Proust's statement that he wrote like a serene god. But he didn't act like one. Sometimes like a god maybe; but about as little serene as a god, or even a man, can be.

In his own time, people who knew him well gave opinions that do not seem to apply to the same person. Here are two examples. Both Chekhov and Gorky became close to him when he was getting old. They were still young themselves, but already experienced men of sharp insight and capable of detachment as well as empathy.

When Chekhov first met Tolstoy, the old man was a world pundit, and that aspect of him, and his entire message, Chekhov found repellent. He wrote: "Every great man is as despotic as a general and as devoid of consideration, because he knows that he is safe. Diogenes spat in people's faces knowing that no one could touch him; and Tolstoy says that all doctors are scoundrels and shows no respect for major issues because he too, like Diogenes, cannot be handed into a police station or attacked in the newspapers." Yet, almost simultaneously, Chekhov was also saying: "Talking with Leo Nikolaevich, one feels utterly in his power. I have never met a more compelling personality, or one more harmoniously developed, so to say. He is almost a perfect man."

Gorky, who saw more of Tolstoy than Chekhov did, was much tougher. He wrote to Chekhov (1900): "Leo

Tolstoy does not love men; no, he does not love them. The truth is that he judges them, cruelly and too severely. I do not like his idea of God. . . ." Gorky remained fascinated and baffled. In another letter, some years later: "Count Leo Tolstoy is an artist of genius, perhaps our Shakespeare. But, although I admire him, I do not like him. He is not a sincere person; he is exaggeratedly self-preoccupied; he sees nothing and knows nothing outside himself. His humility is hypocritical and his desire to suffer repugnant. Usually such a desire is a symptom of a sick and perverted mind but in his case it is a great pride wanting to be imprisoned in order to increase his authority. . . . No, that man is a stranger to me, in spite of his very great beauty."

Perhaps we might call in evidence Tolstoy himself. At the age of twenty-five he was writing: "I must get used to the idea, once and for all, that I am an exceptional being and a person ahead of his time, or else I have an impossible, unsociable nature, easily dissatisfied. . . . I have not met one man morally as good as I am, or ready to sacrifice everything for his ideas as I am. That is why I can find no company in which I am at ease."

None of that prevented him, in the diary he kept with intense self-concern, reporting all his sins in agonies of atonement. The record of fornication goes on, the gambling sessions (at which he seems almost invariably to have lost), the drunken nights, the ill treatment of his army servants (crude, physical ill treatment, for Tolstoy remained for a long time a Russian *boyar* to whom serfs were made to be flogged).

Owing to Tolstoy's own diaries, the complementary diaries of his wife, the hypnotized attentions of contemporaries, there are effectively no factual uncertainties about Tolstoy's life. Very few lives, maybe none, are better documented day by day. The difficulties rest entirely in how to interpret a personality at the same time so overwhelming and so inconsistent. Inconsistent, just to make the distinction, rather than multifariously complex in the sense that Dostoevsky was. Tolstoy's personality mystified the most acute psychological observers in Russia, including at times himself. His nature had its own complexity that was different in kind from Dostoevsky's. However intricate Dostoevsky's was, it was woven together at the root; whereas Tolstoy gave others the impression, and still does, of a whole collection of independent natures, with nothing to rule them except an ego of unsurpassable and unyielding power. Sometimes he must have seemed as much a natural phenomenon as the weather. The texture of his life is there for us all to see. How one responds to it is a matter of one's own moral feeling, and sometimes even more one's psychological taste.

Tolstoy's childhood was exceptionally happy and, as we should now say, exceptionally privileged. His father bore a famous Russian name and, though penniless, had recouped his fortunes by marrying an heiress of even more illustrious origins. She had inherited a largish estate, thousands of acres, several villages, multitudes of serfs, in the Government of Tula, and lived in the family manor house at Yasnaya Polyana. This was in the deep countryside, 130 miles southeast of Moscow.

It is difficult to compare the real wealth of Tolstoy's parents with that of an English landowner of the same date. The Tolstoys would usually have much less ready money, but, if pressed, they could always sell off serfs. Tolstoy himself did just that when he came into his share of the inheritance and had, as usual, got into debt gambling. The Tolstoys' own wide expanse of territory stretched all around them. They had a liberating sense of space and the Russian land. On the other hand, the soil was badly cultivated and even the home estate at Yasnaya Polyana would have looked wild, untidy, and intolerably primitive to the eye of the owner of Petworth or Burleigh. Yet the Tolstoys were high aristocrats, old-fashioned *boyars,* and could behave in a way unthinkable to an English grandee. It was within their power—they didn't do it themselves, but neighbors did—to send off a serf for twenty-five years in the army as a punishment for eating meat in Lent. The standard of sheer personal caprice in such Russian lords took one back to the West of hundreds of years before. So did the standard of material comfort.

The manor house was built of wood, white-painted, handsome in a semiclassical fashion. It consisted of detached parts, like a child's building set. Hence the house that one sees today isn't much like the house of Tolstoy's childhood. In his twenties, debtors more than ordinarily demanding, he sold the middle block to a neighbor, who transported it to his own estate miles away. That left the two side pavilions, but further building blocks in times of prosperity were later added.

There was, of course, no running water. Nearly all the furniture had been knocked together crudely by serf labor. There was very little of it. Furniture was still scarce in nineteenth-century Russia and, moving from one ramshackle house to another, Russian aristocrats tended to take their household fittings with them. At Yasnaya Polyana, there were never enough beds. One night, when the four sons, of whom Leo (Lyov) Tolstoy was the youngest, all happened to be gathered together, there were only three available beds. So, in fraternal equality, they decided they should all sleep on the floor.

In Tolstoy's childhood, the house serfs had to make do at night with any odd corner or cupboard where they could doss down. Many of them—there were a lot—would be dirty, and some drunk. There would be lice around, and cockroaches. The food at the collective dining table, though served by footmen in white gloves, was plentiful but coarse, dished up by a serf cook who swilled away at the *kvass*. Right up to the time, much later, when Tolstoy was one of the most celebrated men on earth, he never knew at Yasnaya Polyana anything like the domestic comfort of middle-class English houses such as, for example, Dickens's at Gadshill or Trollope's at Waltham Cross.

Nevertheless, what you don't know you don't miss, and if he had known he wouldn't have cared. It was a wonderful house for a child to grow up in. His mother died when he was two, but he was surrounded by love. Father, brothers, his beloved Aunt Toinette, house full of people, teeming affection, Russian togetherness, including the introduction of the illegitimate daughter of a rackety bachelor friend of Tolstoy's father. With cheerful good nature she was taken in charge. Lessons in the morning, from a nice old German tutor. His relatives as often as not spoke to the child in French, in which he was as much at ease as in Russian. In the afternoons, an idyllic pagan existence for a young child, the delights of nature in the wild country, the smell of the trees and the river, the games in the winter snow.

We know all about this. In the series *Childhood, Boyhood, Youth,* it is set down with the truth that was his first demand for his own art or, as far as that goes, anyone else's. He didn't believe in invention. In his personal and intense vision, he didn't believe in imagination. That is, imagination as ordinarily conceived. What was *there* was more marvelous than anything one's feeble mind could construct, though one's mind could be given a chance to interpret or analyze the marvel. That was his artistic freedom. It gave him the certainty of his God's-eye surveillance.

Thus we know about his childhood not only from what is in effect the autobiographical trilogy but also from *War and Peace.* For the military history, and the social data of a period the generation before his own, he used, like any sane writer setting out upon an epic, every source he could absorb. His chief source was his own family. There, true to his credo, he invented very little, sometimes comically little. He wasn't, either as a man or as a writer, greatly given to humor, except of a rough earthy kind. But he may have permitted himself a satisfied smile as he changed the name of his mother. She was actually the Princess Marya Volkonskya. With a daring stroke of invention, her son transmuted this name into Bolkonskya, which is how we read it in *War and Peace.*

With comparable ingenuity, Dorokhov, one of Tolstoy's wilder acquaintances, was transmuted into Dolokhov. The Rostov family are the Tolstoys. Tolstoy's father Nikolai appears in the novel as Nikolai Rostov, as faithfully as

Tolstoy could manage, which is as faithfully as any writer could manage. There may have been a faint softening. The marriage of Tolstoy's father and mother was more prosaically arranged, and on the Tolstoy side more nakedly a mercenary bargain, than in the novel. In life, though, as in art, the marriage worked well enough.

Tolstoy loved his father, who became an amiable hard-drinking country gentleman. He died when Tolstoy was nine, one of the few shadows in that happy childhood. Tolstoy's own account of how he reacted to the death reminds one sharply of David Copperfield when his mother died. The boy Tolstoy was full of grief, but at the Requiem Mass thought he cut an interesting figure in his mourning clothes and that everyone felt increased interest in him because he was an orphan.

Before he wrote *Childhood,* Tolstoy—at that stage full of literary ambitions—in his notebook jotted down that *David Copperfield* had an "immense influence." Of course, both men were being absolutely truthful about a child's response to death (though Dickens's was an imagined truth). There are a good many resemblances between Dickens and Tolstoy, as will be mentioned later. Their self-absorption and their egos tower above most of humankind. Tolstoy admired Dickens, whom he considered melancholy and more humorous than he (Tolstoy) was—which is itself more humorous a remark than Tolstoy intended.

His childhood went on a characteristic course for a son of the Russian gentry, modified by the boy's passionate self-absorption. There were stays in the family house in Moscow. There was a move to a relative in Kazan. There were a few terms at Kazan university. Tolstoy soon decided that he could educate himself better than his instructors would. In fact, though his contemporaries seem not to have thought so, he did acquire, in a positive opinionated manner, a comprehensive education. He read English and German in addition to his French. He got interested in philosophy, history, law. He couldn't cope with mathematics, but that seems to have been an occupational weakness of the major novelists, except for Stendhal.

When he was nineteen, the Tolstoy brothers split up the family patrimony. There was no primogeniture in Tsarist Russia, and hence the fortunes weren't preserved intact as with English landowners. Titles were also dissipated, since they passed, with commendable egalitarianism, to all the children. Hence the profusion of princes and counts in Russian literature, including some as derelict as Prince Myshkin. The four Tolstoy brothers were all counts as soon as they were born. Amicably they divided the estate, Tolstoy getting Yasnaya Polyana itself (just because he wanted it), 4,000 acres, and 330 serfs.

Years later, the Volkonsky lands came together again because two of the brothers died unmarried. They were an odd bunch, unconstrained, broad-natured in the Russian sense, and purposeless. The eldest, Nikolai, went into the army and was a good officer until he took to drink on a heroic scale. Tolstoy admired him, except that he didn't wash his hands—Tolstoy was fastidiously clean himself until in old age he took to imitating his peasants. Nikolai and Dmitri both died young, probably from tuberculosis. Dmitri tried to live a Christian life, which he spent with a prostitute, the only woman he had ever possessed. The second brother, Sergei, elegant and superior, whom as a boy Tolstoy envied and hero-worshiped, took up with a gypsy, who was presumably a superior prostitute, and after many years married her. As he grew older, he developed into an autocratic, conservative, old-style Russian nobleman.

At nineteen, then, Tolstoy was installed at Yasnaya Polyana, rich enough to make forays to Moscow and lead the life of his peers. Actually at Kazan he had already begun living the life of his peers—gambling, that eighteenth- and nineteenth-century aristocratic addiction; drinking; having women. The last occupied more part in Tolstoy's existence than even in that of most men, and it was a determining, dark, and, in the end, disastrous part. He had immense appetite for the natural world, and more immense still for women. His sexual passions were imperative. But he doesn't seem to have had much affection for women. That may be a strange or foolish thing to say about one who has produced some of the most delectable pictures of women in all literature. It has to be said with all kinds of qualification. Yet, with reserves, it contains a truth.

He suffered from an extreme form of sexual guilt. After each copulation—and there were very many—he went through agonies of self-reproach. In old age, he told Chekhov and Gorky that he was insatiable, in actual speech using the most brutal peasant words, thereby shocking Chekhov, who was a shade prudish, and also Gorky, who wasn't. *The Kreutzer Sonata* is the fiercest expression of sexual guilt that most of us have ever read. Women were the temptation and the enemy, exactly as they were to Christian saints like St. Anthony. In this respect, Tolstoy makes a black-and-white contrast to Dostoevsky. As we have seen, Dostoevsky was capable of being guilty about many things, but not about sex and women, whom in the person of his wife he worshiped.

In Tolstoy's temperate and less remorseful moments, he behaved, spoke, and laid down the law in the spirit of what would now be called a male chauvinist. Women were made for bed, in lawful marriage, for breeding children, since copulation, even in marriage, was utterly unjustifiable without the object of reproduction; for suckling children, for no woman ought to let her child be fed by another (when at last he married, he inflicted great hardship on his wife by this particular article of faith); for the kitchen, or rather in a lordly household such as his own, for seeing that the serfs produced the food. The final appearance of Natasha in *War and Peace* is the concrete expression of all he believed a woman should be.

With his unassuageable ardor, he had passions in childhood, innocent and intense, for girls and boys. His first sexual experience came at sixteen or so in a brothel at Kazan which the students were fond of. That filled him with a special remorseful horror, and put him off for a while. But not for long. Very soon, the lord of Yasnaya Polyana took women in the fashion of other rich young men he mixed with. Prostitutes, gypsies, most of all serfs from his own estate. Until he married, at the age of thirty-four, unusually late for a man in his position, he did not, so far as is known, have any relations with a woman of his own class. Those he had he either bought or took.

This may have some significance. Before his marriage, though he regarded smart society in Moscow and Petersburg with contempt, he moved in it quite a lot. He had the beginnings of literary fame. He was well born. He had the power of extravagant virility. The eyes of a good many women must have lighted on him. As a boy, and much later, he was often grumbling to himself about his ugliness. He wished he had an aquiline nose like that of his stylish brother Sergei, not his own squashed one. He wished he had big lustrous eyes, not deep-set eyes that looked like a detective's. But that can't have inhibited him. He had the essential attractions. He was shortish by our standards as Dostoevsky was, but not diminutive. He was stocky and exceptionally muscular. In middle age he could outwrestle the toughest of Asian tribesmen in the Samara hinterland, and outlast his own peasants in the fields. He could do a strong man's feat, lying on his back and holding a full-grown male at arm's length. To us, his only physical drawback would be that, like Balzac, he lost most of his teeth very early; but nineteenth-century women must have been accustomed to dental inadequacies. A man of his ardor could have had as many women as he cared to ask for.

Yet he didn't ask for them. He just took serf girls behind the bushes on his own land. It was all violent, short, and succeeded by remorse, by good resolutions, and by a new set of the Rules for Life he kept drawing up and didn't keep. Sex was an imperative need for him, not a supreme pleasure as to Balzac. He would have thought it sinful and the Devil's work to devote Balzac's cheerful attention to the erotic life. Which is why a really experienced woman, like Balzac's Fanny, would have chosen Balzac any time, even though Tolstoy probably surpassed him, or most other men, in sheer physical virile force.

Tolstoy had one semipermanent serf mistress in the midst of the other pickups on the estate. She was called Aksinya, and he had a son by her. The history of this son, or rather his nonhistory, is more difficult for a late-twentieth-century person to accept than other parts of the Tolstoy story. This son looked more like Tolstoy than any of the legitimate children. Tolstoy took no notice of him whatsoever. He did nothing for the boy. The boy received no education. He became a coachman on the estate. At the age of eighty Tolstoy sometimes wondered whether he ought to apologize to him. He called Tolstoy "master," and they didn't exchange an intimate word.

In his early twenties, Tolstoy, who as a boy had made firm statements about his literary intentions, couldn't find any purpose for his life. He went on making Rules of Life, which always included renouncing cards, drink, and women. Sometimes he made a rule that he must obtain a good (that is, an official) position. He had little sense of a vocation. In fact, all through his life, his sense of literary vocation was more intermittent than that of hundreds of minor writers. It was only at intervals that he absorbed himself in art as a worthy activity for a serious man—or more exactly for Leo Tolstoy. In later years he told the world that he thought nothing of art and repudiated it. It wasn't an accident that he found his destiny as a prophet.

It contributed to his aimlessness as a young man, and maybe later, that he didn't have to earn a living. There are professional disadvantages in being a man of means. Simplicities and imperatives are removed. The range of choices becomes so wide that choice becomes impossible, as it was to the young Tolstoy, drifting around Petersburg.

His means were not inexhaustible, we should remember. He was not rich by the side of those he gambled with. He was nothing like as rich as Turgenev, who owned five thousand serfs by comparison with Tolstoy's three hundred. Further, Tolstoy soon dissipated part of his fortune. He wasn't any more successful at the tables than Dostoevsky. Probably his social elevation, which was much more impressive than his wealth, saved him from some consequences of debt, but there were reckonings. He could think of only one way out, which was selling a village or two and a package of serfs. Clearly that couldn't go on indefinitely. By the age of twenty-two he had run through perhaps a quarter of his inheritance. In *The Cossacks* he makes his autobiographical hero run through half his money, but then he was exaggerating. Nevertheless, like Olenin, that autobiographical hero, Tolstoy decided that it was time to skip. He wanted to join the army, alongside his brother Nikolai. It would be a chance to soldier in the Caucasus, which then as now had a romantic appeal for young Russians. That duly happened, and Tolstoy served in the artillery, competently and bravely.

For some time, though he did the work of a junior officer, he was technically a civilian. The complexities of Russian bureaucracy have always been considerable. An aristocrat such as Tolstoy had almost unimaginable privileges, but those privileges didn't extend to evading the bureaucratic grip. Tolstoy's papers were not in order. He had not obtained his discharge from a nominal official appointment that he had never taken up. That was an insuperable difficulty, until a formal discharge arrived from the governor of Kazan (a job that his own grandfather,

the Count Rostov of *War and Peace,* had once occupied).
So Tolstoy couldn't be entered in the army books.

This brought about a penalty that vexed him. He was
a good officer. He was too opinionated, and too lofty, to be
popular with superiors, but he earned professional praise.
The Russians were fighting warlike Muslim tribes, and
this was real war, as risky as patrolling the Indian North-
West Frontier. Tolstoy saw plenty of action, and was
singled out for his courage. He was recommended twice
for the St. George's Cross (comparable with the British
Military Cross or the French Médaille Militaire). He
couldn't receive it, since his papers hadn't arrived and he
wasn't in the army books. Tolstoy would have liked a
military decoration.

In the Cossack settlement Tolstoy lived as he described,
without transmutation, when he wrote the story. For a
time this was another idyllic life, like his early childhood.
He had an attachment for a wild Cossack girl, and slept
with others. By Russian standards, or any other, the Cossack girls were free souls, and free bodies, until they married. It was a frontier society, an untouched preindustrial
leftover, not very different from the Cossack society of
The Quiet Don (known in English translation as *And
Quiet Flows the Don*), placed in the following century.

Tolstoy got tired of it. As usual, he had a relentless
eye for the lie in life, the lie of life—that is, things not
being what they seem, the surface cheating one about the
content, the old conflict between appearance and reality.
Almost for want of anything else to do, he settled down
to write *Childhood*. He knew at once that he could do it.
Truth, no compromise with truth. If it was necessary to

repeat a word in order not to sacrifice the truth, then he repeated it; if a sentence had to lumber on, then it lumbered on. Of course he cared about words. He cared about them so much that he knew when they stood in the way of truth.

He sent *Childhood* to *The Contemporary* (*Sovremennik*), one of the "thick" monthly journals of mid-nineteenth-century Russia. He was twenty-four.

The Contemporary had much prestige. It was edited —it had already been significant in Dostoevsky's career, a few years earlier—by the fine poet Nekrasov, who had the human and literary judgment of another fine poet, Tvardovsky, in our own time. Tolstoy's manuscript had to be carried by mid-nineteenth-century transport from the Caucasus to Petersburg. Within what still seems an astonishingly short time (six weeks), Nekrasov's reply found its way back. He would publish the book. He was certain that the author had distinguished talent, and hoped that he would devote himself to literature.

Tolstoy, for once, behaved like any other young writer. He was full of simple, naïve delight. With the instinct of a true artist, he inquired when he was going to be paid. Nekrasov and his friends knew, though not because of that inquiry, that they had found a writer of the highest originality.

Nineteenth-century literary Russia was eager to recognize new talent and good at doing so. For national reasons, for literary reasons that transcended the nation, they were hoping passionately that the creative explosion of Pushkin and Gogol should produce its successors. They were looking for great writers, and they cheered them on.

It is true that the great writers themselves, when they duly appeared, weren't particularly good at cheering each other on. Worse than their English contemporaries, in historical fact. Tolstoy was generous and wise about the merits of Dickens and Trollope, but couldn't see many in Dostoevsky. Dostoevsky returned the negative compliment. Both thought that Turgenev was an elegant trifler. Tolstoy greeted Chekhov with cheerful abuse, to the effect that Chekhov knew that he (Tolstoy) had an extremely low opinion of Shakespeare, but even Shakespeare could write plays much superior to those of Chekhov, who ought to discontinue writing them immediately.

Persons less world famous and less given to the envy of the great were considerably more sensible. It has been mentioned how Belinsky saw the gifts of Dostoevsky at a first reading of a first book. Nekrasov did the same with Dostoevsky, and then with Tolstoy. Neither Tolstoy nor Dostoevsky had the fantastic public acclaim of the young Dickens in England, but serious opinion in Russia, as soon as *Childhood* was published, was ready for a new master. The opinion was more than confirmed by *Boyhood, Youth,* and Tolstoy's descriptions of the fighting in Sevastopol. Very early, people perceived his great, and in some ways unique, gift—no one before this had been able to tell so much of the unsparing truth.

As an artillery officer in Sevastopol, Tolstoy saw at first hand what war was really like and set it down. It was like this and not like anyone else's adornments. Tolstoy was, as in the Caucasus, an efficient and courageous soldier, concerned for his troops. He also had a strain of aristocratic, or egotistic, irresponsibility. It occurred to him that he was wasting his talents in the battery, and might as well depart to some headquarters job and write more books. The army administration didn't agree with him.

That experience of real war became useful when he wrote his great novel in the following decade—though he himself, always willing to acknowledge literary debts to foreign writers, said that he could never have written truthfully about Austerlitz and Borodino if Stendhal hadn't shown how to do it, in the scene of Fabrice's arrival on the field at Waterloo.

In the mid fifties Tolstoy, his reputation already made in literary *salons*, came to Petersburg, still in uniform, and stayed with Turgenev. Turgenev treated him with the utmost handsomeness, being civilized beyond the limits of civilization. Tolstoy, who wasn't so civilized, didn't behave with such handsomeness. Turgenev didn't really like the young man leaving the apartment night after night to pick up whores, or drink, or gamble, or all those activities combined. Tolstoy, though by birth the more genuinely aristocratic of the two, seems to have been obstinately gauche on social occasions, while Turgenev had beautiful, though somewhat oversilky, manners. Turgenev called his guest "the Troglodyte." They quarreled, made it up, went on quarreling, and did so for the rest of Turgenev's life.

If Tolstoy had been dedicated to literature, or had admitted his vocation, the way was clear. Dostoevsky was still serving as a private in the Siberian infantry. Tolstoy was the most eminent young prose writer on the scene. All he had to do was write.

He did no such thing. He went back to Yasnaya Polyana, set up a school for the *muzhiks'* children, and taught them himself—on strictly Rousseauish principles, people being naturally good and corrupted only by circumstances. He traveled abroad, and like most Slavophile Russians (among whom he and Dostoevsky, unlike Turgenev, fundamentally belonged) was sickened by most of what he saw. London in particular filled him with a loathing for modern civilization. Teaching the peasant children inspired him with a contempt for art—which later, as he became a prophet, became part of his message, though he suppressed it when writing the great novels.

When the Tsar's decree for the emancipation of the serfs was issued (in 1861), Tolstoy explained it, carefully and patiently, to his own serfs, and offered them the most generous terms of peasant tenure that the new laws allowed. The peasants viewed him with suspicion. There was a catch in it somewhere. Tolstoy invented nothing, and observed everything. He could believe that the peasants, lately serfs, were the source of all goodness in Russia and the world. At the same time, with his gift for not sparing himself the lie in life, he understood what they were thinking and what they were truly like. Read the scene where Levin tries to emancipate his serfs in *Anna Karenina*. Tolstoy didn't invent, but all that happened to him was watched.

It was at that time that he decided that he ought to get married. He had thought that before, but, side by side with his intense will, his emotions were not steady. Now they had crystallized—after they had flowed among three sisters, twenty, eighteen, and sixteen, when Tolstoy was thirty-four, all pretty, cultivated, and clever. They belonged to the family of a senior Kremlin doctor called

Behrs. A long time before, there had been a German an-
cestor, hence the name; but they were by now as tradition-
ally Russian as the Tolstoys, Dr. Behrs himself considerably
more so. They were nothing like as socially grand. So far
as there was an upper middle class in Russia, they belonged
to it. Certainly they were not aristocrats. Tolstoy, with
Tolstoy, Volkonsky, and other *boyar* ancestors going back
for generations, would be something of a catch. The girls
called him "the Count" and whispered among themselves
that the Count was coming.

The Behrs were quite well off. Their apartment in
Moscow was cramped, as were all official quarters in the
Kremlin, but they had a comfortable country estate of
their own. The girls were not mercenary or calculating.
They were romantic and idealistic. Tolstoy had glamor, a
brave soldier whom as children they had seen off to the
war, most of all a celebrated writer. The eldest sister fell
helplessly in love with him. That was embarrassing, since
he had fallen in love with the middle sister, Sonya (known
interchangeably as Sofya). Tolstoy brooded that he was
aging, toothless, and nevertheless in love. He accused himself, as he had done in his youth, of having an "ugly mug."

As he must have known, none of that counted. He
overwhelmed Sonya and they became engaged. Sonya's
mother approved. It was a splendid match. Dr. Behrs did
not approve. Carrying all conservative convention to the
limit, he thought that it was intolerable behavior of Tolstoy not to marry the eldest daughter, who was pining for
him and, more essential, was after all the eldest and had
first choice. There were tumultuous Russian scenes. The
entire family, including the eldest daughter gallantly heart-

broken, had to prevail on their father. Realism finally won. At last, not warmly, Dr. Behrs gave Tolstoy and Sonya his blessing.

There was another scene, more private and casting a shadow on the future, before the wedding. Both Tolstoy and Sonya were suspicious of the other's motives. He was jealous of her previous attachment to a young officer. She was jealous of everything about him. They each had an obsession for analyzing their own behavior. They each believed in absolute sincerity.

Tolstoy was getting on toward middle age and had observed most aspects of human feeling. He knew that Sonya was a totally inexperienced girl—intelligent, yes; strong-minded, yes; but knowing no more of men's sexual lives than a Trollope heroine of the same period, Lucy Robarts or Lily Dale, and without their intuition and common sense. He knew all that; and his method of coping with the situation, and of showing his sincerity, was to give her his diaries to read. It is difficult to find a word for this remarkable action. Innocent? Pure-souled? High-minded? Self-absorbed to the point of cruelty? To more corrupt and worldly men, this might appear a time when the pure-souled do more damage than anyone else. The said corrupt and worldly men might say that, if this is sincerity, give us a bit of dissimulation.

Remember that Tolstoy's diaries were a long record of drunken roistering, which she could take easily enough; losses at cards, ditto, though she might have vowed to keep his finances in order; and copulation with tarts and, much more often, his own serf girls. He used the brutish words and described his pleasures with gloating. Then there were repentance afterward, good resolutions, Rules of Life. Back again to the relish of the flesh.

She read the diaries a few days before the wedding. She said that she forgave him. He seems to have thought that she was quite happy. When they were married, as soon as they were alone, he had her. That is the shortest description. He was totally unused to wooing innocent virgins. She was horrified.

A year after their marriage, she was still horrified and writing in her own diary that the physical side of love played a dominating part for him, none at all for her. She had tried to conceal her revulsion, though they had made a pact that their diaries could at any time be read by the other—another pure-souled idea. He was a man of enormous and violent sexuality. He may not have wanted his wife to share his passion.

That was the beginning of one of the most famous and most written-about marriages in literary history. It is not uninstructive to compare it with Dickens's. There are considerable resemblances between the two men, Dickens's personality in action scaled down to something nearer to ordinary human proportions, and lacking most of Tolstoy's leaderlike and prophetic aspirations. Both had egos of adamant impregnability. Both lacked, to an extent astonishing in great writers, passive sensibility. Both had a simple and absolute belief in God, and in no other religious formulation whatever. Among all the strains and stresses of Tolstoy's messianic religious preaching, in which he addressed the world, *urbi et orbi,* for the last thirty years of his life, immersed in conflict, adulated, denounced, excommunicated by the Orthodox Church, it is as well to remember that his actual religious faith was no more spectacular than that of an English Unitarian. That was exactly Dickens's position. They read the gospels with straightforward faith. There was nothing mystical about their faith or them. They believed that Jesus was the Son of Man.

Unhappy marriages, Tolstoy wrote later, were all unhappy in different ways. Perhaps that applied to the marriages of him and Dickens, though there was common ground. Most men would have liked to be spared them, and even more, as we tend to forget, thinking of the calamities of genius; so would most women. As has been mentioned, Dickens was bored with his marriage very early and with increasing desperation had dreams of a heaven elsewhere. Tolstoy wasn't bored. Sonya was a far more intelligent and spirited woman than Dickens's Kate, and took her own part on something like equal terms. But it would have taken an ego as powerful as Tolstoy's own to give her a chance of winning through to a tolerable life.

We know about their marriage in as much detail, including physical detail, as any on record. We don't need to work out for ourselves that Tolstoy was a man of superlative sexual virility. He was also abnormally lacking in sexual consideration. He just urgently wanted her, and grabbed her. She seems almost never to have enjoyed herself, though she was pleased that he continued to desire her, since that was her one hold on him and it made him more amiable when he was satisfied. She may not have known explicitly until she read *The Kreutzer Sonata* (which as usual she prepared for the printer) how much in his thoughts women were the enemy who tempted men into sin, and how intense was his recoil from the flesh and his corroding guilt.

Dickens didn't have much of that. We don't know a lot directly of his sexual behavior, but it is a fair inference that he, too, was a man of extreme physical urgency. When at last he decided to break with his wife, he signaled the fact by having the door leading from his dressing room to their marital bedroom built up, as though even then he might otherwise be impelled into that bed again. Just as after writing *The Kreutzer Sonata,* Tolstoy—and by now to his wife's fury and indignation—showed himself as demanding as ever.

Kate was a passive soul, putting up with constant childbearing and not uttering complaints when she found herself pregnant again a few weeks after another child was born. Dickens sounds as inconsiderate as Tolstoy, and there are no indications anywhere that Kate enjoyed herself any more than Sonya.

The families were large. Tolstoy's was thirteen (that is, the legitimate children), Dickens's ten. Neither went in for contraception. Tolstoy wouldn't have done so on principle, since the only justification for the brute act was the production of children. Dickens, however, could have had no such inhibitions. He frequently cursed at another increase in his family, but as though it were an unavoidable act of God. Victorians weren't ignorant about contraceptive methods, and some of Dickens's intimates are known to have used them. Why he didn't is one of the minor domestic mysteries.

There is another teasing resemblance between the Dickens and Tolstoy marriages. Right from the first months—Dickens already probably disappointed, Tolstoy for once radiantly happy—both of them developed something more than an affection for their wife's younger sister. In both cases this was more than an affection, less than crystallized love. Here the robustness of Tolstoy's nature, and subsisting under all the strain the directness of his instincts, gave him the advantage, as it did in art when these experiences left their mark. Dickens made a mawkish cult of Mary Hogarth, and idolized her in his half-childish characters such as Little Nell. Tanya Behrs was the original of Natasha Rostova, one of the most truthfully drawn and endearing women characters in all fiction.

The Tolstoys had one period of something like married peace. This was during the years 1863–69 when he was writing *War and Peace*. They both realized early on that he was attempting an epic, in scale and in everything else. Even his inquiries and researches were on a gigantic scale. So Sonya took over the administration of the estate. She was much more decisive and businesslike than he was as she demonstrated later, when, like Dostoevsky's wife, but for a different reason, she managed all the Tolstoy literary affairs.

Nevertheless, looking after Yasnaya Polyana wasn't Sonya's real joy. That was to read his manuscript night after night, interpret it, get it into order. A Tolstoy manuscript looks very like a Balzac proof, black with interlinear corrections, insertions in the margins with connecting lines streaming across the page, all executed in a tiny myopic hand. To read it as he intended needed high-class textual skill, or devoted love, or both. She could do it, and it made her as happy as she ever was. She was well educated and well read, and had acute verbal sensitivity. She also had sharp literary insight, and she wasn't afraid to criticize in detail, where he seems to have listened to her, and in the broadest of scope, where he didn't listen to her at all.

It must have been a blessing to her, and it is good that in that conflict-ridden existence she had it. She realized from the first that night after night she was reading a work of great genius, of a different order of genius from anything he had written before. Probably, like so many of us since, she would have been hard put to it to define the nature of his genius. Yes, the end result was certainly, as Proust said, the work of a serene god. She, more than anyone alive, had the best of reasons for knowing that Leo Tolstoy was as little serene as a man can be. She would have understood the delight, the pantheistic immersion in the natural world. That was part of him. But the beautiful calm observation of all kinds of men and women? Generous, totally free from the writer's ego, reluctant to judge? Was this the nature of the man she was living with?

It is hard to say anything about the book that is not jejune—even harder than about *The Brothers Karamazov*. The latter, as has been suggested, is a work of extraordinary psychological insight and also of extraordinary psychological imagination. Psychological imagination, Tolstoy said with revulsion, is a dangerous toy to play with, and distorts the truth. In his best work (though not always) Dostoevsky managed to keep in contact with experienced life. Nevertheless, both his insight and his imagination are unmatchably different from those of other men.

Tolstoy's weren't. That sounds like a reduction, but isn't intended so. First of all, he dispensed with imagination in the conventional sense, when he looked at human beings, just as he did when he studied the gospels. It got in the way of sacrosanct truth. So, when he did look at human beings, it was with the eyes of one of the rest of us but ten times more acute, penetrating, and unsparing. Dostoevsky revealed human beings, with his complicated vision, from the inside out. Tolstoy revealed them from the outside in. That is, of course, how most people try to understand others. He was able to do it with absolute conviction, so that anyone he studied is embossed on the page. Their introspective broodings, which he sometimes allows himself to represent, are of the same nature as any of ours, and on the same level of self-analysis, conscience, anxiety, and hope (compare Natasha before the Rostovs' ball, or, which isn't quite as easy, Prince Andrei, lying wounded on the field of Austerlitz). These introspective passages, anywhere in *War and Peace,* are wonderfully done, but they are recognizable in terms we know and are identifiable with our own.

In this respect, and in fact in most of his art, Tolstoy was as direct and as near ordinary mortals as a great writer can be. That is one of the reasons why the personages in *War and Peace* seem immediately people we know, and don't need interpretative effort on our part.

Thus it is not a surprise that Tolstoy's preparations for the epic were studious and prosaic. He accumulated all the material that he could get hold of. Family documents, of which there were plenty; accounts of the Napoleonic campaigns; memoirs of early-nineteenth-century Russia. He drew heavily on these sources, and it gives even the *longueurs,* such as the masonic chapters, an extraliterary authority.

His language was directed at the same durable, undeviating end. It isn't elegant. If he wants to give an extra shade of meaning, the sentence wambles on. If he wants to catch an expression exactly, as he very often did, working from the outside in, the adjectives multiplied—"a smile good natured, sour, malicious, sarcastic, welcoming." Above all, once he has struck the right word, and the word has no precise equivalent, he goes on repeating it. Time and time again in his original manuscript, he struck out a near-synonym and returned to the original word. This gives a hammerlike quality to his work, very different from, say, Turgenev's elegant and elegiac cadences. But it also gives an assurance of the truth. After a hundred years, there has not been a novel that gives that assurance with such finality.

On its first appearance, *War and Peace* had what we should now call a mixed press—meaning that there were attempts to dismiss the book both in private (Turgenev did so, though he changed his mind later) and in public. It has been mentioned elsewhere that Russian criticism in the 1860s was, as it has always been, passionately political. *War and Peace* was attacked, with curious unanimity, both from the right and from the left. A spokesman for the left announced with heartfelt relief that *fortunately Tolstoy wasn't a great writer.*

Reactionaries accused him of not writing like a true Russian. In the long and absurd history of literary comment, that one deserves an illustrious place. From the middle ground of opinion, there was much praise.

Tolstoy himself appears to have resolved that, though Pushkin had been much distressed by bad notices, he wasn't going to be. He made strong efforts not to read them. He found greater satisfaction in reading a glowing encomium many times over.

All this commotion soon settled down. Even before *Anna Karenina,* which was published seven years later, Tolstoy's reputation was as stable as a writer's is likely to be. After *Anna Karenina,* when he began to give moral teaching to the world, he was listened to, not only because of the strength and impact of his personality, but also because of the general recognition that he was the most eminent writer alive. Just as, two generations later, Einstein was listened to, not only because of his character and message, but also partly because he was the greatest scientist of the century.

War and Peace had been written in cheerfulness. *Anna Karenina* wasn't, the less so as the book proceeded. The book itself is—it doesn't need saying—a great one. There are a good many who admire it, and certainly enjoy it, more than *War and Peace.* But in the theme itself (it isn't by accident that a writer is drawn to his theme), and in the textual treatment, strains and tensions are already showing through. There isn't much, though there is some, of the pantheistic acceptance of the great epic. "Vengeance is mine . . ." is one of the most minatory of epigraphs. It is a supreme example of the abundant contradictions of his nature, which enabled him as a writer to justify Proust's description, that he came to see Anna with loving charity. This was a long way from his original harsh intention.

After the book was finished, when he was nearly fifty, he came more and more to lose his respect for art. At times he couldn't escape from it. He couldn't resist exercising his gift again. He used his gift with searing power to expose, denounce (and, yes, to get a frisson from) the lusts of the flesh, as in *Father Sergei,* when an anchorite, who is aspiring to be a saint, cuts off a finger to kill temptation. But he succumbs to one of the sex-mad women who had become in the later Tolstoy the ultimate enemy. *The Devil,* another novella, is another demonstration of a woman-enemy, through the demon of sensuality driving a man to suicide. Occasionally he got away from his obsessions and wrote, with an inconsistency that it is agreeable to find that he could still show, some pleasant little comedies, such as *The Fruits of Enlightenment.*

At the age of seventy he published his last novel, *Resurrection.* There was a practical reason for returning to novel writing: he wanted to raise a large sum to help the persecuted Dukhobors. He was by this time too far committed to his own conversion and faith to write with the God's-eye justice of *War and Peace.* At the core, *Resurrection* doesn't succeed. The central figure, Nekhlyadov, is another incarnation of Tolstoy himself, like Levin but far less real. Tolstoy couldn't now probe into the old contradictions that had given the breath of life to his great characters. In this novel the panoramic vision of all the ills and injustices of Russia is as brilliant-eyed and marvelous as ever. But all authority anywhere is bad, and all people exercising even the tiniest authority are debased. All the poor and suffering are good, though their physical condition is drawn, felt, smelled by the incomparable Tolstoy senses.

Through his last thirty years, Tolstoy did not know for long any stretches of moral calm. The absence of moral calm was a state he had now become familiar with. Now he lived within it. With his supernormal physical and moral strength he could manage without calm more vigorously than most men. Dickens also didn't know anything like moral calm for the last third of his life; but Dickens, except when he was temporarily saved by distractions, was thrown into active unhappiness. Tolstoy searched for his own way of finding truth and goodness behind the false appearance of this world. It gave him the force to become a world evangelist, to many the symbol of moral hope and redemption. His voice reached beyond Russia all over the world, to an Indian lawyer in South Africa by the name of Gandhi. To those longing for a secular religion, or a practical ethical rule to live by, Tolstoy became a leader and something like a saint. Toward the end of the nineteenth century, and in the first years of this one, there were many sensitive persons hungry for the touch of such a saint, as though they had a premonition of what our century was going to bring.

Tolstoy attained his position simply by the written word and the repute of his personality. Rather oddly, he was no good at speaking and didn't utter in public. But his propaganda writing was as direct and simple as any writing could be. He had his own artistic contempt for false complication. He had an aristocratic certainty that either the ethical rules of life, the world's rules, must be as straightforward as he saw them, or else they were not worth bothering about. He told them as plainly as he saw them, and they were as plain as his reading of the gospels.

The moral life was as simple as the Sermon on the Mount. A man should have faith in God, and live like Jesus. Turn the other cheek. Never offer violence. Killing was absolute evil. War was absolute evil. Punishment, of any kind, was a crime. One should possess nothing and live like the poor. In the poor, in the Russian *muzhik,* was wisdom and virtue; in all humility, one should live like them. The flesh was sinful. By chastity one could avoid the most sinful of sins.

Tolstoyan communes gathered together, in America, in England, in Western Europe. As in other such movements, a disciple more uncompromising than Tolstoy himself arose to keep followers to the faith. He was a retired officer called Chertkov, and had his own group living like primitive Christians in a house not far from Tolstoy's. Meanwhile other disciples, and even interested spectators, came to watch Tolstoy at Yasnaya Polyana. Photographs had now made him familiar—the rugged prophetic face, the savage eyebrows, untrimmed beard. On his own estate he was dressed in a peasant's smock with a peasant's boots. He was to be seen in his seventies threshing as vigorously, and for as long hours, as any of the peasants.

Those privileged enough to be invited into the house would see him at the family table, withdrawn, not participating in the conversation, surrounded by sons and daughters, his wife presiding, as though he were humbling himself among them all. He ate the most meager vegetarian food while the rest tucked into substantial Russian meals. He had long since renounced alcohol.

To an outsider, it might have seemed a beautiful patriarchal picture, the aging prophet and saint at rest in his own home. In fact, that home was riven and seared by the bitterest of family hatred. Tolstoy felt that he was receiving nothing but coldness and hostility from all his children except intermittently from one daughter. He gave nothing but coldness and hostility back. These were not his family, he wrote in his diary. His real family were his disciples.

He had wanted to give away all he possessed. This meant giving away all that his wife and children possessed. They had come to think that he was an egomaniac. Totally affectless, indifferent to all of them, with no emotion except the desire to demonstrate his own sanctity.

They settled on a business compromise by which the earnings on all books written before 1881—thus including the great successes—remained in the family estate. The royalties, becoming worldwide, from *War and Peace* and *Anna Karenina* were vast and increasing, and many times more than the income from the landed property. So the family lived like richer people than Tolstoy's ancestors. And he was living with them, even if he did dress like a *muzhik* and eat nothing but vegetables and eggs.

He detested the negation of the beliefs that he was preaching. This was absurd for one who aspired to be a martyr. The Church excommunicated him for heresy, but the government wouldn't oblige by making him a martyr. He denounced the Japanese war; he called for total non-violence; he hoped to be taken off to prison, to what he kept referring to longingly as "a good stinking prison." There were one or two police searches at his house, which he confronted with all the outrage of an old Russian *boyar*, but otherwise through all the years of his mission he was left untouched in his own manor.

Sonya had taken over, not only the management of the estate, but also his literary business. She got good professional advice from Anna Dostoevsky, and became just as shrewd and practical an operator. Under Sonya's control the income from Tolstoy's books rose in a steady exponential curve. His pamphlets, which had an enormous sale, were not published by her but by Chertkov in cheap editions, since Chertkov was in charge of all Tolstoyan doctrine.

Tolstoy didn't approve of his wife's business competence. She had no moral right to make money from his art. She had no right not to submit to all that he believed. Their relation became anguished. On her side it had long been that. It became anguished with the torment of two people who have lived together for years without communion. The only communion she knew, and wrote about coldly in her diary, was when the sexual insistence was too strong for him and he took her in bed.

This continued into advanced old age. Long after *The Kreutzer Sonata,* the most virulent attack on sexual intercourse written since Tertullian. Even he thought that it would be embarrassing if Sonya became pregnant again shortly after the publication of that book. Embarrassing for him, that is. The most masterly of observers didn't care to observe what she was feeling.

Those two were both of them people of great intelligence and remarkable character. Yet that marital misery, which is distressing just to read about, was very much as it would have been to punier human beings. Some of it, as in marital miseries of the insignificant and humble, was at the same time pathetic and grotesque. For instance, in his desire to live like a peasant, Tolstoy in due course picked up one of his peasants' customs, which was of not troubling to wash. He had most of his life been punctilious about cleanliness, and Sonya was so still. "He smells like a goat," she wrote, with detestation at what was happening.

What was happening to her was destroying first her judgment and then at last her balance. She had always been jealous. Maybe because she wasn't much capable of carnal love herself, she had tended to suspect him of finding it anywhere. She now decided that he was having an erotic relation with Chertkov, which was rather like thinking that H. G. Wells was homosexually attached to Bernard Shaw. She went in for all the ingenious detective work of semideranged jealousy. She searched his diaries for the record of his rapturous boyish passions for other boys. She tracked him down meeting Chertkov in the woods, after she had refused to have the man as a guest. Actually they were planning secret dispositions in the Tolstoyan cause, including a new settlement of the literary estate. Sonya was certain that she had obtained her final proof. She was ill, and she had phases of mental instability. At this time, when Tolstoy was around eighty, she was only sixty-two.

It is hard to resist an antinomian reflection. No one ever tried more strenuously to lead a moral life than Tolstoy, and to exhort others to lead the same moral life. No one ever tried less strenuously than Balzac in those directions. All the evidence tells us that everyone who was close to Balzac, including women who were simultaneously his mistresses, felt that he had brought them happiness. To all those close to Tolstoy, his children, most of all his wife, he brought misery.

In the autumn of 1910, Tolstoy eighty-two, Sonya sixty-four, she had become something like clinically deranged. Tolstoy had had several strokes, and his own mind was failing. The Tolstoy party, which consisted of the daughter who supported him and hated her mother, Chertkov, and Tolstoy's private doctor, Makovitsky, wanted to get Sonya certified and removed to an institution. The Sonya party, which was all the rest of the family, were begging her to separate from the old man. The house became loud with righteous quarrels. Husband and wife shouted curses at each other. At night Sonya rushed into the garden. He stumbled after her, and she cried at the top of her voice, "He's a monster! A murderer! I never want to see him again!"

This furious drama went on for weeks. Mixed up with it, and sometimes triggering it, there were touches of grim domestic farce. Both sides wanted to get hold of some documents. One was Tolstoy's new will, where Chertkov had been successful. Sonya and the others didn't know the details, but in fact it placed all his writings into the public domain and so dispossessed the family. The other documents being searched for were Tolstoy's diaries. There were clandestine searches around the house, people hiding in cupboards, nocturnal prowlings. After an evening of violence, and while such a search was going on, Tolstoy had another seizure.

Both he and Sonya had astonishing fortitude. After one of his strokes, he would be out riding within days. He reread Rousseau and Pascal, whom he found soothing and close to his own inner life. Sonya was capable of smiling for the photographers on their forty-eighth wedding anniversary.

It was Tolstoy who broke first. For some time he had been making vague plans for escaping. He had sounded out his daughter Sasha. Would she come with him? It didn't matter where. Perhaps they could go and live with a peasant who believed in Tolstoyan purity. That would be good. Never mind where. The essential thing was to escape.

On October 28, in the middle of the night, he was wakened by noises in his room. It was Sonya. She was rustling through the papers on his desk. That was enough. He must escape, now, that day, that morning. When she had gone, he got up. He summoned Dr. Makovitsky, and asked him or rather ordered him, to come with him.

The idea of Tolstoy quitting all worldly things had been talked about in Tolstoyan circles for long enough. Makovitsky, who was a fanatical Tolstoyan, a staunch comrade of Chertkov, enthusiastically approved. It didn't in the least worry him that Tolstoy was a very old man ravaged by a succession of strokes, not a suitable patient for arduous travel. This was a triumph for the faith and for them all. Makovitsky has some claims to be the most preposterous doctor so far known. He was a Slovak and, among his other disqualifications as Tolstoy's personal adviser, he was a virulent and persecuting anti-Semite. He had no difficulty in reconciling that passion with the Tolstoyan brotherhood of man.

Where should they go? Again, as Tolstoy had previously agreed with Sasha, it didn't matter. The only imperative was to start at once. Sonya would be after them. As a destination, Makovitsky with his usual fatuousness recommended Bessarabia.

They didn't get to Bessarabia. Tolstoy and Makovitsky set off alone, and Sasha was to follow them. It was bitterly cold, the onset of an early Russian winter. In the carriage to the station Makovitsky thoughtfully provided Tolstoy with an extra cap. They had to wait hours for a train. It was not until the evening that they arrived at Optina monastery.

They couldn't stay there. Sasha joined them, bringing news that Sonya and other members of the family were trying to track them down. They had to get going. That question once more—where? Maps on the table. The Caucasus. That seemed sensible to all of them. They would have to make the railway journey via Novocherkassk to Rostov-on-Don. Railway travel in the Cossack country was not sophisticated. It would take thirty hours to Novocherkassk. Makovitsky was cheerful. Tolstoy could cope with more than that.

Up at dawn. Two hours by trap to Kozelsk, the nearest railway junction to the monastery. Tolstoy was unsteady before they reached it. On the train, in the afternoon, his temperature began to mount. He was developing pneumonia. They had to get him off the train at a little station called Astapovo. Until then, few people even in Russia had ever heard of it. In the next few days it became the most celebrated railway station in the world.

Tolstoy, who had lost consciousness, was put to bed in the stationmaster's living room. The stationmaster and his family were kind and good-natured. They had need to be, for the news of Tolstoy's flight and illness had reached the world press. Journalists poured into the station. So did photographers, among them pioneers from the motion pictures. The progress of the illness was published everywhere. No writer had ever had such a public death, and none will again.

Chertkov and the inner circle of Tolstoyans had been telegraphed for, and duly arrived. Sasha had tried to keep Sonya and the family in ignorance, but a journalist had leaked the news. Sonya, entirely herself in the extremity, mobilized three sons and a daughter, nurse, doctor, medical supplies. Other doctors were being requisitioned. At the end there were half a dozen at the bedside. Sonya discovered that there wasn't a train from Tula that would reach Astapovo on the day she heard the news. She wasn't a grand lady for nothing. She firmly commandeered a special train.

Then there happened the harshest of the confrontations. The Tolstoyans had arrived first, and Chertkov and Makovitsky agreed that at all costs Sonya and the sons must be prevented from seeing Tolstoy. It would add to his suffering, make him worse, damage any chance of recovery. It became Makovitsky's professional duty to give this verdict to Sonya and the family. He discharged this duty with enthusiasm. They accepted it. All they could do was conceal themselves and peer through the windows of the living room.

Sonya was finally allowed to see him when Makovitsky and Sasha thought he had sunk deeply enough into final unconsciousness. Then he couldn't recognize her. He died in the early morning of November 7.

His grave at Yasnaya Polyana is as simple as some of his greatest art. There is no stone or monument—just a mound on which grass grows, set in a glade of trees. It has the harmony and peace and identity with nature that he had, when he wrote like a serene god.

GALDÓS

For a long time, most of the intellectual world seems to have been content to be ignorant of Spanish literature. Galdós is the most striking of cases. Outside academic enclaves, and some parts of the United States where the Spanish influence is strong, very few English-speaking people have heard his name or at any rate could make a significant statement about him. In the 1880s and 1890s books of his were translated into English, French, other languages, without much response. Today there are just two of his novels in print in English translation. Yet he was a great novelist.

He was a great novelist, of the same kind, and of the same stature, as others in this collection. He can be compared with Balzac, and not be diminished by the comparison. That may sound like an overstatement, but it is deliberately made. We ought to realize what we have lost by not reading him. His masterwork, *Fortunata y Jacinta*, is one of the finest of all novels, and no more profound studies of women's personalities (the two women of the title) have been written.

He was born in Las Palmas in May 1843, the tenth and last child of Sebastien Pérez and Dolores Galdós. The father was fifty-nine, the mother forty-three. This was a last child, and after christening his full name became Benito Maria de los Dolores Pérez Galdós. Officially, and on title pages, his style was Benito Pérez Galdós, but from young manhood, and as a writer, it was his mother's name that stuck.

There were two reasons, one matter-of-fact. Pérez is one of the commonest Spanish surnames, and as with López, Martínez, Fernández, García, Hernández, and so on, it is not unusual to drop it in favor of the mother's. Also in this particular family the Galdóses were considerably more eminent than the Pérezes, and Dolores Galdós, who was a woman of formidable personality, was never known by anything but her maiden name.

This must not suggest that there was anything irregular about the marriage. On the contrary, there wasn't a more properly conducted household in the Canary Islands. Dolores brought up all her children as rigidly observant and well-disciplined Catholics should be brought up. It was an orderly and quietly prosperous household, professional middle class, and with relatives rising in the world. Dolores's father had come to the Canaries as secretary of the Inquisition, which was a dignified job and rather surprisingly could be held by a layman. Sebastien Pérez came from substantial peasant stock, fought as a volunteer officer in the Peninsular War, did well, was decorated, and was rewarded with a grant of land. Before he married Dolores, he was already successfully growing vines. He was obscured by the personality of his wife, but he was shrewd and decent, and kept the big family in comfort. Two of Benito's brothers later became generals in the Spanish army.

As the Benjamin, and as a delicate and unassertive child, Benito was overprotected. His mother watched over him through his boyhood with possessive care. They all knew that he had gifts. She was anxious that he should add to the credit of the family. She tried to make sure that he got the best education that Las Palmas could provide. He probably learned a little English, a fair amount of Latin and French. He read a great deal. He did just adequately at his schoolwork, enough to get by. His mother worried about his wasting himself. He seemed to be writing away in secret, and articles and poems may have appeared anonymously in the local press. He showed considerable talent in the visual arts. His cartoons were so original that the headmaster of his school preserved them. Later in life, Galdós often ornamented the margins of his manuscripts with drawings, as Dostoevsky did his. He won awards for small oil paintings at Las Palmas exhibitions. He could have made a living at most arts.

His mother continued to be worried. None of this was what she expected of him. She would have been even more worried if she had realized that, from early in his boyhood, he took time off from school to explore the backstreets, the waterfront. He was abnormally quiet both at school and at home, but he observed. Little escaped the eye he was born with, a preternaturally accurate eye.

His mother made her decision. She wasn't going to let him dribble his intelligence away. He must train to be a lawyer. He had all the abilities to be a high-class lawyer. The law was an honorable profession and the best route to get into some of the most illustrious posts in Spain. He must go to the university in Madrid and read law.

Benito did not wish to become a lawyer. He would prefer to be an architect. They argued, she with emphatic eloquence, he in his tongue-tied fashion. He knew the strength of his mother's will. They reached agreement. He went off to Madrid to read law.

That sounds like a somewhat one-sided compromise. In fact, underneath his shyness, he had a will as strong as hers. Going to Madrid suited him very well. Already, under the surface of his mind, a secret planner had been at work. It didn't matter much what subject he read, or affected to read, in Madrid. It was being in Madrid on any pretext, with enough funds to exist on, that was the point. He knew what he wanted to do.

More certainly than any other of the greatest nineteenth-century novelists, he was in no shadow of doubt about his vocation. It gave him his driving motive. He was going to be a writer. To almost everyone who met him, he seemed unassuming and modest. Certainly he was unassuming, beyond the common. In company, he was often genuinely humble and what some people might have called *chétif*. But modest he was not. In Spain he was going to be the great writer of his time. Whatever the anxieties and qualms of youth, he didn't really doubt that he would make it.

That was his state at nineteen, when he arrived in Madrid. It was still his state when he died, old, blind, after he had fulfilled his vocation. He had obtained immense popular success, he had done what he had set out to do, and he was dying—for a singular and hidden reason—nearly as poor as when he started. As a young man, he kept his intentions to himself. Year after year, he duly enrolled as a law student at the university. With a pleasing symmetry, year after year, the law faculty reported that he had failed the course on account of insufficient attendance. He managed to conceal from his family what he was up to, though one sister-in-law had something of an idea and became his most enthusiastic backer. He also managed to conceal his doings from his student acquaintances, which to a normally spontaneous young man of twenty wouldn't have been possible.

He wasn't a normally spontaneous young man. He sat with a café group (*tertulia*) amiably enough, listening, watching, speaking so rarely that they said he didn't open his mouth to order coffee. Yet he was liked. There was something benign about him, as people felt, however reticent he was, all his life. He had presence. He wasn't handsome, but he was presentable, with thick dark hair, expressionless visage, watchful and penetrating little eyes—where there must have been one of several resemblances to Dostoevsky. He was tall for a Spaniard, slim, probably a trifle gangling. His physical makeup would be regarded by Sheldonians as a classical example of an ectomorphic constitution. He had a habit of twisting one leg around another under the table. On the rare occasions when he uttered, his voice was strangulated and didn't flow.

He had an accomplishment that added considerably to his popularity as a *tertulia* member—added more considerably than would seem entirely reasonable to a modern Anglo-Saxon. While the other young men talked for hours about politics, religion, women, he sat unobtrusively making paper birds. With his visual eye and clever fingers, he was very good at making paper birds. That was a trick that Miguel de Unamuno, a less endearing character than Galdós, may have picked up from him. Unamuno behaved with much ungenerosity to Galdós's reputation. When he thought that his own ego wasn't being sufficiently recognized, he too proceeded to make paper birds.

Galdós also made paper figures of celebrated Madrid prostitutes. In most student circles, that must have been even more popular. Some of them nicknamed him *"El chico de las putas."* This is said to be an unusual phrase in Spanish. Literally it means "the child of whores." It is possible that Galdós's companions had been trying to guess about his wanderings.

It took them a long time to guess what he would do for a living. Was he a government spy? That was one bright suggestion. Then someone saw him entering a newspaper office. That must be it. The silent, shy, impenetrable Galdós meant to be a journalist.

So he did. But only as a step on the way. He was actually taken on the staff of a couple of papers. He was a good journalist, like Dickens, one of his heroes, and like Dickens was employed as a parliamentary correspondent. He was also used to collect stories around Madrid. This brought in a little money. It also brought in knowledge. He may have been a Canarian born, but he soon knew Madrid better than any native. In later years no one—except Canarian patriots, who felt neglected—thought of him as anything but a Madrileño, but one is told that in the midst of his pure Castilian there occur a few dialect (originally Portuguese) words.

Journalism took up only a fraction of his energies. He wasn't wasting his time. He read with the voracity of all young writers. Like Dostoevsky and Tolstoy twenty years before, he read Dickens, Balzac, Schiller—the fashionable writers for young intellectuals. He also read Spanish writers now forgotten. It is desirable to remember that potentially great writers may read great writers, but not great writers only. Often they learn enduring lessons, good or bad, from the ordinary ephemeral reading matter of their time. Graham Greene has said wise and honest things about the writers who had the most effect on him, and not many of them are studied in college courses.

Alongside all else, and above all else, the young Galdós wrote. He wouldn't have been a child of his time, of the literary nineteenth century, if he hadn't begun by writing plays, verse plays in the manner of Schiller, who was one of the more dangerous models of all master figures. Galdós duly composed a verse play about the expulsion of the Moors from Spain, and other dramatic works. They have never been performed, and are said to be dreadful. Determining whether they are more dreadful than the other plays executed by the greatest nineteenth-century novelists and poets would be a nice exercise in comparative literature.

Galdós's first published work of any length was a translation of *The Pickwick Papers*. That was an odd venture. We know that Galdós never came to speak English. There is no evidence that he had a real command of the language, but the translation is said to read quite well. It was published in the newspaper *La Nacion*. Dickens's English is very far from straightforward.

Then Galdós took to novels. He would, of course, have done so anyway, for he was too sensible not to discover what his real gift was. But the choice was accelerated by others' good intentions—good intentions, that is, in the reverse direction, meant to fend him off from writing and get him back to a good, safe, honorable career. His family still thought that he was studying law, though with not such single-mindedness as might be wished. At the age of twenty-four he went back to Las Palmas for a holiday (there was to be only one more visit home in the course of a long life). Family conferences took place, mother presiding. Could law and literature be mixed? General opinion, no, with a dissenting voice or two from the half-American sisters-in-law. Galdós didn't make it clear that he would become a lawyer about as willingly as he would become a sanitary inspector. Arguments went on. Someone had a flash of inspiration. Why not take up a collection and send Benito off for a trip to Paris?

It is puzzling that this was thought likely to redirect him toward the law. Galdós, staying silent, thought that the least likely result on earth. On the other hand, staying a little less silent, he thought the trip to Paris a very good idea. For his own purposes, it was. It was on that trip that he really understood Balzac, and came to realize what his own life work must be. Like Balzac, he started with a historical novel. It wasn't a historical romance, in the fashion of the day, but it was set in the past. He wasn't yet able to reach down to his deepest creative springs. It took him ten years more before he could attempt to bring together his social and psychological insight, so that he could explore and project the life around him. When that happened, it was his great period, though it lasted only a few years in a long literary career, and it gave him his triumphs of realism.

Except in that period, he had divided aims. He had ultimate confidence that he was to be the great writer of Spain; but he hadn't so much confidence about most of his books as he wrote them. He was sensitive to critics, which didn't sharply distinguish him from other writers: Tolstoy could brush them off, but not many had Tolstoy's character. Further, and much more significant, Galdós was living in a society dominated by a brilliant past, and a past that appeared in retrospect more brilliant than it was. Galdós's Spain was existing in stagnation compared with the rest of Europe, and men like him were searching frenetically for a decent future.

On the political surface, Spain in Galdós's lifetime was constantly changing, getting rid of monarchs, trying a republic, restoring dynasties, tinkering with institutions. Galdós had no faith in institutions. He was a liberal from his earliest youth, and stayed a liberal until he died. He loved everything about Spain—the language, the countryside, the people in the Madrid slums, at times even the anachronisms. He was the most devoted of patriots. He knew more about history and politics than most writers. He wanted a national rebirth. But he was skeptical about any political solution. He seems to have thought, exactly like Dostoevsky in Russia, that rebirth could come only from inside individual men. Modest as he appeared to those who met him, he believed that he could start this rebirth with his own novels.

That strikes us as a strange illusion for a reflective and skeptical man. It helps perhaps to recall that there was much in common between nineteenth-century Spain and nineteenth-century Russia. There was one deep difference. Spain had a great past. Russia would have a great future; Russians disagreed on everything else, but not on that. Otherwise the two countries were primitive, in material living centuries behind England, Germany, France. That, their intellectuals knew whenever they traveled. They didn't travel to the United States, or would have been still more depressed.

In both countries, Spain and Russia, all thinking men were split by politics. Politics must be the remedy, but what kind of politics? Literary controversy had to be political. Maybe as a consequence, they had an abnormal faith and pride in their ideas and in the printed word. Will and intelligence and the printed word could somehow make the change. Through Galdós's novels, telling the people the truth about themselves, he was sure he could lead them.

One of the ways he could lead them—and this was to be the most direct of his messages—was against the Church. It was the Church, untouched in its medieval power and in blank ignorance, that kept Spain primitive. Galdós was immovably anticlerical. In a Protestant or secular country, it seems perverse to add that he was also a man of strong religious feeling. In some of his later novels, notably *Nazarín,* the feeling is intense. This combination of anticlerical ferocity and religious emotion wouldn't seem odd to many Europeans. Galdós wanted a Catholicism stripped of its decorations, superstitions, complacency, and power. He might have been surprised by the direction that Spanish Catholicism has taken in the last twenty years, but he might also have been happy in it, and reconciled.

The first historical novel, *La fontana de oro,* set in
the period 1820 to 1823, grappled with the peculiar problems of a Spanish liberal. To get it published, he had to
come clean with his family at last. He was twenty-seven.
He was going to be a writer, he let them know, and nothing but a writer. He was making a living as a journalist,
but hadn't enough money to pay for his novel's publication. To his mother's chagrin, money was immediately offered by Madrina, his sister-in-law, half-American, his
nearest intimate and most faithful admirer in the family.
Actually, Galdós had at no time been really poor in Madrid,
quite unlike the young Balzac or the young Dostoevsky.
Very soon, he was to become, by Spanish professional standards, well-to-do.

Publishing novels in the Madrid of 1870 wasn't an encouraging prospect. Writers of popular romances issued
their books in installments, but only to subscribers. For a
beginner, hardback publishing meant paying the initial cost
and persuading the bookshops, not to buy copies, but to
exhibit them. That happened to Galdós's first novel, and
for months nothing else happened. He did some useful
personal publicity in a paper edited by himself. Then he
was lucky. Somehow a couple of influential writers came to
know of the book.

He was launched. He was talked about. It all bore a
family resemblance to the reception of Dostoevsky's *Poor
Folk.* Liberal intellectuals were numerically thin on the
ground, but their opinions counted; and they said, and
went on saying, that Spain had thrown up a major writer.
That book, *La fontana de oro,* didn't sell much. Shortly
afterward Galdós became the best-selling novelist in Spain.

He had a conception that both fitted his hope of national
rebirth and brought him wealth. He was immersed in Spanish history. The history of the nineteenth century in Spain
was something that the people must learn, truthfully, without false gloss, but still with self-respect. He could tell it
to them in a series of novels. He began the series in 1873 at
the age of thirty, wrote ten of them, followed with another
series of ten—all those twenty books in half a dozen years.
That was the first installment of the *Episodios nacionales*.

The *Episodios* were initiated by a dashing overture—
Trafalgar. The second volume was *La corte de Carlos IV*.
That was enough to establish Galdós as a national figure.
The ten novels of the first series appeared at spectacular
speed, ten in just over two years. They were even spectacular to the eye, since the covers were adorned by the national colors. The books touched the hopes of Spain. They
were what the literate public had been craving.

The history was sound. Galdós was a conscientious
and scholarly man, and though he didn't disguise his own
ideological position (which was founded on something like
the Whig interpretation of history), he wouldn't distort
the sources. He was too good a writer not to inject his
human insight, which, although subdued in the early *Episodios,* was already formed, by experience as well as natural
gifts.

It is possible that becoming a national hero made it
more difficult for Galdós to become an international one.
Spain was a backward and powerless country, right outside
the mainstream. No one in England or France was likely
to be interested in a series of novels about a history of
which they knew nothing and cared less. What was all the

fuss about? There were perfunctory attempts by English and French publishers to issue translations of the immediate successors to the first twenty *Episodios*. They didn't work. If the early translations of a foreign writer don't catch on, it isn't easy to revive him. Thus the major novels of his maturity, written in the next decade during his forties, fell obscurely flat in London and Paris, and the greatest ones have not been adequately translated until the last few years.

Nevertheless, in Spain at the age of thirty he was already established as the voice of the liberals' conscience and their supreme professional writer. Except for one singularity, which we shall be coming to later, he was the most disciplined of professional writers. He needed to be, for he proceeded to write over eighty novels and, late in his career, over twenty plays.

No one could write eighty novels, some of immense length (his masterpiece is slightly longer than *The Brothers Karamazov*), without sitting down to his work. Galdós did sit down to his work. He did so as methodically as Trollope, and wrote more hours a day, and wrote more words. As with all great professionals, his routine may have struck romanticizing admirers as disconcertingly prosaic. He got up at dawn. There was coffee and hot milk waiting for him on his writing table. He had the tic, common to many writers, of insisting that that table had to be kept pernicketily tidy, papers in precise order (the same was true of Balzac, Dickens, Dostoevsky, Tolstoy). He was a bachelor and his household was managed by two of his sisters, who kept it with fastidious cleanliness and bourgeois austerity.

With sips of coffee he started in. He had an accurate

memory, visual and verbal, and he didn't need to read over the previous day's writing. Once he had got over the difficult part—that is, getting the book going at all—then writing went steadily on. He wrote until one o'clock. Then a meager lunch with his sisters, at which he wasn't communicative. Words, food, drink, entertainment weren't wasted in the Galdós house. The rest of the day was his own. His timetable was as methodical as his writing—evening visit to a café, dinner at a restaurant—but it provided for his one singularity.

Being a good professional, he didn't leave the practical side of publishing to chance. He was responsible for the advertising campaign for the first *Episodios*. The national colors on the cover, they were due to him. He had most of the ideas for new editions. His personality suggested to some, particularly to hero-worshipers, that he was remote from mundane concerns, such as money. That can be regarded with mild skepticism. He may not have been clever with his contracts, but he certainly wasn't remote from the need of attracting, and keeping, the largest possible readership. That was imperative both for the cause and—he wasn't self-deceiving—for himself. No Spanish writer could expect from his books what Dickens or Tolstoy earned, but from thirty onward Galdós did remarkably well, and, for any nineteenth-century novelist, the size and loyalty of his public had deep emotional meaning. To have dim reviews was bad enough; to see one's readership dwindling was very much worse.

The *Episodios* established him with fame and money, but he hadn't yet worked from his deepest springs. When he was thirty-eight, he could begin. That was the year,

1881, when he published the first of his *Novelas contem-poráneas*. He didn't find an equivalent of *La Comédie humaine* as a title for this series, and with his usual literary tact was content with that commonplace one. It was in this series that Balzac had taught him most. He had nearly all the talents to do for Spain what Balzac had done for France. He could even brandish some of the same faults, such as a pleasure in the occasional absurd generalization. He had already used characters recurring from book to book in the *Episodios,* and had probably at that time formed the conception of this contemporary panorama.

As a rule, he was under better control than Balzac. He was much less extravagant. He didn't lose his sense of fact, which in him was difficult to shift. Balzac knew a great deal. So did Galdós. About individual human beings, there wasn't much to choose between them. Each had percipience at full stretch—that is, insight, intuition, experience, all in harmony. Balzac had the greater projective power, partly because he simplified more, but Galdós at the height of his gift had plenty. In social range the advantage was slightly on Galdós's side. Balzac could explore most of Paris with complete familiarity. Galdós did the same with Madrid, and was intimate, as Balzac wasn't, with the lower depths. No writer has known so much, in so many different strata, of a big city. Balzac wrote with mastery of the aristocracy, the middle classes, the professionals, the artisans. Galdós was at home from the aristocracy down to the seething slums, though he wasn't at all beglamored by the *beau monde.*

As a minor piece of equipment, he had the city in mind with geographical exactitude street by street. Spanish scholars such as Pedro Ortíz have occupied themselves drawing maps of the settings of his novels. James Joyce proclaimed that, if Dublin were destroyed, that wouldn't matter. It could be reconstructed from the text of *Ulysses*. It wasn't in Galdós's style to make that kind of boast, but he could have done so about Madrid, and with more justification.

Galdós's ultimate merit depends on the *Contemporary Novels*. The international recognition he would have liked, made considerable efforts to help on, and didn't get in his lifetime won't be adequate, until the best of these are properly read and comprehended.

The first of the series, *La Desheradada,* is possibly the right introduction to Galdós for English-speaking readers. There is an effective translation by Lester Clark, called *The Disinherited*. The narrative is less densely packed than in some of the successors, but the characteristic virtues are nearly all there. The central figure is a girl, one of Galdós's splendid gallery of women, living in a simple provincial home, but brought up to believe that she is the illegitimate granddaughter of a great aristocratic lady. The girl, Isidora, has some objective reasons for believing this story. She is shown documents by her father (who, if the story is true, isn't her father) and by a kind of adopted uncle who is at the same time a comfortable dreamer and a miser.

Isidora is only too willing to believe. She is generous, romantic, aspiring, certain that this humble home isn't her natural place. She may be penniless, but she is snobbish, reckless, spendthrift, like some of Galdós's other girls. Shades of the old Spanish fascination with the rift between fantasy and reality prevail over the book's opening, delib-

erate shades from Cervantes and Calderón. But soon we are
plunged into Galdós's total immersion in his people and in
his social scene.

Isidora, in an underplayed meeting seen with the
sharpest of eyes, is told not to be silly by her putative
marquesa grandmother. Isidora, incapable of being convinced, goes to law; but, on the way to what she is certain
are her rights, she takes a lover, for she is a sensual girl and
needs to devote herself to a man as totally as most of
Galdós's heroines. Another man takes her over, this being
her way to keep alive, before the case is settled. At long
last, she has to realize that her precious documents are a
forgery by her lunatic father. The trauma is shattering.
She hates the hope she has longed for as passionately as she
would have once groveled for it. This sounds melodramatic,
but is written with consummate quietness. She is a pauper,
with no skills. There is nothing for her, in Madrid in the
1870s. She goes on the streets.

Throughout the *Contemporary Novels,* the history of
Galdós's modern Spain is heard offstage. In *The Disinherited,* people are commenting on the abdication of one king
and, often with the sort of irrational hope that accom-
panies a presidential election in America, on the restoration
of the Bourbons. Again, as usual in Galdós, some of the
incidental chapters light up the book. He hadn't been
stimulated only by Balzac and was allowing himself minor
reflections from his other great hero, Dickens. There is a
wonderful derelict family, the Relimpios, like toned-down
and semirealistic Micawbers, and their Christmas dinner is
Dickensian with a harder irony thrown in. There is also a
less successful reflection of the Circumlocution Office, just

as repetitive and heavy-footed and not as lively, though Galdós knew much more than Dickens of how an administration really worked. The very fine young doctor, Miquis, must owe something to Balzac's Bianchon, but he is one of the best-realized people in the book; which is saying a good deal, since Galdós's characters fail to be three-dimensional as rarely as those of any novelist.

The doings of Isidora's young brother are told with clinical confidence: this is what gang warfare among slum children in Madrid was really like, seen by someone within touching distance.

Several interesting novels are set in the genteel lower middle class, for example, *Tormento* and *La de Bringas*. *Fortunata y Jacinta* stretches over a much wider social range and is altogether richer and deeper than anything that came before or was to follow. It was written when Galdós was between forty-two and forty-four and was published in four parts, each of them more substantial than the standard twentieth-century novel. The entire work carries the modest subtitle *Two Stories of Married Women*. That is true as far as it goes; but, as the author knew better than anyone else, it doesn't go far enough. He didn't expect, and didn't get, a rapturous reception. Since his reputation was still high, he also didn't get abuse, but something more like an absence of praise. As a rule, he was hurt by critical opinion. Not so much this time. He knew that, if he had written nothing else, this one was good enough.

The two women are investigated with loving ruthlessness. They have an existence as solid and as totally projected as any women characters in fiction. Their marriages, one unhappy, the other disastrous, are alive through the same loving, detached ruthlessness. The overall effect is not depressing, unless extraordinary percipience about human beings is depressing. We are in the presence, often high-spirited, illuminated by experience, the level of sheer curiosity always sustained, of life as it is lived.

Jacinta has made a marriage with her cousin Juanito that is not only good by the standards of their *haut bourgeois* Madrid world, but also on her side full of love. Juanito is an engaging frivolous young man, pleasing to women, good-natured when it doesn't cost him much. He is the heir (the Delfín) to the Santa Cruz fortune, which has been made out of the drapery trade. Galdós, who makes us interested in anything he was interested in himself, gives a professional sketch of real commerce in mid-nineteenth-century Madrid. He knows more about it than Juanito could have, for the young man hasn't application or ability, except in amusing himself with girls. For a time he makes the young girl happy. There is a cheerful account of the first months of a youthful marriage, the day-by-day frets and pleasures. It is more vivid than the comparable Oblonsky marriage in *Anna Karenina,* partly because Galdós has affection for the domestic interiors, including the silliness of the ordinary.

Before the marriage, Juanito has noticed—more than noticed—another girl, Fortunata. He has been roaming through the slums. He sees a beautiful, strapping young woman outside a shop, eating a raw egg. She radiates vitality, sensual vitality, which is what Juanito can respond to, and much else that he can't. She has come from the very poor. Her parents died when she was in her early teens. She had no one to support her. A man did, and after him a succession of men. She hadn't loved any of them, but with some there had been fun.

In her early twenties, when Juanito appeared, she hadn't many constraints. She wouldn't sell herself for money, but would give herself for love. She hadn't been in love, and she soon loved Juanito as devotedly as did his innocent young wife. Jacinta's senses were far from cold, but there was something maternal about her love; she craved a child, but she didn't conceive. Whereas Fortunata's love was erotic, sacrificial, and totally self-forgetful.

The counterpoint between the two personalities is the deepest layer in the whole massive work. Juanito pays enough to keep Fortunata going, and makes sporadic visits. She has two children by him. The first doesn't survive. She believes in his promises with passionate fidelity. To begin with, Jacinta, discovering little by little that Juanito has a mistress, also believes that he is extricating himself. There are passages of much subtlety about the intermittences of emotion—how jealousy, with one in love, can be dissolved in an instant, and replaced by absolute happy assurance. Then jealousy returns. The same happens with moods of guilt, suddenly washed away by floods of absolute innocence.

Jacinta, however, is a person of far more substance than her husband. At the end of the book, after Fortunata has died following the birth of the second child, Jacinta sees Juanito with no residue of any illusion. Now she is in control.

There is a very large cast of personages in the novel, examined and displayed with Galdós's insight, irony, and respect. Each human being is a human being, even when, as sometimes happens, there isn't much else agreeable to say. The technical control in a work of such complexity and confusion is masterly, though one ceases to attend to it under the cumulative impact of the whole; which, by the way, is a high tribute to the technical control. Galdós doesn't try many of the technical tricks he used in other novels, such as writing occasional scenes as though they were the scripts of plays. He does sometimes, as he had done on a much larger scale in *La desheradada,* let his people express themselves in interior monologues—which later became known as streams of consciousness, incidentally a misleading term. There is a characteristic one when the rich Anglophile Moreno, hopelessly in love with Jacinta, is walking, rather surprisingly in a novel that is the essence of Madrid, from Hyde Park to Cromwell Road.

Galdós didn't interpose his play scripts in the book, but several of the major scenes could go straight onto the stage. He was a born dramatic writer and shows it in some of the cardinal dialogues. A poor shadow of a man, adoring Fortunata, possibly impotent, wants to marry her. When Juanito seems to have dispensed with her for good, she is made to accept this man, in order to reclaim her respectability. It is a dreadful marriage. Both are fundamentally kind, and would like to be good. He is unavailing, a semi-intellectual. She can barely read, not write. There is scarcely a word in common. Before they marry, she tries to explain what her life has been, and what she feels for Juanito. Then a grimmer scene when she has married the man and left him. His brother, a priest, is forcing her to go back.

This might be a dialogue from Dostoevsky. The priest,

who is not without self-interest, as Galdós keeps his detachment in the midst of spiritual drama, is telling her about
the need for redemption. She knows the word only vaguely,
yet somehow she understands what he means. She has
learned nothing of religion, but she is listening as though it
were a kind of music. It is a scene of disquieting power.

It seems unlikely that Galdós can have read Dostoevsky, who didn't reach Spain until some years after *Fortunata y Jacinta* was published. But he knew all about Emilia
Pardo-Bazán's lectures on the Russian novel. Certainly
Dostoevsky and Galdós had something in common. There
is one article of faith of Fortunata's, however, the only one
she is certain of, that would have been foreign to Dostoevsky. It baffles the priest. It is simple. It is that love, the kind
of love she bears Juanito, can never be wrong. That might
be a voice from the America of our own times.

When the book was first published, Galdós was accused of going over to Zola-type naturalism. This was a
misunderstanding that is worth more treatment than can
be afforded here. The line between realism and naturalism
is a quavering one. All literary categories are bound to be
simpler and more cut-and-dried than the works they
attempt to define. It is perfectly true that Galdós piles up
more factual data, more inventories of furniture and cou-
turiers' descriptions of women's clothes, than a writer could
allow himself in 1978, even if there were one with Galdós's
thrust and appetite. He allowed himself more of that material, in fact, than the other realistic writers of his own
century, except for his teacher Balzac. But in Galdós—
and this is the distinction between realism and naturalism
—there is always an interpreting and personal intelligence.

When naturalism is carried to a limit, there isn't. Zola

didn't carry naturalism to the limit, and so has remained interesting. But a good deal of committed naturalism has gone to the limit, and beyond it, giving us the delightful prospect of a pile of data, mindless, porridgelike. That is no more true of Galdós than it is of Balzac. One illustration: in *Fortunata y Jacinta* Galdós indulges himself in a chapter called "Coffee-drinking Customs." This chapter develops into scenes that are relevant to the book's themes and multiple narratives, but at the beginning it is a description of the café habits, the way *tertulias* migrated from one café to another, these cafés being indistinguishable, in Galdós's Madrid. This could be tedious porridge naturalism. It is very far from that. Galdós, with his usual watchfulness, observes these phenomena and then speculates about them. Just as Proust might have done a generation later.

Such ruminations are an agreeable distraction from the pressure, throughout the book, of so many individual human beings. He maintains the intense concentration on each one, as he looks at them and into them. They are human beings like himself, and that is where the accent of his own personality is always present. He is never sentimental. Sentimentality, someone once sagely observed, consists of leaving things out. Building up his major climax, which he is the last man to evade, he doesn't leave out things that a lesser, and less realistic, writer might have felt would minimize the impact. At the end of *Fortunata y Jacinta*, Fortunata is coming near death. She cannot feed the newborn baby. She is meeting her bleak fate. In lucid intervals, she is trying to see that the child is looked after; she wishes to send messages to Jacinta.

This is the drama of Fortunata's highly charged nature. It is written with extreme quietness, and is difficult to read without emotion. But the writer, not leaving things out, doesn't forget that Fortunata, the least petty of all his people, in the tumult of her passion also has a streak of a poor waif's snobbery. A friend tells her about a rich visitor—"Do you know what she said to Placido [one of the Santa Cruz domestics] as she left? That, if you want anything, she has given instructions that your orders are to be obeyed if it should be necessary."

"Quite so," says Fortunata, bursting with innocent pride. "Placido is a servant of the house, and ever since he was a small boy he has done nothing but run errands for the gentry. . . ."

It puzzled people in Galdós's own time, and has done since, that he knew so much, with such intimate certainty, of the down-and-out poor, the cheap prostitutes and derelicts of the slums.

To get into the homes of clerks only just above the subsistence level—that was easy enough; Dickens and Dostoevsky had done it. But this whole assembly of the Fortunata world—however did Galdós come to know it? The answer is simple. By the most direct means conceivable. Galdós had an indefatigable appetite for women. He appears to have had a special addiction to women of the lowest classes—prostitutes, semiprostitutes, women of the slums who heard gossip about this nice, kind, rich, and generous man. He didn't much want anything in the way of a sustained relation. He did have several upper-class mistresses, but seems to have extricated himself with some dexterity. He had affection for most things about women, but above all he wanted women's flesh, as quickly and easily as it came.

This was kept extraordinarily secret. He gave plenty of interviews, but talked about literature and politics, not about himself. One feels that in America and England some of those journalists who interviewed him would have moved onto the track. A few friends had their suspicions, in particular his partner in the firm that published his books. That partner couldn't help noticing that Galdós was constantly extracting from the firm sums of money inexplicably large for a man who lived so modestly.

When at the age of fifty Galdós was known to be in financial straits, and got into worse trouble as the years passed, though he was still by far the most successful writer in Spain, others began to guess. It is possible that his student acquaintances had made their guesses very early in his life, and the nickname they gave him suggests as much. Spanish students at the age of twenty wouldn't be incurious or unknowledgeable about dealings with prostitutes. They may have had an inkling that Galdós, nineteen years old, was abnormally dependent on women he could pick up. It is possible—more than possible, for a young man with such an impulse—that he had already started before he left Las Palmas.

This passion, habit, necessity, or whatever we like to call it, was fitted methodically into the routine of his days. A certain lacuna, which for a long time mystified his household, isn't a lacuna anymore. Writing all the morning—the first of his necessities. Decorous lunch at one o'clock, sisters present but not disturbing his thoughts, rather as though this were the domestic pattern of a pious priest. Off before two each afternoon, each and every afternoon through the decades, off alone until he was no longer able-bodied, when a discreet servant took him. If he had given an explanation at home, it would have been "business," "literary affairs." Scattered through the Galdós corpus, there are a few hints, which may be obscure jokes at his own expense.

Two women are exchanging amorous gossip. One of them, a friend of Fortunata's called Aurora, complains that bachelors, especially well-to-do bachelors, are always inconsiderate. They insist on making appointments for the middle of the day, two in the afternoon. What a time to choose!

That was Galdós's time. It is now known that he had two or three hideouts in Madrid, rooms that he must have rented, where he could have his women. The names of most of the women are lost in oblivion, presumably forever. Nearly all of them would have been illiterate, and there is no chance of any record. Fortunata could read a little, though with difficulty, but couldn't write. Of course there was a Fortunata among Galdós's collection. The exactness of the account, the minute particularity of the way she explains, simply and honestly, how little she knows (she thinks the Virgin, Jesus, St. Peter were good people, but nothing more). She asks what some long words mean, and can't pronounce them. It wouldn't be difficult for a romantic writer to create a magnificent savage, but here is a magnificent savage drawn from life. One would bet that, as he looked through the slums, there was a day when he saw this strong figure of a girl eating her raw egg.

As has been mentioned, he didn't restrict himself entirely to the women of the slums. There was a pleasant and cultivated Swede, Juanita Lund, with whom he went to bed on and off over a period of years. There was a less

pleasant but more picturesque Spanish contessa, Emilia
Pardo-Bazán, who had literary talent and was something
like a hispanic George Sand, books, men, and all. She was
a genuine writer, and a considerable one. She wrote him
exuberant love letters, which have been published. She
made up for lack of physical charms (she was uncommonly fat) by an ardent temperament. Galdós, who had a
strong sense of self-preservation, seems scarcely to have
written love letters at all to her or anyone else. If he did,
they haven't been traced. His correspondence on any subject was, from available evidence, as guarded and reticent
as his talk.

Like Balzac, and like a good many writers who touch
emotional nerves, he received letters from adoring women.
Some of these were by way of being offers. Middle-class
Spain in his time was not so purdah-bound as Anglo-
Saxons have been taught to believe. Some of these offers he
no doubt accepted. But none of those distractions appears
to have interfered with his dutiful daily visits to the Barrios
Bajos.

He knew those streets, alleys, courts, as no bourgeois
had ever done. He listened, not only to the women he
picked up, but to the men, peddlers, beggars, street ven-
dors, petty criminals. He heard their language and used it
richly in his novels. He was probably easier with the people
there, more open, than in any café *tertulia*.

Anyway they loved him. He couldn't help being an
unusual sight, walking in his dignified style, past broken-
down shops, entering rickety doors that led upstairs with
missing treads. He wore his correct black professional suit
among the rags of that lumpen proletariat, all around him,

yelling at each other, not at him. They loved him. Of course, among his acquaintances there was some cupboard love. It didn't take them long to discover that he was not only generous but also careless about money, and not only to his girls but also to anyone who seemed to need it. That was true, though they couldn't know it, with his fellow writers. In several of his novels, there are studies, understanding and amused, of women who get into trouble because they can no more keep hold of money than if it were liquid. He knew all about that minor affliction since it was true of himself. He looked so prudent and wise. He spent so little on himself. The money disappeared.

Even so, it is still something of a puzzle how he got into such a financial mess. His own expenses must have been very small. Some have suggested that his partner did contrive—as Galdós himself believed in fits of paranoia—to get away with some of the firm's money. The weight of evidence is right against that, but one would like to see a good professional audit of their accounts. It would tell us how much Galdós really earned. It may have been much less than we, accustomed to the literary incomes of America and England, are inclined to imagine. If so, this would explain some of his money worries straightaway.

Though assignations were arranged in his clandestine hideouts, he also liked visiting his women in their own rooms. Hence the pictures of such interiors in his books. His eye was watchful and accurate as ever, and he enjoyed the sight and smell of everyday existence, whether it was squalid, or luxurious, or just pretty. He seems to have enjoyed reading proofs in the room of one of his favorite girls. This may have happened with his original of Fortunata. The words would be too difficult for her to read, and so he would explain and, since she had her native brightness, make her laugh.

This singular life of his raised a question before he died, among people who knew him well. He had never married; but how many children had he had? No one knew. To this day, no one knows. There was certainly one daughter. He jotted down the date of the baby's birth in his notebook and apparently talked to the child now and then. Presumably some of his money was spent on her. She acquired an education, and grew up a clever, presentable woman. She was quiet, shy, and determined, and insisted on seeing him as he lay on his deathbed. She called herself Maria Galdós, and years after his death was invited to Galdós celebrations.

It isn't doubted that there were other children, but no one has discovered what the number was. It was strongly suspected that a clerk in his own publishing house was a son of his. Others presumably lived out their lives, money mysteriously drifting down to them, in the slum streets. He seems not to have felt more responsibility than Tolstoy did for his illegitimate offspring, though Galdós was embarrassed when Maria forced her way into the family. Some Spanish authorities guess that there were at least six Galdós children, and others that that is a gross underestimate. It is unlikely that anyone will know for sure.

To remark that this was a singular life is understating the case. It isn't easy to think of anything much like it among major writers, and it can't be commonplace anywhere else. It is similar in form to the life pattern of one kind of homosexual, the camp term being *cruiser*, trans-

ferred to a hyperfervid heterosexual. Maupassant picked up
many women with an addiction as compulsive as Galdós's,
but he was uncontrolled in all respects, while in any other
respect Galdós was a model of control. As a footnote,
Maupassant acquired syphilis, and died in his early forties.
Galdós didn't acquire syphilis, and lived to be seventy-
seven, not altering his habits, as we shall see shortly, until
very near the end.

Spanish friends tend to say cheerfully that Galdós had
two devotions, writing and women, and that the explanation for the hidden part of his existence is simply biological.
Biological, they say firmly, like sensible Mediterranean men.
Well, that seems just a shade reductive. Galdós loved women
and everything about them. Not only their bodies but also
their minds and tastes. He reveled in the sight of women
dressing and undressing, and he wasn't unusual in that, but
he also shared their delight in what they wore.

It does seem strange that he didn't wish for one permanent relationship, whatever he did elsewhere. It may be
that he drops one of his clues, or his subliminal confes-
sions, in *Fortunata y Jacinta,* though few writers have confessed less. In that book, Juanito says that variety of women
is for him the only support by which he can go on living,
and we are led to infer that he means he needs variety as an
aphrodisiac. Without variety, the sexual tide isn't in full
flow. Juanito is a waster, and Galdós was the opposite.
Juanito has very little imagination, and Galdós a great deal.
The need for variety is the kind of self-excuse that wasters
without imagination have been known to make. In this
specific matter, is Galdós for once identifying himself with
such men?

In his forties, Galdós was beginning to receive honors

in the public life of Spain. There was opposition from conservative forces. His election to the Royal Spanish Academy
of Language was delayed. He had some capacity for um-
brage, and after he was elected, it was years before he
occupied his chair. He was found a seat in the Cortes, as
was thought suitable for the most eminent liberal writer.
He attended conscientiously and spoke just once. His shyness or timidity in personal expression remained extreme.
It has been suggested, though it seems too schematic, that
this was the reverse side or complement to his lack of
timidity with women.

In the Cortes, much respected, vigilantly observant,
he behaved like a humble member of his party, staunch
lobby fodder. Much later, when he had abandoned hope in
monarchical liberalism and become a republican, he had
another term in the Cortes, and in a stately fashion sat
just as silent and obeyed another party whip. He couldn't
face public speaking. As a rule, he wrote out a speech very
carefully, even on a minor literary occasion, and had it
declaimed by someone else. No one had less natural apti-
tude for the public life.

Not that he didn't want public applause. On the contrary, he wanted it rapaciously, the more so as he got older.
He was painfully shy, but we have to remind ourselves
again that he wasn't modest. He traveled all over Europe
to help his books get international fame. A writer helps
that by his personality only if he is a bit of a film star, like
Byron or in our own time Yevtushenko. Galdós didn't
have much success. But he wasn't easily put off, either in
his public ambition or in his creative one. Both were more
organically part of him than in less unassuming men.

His creative ambition had been honorable and also

voracious from the beginning, had led him away from comfortable popular success to relative neglect with *Fortunata y Jacinta,* though that book was gradually making its way. His ambition wasn't going to sleep as he approached his fifties. It was something to have regenerated the Spanish novel. Now it was his job to regenerate the Spanish drama. He felt that he had written the best Spanish novels, and he had better try to write the best plays.

So he wrote plays, twenty-one between the early nineties and 1918, when he finished, the last at the age of seventy-five. He had some enormous successes (that is, by Spanish standards, where runs were not long), and a few total flops. He became the best-known playwright on the Spanish stage. To one of his temperament, first nights meant acute suffering, acute even compared with those of other playwrights anywhere. He sat in the wings, inarticulate, smoking packs of cigarettes, unable to comprehend. To much of the public, in Spain and Spanish America, he was soon more famous as a playwright than as a novelist. Here an Anglo-Saxon commentator is at a disadvantage. The Galdós plays didn't reach our stage, and it isn't possible to guess how they would have struck us at the time, or how they would strike us if they were now put on.

Passages of his novels are intensely dramatic, in the best sense. We know for certain that he was a master of dramatic dialogue—which is quite different from naturalistic dialogue. Adaptations of those novels should have worked on the stage, and we are told that some of his own did so, through the efforts of professional playwrights.

From what we know at second hand of his own original plays, it does appear that they are not of the same

quality as his best novels. Like other realistic novelists turn-
ing to the stage, like Henry James, he may, despite his
strong literary conscience, have taken the form too lightly.
That is, he may have become too mechanical or abstract,
where his novels are rooted in the twists of motive that no
one could foresee; he may have been too linear in the narrative sense, and probably too propagandist. That is the
impression one receives from accounts of his great success,
Electra, which became a kind of national anthem for
liberal Spain. In cool blood, and in a different culture, it
sounds like a crude piece of anticlerical melodrama—vil-
lainous priest, innocent girl sequestered in a convent. People in Spain said that here is our Ibsen. One has to make a
confession of ignorance, but from this distance that is hard
to believe.

Still, the plays swelled his national fame. He had two
other reasons for deciding to conquer the stage. One was
that plays traveled more effectively than novels and perhaps at last he would see his dearest wish come true, which
was acclaim in Paris. It didn't happen, though he did get
acclaim all over Latin America. The second reason was
that plays brought in money.

That did happen. This, however, didn't make him
solvent. From his early fifties onward his finances were
going from bad to worse, and he slid on a decline into
desperate need—owing to circumstances, as embarrassed
biographers delicately wrote after his death, connected with
his intimate life.

The more he earned, he complained bitterly, the more
poverty-stricken he seemed to be. As has been said before,
there is some mystery not yet clarified. How much did he

earn? Certainly much more than Dostoevsky, but he was as incompetent with money and, in his hidden fashion, much more spendthrift. He was writing novels as well as plays, for his passion for creation, as well as his other consuming passion, never flagged. To beat off cascades of debt, he wrote a third series of the *Episodios nacionales,* from which he could count on big returns. Those duly arrived, but they didn't beat off the cascades for long. The consensus view is that these *Episodios* were nothing but potboilers, though nonconformist voices say that they are much better than the first two series, and the work of a mature artist, with the fourth series better still. Among his troubles, his gifts stayed serene. *Realidad* is one of his best novels, and so are works like *Nazarín,* spiritual and dissenting, in his last years.

At the age of sixty, he was in one of those creeping crises in which no one could see the end. He was the most celebrated writer in his country. He was also the moral leader of liberal Spain. For a writer, being enshrined as a moral leader brings its own liabilities. These may have accrued to Galdós as to Tolstoy. They don't conduce to the highest creative art, and they tend to inflate and coarsen the personality. There were signs of that in Galdós. His great works were behind him, although good works were still to come.

But he was affected more by the incessant siege of creditors and dependents. Demands for money pressed on him week after week. The supply got less. Sales declined, not dramatically, but enough to worry an aging writer. The afternoon visits became the one blessed interval, anxiety-free. With his women, whatever he spent on them, he could forget the cares.

Everywhere else, he began to feel persecuted. He believed his publishing partner had been cheating him. That partner was the person who knew most clearly how and where the literary income had oozed itself away. Galdós started litigation. Friends had to be stern with him, and the affair was settled out of court. He was declining into genteel poverty, or, in real terms, concealed from others, something more precarious than that. His judgment was showing dangerous signs of wear.

It may have been out of defiance, or the need to rely on his public fame, that he took a step to the left. He was the moral leader of liberal Spain. The young loved him even more when he announced that he now believed in a republican Spain.

The fates hadn't finished with him. In his mid-sixties he had a minor stroke. Far worse, his eyesight was failing. For a long time, this he concealed, and managed to write most of the novels by hand. At last it was diagnosed that he had cataracts in both eyes. He was told that operations would cure him.

The news of his poverty was spreading among friends and admirers. Probably rumors of its causes were spreading too, though they were kept very quiet. Few persons, not even his clerical enemies, appear to have been censorious about what they heard, though enemies were censorious enough about his politics. There were plenty of people who told each other that something had to be done for Galdós. The grand old man couldn't be allowed to get poorer. He had been a major literary figure so long that he seemed older than he was. To have an indigent patriarch was intolerable.

What about the Nobel Prize? It would be good for

Spain; it would restore his credit (only for a while, skeptical intimates may have muttered, the Nobel Prize being smaller then, even in terms of 1912 money). Literary support was mobilized, from nearly all the writers in Spain. But the conservative opposition wouldn't play. The Catholic press became violent. The Royal Spanish Academy of Language said it would be improper for it to give official backing. Overall, there was national enthusiasm, shared by Galdós himself, less reticent as he grew older and sadder.

He didn't get the Nobel Prize. He was not much known outside his own country. Possibly a greater difficulty was that he was, as modern journalists would call it, a controversial figure in his own country. In comparable circumstances, Tolstoy had not been given the prize. In the gaze of literary history, that looks like the most bizarre negative decision of all. The one about Galdós now seems bizarre enough.

His supporters were not at a loss. Why not initiate a national subscription, to bring in as much as the Nobel, or more? Galdós once more enthusiastically approved. The subscription was promptly floated. The King, Alfonso XIII, started it off with a handsome donation. Alfonso didn't pretend to know much about books, but he behaved chivalrously about Galdós. Whereas Galdós, now infirm, sight going, showed that he was losing his hold on reality. He complained because the King hadn't invited him to the summer palace on the coast, where Galdós himself in less harassed days had himself built a house. It didn't occur to him that the most prominent of republicans wasn't a particularly obvious subject for regal hospitality.

The subscription list opened brightly, and tailed off.

A subscription for almost any writer in any country wouldn't have been a good prospect. In Spain it must have seemed bewildering. Here was Galdós, their most famous writer, whose books many of them had seen around them since childhood, apparently asking for help. It might have struck Americans likewise, fifty years later, if required to give dollars for the support of Ernest Hemingway.

In the end, the government saw to it that Galdós didn't die in poverty. He was given a sinecure appointment, as auxiliary delegate for the Cervantes Tercentenary. This carried a salary large enough to keep Galdós in something like decency. The Tercentenary celebration was canceled, but the salary continued until his death.

Meanwhile he had gone blind, or near enough blind to prevent him from reading or writing. Operations on the cataracts had failed. Eye surgery might have done better sixty years later, but the condition appears not to have been straightforward. For his last seven years he had to exist without his sight. Not many people have lived more through the eye. It was a dark and at times a Lear-like end.

He was driven into himself. Interminable reveries, and, when his stoicism broke down, accusations and demands. He became certain that he had been robbed over the subscription. The organizers had got away with the money. That quarrel became public, and had to be damped down.

Yet he dictated indomitably away. He didn't attempt a novel after blindness struck him, but plays were possible to dictate, and he did four of them and one long dialogue. He also continued indomitably with his second life-long passion and wasn't to be stopped visiting his girls. Blind, he couldn't go alone, and was escorted by a manservant who could keep secrets. They became a familiar sight in the streets of the Barrios Bajos, the tall old man on the arm of his attendant. Galdós was greeted with the love that he had always found among the derelict. The servant had to ask the way to some of Galdós's rendezvous. He was answered with respect and without inquisitive questioning. People of the slums must have known about it long since. They venerated the old man, and they behaved as though to preserve his dignity.

He hadn't changed his ways. His appetite remained. There was just one modification of the familiar routine. Before he was blind, he used to make his visits in the afternoon. Now, for reasons that are not immediately obvious, the timetable was modified and he started off with his servant in the morning.

Back in his own house, he sank into his thoughts. When friends called on him, he was often more talkative and self-absorbed than in the past. As with others in extremity, his personal self, so long controlled, made its way out. Major concerns: his work; his needs—often the trivial insistences of an invalid.

The King, learning that Galdós had been hurt because he was not invited to the palace, invited him now, which was good manners of the heart. Galdós talked of the occasion to all his visitors, repeating himself time after time.

Finally he died of uremia. It wasn't a peaceful death. In the terminal months he was often delirious. He was lucid, though distressed, when his daughter Maria insisted on seeing him. Perhaps it was fitting that the last days should provoke a violent public argument, never resolved. Did he or did he not receive the last sacraments? Did he, the enemy of the Church, finally return to its arms?

His public, his own people, his readers, the poor who knew only his name but loved him were faithful at the end. He had a funeral procession such as no writer had ever had in Spain, perhaps twenty thousand following it, as Russians did for Dostoevsky and Parisians for Hugo, the three great public demonstrations of grief for literary deaths. We are always overconfident about the retrospective satisfactions of the dead, but one can't help thinking that that would have pleased Galdós more than most kinds of praise.

HENRY JAMES

IT is difficult in the records to discover anyone who knew Henry James and didn't like him. He was the most decorous and responsible of great writers. He was polite beyond the limits of politeness, and he was also very kind. As he became eminent, and had set himself up as the great master of the theory of fiction, he was sent floods of manuscripts by fellow novelists. He read them all, and wrote letters of immense length and labyrinthine praise trying to find something good in them; though, as he couldn't help being true to his own view of art, he usually had to include, concealed under the ambiguities of his prose, a line or two of doubt. He had natural authority, and in England attracted more respect from his contemporaries than any other writer then or since.

He was the literary pundit of his time. Certainly some people, listening to him, had to suppress a grin. There was a trace of absurdity as he struggled, like a computer gone wrong, to find the exact, the perfect word; which, after minutes of strain, finally emerged. Surprisingly often, he was at last satisfied that it was the perfect word, but it didn't produce the right effect.

In the midst of this veneration, the more perceptive of his friends (none really close, which carries its own message) must have realized that he hadn't had much happiness. In the external sense, he didn't have an eventful life, not much more so than Jane Austen's, except that he had been a dedicated professional writer from his early twenties, and taken all the disappointments and occasional victories of the writing life. In many ways, he had lived rather like a bachelor don of his own period, granted that the don was as devoted to scholarship as Henry James was to literature—not too strenuous travel, almost entirely in France and Italy, taste well informed but not original in architecture and pictures, dining out in London, visits to country houses, and as he grew older romantic friendships with young men. This last point shouldn't be dismissed in late-twentieth-century terms, and will be considered later.

None of that was enough. He hadn't touched the simple or the supreme joys—above all, not the simple and supreme joys when they might fuse together. He hadn't even had the literary rewards he had worked for so obsessively. Yes, there had been, and remained, devoted acclaim in the world of letters. He had more of that than Dickens ever had, or Dostoevsky. He didn't doubt that he had written splendid novels. He had his own brand of egotism, and didn't doubt, either, that all he had pronounced about novel writing was absolutely and finally right. But he had wanted, with unusual intensity, the most complete and spectacular of popular success. He hadn't compromised or made concessions in his search for writing novels that satisfied his artistic conscience. But he had compromised— more than writers of less exalted principles would have done—in his pathetic attempts to write plays. That had failed, in the most painful experience of his career.

The popular success hadn't come. His friends had achieved it—when he was young, Turgenev, later Paul Bourget; then as he grew older, H. G. Wells, Edith Wharton. He envied them, and all who had won a great public and much money. In reality he had done pretty well. He had earned not only the highest of reputations, but also a comfortable living. For a novelist who presented considerable difficulties, his income had been substantial. That didn't placate him. His expectations were not fulfilled. He was a good and strong-natured man, and he bore stoically all that happened to him, but in his last years there was a dark tinge of disappointment.

It has often been thought that Henry James came from old English stock in New England, and always had large private means. Neither statement is true. As for private means, he had none of his own until he was nearly fifty, when he came into about £300 a year. Three hundred pounds a year meant more at the end of the nineteenth century than it would now, but it wasn't wealth. It was the income of Trollope's Mrs. Dale, living modestly as a widow at Allington. Henry could have had this money ten years earlier, but with the maximum of generosity and brotherly feeling, of both of which he had more than his share, he insisted on the money going to his invalid sister Alice so long as she lived.

From his early twenties, he existed on what he earned by writing. He often did hack work that nowadays a writer as serious as he was wouldn't look at. He worked excessively hard, at reviews, articles, letter pieces to American papers, a commissioned biography of a rich man he thought nothing of, ephemeral stories, as well as the fiction by which we know him. It is true that until his father died, when Henry was thirty-nine, he could draw minor sums from family funds. He did this little, but it meant that there was a support behind him. Not that the Jameses were really rich, though Henry's father, after his own father's death, had announced, in his expansive Irish fashion, that he was "leisured for life."

The Jameses were all Irish, or more precisely, what Americans call Scotch-Irish. That is, they were descended from Scottish settlers, who in the case of the Jameses hadn't stayed in Ulster but had moved south. They were Presbyterian Calvinists, and Henry's grandfather, the founder of the family in America, a stern and inflexible one. He had emigrated to America in the late eighteenth century, soon settled in Albany, and made a fortune in land dealing in upper New York State. It was a large fortune for the period, but there were thirteen children, so Henry James's father, also called Henry, was ultimately equipped with about $10,000 a year. We have to remember that there were then five dollars to the English pound. Even £2,000 a year was enough to keep Henry senior leisured for life, and he did not find it necessary to earn a penny.

Not that he was idle. He, like his son, wrote away all his life, with considerable eloquence but not much avail. He talked with even more eloquence. He seems to have been a most endearing man, and very Irish. The accents that Henry James heard in his childhood must have been largely Irish, though he obliterated any trace of any such accent himself. Not only in that way, it would be hard to imagine a man who, to an outsider, appeared less Irish. He went to Ireland once or twice and detested it.

He had a vehemently loving family life. His brother William was only a year and a half older than he was. He was to become as famous a philosopher-psychologist as Henry was a novelist. In childhood he was aggressive, dominant, dominating, willful, and Henry was the retiring and best-loved son. Thanks to the father's eccentricities and his passion for ideas, their childhood, however loving, was scarcely restful. They were constantly on the move.

The notions of Henry James senior were expansive and benevolent. He was resolved that his children shouldn't suffer from the bleak religion that had made his own childhood somber. He discovered, or invented, a kind of universal faith for them all, and for the human race, and for everyone's social betterment, derived from Swedenborg, but lighter-spirited and entirely optimistic. He wrote many books about his credo, but didn't find anyone to listen. That didn't distress him overmuch. He applied himself to his children's education.

He went on the move. Many changes of houses— Washington Place (near Washington Square)—14th Street, at that time uptown New York—Newport, Rhode Island. He became seized by the virtues of a European education, hence sojourns in Geneva, Paris, London. Since it was always greener on the other side of the hill, his thoughts reverted to the beauties of American schooling, its pure democracy. So back to Newport. A year of that, and once again he saw very clearly that European rigor was the proper form of education. Henry at sixteen was dispatched to a training school for engineers. He was a clever boy, but remarkably unadapted for applied science. That was the least successful of his father's bright ideas.

On that procession of travels, both he and brother William managed to accumulate a good, if unorganized, education. Father Henry took much care about their languages. There were French-speaking governesses and French schools. William became proficient also in German. Henry, who was a fine natural linguist, as well as being well trained, from his youth onward spoke French about as well as a foreigner can. The only oddity, according to his French literary friends, was a curious hesitation, not quite a stammer. Alphonse Daudet passed him one of the most handsome of all linguistic tributes: "If he can handle his own language as well as he does ours, he is the hell of a fellow."

As boys, the young Jameses lived in Paris of the Second Empire and London at the high hour—short-lived but real—of British prosperity, power, and confidence. The boys imbibed a good deal, as it were out of the air. That peculiar dromophilic education helped to give Henry the nature of his art. On the whole, their father's good intentions, often dotty, turned out well. But there was a price.

They hadn't a place to stand, or more exactly, anywhere in which they were instinctively at home. They didn't belong, not quite, to old New York, unlike the friend of Henry's later life, Edith Wharton. They were brought up, eccentrically, as gentlemen, but they weren't as socially elevated as she was—and nothing like as rich. It might have been difficult (an Englishman so long afterward can't begin to have an opinion) for an Irish family to reach the inner circle of that odd and closed society, even if Henry James senior had wanted to. But that was about the last thing he wanted, as he expounded on the glorious community of all men. He was friendly with Emerson and his circle, and in England with the high literary figures. That was the kind of company he liked. He didn't have any of the interest in fine-structure gradations of society that his son was, for a period, to revel in.

They could go, and did go, everywhere and didn't belong integrally anywhere. That is a splendid starting point for a detached observer, or for the kind of novelist that Henry became. He made the most of it. But it is probably one of the worst of starting points for a contented domestic life. It makes intimate relations, marriage or any other, harder to settle into, except for people in whom the sexual tide is running high. In Henry, where the tide was probably pretty low, and who anyway had profound constraints and inhibitions embedded deep, it weakened any desire he may have had for the direct intimacies and gave him an excuse for evading them. It may have contributed to the lack of fundamental instinct that is the single great weakness of his art.

He was a remarkably unobtrusive young man. He was short, like most of his family, and stockily built. In the photographs his face appears delicately handsome, startlingly different from the Mussolini-like visage of his middle age. Probably his looks as a youth were not striking enough to attract the glances of many women, but he was presentable enough, with acute, penetrating light gray eyes. With those eyes he watched everything, the most attentive of spectators. He was extremely silent. All his life, he remained the most attentive of spectators, but not so silent.

When the Civil War started, he was eighteen. He and

William couldn't make up their minds what to do. Upper-class young men in the North appear not to have gone to war with the enthusiasm of their Southern counterparts. The two younger James brothers, when they were old enough, did become soldiers and distinguished themselves. William and Henry were not assisted by an utterance from their father, who wrote to a friend: "I tell them that no young American should put himself in the way of death, until he has realized something of the good in life" (that is, until he had married and had a child).

There isn't much doubt that Henry was ashamed of holding back. The problem was solved in a manner that has provoked more crass comments than anything else in his life. He was called on to give a hand in fighting a fire at Newport. It wasn't a particularly grand fire—not like that in which his father, by a bizarre coincidence, had lost a leg at the age of fourteen. Henry called this Newport one a "shabby conflagration" (when he is writing in that idiom he is always uneasy). That night, no one noticed that, in the shabby conflagration, Henry damaged himself. He was well enough to travel to Boston within three days. Some months later he went to be examined by a leading surgeon. In his own account, which is evasive even by his own high standard, he gives no dates, though they are now established. "At the same dark hour"—it was actually October 1861—"I suffered a horrid even if an obscure hurt." He wraps up the incident in a gauze of words. "To have trumped up a lameness at such a juncture"—in the war—"could be made to pass in no light for graceful."

Henry often lacked introspective candor, or even introspective insight. He was much more perceptive about other people than himself. That passage was written in old age. No good writer could write so deplorably, or obfuscate so clumsily, unless he had something to cover up. American critics have leaped enthusiastically to the conclusion that Henry's accident had castrated him. Those solemn judgments were published before all the facts had been established; but, even so, only people, highly intelligent people, so bemused by psychoanalytical thinking that they had lost contact with physical reality could have thought anything so foolish. It would be something of a feat to castrate oneself working a pumping machine. It would be even more of a feat to act manfully for a matter of months as though nothing had happened. Finally, instead of the surgeon being baffled, as he was about Henry's condition, and as his brother William (who had been trained as a doctor) was in later life, the diagnosis of castration would really not have been all that difficult to reach.

It is now fairly certain that Henry had contracted a back injury, possibly what we might now call a slipped disk and his own time would have thought of as chronic lumbago. Very unpleasant, and sometimes agonizing: but also a psychosomatic condition that could relieve one of moral problems about getting into uniform (he is likely to have become quite unfit to soldier) and perhaps, later in life, about testing his virility.

Obscurely emancipated by the obscure hurt, Henry went to Harvard. As usual in the nineteenth century, it was difficult to decide what a young man of literary interests and talent should study. As usual in the nineteenth century (compare Balzac, Tolstoy, Galdós, and, a generation after Henry James, Proust), there was just one conclusion: law. Like all the others, Henry escaped. He endured one year in the Harvard Law School, did not distinguish himself either positively or negatively, and at twenty-one took steps, remarkably undiffident steps, toward becoming a professional writer.

More than with any other major novelist, except maybe Galdós, the rest of his life consisted of being a professional writer, and nothing else. He found those first steps surprisingly easy, and in fact lived on his literary earnings early on. Living was, of course, cheap in the nineteenth century. In spite of all his cries of poverty, which in his old age drove Edith Wharton to charitable efforts on his behalf, his work brought in a steady income from his twenties until he died—not a tenth of what accrued to Edith Wharton herself, or friends such as H. G. Wells, Bourget, Howells; but a good deal more than if he had been an academic of international reputation such as his brother William. Henry walked into a literary scene, without realizing how lucky he was. Most of his living for a number of years came from high-level literary journalism, and he wouldn't have found it anything like so easy in London. The New England cultural climate was made for him, though he wasn't especially grateful to it. Men like James Russell Lowell and Charles Eliot Norton looked after him. There was a market for his finespun criticisms in the *Atlantic Monthly* and the *North American Review.* William Dean Howells went onto the staff of the *Atlantic Monthly,* and that meant a friend and supporter who was eager for Henry's stories as well as his articles. Godkin of the newly established *Nation* gave him commissions for journalistic pieces—no one could regard Henry as a journalist with a popular flair, and in England it would have been hard to find a paper prepared to be so patient.

The Boston culture of Lowell and Norton was a high one, though too ethereal for its own good. It is hard to think that in the 1860s any other cultural group in the world would have encouraged an entirely unknown young man to start his career with a very long, pontifical, intricately worked-out essay on the Art of Fiction. Henry had conceived most of his theory of fiction before he wrote fiction himself. He was also a fine practical critic, better in those early days than when he had become hypnotized by his own theory. Like all writers who expound a critical theory, he was, of course, staking a claim for his own work.

But he had a generous spirit, and his capacity to admire spread much wider than his theory. He could say as a young man that Dickens was "the greatest of the superficial novelists," which was a judgment strictly in line with the theory, and not sensible. It was also not sensible to remark that the novels of Tolstoy and Dostoevsky were loose, baggy monsters, which meant that he didn't understand their art at all. At the same time, he could believe, and did so all his life, that Balzac was the greatest of all novelists. Whatever the arguments about that judgment, there isn't any doubt that, of great novelists, Balzac is about the last to be fitted inside the Jamesian confines. Yet, as an old man, Henry stumped around America, saying how wonderful Balzac was. There was something very handsome about Henry James.

Did he ever wonder what his hero Balzac would have written about, if set down in his (Henry's) environment? He shouldn't have wondered long. Balzac would have rev-

eled in the America of the 1860s and 1870s, from cultivated Boston, the New York slums, out to the frontier. It
would have been a marvelous prospect for a novelist of
Balzac's passion and indelicacy. It wasn't a marvelous prospect for Henry.

He seems to have known that his chosen field would
be the interactions of Americans—that is, Americans of
his own kind and class—with Europeans. In his mind this
was already the meeting of innocence and experience. It
was a field that his childhood travels had prepared him for,
but the choice came from deeper in his nature. The innocence of the Americans was a romantic conception; he
might have taken a glance at his friend Fullerton, who was
about as innocent as Maupassant. Henry wasn't really innocent himself, though he could transform the disquiets
of his own temperament and make them appear like a form
of innocence. He could observe Americans who were genuinely innocent, such as his cousin Minnie Temple, who was
the original of Isabel Archer. Henry was half in love with
her, but when she died in her early twenties he was re-
lieved. He rationalized that relief into the thought that
women, and love, were destructive of art. That was a
classical statement of extreme sexual timidity.

Not that he had too bad a time as a young man. It was
only later that he came to a dark, and even then half-
hidden, realization of what he had missed or starved himself of. Up to well into middle age, it didn't seem like
that. He became an expatriate, which suited him well. He
had plenty of sedate, donnish satisfactions. Railways were
spreading over Europe, travel was becoming comfortable.
On his journeys, Henry's chief affliction was a tendency to

constipation, which, with a bachelor's hypochondriac ner-
vousness he regarded with a gravity more suitable for terminal cancer.

When he was in his mid-thirties, he made London his
base. It was there that for a few years his period of high
expectations appeared to come true, and England became
his permanent home. On the way, he had tried Italy, which
he didn't cease loving. He even tried New York, to explore
whether he could fulfill himself as a writer there; the answer was no, and he didn't attempt to write in his native
country again. He spent a whole year and more in Paris,
but didn't achieve the social *entrées* that, a little later, he
found waiting for him in London. Henry was as anxious
to reach high French society as the young Proust twenty
years after; but Henry didn't have the advantages of the
young Proust, French society was more closed than English,
and an American, even an American with good connections, presence, manners, and admirable French, couldn't
get far.

He did get accepted into literary circles, but he didn't
like them much. He decided that many of the Paris nota-
bilities were blinkered and second-rate. He wasn't altogether wrong. One also has the impression that he found
their talk too coarse for him—neither aesthetic nor intellectual enough, just repetitively ruttish. His only genuine
admirations were for Flaubert and, above all, Turgenev.
Turgenev became one of his idols, and he learned a lot from
him, both in person and in art. Their feelings about novel
writing were similar, though Turgenev was more flexible
and didn't become so theory-bound. In tone, and ultimately in stature, Henry's novels can stand beside Tur-

genev's, as they cannot, in spite of his attempts at critical
demotion, beside those of Dostoevsky and Tolstoy.

In Italy he didn't know many Italian writers, but he
had a much better time. Rich Americans had, before the
middle of the nineteenth century, decided that this was the
most agreeable country to live in. Even people just comfortably off, like the English colony in Florence, the Brown-
ings and the Tom Trollopes, could live in some sort of
state. One could maintain a palazzo in Rome or Venice on
less than $1,000 (£200 to £300 in 1870 English money) a
year. So Henry could perform a dignified circuit, Rome,
Florence, Venice, the last his favorite spot on earth, being
entertained by American acquaintances.

Many of these were cultivated. Some were searching
romantically for European civilization. A few, with talent
or without, were hoping to become painters or sculptors.
One or two, such as the grandiose Isabella Gardner, were
buying stacks of Italian pictures and taking them back to
America. As one can now see in Cambridge, Massachusetts,
Isabella Gardner had excellent taste. And so did many of
the others. Henry himself had, as is obvious in his novels,
a fine eye for the visual arts, though not an enterprising
one. He never understood the Impressionists, or any painters who came after them; but what he knew, he knew with
exactness. He had the same eye for architecture and the
Italian landscape, and he knew more history than most
Italophiles. The 1870s were good years for a cultured amateur on gentlemanly grand tours, and Henry made the
most of them.

It was not only Henry's comfort that was helped by
the network of privileged Americans, but also his social

triumphs. He had a high and proper literary ambition; that was the only ambition inseparable from his nature, part of him. But as a man in his thirties he also felt that it was worthy of respect to aim at a position in society. In this he was, as we shall see, something like the young Proust, and there are some coincidences between their lives. Henry was much less shamelessly snobbish than Proust at the beginning of their climbs; and, though they both got bored with the game after a few years, Henry was accordingly less harshly disillusioned at the end.

Henry always had a tincture of detached radicalism. Still, there is no doubt that in the years leading up to the writing of one of his finest novels (to some of us the finest without qualification) he wanted to carve out a place among "the better sort of people." He achieved this simple ambition very quickly, with much more ease and completeness than he achieved any literary ambition (which might have led him, though it doesn't seem to have done so, into some ironic reflections). For his social conquests, he had many advantages. He had a growing literary reputation, which in the late nineteenth century counted for something. He was, as Trollope would have said, a gentleman. He was an accomplished talker by now, and, in his elaborate way, very witty. He was polite, considerate, and exceptionally good with elderly women. He was a bachelor, which made him useful for dinner parties. He wasn't assertive but he had subdued authority, and no one ever thought him negligible. But it helped more than may appear that he had powerful American patrons who, particularly in London, were already popular and respected.

The Lowells and the Nortons could go anywhere. The

New England upper class were welcome in London, regarded as insiders, and liked. Much more, if one can judge
from memoirs, than the other way around. Boston and
Cambridge cultivated circles don't seem to have liked their
English opposite numbers very much. They thought that
Dickens was a bounder and Trollope ill-bred (that judgment would have infuriated Trollope, whose origins were
more than respectable). Nearly all the Adamses seem in
private to have had little use for the Englishmen they met.

Introductions from Henry's New England grandees
worked like a charm. When he settled in London—taking
rooms in the Victorian manner, as bachelors such as Holmes
and Watson did, in Henry's case in Bolton Street, just off
Piccadilly—he was within a dazzlingly short time dining
out night after night. He wrote each morning; no more
conscientious a professional has lived the career of letters.
Evenings were free for social engagements. In one London
season, a year or two after his arrival, he dined out 140
times—that is, about three nights in four.

Men took him to clubs. Hostesses had him, of course,
at their London homes. He went for long Victorian visits
to country houses. His closest contacts were with people
like himself, the Victorian intellectual eminences—Leslie
Stephen and his circle, George Eliot, T. H. Huxley, Tennyson, Browning (both of those last two disappointed him)—
but he made acquaintances in the smartest of society. He
didn't know the English aristocracy as intimately as Proust
was to know the Faubourg Saint-Germain. The magnates
who took him up tended to be a shade offbeat—Lord Rose-
bery, Lord Houghton (once Richard Monckton Milnes, and
not entirely reputable), Charles Dilke. Nevertheless, Henry

studied at first hand most strata of upper-class England, from landowning gentry to professional writers and academics. For some years, when he was between thirty-three and thirty-eight, he enjoyed himself, and it may have been the happiest period of his life.

He had one objective reason. For the first time, he had written something like a popular success. Perversely, he was not to have a success on this scale again. The novel was *Daisy Miller*. It is fresh and lively, but nothing like so considered or mentally scrupulous as his best work. The name-heroine is a bright American girl, positive, active, certain that her behavior is above reproach, forthcoming, flirtatious, who gets misunderstood in Europe. She is the most innocent of all the Jamesian innocents. She is contrasted to Europeans of her own age. She has an almost incredibly innocent love affair in Rome with a virtuous young Italian. They walk about the gardens at night, and suspicious persons assume that they have been sleeping together.

Henry had stirred a nerve. He was acclaimed for having brought into fashion the "American girl," almost for having created her. Daisy Miller became a catchword, and Daisy Miller couturier articles were sold in New York shops. In fact, like a good many originators, Henry was not the first in the field. Trollope, with much more subtlety and insight, had introduced an American girl into *The Duke's Children*. Isabel Boncassen is as positive and outgoing as Daisy Miller, and she, too, is contrasted to her English contemporaries. But in Trollope both the American and the English girls around her have feet considerably nearer the ground than Daisy's. They do know the facts of life; and Trollope, who loved young women, wrote of them with the affection of one who didn't expect them to be disembodied. Isabel Boncassen is the first lifelike American woman in novels in English. Her father is the first authoritative American male character produced by an Englishman. It is probable that Henry had read *The Duke's Children* and had learned something from it. He didn't imitate, but as the most attentive of readers he assimilated. This, of course, good writers have always done, with complete propriety.

He relished the *réclame,* even the noise—there were some reproaches in America for his having abused American womanhood—that *Daisy Miller* brought him. It didn't bring him much money. That was because Henry's publishing arrangements were similar to those that have been described for his Russian contemporaries. His first sale was usually as a serial to a magazine. If he could arrange simultaneous publication in American and English magazines, he might collect payments in all of just over £1,000, on which he could live very nicely for a year in his London apartment, and afford to travel.

With *Daisy Miller* there was a slip, which meant no American serial. Instead there was a pirated paperback edition that sold, inordinately for Henry, either then or later, in many thousands. The sale of any of his novels in hardback editions, after they had been serialized, was very small. Not bearing much malice, since he was jubilant about his success, he told his brother William that his total earnings from *Daisy Miller* in America were less than $200.

He didn't make the same mistake with what he began to call his "big novel." When he found the title, it was *The Portrait of a Lady.* He was riding high. The short book

Washington Square had been well received. After that, and *Daisy Miller,* he could bargain for good terms for the big novel. The *Atlantic Monthly* was to run it as a serial. He could count on realizing more than he had ever made from a novel. He began to write *The Portrait of a Lady* in Florence in 1880. He was totally confident from the start. This was the confidence that comes to most writers only once or twice in a lifetime, just as it came to Dostoevsky only as he brooded on *The Brothers Karamazov.* Henry was to know plenty of intellectual and technical confidence later on, but this was the confidence of the fingertips. The book was certain to be all right.

He had all the justification in the world for being confident. People can and do disagree about other works of Henry James; this novel is, however, recognized as one of the best ever written in English. Under the surface, and perhaps more than he knew, it tells a good deal about Henry himself. Half-hidden, some of the psychological climate is singular but, then, he was a singular man.

Standing by itself as an independent work of art, the novel is immaculate. Though it is a long book, with a fair amount of the dramatic invention that often breaks through the Jamesian surface, the story is essentially simple. The "Lady" herself, Isabel Archer, is the apotheosis of Henry's American girl. She is highly intelligent, strong-willed, idealistic, determined to have her freedom and be herself, though she has no conception what such liberation means. She is attractive to men. She responds to the men who are attracted, but in a fashion that gives a curious and a somewhat disquieting impression. She is innocent all right, which is natural enough when she comes to England from upstate New York, Puritanism and all, at the age of twenty-two. But she is innocent in a much deeper sense than the heroines in English nineteenth-century novels, though those girls (compare Lucy Robarts, Dorothea Casaubon) have known just as little emancipation, or less. She is inhibited to the edge of sexlessness, which the English girls are not. For this Henry may have had objective justification: Minnie Temple, who was his original, came from that same New England culture. But that aspect of Isabel gives an oddity to a book that hangs on her choice of a husband.

Isabel, who at this stage has no money at all, comes to England to visit some rich American relatives. The setting is beautifully done, like all the settings in the book. Henry was at the peak of his gift in the external arts of a novelist, as with the projection of his people. Her uncle-in-law, who has made a big fortune and who is now dying, has acquired a house something like Cliveden. He comes to love Isabel. So does his son Ralph, who is tubercular; otherwise he would have tried to marry her, which would have been her best chance, for he is cleverer than she is, cares for her, and has the insight to understand her. Other suitors appear: a straightforward, simple, dominant American whose masculinity puts Isabel off, and an agreeable English peer, whose life, she feels, would absorb hers.

Her uncle-in-law dies, having been persuaded by Ralph to divide his own inheritance in two and give half to Isabel—Ralph rationalizes his motive and says that he wants to see her given liberty, so that he can watch what happens to her. In the book, this legacy is said to make Isabel a rich woman. The period of the book is the 1870s, and the actual amount is between £60,000 and £70,000.

She is certainly regarded as a prize by fortune hunters. She goes to Italy, and there is captivated by one. He is an American expatriate, corrupted by Europe in the Jamesian style, an aesthete who has done nothing except cultivate his sensibility. Isabel wants to do something perfect with her freedom. In this, she is a personification of Henry James himself; but, then, he had the luck to discover his salvation, and also to achieve material freedom, through his art. She has no such expression. The best she can do is to marry this man, and make his life.

It is a wretched marriage, of which the rest of the book is a bitter and brilliant description. He comes to hate her. Her own delight in his delicate cultivation fades, and she comes to hate him back. He is determined to break her psychologically, but she is too strong for that. In a chapter that Henry himself thought the best thing in the book, she sits late at night in the great drawing room of the Roman palace she has bought for him, and thinks about why she made her choice and where it has brought her.

> That he was poor and lonely and yet that somehow he was noble—that was what had interested her and seemed to give her opportunity. . . . But for her money, as she saw to-day, she would never have done it. . . . At bottom her money had been a burden, had been on her mind which was filled with the desire to transfer the weight of it to some other conscience, to some more prepared receptacle. What would lighten her own conscience more effectively than to make it over to the man with the best taste in the

> She could live it over again, the incredulous terror with which she had taken the measure of her dwelling. Between those four walls she had lived ever since; they were to surround her for the rest of her life. It was the house of dark-

ness, the house of dumbness, the house of suffocation. . . .
Of course it had not been physical suffering; for physical
suffering there might have been a remedy. She could come
and go; she had her liberty; her husband was perfectly
polite. He took himself so seriously; it was something appalling. Underneath all his culture, his cleverness, his ame-
nity, under his good nature, his facility, his knowledge of
life, his egoism lay hidden like a serpent in a bank of flowers.

It is a sad scene, for though Isabel herself has the egoism of an aspiring opinionated girl, she is fundamentally
generous and bright. The whole chapter—the preceding is
only a short extract—does suggest a young woman with
extraordinarily little instinct for men, and one who even
now hasn't learned much. As a matter of fact, one need
not share Henry's own high opinion of the chapter. It
doesn't suggest introspective brooding very well, and is
much more heavily written than most of the rest of the
novel. What it does suggest is the closeness of the author's
identification and perhaps his as yet unrealized discontent.

For anyone who does not know the book, that quotation is not representative. Most of the novel is brilliantly
written, more brilliantly than any of his future books
(some short stories and one or two essays approach it). In a
fashion slightly stylized but admirably effective, the dialogue is often witty. When he was not overcome by the
need to lucubrate, Henry could be both brisk and sharply
funny, and in this novel he is both. Most of all, Isabel
Archer may lack instinct, may seem to us, a hundred years
later, without an elementary sense of life; but the curious
thing is, we know that there are still girls like her and that
she remains wonderfully alive.

Not long after the publication of *The Portrait of a*

Lady as a book, Henry's mother and father died in quick succession. By another coincidence with Proust's life, this happened to Proust twenty years later; but, though these deaths were griefs to Henry, it meant nothing like the prostration that Proust sank into when his mother died. The main consequences for Henry were that he took responsibility for his sister, invalid and at times mentally unstable, and that he could now settle in England for good.

His life in his forties seemed a model of artistic success. It seemed so to his literary colleagues. He had had great critical success with *The Portrait of a Lady*. He was adequately prosperous, and had now moved into a handsome bachelor apartment, with a suitable Jamesian vista of Kensington Gardens. Often he must have felt, and from the documentary evidence did feel, that he was getting what he had worked for. And yet, within himself, he was inexplicably restless.

There were some simple reasons for restlessness. The prosperity—he had a professional's anxiety—was fragile. His American publisher went bankrupt, and he lost most of a year's earnings. More serious, his novels in the eighties weren't received as *The Portrait of a Lady* had been. *The Bostonians, The Princess Casamassima, The Tragic Muse* had the virtues of his gift, but didn't strike his admirers as utterly right. Nor were they. He wasn't the most adroit of theoreticians for nothing, and he could put up elaborate defenses, but he may have known that there was something faulty at their roots.

He certainly did know two brutish practical things. The magazines weren't pressing for him quite so eagerly (to an extent, with articles and short stories, he was flooding his market). Much harder to brush off, his sales in book form weren't even earning the tiny advances that his English and American publishers were giving. The advances they offered began to get displeasingly smaller. He had not won a public; and not only for money and security, but also for sheer response, a public would have been a consolation to him in those years. For, apparently without examining his own nature, he was suffering from something more than professional misgivings. There was developing a deep disquiet. It hadn't yet crystallized in the Stendhalian sense. In the Stendhalian sense, there can be a crystallization of disquiet and discontent as definite as the crystallizations of love. Very slowly, almost imperceptibly, this seems to have been happening to Henry.

It might have been detected by quite small signs. He was shaken by meeting and reading Maupassant. That hard and explicit sexuality couldn't be the way to understand people, Henry reflected on paper. It was the enemy of all other psychological explanation. There may have been an instant of doubt, when Henry suspected that some reading his own work might turn that thought the other way around. No one can be sure. What is established is that Henry was walking, half blindly, into a tenuous relation with a woman. Nothing happened. It would have been better if it had, for through his negligence the woman suffered great harm.

Her story is pathetic. She was a very nice, lonely, intelligent American woman, a little older than he was, and of his own kind of upbringing. Her name was Fenimore Woolson, and she was a family connection of Fenimore Cooper. She had made a considerable popular success in

America out of writing regional novels, a much more popular success than Henry had achieved. She devotedly admired Henry's work. She contrived to meet him. She
promptly fell in love with him. Henry had much charm
for women. He was sensitive, authoritative, vaguely mysterious, and had all the appearance of gentle masculinity.
He took her around Florence and Venice and showed her
the sights. As it were absentmindedly, and perhaps care-
lessly, he gave her some encouragement. Not physical encouragement, that is certain. But he had a wooing tongue.
He performed a series of withdrawals and returns. After
an interval of six months, he would discover her in Italy
once more, and pay what she thought of as attentions.

She wrote him adoring letters. It is likely that he
wrote letters back, no doubt ambiguous but—there has to
be a suspicion—warm enough to give her hope. It is not for
anyone outside the situation to blame him; he, too, was
starved of affection. He was obtuse and, if you like, egocentric not to realize that to her he was the one home for
her emotions. She existed for their meetings, which did not
happen often, over a stretch of years. At last, alone in
Venice one winter, she threw herself out of a window.

We had better think for a moment of Henry's sexual
temperament. It is now the conventional wisdom to regard
him as a homosexual in the Proustian mode. That, like a
great many attempts at putting people into categories, is
almost certainly too simple. As we shall see, Proust probably was a genuine homosexual. He also was not at all
timid about sex, very likely not timid with women, and
quite surely not with men. Henry was abnormally timid
about it, so timid that it wouldn't be unreasonable to

guess that he never tried. Instead of thinking of him as a homosexual, we may be nearer the truth to change the term. He was more like a crippled, profoundly inhibited, frustrated male.

In nineteenth-century celibate societies, among schoolmasters, academics, clergymen, there were a good many such, and one can find a few today. There has been a thoughtful analysis by one of the more percipient psychologists, Edgar Friedenberg. It is possible to make qualifications, and give examples—there are plenty—where such frustrated males have broken out and, to their own astonishment, have attained highly satisfied sexual lives. But this analysis of Friedenberg's does describe what happened to Henry in later life, and he is actually cited as a specimen. The description is:

> There are men who have great anxiety about heterosexual relations and therefore retain the erotic attitudes of preadolescence. They see young adolescent boys taking the next step of development which they were unable to take, and identify with them. The feeling of a man of this sort towards boys is tender, and often overprotective, since he is by definition over-anxious. . . . [His eroticism] initially has no specific object—he loves boys generally because it is a way of loving the "boyishness" in himself, and is also a way, by identifying, of reminding himself of the time when he was last sexually "happy." He is not exactly adolescent all his life, but he is caught, sexually, by the predicament of early adolescence and escapes by loving the young man he might have become. He is often a very good teacher . . . because he is intensely subjective, he is very good at close analysis of his own condition, hence he is frequently an artist.

It is here that Henry James is given as an example.

As a general rule, that kind of diagnosis needs inspecting with a hard empirical eye. But this one is pretty near what we know of Henry's relations with young men (not boys) as he grew older, and perhaps tells us something of those features of his art that, unlike anything else by the major novelists, appear to come from nowhere except a region in himself that he didn't understand—as in *The Turn of the Screw*.

It may have taken him a long time to cope with, or even to accept, that he was cut off from primary satisfactions that in most men come easily. Nevertheless, some of that disquiet mingled with his practical worries as he got nearer fifty. That was part, perhaps not yet the darkest part, of the crystallization of discontent. It helped him make the most mistaken literary decision of his life, and the one that brought him most misery. He made up his mind to solve his problems by writing plays.

He saw people all around him getting fame, money, excitement out of plays. His novels hadn't found an audience. He would try plays. Not one, but several, so as to give them a fair chance. He knew that his novels showed a natural dramatic sense. The scenes worked. He had hopes, more than hopes, that he could take the theater.

He soon discovered that the theater presented certain difficulties. Managers encouraged him, but there were inexplicable delays. When he wrote a novel, it got into print within a couple of months (much faster than in the late twentieth century). No one interfered or wanted to alter the script. Not so with the stage. Plays seemed to be accepted, or at least welcomed, and then hung about for years. Managers had views. Actors had views. Words didn't seem to have their normal meaning. He was told a play was wonderful. He discovered that that didn't mean it was going to be put on. Henry, who expected a writer to be treated with respect, and such a writer as himself with more than respect, didn't like all this. How could the theater be a form of art?

One actor-manager took much trouble with him. This was Edward Compton, whose son later adopted the name of Compton Mackenzie. Mackenzie didn't take much enticement to give imitations of Henry James, thus spanning a couple of generations. Edward Compton paid Henry to adapt *The Traveller* (an interesting novel if one doesn't read it in the New York Edition) for the stage. Compton cut it about, much to Henry's bewilderment, acted the main part in the provinces, took it into London, where it didn't make money, but wasn't a total flop. Other plays were less successful. One somehow became discreetly forgotten by an eminent actor-manager. The American impresario Daly had contracted for another, announced it for his new theater in London, got more depressed the more often he looked at it, and finally arranged a reading, not a rehearsal, in the hope of persuading Henry to withdraw it.

With immense bitterness, suspicious, feeling afraid, Henry did so. But he had implicit faith in yet another play, *Guy Domville*. This was based on an anecdote from Venetian history, in which a young nobleman had to leave his religious vocation because all the males in his family had died in an epidemic. He was ordered to leave his monastery, marry, and continue the line. Henry transferred the setting to the eighteenth century, made the hero a young English aristocrat being educated in France and dedicated to becoming a Benedictine monk. Henry was happy about his creation. So was George Alexander, the most successful of the young actor-managers in the great age of that breed. Alexander saw the hero Guy Domville as a dazzling costume part for himself. Like Compton, while Henry sat uneasily by, he got to work on the play, shortened it, tightened it. It has to be said that he probably improved it. He opened with it at his fine theater, the St. James's, on January 5, 1895. That became one of the most memorable nights in theatrical history.

Henry couldn't bear to attend. For five years he had been set on conquering the stage. This was his chance. A great star in the lead, a beautiful theater. His own name was a major draw to cultured London. In fact, the stalls were packed with his friends, admirers, supporters. Himself, he went, to wear away the minutes of anxiety not to see it, to Oscar Wilde's new play—which was *A Woman of No Importance* at the Haymarket, a few hundred yards away. So far as he could watch the play at all, he thought it worthless. How could his own wonderful work survive?

He had to go along to the St. James's to hear. From the wings he could see Alexander taking a curtain call. Applause, cheers from the stalls, from his following and Henry's. Boos from the gallery. Everyone backstage seems to have been too distressed to tell Henry anything. The night had been a disaster. Jeers and shouts, which Alexander had never had in his career before. Tempers hadn't been improved by the mundane fact that he had increased the price of programs. Henry was too stupefied, too blank

with anxiety, to pick up what had happened. Cries of
"Author" from loyal friends. Alexander, who must temporarily have lost his head and sense of the stage, led Henry
forward. Loyal applause from the front rows. Ferocious
yells, hisses, shrieks not often heard in a London theater
then or now, from the cheap seats. They might forgive
Alexander, who was a popular pet, but they had come to
hate the author. Alexander had to take Henry back into
the wings, and then return, his actor's nerve restored, in
order to quiet the audience down.

It would have been a terrible night for anyone. It
brought out complex responses in Henry's nature. Some of
them would have shown themselves anyway, but it quickened and hardened the process. It was the end of him in the
theater.

Was the play really so bad? Probably not quite. The
press was tolerable. The orthodox critics gave temperate
praise, and the young men, Shaw, Wells, Bennett, who all
happened to be present in their first jobs as dramatic critics, did their best to be kind. But Henry wasn't made to
write good plays. True, very few novelists have had more
dramatic instinct. His inhibitions wouldn't have been a
hindrance: Shaw had no more primary feeling than Henry,
and turned the deficiency into a theatrical bonus. But
Henry had another deficiency that was fatal. He despised
the drama as an art form.

It is pretty well certain that one can't write anything
valuable, or catch any audience of any kind, if one despises
what one is doing. Henry may have thought that no plays,
except maybe Shakespeare's, could compare, in depth and
richness of effect, with the best novels, including his own.

As a theoretical case, that could be argued. What Henry didn't realize was that good plays are more difficult, perhaps more chancy, to write than good novels. At any rate, there are far fewer of them in the world's repertory.

The peculiar result of Henry's attitude was that he vulgarized his plays more than a commercial playwright would have dreamed of doing. His adaptation of his own *The Traveller* is quite unnecessarily cheapened, as a professional adapter would never have made it. There was always a streak of suppressed melodrama in Henry, and he thought so little of the stage that he let it rip. The curtain line of the first act of *Guy Domville* is the hero declaiming: "Long live, long live the Domvilles!" Alexander must have left that in, feeling that it suited his fine voice. Can anyone imagine Henry using that egregious speech in a novel?

There has been a classical irony. After that first night, Henry gave up the stage; but the stage was not to give up Henry. When he was dead, people who understood the theater perceived the dramatic potentialities in his work. *Washington Square* was made into a satisfactory play. So was *The Sense of the Past*. More impressively, writers with dramaturgic skill saw the novels as beautiful quarries for drama on the television screen. *The Portrait of a Lady* became a supreme television achievement, aesthetically and in all other ways. So did, only a short way behind, *The Ambassadors* and *The Golden Bowl*. The interesting lesson is that none of the adapters tried to coarsen the material. They have shown far more respect for drama, and artistic tact, than in his own theatrical efforts Henry did himself.

The humiliation of *Guy Domville* both was, and represented, a crisis in Henry's life. Fenimore Woolson had

killed herself. Now the crystallization of discontent had
become sharp. He knew what he had missed, and feared
what he was going to miss. On and off for years he was near
a breakdown. But he was a man of exceptionally strong
character and, somewhere beyond the will, set to work to
rebuild an existence. His ultimate resource was, of course,
his art. He had lost his gamble for popular success. Very
well. Not obtrusively but with all the authority he carried,
still great, and soon made greater, he consolidated his claim
for his own kind of unpopular art. Pure art, his own version of ideal fiction. So, year by year, emerged the legend
of Henry James that in the first half of this century we
all knew. Like all such legends, it was a good deal simpler
than the truth, but there was something in it.

He was a born teacher, which fits neatly into the psychological analysis we have seen. He had command, pa-
tience, certainty. What he taught was what fiction should
be. He is the only major novelist who has developed a
defined ideological theory of the art. Proust wrote about it
more subtly, but not in a way suitable for the instruction
of young students.

On the whole, it is perhaps fair to say that the James
theory did harm rather than good. It was made too restrictive. His insistence on the point of view would have
made the whole of Dostoevsky, Tolstoy, Dickens impossible to write; as has been mentioned, Henry in critical
asides did manage to put those works aside. Above all, the
theory couldn't have accommodated Balzac—to whom, as
has been stressed, Henry with generous inconsistency produced the most passionate of all tributes.

In his own case, both for his legend and his art, the

theory did good. People are impressed by certainty, and when they are impressed are remarkably unborable, even those not easily given to deference. That was true of Wells, who in spite of one ill-natured outburst cherished unusual respect for the old master. Everyone listened to the tortuous discourses, fingers clutching the air, trying in long pauses to catch the only fitting word—which it was unforgivable for anyone else to try to provide. It was all pleasingly similar to Niels Bohr in Copenhagen a generation later, treating theoretical physicists to corresponding lucubrations, equally involved. The speeches must have been just about as long.

For Henry's own art, the theory served a more direct purpose. It should be said that what follows is a minority view. By late middle life, Henry's art was tending to run thin in substance. He wanted to say some difficult, or certainly complicated, things, but there were not so many of them as appears. When a fine and conscientious writer runs thin in substance, he falls back on his technical virtuosity (there are signs that this was happening to Dickens). Henry had great technical virtuosity, which was more than reinforced by an ideology of technique. He had been allured by Ibsen's symbolism, and used it, as in *The Wings of the Dove* and *The Golden Bowl*. It didn't really suit him. It did, however, help out a substance wearing thin. Similarly with the language of the later novels. Often it did not say more than he had said already, though not in such Alexandrian profusion. The technique gave invisible assistance. The comparison with Dostoevsky comes to mind. The later Henry was using all conceivable resources to fill up a form that could have contained more substance. Dostoevsky, except in *The Brothers Karamazov,* couldn't find a form that was expansible enough for all he had to say.

One can identify some of these processes in the famous prefaces to the New York Edition, and in the revisions. The prefaces show piercing and truthful insight into his own creative operations, particularly into his work of many years before. No writer has written so articulately about how he wrote. The revisions usually make the earlier work more elaborate, different in tone, but not better. Several of the books are distorted or spoiled by the revision. Though this is a different point, the most significant revision in psychological terms is at the end of *The Portrait of a Lady* when, in the New York Edition, Goodwood's kiss makes Isabel fully aware of him as a passionate man, and gives her a sense of what physical love could be. She recoils, but she has an intimation. This isn't done well, for it was still too much of a strain on Henry's temperament. The interesting thing is that it was done at all.

For the present writer, the best of the later James is *The Ambassadors.* To a considerable extent that book is a reworking of earlier themes, but a much more sophisticated and experienced one, and it ranks high within the *oeuvre.* The other late novels stand uneasily beside the shorter stories, above all *The Turn of the Screw,* where Henry wasn't consciously trying too hard and where the substance produced itself.

So, as masterly literary lawgiver, explaining his own art, still creative, Henry endured his last twenty years. He had expected more. Much of life had proved to be a disappointing business. But under all the agitated nerves he had a tough spirit, and he made the best of it.

He made the best of it in his domestic arrangements, too. Once upon a time he had probably hoped to finish in the princely style of Paul Bourget down at Hyères. Henry had to settle for the modest state of an elderly man of letters, rather like that of a Cambridge professor with a small supplement of private means. He bought a decorous Georgian house in Rye, and there he could dictate away (the change from writing by hand to dictation made his language considerably more parenthetical and unedged) and entertain his friends. He could provide adequate food and, though he didn't drink overmuch himself, better and plentiful wine. The regime at Rye was punctilious and modestly dignified, and he was earning just enough to support it. He had one major practical disappointment. This was the failure of the New York Edition. There he had invested his last great hopes and spent years of luxuriating, anxious work on the final, the definitive qualifications. This edition was to bring in an income to support him in his old age. It was handsomely produced and floated by Scribners in New York. It sank with next to nothing of a trace.

Still, in 1913 he could afford to take a sizable apartment in London, keeping the Rye house for the summers. The London apartment was in Carlyle Mansions, at the Embankment end of Cheyne Row, and Henry's drawing room overlooked the river (within a few years, T. S. Eliot also went to live in Carlyle Mansions). Henry was not poverty stricken, and there was no danger that he would be so. The trouble was, Edith Wharton thought he was, and when Edith Wharton got an idea into her head, action was taken.

The relations between Henry and her always had

strains of high comedy, and Henry was, in his hyperbolic manner, very funny about them himself. They were both good and generous people, but it would be an error to think that they were made for one another. As has been said earlier, she was very grand, very rich, immensely successful as a writer—and immensely active. She descended on Henry at Rye, together with one of the latest large motorcars, chauffeur, and establishment, and disturbed his settled and sedate routine. She became known, in letters to his intimates, as "the Angel of Desolation," or sometimes as "the Firebird." She whisked him away in the car, and took him around England on journeys he had no desire to make. She seems to have regarded Lamb House, Rye, as a humble village dwelling: in that she was being fairly lordly. She heard Henry complain about money, which he did rather too often. Something had to be done, Edith decided. Henry must get the Nobel Prize.

That was, of course, an entirely reasonable idea. She mobilized backers with her usual energy, efficiency, influence. This was just about the time that Spaniards were doing the same for Galdós. The objections to both were similar, though Henry was not a controversial figure in a political sense. Like Galdós, however, he was not known outside his own country, or more precisely in Henry's case, outside the English-speaking world. Which is, one has to say, still largely true. Like Galdós, Henry didn't get the prize.

Edith, not deterred, had another idea. She had the same New York publisher as Henry. She entered into an amiable conspiracy with Charles Scribner. A largish sum of money could be secretly diverted from her account.

Scribners could offer Henry this sum of money as an advance on a novel not yet written and, since his health was now precarious, not likely to be written. An offer like that would cheer him up. Charles Scribner was glad to play. To Henry's astonishment, he received a tactful letter, full of affection and admiration (both genuine), saying that Scribners were eager for another novel, and as a sign of their eagerness wanted to pay $8,000 in advance. Henry had never been offered anything like such an advance in his whole career. He may have been a shade suspicious. He took the money.

Then Edith, indomitable, had another idea, and a much worse one. Again as with Galdós, and at exactly the same period, she proposed to raise a large subscription. The result was different. Henry, in spite of his grumbles, wasn't at all in need, and, if he had been in need, he would have still been outraged. He was a very proud man. He squashed this suggestion without any Jamesian qualifications whatsoever.

Edith was as kind as he was. Whether he knew that there was another and deeper resemblance between them isn't clear. In fact, she, too, had had a frustrated life— frustrated, that is, in love and sex. Her marriage had given her nothing. Her long love affair, so-called, with Walter Berry, had given her very little, or not what she hungered for. She was, however, a little luckier than Henry, and not so timid. She did have an episode, not very long, of rapturous sexual joy, with Henry's old acquaintance Morton Fullerton. Fullerton was a shady character in most respects, especially with money; but like Balzac he brought moments of happiness to all the women with whom he went to bed, and conceivably to some men. He was a kind of erotic do-gooder. He reveled in giving pleasure, and did so to Edith.

It is as certain as such guesses can be that Henry didn't have that gift of fortune. Yet, in those last twenty years, he drew emotional compensation from affectionate young men, and that was much better than nothing. There was a series of these young men, and the first, in other respects an egomaniac Norwegian-American by name of Hendrik Andersen, seems to have given Henry a sense of the simple physical life and of what had been evaded both in his art and in his existence. Apparently there was nothing climactic about any of this, but plenty of hugs and caresses. From that time on, Henry's letters, not just to Hendrik but also to succeeding young men, are packed effusively with both. That wasn't a sign of total erotic liberation, much more a sign of aching, but there it is. In spite of pleading letters, which have their own pathos, Henry couldn't get Andersen to see him very often. They met only about four times in all. The fact was, Hendrik Andersen had a lunatic illusion that he was, or was going to be, a great sculptor. He asked for advice, and didn't take it. He had the same kind of megalomaniac ambition as another sculptor of Norwegian origin, Vigeland, who did manage to populate an Oslo park with monstrous pieces.

The pleasantest of the young men was Jocelyn Persse, son of Anglo-Irish gentry in County Galway, nephew of Lady Gregory. He was handsome, cheerful, beautifully mannered, considerate, and very simple. Long afterward, he said that Henry was the dearest human being he had ever known. He added with honest puzzlement that why Henry should have liked him so much he couldn't say.

That was the most tranquil of Henry's loves and

semiloves. The last was Hugh Walpole, which provoked acidulated scorn from the English homosexual pundits. Actually the young Walpole, ingenuous, on the make, spontaneous, utterly unconstrained, brought a great deal of consolation to the aging Henry. Henry could advise, lay down the artistic law, give worldly guidance, moral guidance, be half-fatherly, half-loverly, all according to the psychological profile. There is a story, attributed to Hugh Walpole himself, that he once suggested that they should go to bed. Henry had shrunk back, saying that he couldn't. That is gossip, but there is nothing improbable about it. Walpole was quite uninhibited and fully homosexual. In any sense that governs instinctive behavior, Henry was neither.

In the summer of 1914, Henry was already ailing. He was passionately involved in the war. For him, England, as it had been all his life, was the home of civilization. He couldn't bear to hear about American criticisms, much less about Irish-American aid and comfort to the enemy. Many friends of his, Jocelyn Persse among them, were fighting. He wanted to do something. He volunteered to spend time with Belgian wounded, since people were wanted who could speak to them in French. That wasn't much, but it was something, for an ill and fastidious old man.

Then he decided to do a little more. There was a faintly ridiculous piece of bureaucratic routine that acted as a trigger. Down in Rye, in the summer of 1915, heart and soul immersed in the war, like other sensible men not able to foresee the end, Henry was required to register as an alien. This distressed him. He had lived in England for the past thirty years, and in all for more than half his lifetime. His affections were in England, and nearly everyone he loved. He loved the country. Sometimes he viewed it with detachment; but, then, he viewed everything and everywhere with detachment. So far as he had a total loyalty, it was to England.

He didn't hesitate. There was only one step to take. He applied for English nationality.

He would not have done so, except for the war. Henry wasn't the man to change his nationality, any more than his name or anything else about him. It was not in his style. He must have known there would have been advantages for him in making the change years earlier. He was much more of a figure in England than in America. He was profoundly respected by the leading politicians, particularly by the Prime Minister, Asquith, who was a man of literary culture. As an Englishman, Henry would have been offered any honor that the state could give. But there is no indication that Henry had considered it.

Now he did, in that black year of war. He acted with extreme promptitude. It was a chivalrous gesture. His name was all he could give. It was right to give it. He explained to his relatives in America, but told them that the decision was made. The papers were rushed through, the Prime Minister himself as one of his sponsors.

The English were delighted. For them, it was, of course, a propaganda coup. To the cultivated world, Henry was the most eminent living American. There was a headline in *The Times*. The official and upper-class England that he had written about, and known so well, was gratified.

Soon he was very ill. Death came nearer, and lingered near him for months. It wasn't an easy way of dying. His mind left him, sometimes brought him back to the present, left him again. On New Year's Day, 1916, there was an announcement. Mr. Henry James had been awarded the Order of Merit, the highest civilian order open to an Englishman.

He seems to have been aware of it, and gently pleased. He was not often conscious, though he sent a message to a friend saying that he was determined to survive. He had hallucinations that he was traveling on a ship, and that he was Napoleon. He clung to life for weeks, and died on the last day of February.

His funeral service was held in Chelsea Old Church, and his ashes taken to America. Sixty years later, a plaque bearing his name was placed in the Poets' Corner of Westminster Abbey, the modern equivalent of being buried there. Sixty years was a long time; it wasn't so much of a tribute, but it was all that could be done and carried its own meaning.

PROUST

IT used to be common form for literary people in Eastern Europe to talk with disapproval of a curious triad —Kafka, Joyce, Proust. They had taken the European novel onto a wrong course, it was said, as though they were indistinguishable, a kind of three-headed monstrosity. Protests that they were about as different as three writers could be, that Proust was in essence a novelist in the greatest realistic tradition (that is, he was what these same Eastern Europeans would call a critical realist), didn't appear to make much impact. Fortunately, those arguments are now dead, and Proust is being read in Moscow as a great novelist, and understood.

It is true that the metaphysical frame into which he finally fitted *A la Recherche du temps perdu,* the formulation of time and memory that he abstracted from experience, sometimes conceals the most wonderful and inherent of his gifts. That frame didn't come from experience, and was decided on before the substance of the novel was written. The famous end—where all his people are like giants immersed in time—was composed before much of

✕ *297*

the first book was written. That ending gives aesthetic shape and neatness to the whole work, and, though the statement isn't original, probably (to some of Proust's committed admirers there is still a certain intellectual doubt) it justifies itself. It ought, however, not to act as a distraction from elements in the great *roman fleuve* that are as valid and universal as a novelist has made them. Time puzzles have been juggled with by many people—involuntary memory wasn't a new discovery—but Swann walking outside Odette's house, the stripping away, as though they were onionskins, of layers of the personality of M. de Charlus, the highspirited absurdity of a Verdurin dinner, the heartbreak at sunrise, those could only have been written by this one and this great novelist.

Perhaps it helps to remember one simple thing. Proust imbibed the work of Balzac with complete comprehension. Balzac is the least ethereal of all great novelists. Proust was confident that anything that Balzac could do, he, Proust, could do better. That wasn't entirely borne out in the event, though Proust's social analysis of circles that Balzac had also penetrated sixty years before is both more accurate and more brilliant, and Proust's analysis of individual persons often goes deeper. Anyway, to excel Balzac was one of Proust's literary ambitions, and one that he could set for himself without falsity or conceit.

He grinned inwardly to himself with characteristic self-mockery, in the process. In *Contre Sainte-Beuve,* which he wrote but did not publish before he was certain what his masterwork would be, there is a chapter of magnificent applied criticism called "M. de Guermantes' Balzac." In this chapter M. de Guermantes is being rehearsed for his part as the duc de Guermantes in *A la Recherche*. He is a lofty aristocrat, quite uncultivated and unliterary, positive that his views on Balzac and his reasons for loving the novel must be shared by any sane person. The young Proust, the most sophisticated of literary intellectuals, adds with subdued amusement that to his own astonishment he found himself agreeing with M. de Guermantes. The young Proust had read Balzac for just those same reasons, and was at one with this simple soul against the whole literary world.

Incidentally, for anyone who wants to get a foretaste of Proust's humor, there is a good example in that same chapter. Proust is the funniest of the supreme novelists, if we except Dickens. The Proustian humor is gentler than Dickens's, less hectic, and often wears better. The passage about M. de Guermantes being prevailed upon to demonstrate his stereoscope is pure innocent pleasure. In *A la Recherche* this comedy is transferred to another character, and given a faint social connotation, which somewhat takes away from the undiluted human joy.

It wouldn't be sensible to pretend that Proust was as hearty a man as the Balzac he admired and wanted to excel. Proust was about as little hearty as a great writer can be. He was a chronic neurasthenic invalid from the age of nine. In his last twenty years he made invalidism a way of life. Sometimes he triumphed over it, and by the effort of an immensely strong will, which he didn't always recognize that he possessed, he triumphed over it in his art. But his was an existence so different from those of his literary peers, Tolstoy, Dostoevsky, Dickens, Balzac, that he might have belonged to a different species.

There was even less overt drama in his life than in that of Henry James. He wasn't precisely a hypochondriac, and he died at fifty-one of his afflictions; but he certainly cherished his afflictions like a hypochondriac, and made some of his art out of his hyperaesthetic nerves. To adapt a phrase of Malcolm Cowley's, he was the only great writer who could make the railway journey from Paris to the Normandy coast sound as much an adventure as the Charge of the Light Brigade.

In his early childhood, his parents couldn't help recognizing that he was both abnormally bright and abnormally sensitive—and here *abnormally* isn't a loose word. In fact, both his father and mother were very intelligent; he was their first child, and his mother in particular worried about him from infancy until his middle thirties, when she died. She worried about her Marcel rather as another mother worried about the young Galdós, with some formal similarities but with different objective results.

There was plenty of money around, and all his life Proust could draw on substantial private means, more so than any major writer of his time. Not that his father's family were at all elevated. Long lines of Prousts had been shopkeepers in the small town of Illiers, out in the featureless Beauce countryside to the southeast of Chartres. Father Proust was the first of them to emerge into a profession, by the nineteenth-century French (and English) meritocratic method of being very good at competitive examinations. He became a doctor and at thirty was already an eminent one. He showed himself both brave and scientifically acute in cholera epidemics, and that made his reputation. He was a conforming Catholic, a conforming Conservative, provincial France at its sturdiest and its most lucid.

Aged thirty-six, established in his profession, he married a girl fifteen years younger than he was, Jeanne Weil. As the surname tells us, she came from a Jewish family. Her father was a wealthy stockbroker. Dr. Proust earned a considerable income, but it was from the Weils that most of Marcel's money was to come.

Nearly all the Weils had been assimilated, in some ways even more completely than their nearest English equivalent. Jeanne Weil was highly cultivated in a manner indistinguishable from any privileged French girl. Apparently out of deference to family proprieties, she was not received into the Catholic Church; but, since neither she nor Dr. Proust was concerned with religious beliefs, that was not a problem. It was taken as a matter of course that the infant Marcel, born in 1871, just after the Franco-Prussian War and the Commune, should be baptized as a Catholic. At the appropriate age he took his first communion. He was no more concerned with religious faith than his parents were. In *A la Recherche,* where the content is in essence autobiographical, though maneuvered for the purposes of art, Proust is fundamentally as truthful as Tolstoy. There is no indication whatever that his mother was Jewish.

All kinds of inference have been drawn from this, as from the failure to mention that the narrator was homosexual. Proust must have been dogged by those two fatalities, it has been argued, and he was concealing the shame of being half-Jewish. That seems to be far too simple. It is possible to read the book, and the historical evidence, quite differently. Proust's origins, and later on his sexual behavior, were entirely known not only to his intimates, but also in all the circles he moved among. The Weils were as prominent in Paris as, say, the Montefiores in London. He couldn't have concealed his mother's family even if he had wanted to. Further, a high proportion of his associates were themselves Jewish: Madame Straus, one of the first hostesses who aided his progress into smart society; Charles Haas, the original of Swann and a leading figure in the *beau monde;* companions at school such as the Blums and the Halévys; Reynaldo Hahn, whom he loved; Madame de Caillavet, Anatole France's mistress, who presided over another salon. Plenty more. In many sectors of Paris society, social and artistic, there appears, until the Dreyfus case, to have been very little effective anti-Semitism—possibly less than in London at the same date.

Finally, and much more important, Proust was not given to shame. He had the inner, and ultimate, confidence of someone conscious of great gifts. Part Jewish, homosexual—though not altogether so—what did that matter, when he was himself? His nerves might prostrate him, but he was, from youth onward, a man of almost reckless courage, as he demonstrated in the Dreyfus period.

It is far more likely that, in the novel, he found it more aesthetically satisfactory not to have a Jewish mother. He wanted a devoted, obsessive mother there; it took nothing away from that, and added familiarity, to place her as a pure French *haute bourgeoise.* His literary tact—an underestimated quality and one to which he, one of the most conscious of artists, paid great attention—was usually impeccable, and was so here. And so it was, in a much more important matter, when he came to his own (that is, the narrator's) erotic life.

One can follow this literary tact at work in his de-

scription of childhood visits to Combray, his fictional version of Illiers, now known officially as Illiers-Combray,
which is a modest tribute to art. Those passages about
childhood are perhaps the most haunting in fiction. They
preserve, with absolute fidelity, the essence of his experience, but they have been a good deal simplified from the
historical facts. In his own childhood, Proust actually spent
summers with two sets of relatives: one at Auteuil, with a
Weil uncle; one at Illiers, with a Proust aunt.

It was at Auteuil that occurred the incident of his
mother being too much occupied to come up for his good
night kiss (which is beautifully dramatized, but, except in
the minds of simple psychiatrists, didn't determine his future life). It was also at Auteuil, not Illiers, that at the age
of nine he had his first attack of asthma, which genuinely
did at least foreshadow his invalid existence. For the purposes of art, Proust required something more provincial
than Auteuil for these childhood sorrows and joys, and so
everything was transferred to Illiers. There again, reenter-
ing with total involvement into childish imagination, he
proceeded to magnify the place and its wonders as a child
would see it. To an adult, Illiers is, as M. de Charlus observes, a small town like many others. Tante Léonie's house
is perceptibly humbler than one would imagine from the
novel—the house, as in fact it was, of a superior tradesman.
How Tante Léonie saw the street at all from her bedroom
is something of a mystery, but that she finally relapsed into
permanent invalidism, not leaving that little room, isn't a
mystery at all, and prefigures Proust's own final state. It
looks as though there may have been a genetic frailty running through the Proust strain. The garden, through which

Swann walked after ringing the outside bell, is tiny, about the size of a Chelsea patio. The young Proust could make all this into the earliest and best of life's heavens, and so could the creative artist.

One other piece of literary tact, or in this case literary sleight of hand. It isn't always realized that Proust was a master of the *faux naïf*. Any observant child of eight who wasn't a fool (and the young Proust was as observant and as little a fool as any child known to man) would have grasped after exactly two walks, both quite short, that the famous Two Ways led back to the same place. Madame Proust's astonishment at her husband's sense of direction cannot have been stimulated on more than one arrival back home. Proust's wonder at such miracles is a favorite trick. Behind the apparently simple-minded narrator is a mocking observer over his shoulder, and this gives one of Proust's many forms of humor. Exactly the same effect is produced when the narrator professes, and appears to feel, absolute incomprehension at M. de Charlus's behavior. Is he a detective? What can he be doing? The observer over the shoulder is giving Mephistophelian grins. Actually, of course, Proust as a schoolboy would have known all about M. de Charlus's predilections in half an hour.

After the age of nine, when he had his first diagnosable attack of asthma, he couldn't be allowed the smell of blossom, which in later years he celebrated as one of the heavenly joys, the smell of hawthorn, apple, lilac. Illiers, beloved Illiers, was not for spring or summer holidays. He wasn't continuously ill. The English of the period would have called him "delicate" and thought him overindulged. It was sensible, they might have conceded, to guard him

from the effects of pollen, as one did with those susceptible
to hay fever. Instead of Illiers, he was taken for vacations
by the sea, supposed to be good for asthma. Many years
later, his readers were to be allured by the Normandy resort of Balbec (actually Cabourg).

In his boyhood, and until he was getting on toward
thirty, he was able to live a fair approximation to a normal life. He went to one of the best *lycées* in Paris, where
the intellectual level of his contemporaries would be considerably higher than that of any English school. These
great *lycées* were institutions for the upper class— that is,
the sons of well-to-do professional men such as Dr. Proust
mixed up with the socially smart and the aristocracy. Some
of the teachers were, in the French fashion, part-time
writers attached to the Paris literary journals, and one of
them detected quite early that the young Proust had a
startling talent. He was often away ill from school, and his
academic record was spotty, sometimes brilliant, but with
phases of it lost between absent-mindedness and idleness.
This his anxious parents attributed to lack of willpower, a
definition that he may have partly believed, and that certainly saved him from efforts he didn't wish to make. Little
did anyone know.

He fascinated some of his classmates, but put more of
them off. He already struck them as in some mysterious
sense different. He looked different. He had jet black hair
and a chalk white skin. His eyes were enormous, both
probing and engulfing—someone said that they were like a
man-sized insect's many-faceted eyes. He was something
like middle height, but he didn't carry himself well. Perhaps the seeds of illness had begun early to sink into his

chest. He was a marvelous talker for a boy in his teens; not a monologist, since he listened as intently as he talked. He was a good mimic, preposterously well informed, exuding mental energy, embarrassing others with elaborate flattery, giving out affection and demanding it. A lot of that was too much for some schoolboys, even clever ones. They may have had the intuition to feel, while the flattery, even the sycophancy, was pouring out, that there was a skeptical, amused, mocking, detached watcher somewhere over his shoulder or behind those hypnotizing eyes. He was beginning to develop his singular manner. He was rehearsing it, as it were, among boys. Sophisticated men would later find it so hard to resist. He had himself a good many of the occupations of a schoolboy—that is, of a cultivated French schoolboy. There were no games, compulsory or otherwise, at the Lycée Condorcet; that would have been barbarous, and in later life Proust appears to have thought that the object in golf was to achieve the maximum number of strokes. He was once photographed holding a tennis racket belonging to someone else, which was the summit of his athletic prowess. He did fall in love, rapturously and eloquently, with a girl his own age.

That was the episode that occurs in *A la Recherche* as between the narrator and Gilberte. It is perfectly well authenticated in biographical terms; the girl is established; it happened so. Proust altered, amended, fused, much more than Tolstoy, but in principle he told a similar truth. Occasionally he showed the kind of invention that must have pleased them both, as in changing the place name Méréglise to Méséglise.

Proust had several genuine attachments to girls, and

he writes about them, without any homosexual diffidence, as a man who could love girls. Just as his women characters, in spite of some improbabilities in the incidents, don't suggest a transference from young men. The most experienced of his women readers have testified vigorously that they have detected no such transference. There is no doubt that he had physical intimacies with women. It is necessary to use that kind of coy expression because the evidence isn't clear as to what did happen physiologically, and Proust could be a master of ambiguity. One of these intimacies, a pleasant, offhand amorous diversion, was with Louisa de Mornand, an actress, mistress of a close friend of Proust's, and the original of Saint Loup's Rachel. That affair took place long after Proust had become a committed homosexual.

While he was at the *lycée,* his parents were fretting about what would become of him. This was much like Señora Galdós's fretting about her son, though with the Prousts it was the father who was the more anxious to get the boy going in a respectable profession or career. Ironically, Proust's brother, two years younger, gave no trouble at all, was stable and competent all the way along, and finally became a surgeon, as much a dignitary in French medicine as Dr. Proust himself. He was a source of comfortable family pride; but it was Marcel who was the more loved, and who, among the distresses, was the object of more hopes, however baffled his parents were.

School hadn't been a failure. He had written a few articles in an avant-garde student publication. But those, to Dr. Proust, didn't point toward a sound future. Literature obviously wasn't a career, not even to a young man who had no practical need to earn a living. To Dr. Proust, a good conservative Frenchman, there was nevertheless a moral need to work. Dr. Proust was temporarily appeased when Marcel, after getting through his *baccalauréat*, insisted on doing his year of military service. That was a good conservative thing to do. Proust thoroughly enjoyed it. His health improved, rather like Dostoevsky's in Siberia. On the other hand, he was not a dazzling success as a soldier. He passed sixty-third out of sixty-four. Perversely he wanted to stay longer in the army, but, though as a rich clever young man he had been a good deal entertained by his senior officers, his military promise didn't seem quite good enough for that.

What should he do? This was precisely the same as the Galdós question thirty years earlier in Las Palmas; and Dr. Proust, with some aid from his wife, came up with precisely the same answer. Marcel must read law. He was clever enough for anything, as no one ever doubted. After he had read law, he would have an illustrious career.

Accordingly Proust entered the Faculté de Droit. In an uninterested fashion, he managed to pass, though he did fail in one oral exam. That is a minor puzzle, since there can't have been many more articulate and persuasive talkers alive. As for a career in law, he had a talent for evasive tactics even greater than those we have seen in the young Galdós. He did give his parents intimations of what he really wanted, as the young Galdós didn't. Their response was that literature might be a pleasant hobby. They thought of him, as people went on thinking of him when he was being recognized as the most original writer in Europe, as an idle dilettante. Some of the family atmosphere is conveyed in *A la Recherche* in the bizarrely humorous dinner party with M. de Norpois.

Evasive tactics continued. He still hadn't started a respectable career. He was living on allowances from his parents. They were very large allowances but, in theory at least, could be cut off. He obtained permission to study for his *Licence ès lettres*. That obtained some sort of approval at home. Dr. Proust understood about examinations. Letters were Proust's home ground, and he performed with credit.

Still, nearly twenty-four, no respectable occupation. Though his parents presumably didn't know it, or blinded themselves, he was beginning his social triumph, moving from smart *salon* to smarter, and also beginning his active homosexual existence. His health wasn't too bad, and he was happier, except in his creative depth, than at any other time. Still, he had no occupation. His parents attributed this to his famous lack of will.

The words they used, such as *"manque de volonté,"* and the words we still use are deceptive. No one has found the right concepts for some of these mental qualities. Certainly Proust didn't possess the adamantine ego of Tolstoy or Dickens. His psychological structure was more fluid and permeable, which gave him some of his receptivity, perhaps his suspect charm, and his ability to merge other personalities into his own. But, in an amorphous fashion, his will was immensely strong.

Without assertion or anyone noticing, he was set on not doing anything he didn't want to do. It looks as though he never did. That is, he used every trick of a chameleon makeup to get his own way. And he got it. He wasn't egocentric, even less so than Balzac, but he was, underneath his mellifluous and sensitive apologies, remarkably selfish, as much so as Balzac. So, despite appearances, he was extremely strong-willed, if strong-willed means getting one's own desires. He was also inordinately self-willed, and somehow, as will be mentioned later, others couldn't help letting him be so. They sat by powerlessly, watching him with superb apologies inflict on them maximum disruption of any organized existence.

At twenty-four he appeased his father and took a job. He held it, if that is the right term, for four years. This went on simultaneously with his social glories, his secret sexual life, and the beginning of an even more secret literary life. But it was the only job he ever had, and it is convenient to refer to it here. Proust became an honorary attaché to the Mazarine Library. As the title indicates, he received no pay. His method of interpreting his duties, and placating his family, was his own. In the first few months, he called at the library several times, and had a chat with some of his colleagues. That seems to have proved too much for him. So then, for each of the next three years, he punctiliously applied for, and was granted, leave of absence. This eclipses any of Galdós's somewhat similar exploits with the law faculty at Madrid. At last Proust was told that he really couldn't be given more leave of absence. They had to ask him to attend the library now and then. With the same punctiliousness with which he had applied for leave of absence, Proust formally resigned.

During those same years, the honorary attaché at the Mazarine Library was making his way into the topmost layers of Paris society. He was entertained—and of course took pains to be entertained—all over the Faubourg Saint-Germain. He was received into the *gratin,* the social elite, and saw it from the inside.

That sounds an astonishing feat for a young man of the middle class, half-Jewish, with no obvious fame or credentials of his own. In *A la Recherche* he doesn't refrain from making it sound astonishing. In fact, it wasn't as difficult as all that. The Prousts might be middle class, but Dr. Proust through his medical crusades knew most of the French politicians. It helped that the Prousts were distinctly rich, probably more so than Charles Haas, who had made even more startling social conquests a generation before. Proust was one of the most ingratiating and amusing of young men, and a good many French hostesses had an eye for what their English equivalents would at the time have called "brilliant" arrivals.

Most of all, at the *lycée,* some of his closest associates had mothers who presided over *salons,* including the admirable Madame Straus. The fact was, Proust had the *entrée* from the start. It was an easy step from one *salon* to the next, socially a shade more exalted, intellectually a shade less exacting. A bright young man, if he had something about him, could do it, provided he wanted to enough.

Proust wanted to very much. Why? We needn't be too nice about that. He wasn't too nice about it himself. In his novel *Jean Santeuil,* written shortly after this sojourn in high society, but not published in his lifetime, he is completely candid. He wanted to climb. He was beglamored by the aristocracy. He was inquisitive about them, as he was about all people, but even more about people who seemed to possess grandeur. He was a snob.

There are worse vices than snobbery. One has to be pretty self-bound when young not to imagine that there must be some life more glamorous than one's own. Some young people of Proust's origins have searched downward in society, feeling that in the very poor, or most of all in the derelict, there will be wisdom denied to themselves. Others have plunged among different races. Others have taken the Proustian course. The emotional drive, and the search itself, is very much the same. The realistic and wise, as Proust was or became, emerge having made the somewhat flat discovery that people anywhere are disconcertingly more alike than different. It didn't take Proust long in the Faubourg Saint-Germain to conclude that the very rich and very lofty were no more admirable than those he had known elsewhere. They might be sometimes colder-hearted—as when in *A la Recherche* the narrator hears the Guermanteses, so as not to spoil their evening, assuring Swann in his terminal illness that he is as right as rain.

In his very early twenties, just before he was winning those social victories, he began his first homosexual affairs. No one can be certain about how he really regarded his own homosexuality. It is easy to be overwhelmed by his grave prophetlike rhetoric about Sodom and Gomorrah, the cities of the plain, and his moral horror at "a cursed race," "a race apart." That must have been a phase of his feeling. However skillful a literary strategist a writer is, he can't manufacture feelings he doesn't have, or manufacture them for long. There is a chapter in *Contre Sainte-Beuve*, harsher than anything in the novel, where he is judging the race of homosexuals, with sadness and without mercy. To him that must have been part of the truth. Yet it seems unlikely that it was all.

Proust had a remarkable capacity, which gave much of both the joy and the resignation to his art, of entering an experience, either with an individual, as in a love affair, or in a social exploration, as in the Faubourg, first with suspicion, then with total immersion and delight, and then finally reappearing having once more discovered that appearances cheat one. In the case of Tolstoy that has been called discovering the lie in life. This may have been part of his response to homosexual love.

All this is speculative, and it would be foolish to suggest that it is more than a dubious guess. We don't know much of the detail of Proust's sexual relations—far less than we know of Tolstoy's or Dostoevsky's. A little we can infer with fair certainty. He didn't find sex difficult. He may have been a bit of a voyeur (he took extravagant pleasure in studying a love object in bed), but he enjoyed himself in directer ways. He had none of the crippling restraints that kept Henry James virginal so long.

At twenty-two he had his first, and perhaps his pleasantest, fully consummated affair: that was with the amiable Reynaldo Hahn. Reynaldo was three years younger than Proust, a talented musician, and a loving and gentle soul. He put up with Proust's demands, always excessive in the first stage of any kind of relation, for total emotional surrender. They had their scenes, impossible to avoid when Proust was one of a pair, but they were happy for a couple of years. The more uncensorious of hostesses let Proust bring Reynaldo along with him, and his music was an asset to a party. When sexual enthusiasm ebbed away, probably first on Proust's side, they became loving friends, and continued so for life. It is curious, and possibly indicative, that this consolation wasn't allowed into any homosexual relation in *A la Recherche,* though one sees something like it in the beautiful lifelong love of M. de Norpois and Madame de Villeparisis.

In his twenties, the least-clouded period of his life, Proust had attachments, similar to that with Reynaldo, to one or two other young men, such as Lucien Daudet, one of Alphonse's sons. These young men were of his own kind and class, genuinely homosexual and making no pretense about it. The affairs were, by Proustian standards, quite cheerful. It was because a journalist made a sneer at his relation with Lucien that Proust fought a duel. No one could have been less equipped to fight a duel. He hadn't handled a weapon of any kind at any time. Duels in Paris in the 1890s were usually not very dangerous, but if they had been he wouldn't have been deterred. He comported himself with honor. His seconds were of high social distinction, and an aristocratic friend reported afterward that Marcel had been brave, frail, and charming.

Once he had expected heaven out of ecstatic friendships without sex. The promise of that heaven was one of the lies in life. Now he had tried loving friendships with sex. Had that promise, too, turned out another lie? If so, it meant that he hadn't, and maybe couldn't, come to terms with the human limits.

After about five years of the *beau monde,* the highest society that he could reach in Paris, he had found a similar lie in life. The *beau monde* was no good. It wasn't always stupid, but it often was. It was heartless. It was empty. It had no reason to exist, except to preserve its existence. He would have reached that verdict anyway, for none of his romantic dreams could survive his honest and relentless

mind; but his disenchantment was quickened by the Dreyfus case. Most of the Faubourg society (not quite all)
showed itself at its worst—intellectually dishonest, morally
cowardly, and without human virtues. Anti-Semitism became fashionable. Proust, like others with Jewish origins,
was reminded of them.

He behaved with absolute guts. He might be risking
his social position. He had clambered there, he had charmed
them, but after all he was an outsider. He dismissed any
kind of prudence with bitter contempt. If that was society, and it probably was, he wanted no part of it. In
historical fact, perhaps because he was so odd a fish, his position doesn't seem to have been much affected. He took
part, as his brother Robert did, in pro-Dreyfus campaigns
from the start, and went on until the end. He helped
Dreyfus's lawyers. He quarreled with influential persons—
influential, that is, not in society, which didn't matter, but
in the literary world, which, in view of his secret plans,
mattered where it hurt. He wrote a savage letter to Mon-
tesquiou, a patron of his, the original of M. de Charlus,
formidable and powerful, if also grotesque, and forbade
him to make anti-Semitic remarks in his (Proust's) presence.

Like a good many Dreyfusards, he found that their
success left a sour taste. People who had behaved nobly—
Picquart above all—turned out to be idiots. The great
campaign was another of his hopes gone wrong, like his
social triumphs. At the turn of the century, his health was
getting worse. Asserting his self-will, he let his habits become more unusual. Since he believed that he got worse in
daylight, he began to live like a nocturnal animal, not get-

ting up until the evening. His personal dominance was so strong that family and friends adjusted themselves, and hostesses waited at their evening parties for the sound of dear Marcel's carriage arriving after midnight. He had not quite withdrawn from society, and his mother occasionally had to arrange one of his "little dinner parties"—little dinner parties of fifteen to twenty people, eminent persons responding to Proust's commands.

In those same years, not fully revealed to anyone, though there are gnomic references in letters to his closest friends, he was writing a novel. Not *A la Recherche,* but what now seems like an enormously long preliminary sketch, as straightforward as an autobiographical novel or *Bildungsroman,* with none of the interventions of time and memory, few of the embellishments of sensuous delight and humor, and written in fairly direct language, without the later hypnotizing sentences. It took him years of work, and was so carefully concealed that the manuscript was not discovered until thirty years after his death.

We know the book as *Jean Santeuil.* It isn't complete and tidied up, but it is nevertheless twice the length of a substantial novel today. He decided not to publish it. It is good. It would have made him a solid reputation, different in kind from that of the society idler who, in the nineties, had produced the trivialities of *Les Plaisirs et les jours.* Standing on its own, *Jean Santeuil* is somewhere in the same class as an English novel published not so long after Proust had put his manuscript away—Maugham's *Of Human Bondage,* which is at present undervalued.

It is something of a puzzle that Proust wouldn't publish *Jean Santeuil.* After all, his other aspirations had failed him, and he was approaching the stage when the desire to create a work of art, and to find recognition for his art, was to be the only drive he had.

One reason for holding the book back may have been domestic. His father and mother were still alive. The chief interest of *Jean Santeuil*, to us who are familiar with the great novel for which it was a trial run, is that the precursor tells us more about the factual circumstances of Proust's life. In *A la Recherche* he is harder on himself, gentler to his parents, particularly to his mother. She is nothing like so sanctified in *Jean Santeuil*. There are rows, on her part intrusions, failures of sympathy, pieces of crude obtuseness. There is very little reference to homosexuality, direct or indirect, which makes it look as though, when writing, he had his mother's sensibilities in mind. Even so, the book would have hurt her.

Another reason for holding back may cut nearer Proust's artistic core. People may differ about some of his gifts, but it is difficult to differ about his insight as a critic. When he cared, it was as powerful and as certain as anyone's has been. It is reasonable to suppose that he cared to apply it to his own work. He knew, more exactly than anyone else, that *Jean Santeuil* was a passable work, maybe a good one, emphatically not a great one. If he was going to justify his existence through art, this wasn't enough. He may already have foreseen that it would stand in the way of the great work. Possibly he had intimations of how he could use it as a sketch for the great work.

At that time, *Jean Santeuil* shelved, Proust was suffering griefs more acute than he had known, though some he already knew as it were by heart. With young men like

Reynaldo Hahn and Lucien Daudet, he had obtained an intimation of response and ease. But now he began a process that has ravaged other temperaments similar to his own: falling in love with entirely masculine characters. He commenced this process with handsome young aristocrats. On several in succession he lavished all his effusive, overpowering, jealous emotions, and they could give nothing back. Years later, one of them, Bertrand de Fénélon, said that Proust was a Saturnian (their circle's term for homosexual) and a very difficult friend. This hopeless love of a homosexual for the unobtainable male was christened by Victor Hugo the "tristesse d'Olympio." M. de Charlus, who must have been an expert, applied the phrase to Balzac's Vautrin yearning outside the birthplace of Rastignac.

Then Proust's father died in 1903, and his mother two years later. Proust was then thirty-four. He was prostrated by a complex of misery. His love for his mother—though love is too simple a word—was the deepest, longest lasting, and most fateful of his human relations. He never contrived to write it straight. For the only time, the introspective candor couldn't get free. In *Jean Santeuil,* he revealed some of the protests and resentment. After she was dead, he tried in *A la Recherche* to release himself by transferring many of the narrator's emotional ties to a grandmother. Usually, in spite of what looks like profusion, he was, in structural terms, one of the most economical of writers, and it cut against all his artistic instincts to use two characters where one would serve. Here, in real life, one character had served, but the pain hadn't left him, and in art he had to move it a distance away. The grandmother is marvelously done, but the ambiguity remains.

It looks as though, during his lifetime with his mother, and after her death, he felt a disentanglable set of passions: self-reproach, injury, guilt, dependence, desire to be avenged, remorse, separateness, the opposite of separateness, longing to obliterate or humiliate the memory, sheer childish love. Perhaps he felt the disappointment of one receiving absolute and exclusive love and finding that it was not enough. Perhaps he also felt the disappointment of one giving absolute and exclusive love (as he did in his childhood) and finding that that was not enough, either.

After the death of his parents, there were changes in his day-by-day existence. He still lived in the old family apartment, but he had no watchful eyes around him. He could have young men, and women also, to call on him at any time of the day or night. Again with a family resemblance to some other homosexuals, he had now turned away from handsome noblemen and was thinking of vigorous youths from the lower classes. This progress within a few years led him to the most passionate of his erotic loves, which we know in the final episodes with Albertine.

Proust had now become a rich man in his own right. It isn't clear just how rich, and he appears once to have thought that he had ruined himself by speculations on the Bourse. But the speculation was really quite minor, and he may have lost not more than a few thousand pounds. He wasn't clever at managing his affairs, and even worse at delegating them. That didn't count. He remained rich until he died.

When the mourning for his mother was easing, he was ready to turn back to art. Two years after her death, he wrote *Contre Sainte-Beuve*. *Jean Santeuil* had been a kind of primitive sketch for the ultimate novel. *Contre Sainte-Beuve* was much more. Sainte-Beuve himself was a critic who represented most of what Proust considered destructive, and in his attack Proust was setting down his own theory of the novel. He did it, characteristically, by various techniques: parody, satire, chapters that later could be used with trivial amendment in *A la Recherche* itself. It all sounds casual and amateur. It isn't. It is fluid and deliberately conceals the intellectual bone beneath it, but it is a masterly treatment of novel writing. By his side Henry James as a theoretician seems to be trying altogether too hard. In *Contre Sainte-Beuve* Proust is writing like a supreme novelist, and with intellectual dexterity that no critic has surpassed.

After that, in 1909, at the age of thirty-eight, Proust had finished with sighting shots and begun *A la Recherche* in earnest. Much of it was already in his mind. *A la Recherche* reads, and was intended to read, like a process of exploration and discovery. This is aided by Proust's mocking use of *faux naïf* surprise. But it really wasn't that at all. Like a good many scientists, Proust knew what his discovery was before he proved it.

As has been mentioned, the last words of the novel were written almost simultaneously with the first. "For a long time I used to go to bed early. Like giants immersed in time." Proust knew precisely where he was going. The last chapters in *Time Regained* were on paper before Proust had got thoroughly going in *Swann's Way*. Involuntary memory had appeared to him as what was missing in *Jean Santeuil*. It gave him his architecture or his framework. Both *architecture* and *framework* are terms too mechanical for a work of art that finally grew into something so beautifully organic. Biological metaphors might be more appropriate. Anyway, the architecture or organization, whatever one likes to call it, of *A la Recherche* is a major triumph. That is unarguable, even with those who don't feel comfortable with the ideas or wonder how valid they really are.

As he began, Proust knew the beginning and the end, but not the middle. Originally, that middle section wasn't intended to be anything like so long. He was thinking of *A la Recherche* as less than half the present length. It grew. He went on writing from 1909 until just before he died in 1922. The novel, always conceived as one single work, which it remained, finally became twice as long as *War and Peace*. Conceiving the framework was a marvelous feat; but it was just as marvelous, perhaps more so, to fit all the content, much of it entirely unanticipated, as he wrote the famous first and last words, into the artistic whole. It was a feat both of literary intuition and, it sounds prosaic, of administrative competence. Only a supremely gifted artist could have done it, and also, at a more rudimentary level, only a very clever man with an exceptionally good memory.

There were some oddities along the way. During the thirteen years of composition, not only thoughts and memories, but experiences happened to Proust, which he couldn't resist tying in, as in fact no writer could. The first volume of *A la Recherche* was published late in 1913, as *Du Côté de chez Swann,* and came to be known in English as *Swann's Way.* While Proust was completing that volume, he was living a later one. It is important to remind ourselves of

Proust's structural mastery. The part that Albertine plays in the narrator's life was mapped out very early, long before he had set eyes on the ultimate Albertine. He had realized the necessity of a Marcel-Albertine relation as one of the climactic themes of *A la Recherche,* to balance and chime with the Swann-Odette relation near the beginning. Otherwise *Swann in Love,* fine as it is—it would have made a perfect independent novella—wouldn't justify itself as part of the whole. Proust had contemplated the artistic consequences, and built up an Albertine largely from the girls of his youth, supplemented by various young men. The character was to be the Albertine much as we know her when she is first introduced—very much a living girl, and if we didn't know Proust's own history, few people would have doubted it. As for the counterpoint of jealousy between Swann and Marcel, Proust had learned enough about jealousy for any one lifetime.

During one of his stays at Cabourg, Proust, captivated by the miracle of that new contrivance the automobile, had hired a couple of chauffeurs. One came from Monaco, and was called Alfred Agostinelli. Proust found him agreeable, as he did a good many young men, but didn't take any special notice. Then, some years later, when Proust was in the middle of months-long maneuvers to get *Du Côté de chez Swann* published—which in the end required the use of all the social influence he could mobilize, blandishments, personal pressure, and finally money, and even then took well over a year—Agostinelli arrived in Paris and asked for a job. Proust took him on, set him to work typing the second volume of *A la Recherche,* and fell in love. Fell in love more helplessly than ever before.

This was in January 1913. Agostinelli was about twenty-two. He was a kind and honorable man. He is said to have borne a faint physical resemblance to Proust himself, with dark-rimmed lemurlike eyes. He wasn't educated, but he was highly intelligent, probably the most intelligent person that Proust had deeply loved. He wasn't only a natural mechanic, but also had a feeling and a gift for words. The chief contribution he made to the character of Albertine, as opposed to the events, is in the improvement in the articulateness and sensitivity of her talk and her understanding of what the narrator implies. That came from Agostinelli.

It is clear that he venerated and cared for Proust. The trouble was he almost certainly was not in the least homosexual. He may have been free and easy about sex, like other Mediterranean youths, and if Proust wanted it, he didn't mind. But his taste, and perhaps an ardent one, was for women. He had a wife, whom, as it later became known, he had omitted to marry. It seems as though there were plenty of other women, and it is they who were the objects of Proust's frantic and obsessive jealousy just as they are for the narrator in *A la Recherche*, except that there Albertine happened to be a girl chasing other girls.

It was a situation for which no one in Agostinelli's role, or in Proust's, could have contrived a happy outcome. For a time Agostinelli did his best. He was good-natured, as we can see from some of Albertine's pain-filled and tender remarks to Marcel. That wasn't enough. He was surrounded by a spider's web of love. Proust used all his insensate strategies. It is described, in minute and hyperaestheticized detail, in the novel, and something like that actually happened. In the end Agostinelli had to escape. Aircraft were just catching the world's imagination, and he wanted to be a pilot. On one of his first solo flights, he crashed into the sea and died.

Hence *La Prisonnière* and *Albertine disparue*. If Agostinelli hadn't reentered Proust's life, something would have taken the place of those works, but possibly not with the same piercing desolation. Proust had dismissed all the hopes of what love could give long before, but until now he hadn't reached this dead blank.

And yet, racked by misery as dark as when his mother died, Proust was showing untiring energy, perseverance, acumen about getting his first volume published. In a sense, the novel was inseparable from his innermost self, as no experience was, neither love nor grief. This may make him appear less than human, but it has been true of writers nearer the mainstream of existence than he was capable of. Think of Conrad, writing away in full creative fervor while his son was dying in a room close by.

As has been indicated, it took all Proust's resources to find a publisher. He wanted the Nouvelle Revue Française, which was the obvious house for a new kind of novel. The N.R.F. duly turned him down, with a letter from André Gide, who may not have found it obligatory to read more than a few pages. Others rejected it. Friends were called into action. At last an ambitious young publisher, Grasset, took him on, though on terms that only a rich man could have considered (incidentally, if Proust hadn't been rich, he wouldn't have been so much at liberty to shelve *Jean Santeuil* and *Contre Sainte-Beuve*).

Publication was fixed for December 1913. Proust took all possible steps in what Americans would now call ad-

vance promotion. To say that he wasn't overscrupulous is
being miffish. He did things that no kind of professional
etiquette would have permitted. He was, as in other aspects of life, remarkably free from shame. He could have
given points to any literary careerist. Of course, the novel
was now his life, and stayed so. He knew what it was
worth, and he was going to give it every try. But also, as
we have seen elsewhere, it is wrong to think that great
writers, when undressed and in their ordinary operations,
are different from common flesh. Proust not only wished
for his work of art to endure. He wanted fame, recognition, prizes, all the rest. He took remarkably resolute steps
to achieve this desirable end.

So far as we know, money didn't pass. Nearly everything else did. With his social connections, he had access to
most editors in Paris. He used it. He suggested suitable re-
viewers, including, as was appropriate, some of his most
fervent admirers. He suggested the most useful tone that a
review should take: it would be a mistake to overdo such
words as *subtle* or *delicate*. The *Figaro* deserved special
attention, and so the Empress Eugénie was invoked. She
wrote what was in effect a command, and no fewer than
three reviews appeared—all glowing.

Perhaps not surprisingly, the book had a good press.
No such campaign had ever been mounted for a great
novel. News of the book reached England that winter. In
Paris it was selling well, very well for a work so unfamiliar.
Several impressions were printed before August 1914. The
N.R.F. wrote an abject apology, and offered to take over
the whole of *A la Recherche,* on handsome terms. If the
war hadn't intervened, Proust would have had international fame within two or three years.

As it was, the rest of his life was spent with his novel. He had to fit in wartime scenes, of which obviously there couldn't have been prevision. Details—even minute detail of a hostess's dress—needed to be checked. If he was too ill to move—he was by now often bedridden—he dispatched helpers and spies. He increased the length of the novel yet more, perhaps by another third, and still had the power to keep it under artistic control. There was no weakening in his literary judgment. It is halfway incredible that anyone working in his state, in what became a famous cork-lined bedroom, illness gaining on him, alone at night with paper-chains of proofs, muddled manuscripts, no secretary, could have performed the sheer bureaucratic task of getting the novel into order. The mechanical office work would have defeated anyone of less spirit. It was like filling in a jigsaw puzzle to end all jigsaw puzzles.

His writing habits had always been an extravagant parody of Balzac's, slogging through the night, composing very fast, correcting or in effect rewriting on the proofs. To interpret the corrections would have been a full-time job for a good secretary. With a little help from the devoted Céleste Albaret, his housekeeper, uneducated but very bright, and one of the admirable characters in the Proust story, he did it all himself. There were some slips and contradictions left in the final version. If he had lived longer, the definitive text would have shown some differences from the one we have, but that has bequeathed agreeable problems for Proustian scholars.

He was as pertinacious as ever about the novel's publishing fortune. *Du Côté de chez Swann* had been a success. He knew for certain that the second volume would have everything in its favor. That, however, was again not to be left to chance. He was not prepared to release it until the war was over. Meanwhile the campaign must be organized.

He would, of course, change publishers. The N.R.F. could do far more for the book than Grasset. By the side of the well-being of the work, personal obligations didn't enter. The change would be good for the novel, good for Proust, good for the N.R.F.; bad for Grasset. Grasset, who had behaved impeccably, was got rid of. Grasset continued to behave with dignity and generosity. Proust didn't. He assumed a posture of moral rectitude, as though his own finaglings were irreproachable and Grasset in the wrong (very much as Dickens and George Eliot did in comparable situations). It is interesting to reflect on the mocking humor Proust would have extracted from one of his more pompous people in *A la Recherche*—say, the prince de Guermantes or Norpois—conscious of their moral superiority after bringing off a piece of business both shady and callous.

The second volume, *A l'Ombre des jeunes filles en fleurs* became, after a slow start, an unqualified success. The word went around literary Europe: a great novel, an astonishing one, was coming out under their eyes.

He had, and knew he had, the justification of a lifetime. But he wasn't satisfied. That volume must win the Prix Goncourt. The Proust machine, as well organized as the Democratic machine in Boston at the same period, was once more set in motion. The Prix Goncourt was secured. It was, of course, more than deserved. If he had survived longer, all other prizes within reach would have been secured.

He didn't survive much longer. He seems to have been

abnormally indifferent to mortality, though he talked about it often enough. He had lived as an invalid more than half his life. His brother Robert, an excellent doctor, tried to look after him. Whether a hospital existence, or today's medicine, would have kept him alive, no one has been certain. Neither Robert nor anyone on earth could persuade him to change his ways. As the illness increased, so did his self-will.

In the war, he showed himself, as he always had been, careless about death. In air raids he walked through Paris streets, infirm, spectral, huddled in his fur-lined coat (apparently he suffered from chronic hypothermia), taking a calm spectator's interest in the proceedings. Like other brave men, he enjoyed a new face of danger. And, like other men who had run through the repertory of sensations, he seems at times to have enjoyed, with a voyeur's interest, a new face of sex. The scene of M. de Charlus being whipped in Jupien's homosexual brothel wasn't invented; it was something he had watched. It is now known that he had financed that brothel, and got a spectator's interest out of it. Just as he did out of the killing of rats.

In his magnificent biography, George Painter tells us of these distractions with passionate and poetic regret, seeing Proust simultaneously climbing to the loftiest level of his art and also, in Painter's phrase, descending to the pit of Sodom, his life maybe atoned through art, but only there. That is a possible rendering. But one feels that the jeering observer over Marcel's shoulder in *A la Recherche,* and of course in life, may have taken a less romantic view.

In those last years, there was also, and taking up far more of his time than those visits to Jupien's establishment, a resumption of his social life, though in a singularly eccentric form. His self-will, as has been suggested, had become inordinate. He was hypersensitive to others' feelings, but he didn't see why those others shouldn't accommodate their habits to his, even if they did seem a trifle unusual. Here his capacity for the *faux naïf* came in useful. He would arrive in a taxi at a friend's house in the small hours, and express indignation that the place was dark and that there was no one to welcome him. That must have been one of the jeering observer's gibes. He invited people around to his apartment in the middle of the night, and treated them to fried potatoes (Céleste had many virtues, but skill at cooking was not one of them) and cider or iced beer. He seems not to have drunk wine or to have cared about it. He took to giving dinner parties at the Ritz at hours that only he could bribe the staff to keep. He wore his fur-lined coat, and didn't eat.

The Ritz put up with anything he did, and had solid financial reasons for doing so. His friends and admirers put up with anything also, just because of the aura of his personality, and in those last years because of his fame. Perhaps it is worth remembering, though it tends to diminish the magic, that pure self-will tends to get its own way, if it is firm and shameless enough. Writers insignificant by the side of Proust have managed to get people around them to accept similar inconveniences.

His real existence was in his austere bedroom with his proofs and manuscripts. He still wanted the time to make *A la Recherche* as perfect as he imagined it. He was getting weaker, his lungs were failing at last. One night Céleste, sleepless by the sickbed, copied in her firm strong hand

passages from his shaking one, adding them to the manuscript of *Albertine disparue*. He died the next day, November 18, 1922. At the funeral, Barrès remarked, "Well,
he was our young man."

Barrès had been the bitterest of enemies in the Dreyfus
time, but they had become reconciled and it was a good
thing to say. Despite all that happened to him, there was
unquenchable youth in Proust to the end. *A la Recherche*
has intense wisdom, but it is a young man's wisdom. As
with Stendhal, the book is best read—for the first time,
that is—in one's early twenties. Then one gets the full en-
velopment of a work of art that, much more than any
single book of any great writer, is inseparable from the
man himself.

It is more than a rhetorical flourish to say that the
book really was his life. We shouldn't be much interested
in him if he hadn't written *A la Recherche*. We should
have been interested in some writers if they had not produced their major works or (as with Dickens, Dostoevsky,
Tolstoy) any literary works at all. Our only interest in
Proust, however, would have been if he had been entered
in medical records as an unusual clinical case, and people
had disagreed about the etiology. But, after reading *A la
Recherche,* we are as close to Proust as to any novelist, perhaps too close to see clearly.

He himself had a young man's passion to see through
falsity. No one could have had a harder eye for nonsense.
The book is invigorating, not lowering, because of the
power of intellect and feeling with which he demolishes his
own false romantic hopes. Yet he is left with one indomitable surging hope—in art.

That is, of course, as romantic as the ones he has dismissed. In the reflections of the narrator as he decides to justify himself through a work of art, and in the sonorous cadences at the end of the novel, the reader is swept along with him. It takes an effort to remind oneself that the relentless scrutiny that saw through so many human illusions would have been equally destructive if applied to this. If Proust had lived as long as Tolstoy, would he still have believed in salvation through art?

Salvation by art was not an original idea of Proust's. It had begun in the early 1800s and by 1890 had become a cult. It was in the air of Proust's period, but it may have been for him a special faith. This is one of the places where we are too close to him. He wanted a personal salvation; that is certain. Whether he really believed in art as in a universal testament is less certain. We probably ought to be skeptical as he was skeptical. Remember, he had the acutest nose for aesthetic form. He inhabited any kind of experience, but for his art he needed outlines, envelopes, to contain it. Because he hadn't found such forms for *Jean Santeuil,* he kept it secret, abandoning years of work. In *A la Recherche* he found his form. Salvation through art was a splendid formal end. How far he would have been prepared to defend it, if examined by his own ruthless eye, is another matter.

The same is true of his formal use of involuntary memory. Yes, such memories shape the book, and no one in his aesthetic senses would dispense with them. People innocent of idealist philosophy, and particularly of the kind that Bergson was teaching in Proust's period, swallow them whole. They do their work. Proust was a great master. But, since he was a great master, they deserve a slightly more rigorous glance.

There are several of those involuntary memories, carefully distributed. The occasions that invoked three of them are these. One is the taste of the madeleine, recalling with supreme actuality the Eden of childhood. The second is the slip of a foot on a curb in Paris, recalling the Baptistry in St. Mark's. The third is a knife tinkling on a plate, recalling the sound of hammers on train wheels during a journey to Balbec.

They are presented as though identical in force and emotional impact; they bring back, with a kind of three-fold symmetry, time lost, and then regained, through these chances of memory. That is marvelously contrived, but it is contrived. Taste—that is, the madeleine—or smell, which is effectively the same thing, is incomparably more powerful in touching memory beyond the will than is any other stimulus. That is the experience of any human being who has ever reported, and there is no reason to imagine that Proust was different in kind. The other two of the Proustian cases, if they touched deep memory at all, would require considerable encouragement, and for the sake of Proust's formal patterns were actually given considerable literary encouragement.

Without the formal patterns, though, *A la Recherche* wouldn't capture us as it does. Even the skeptical surrender. And even the skeptical accept, and willingly, that there couldn't be a more rigorous treatment of jealousy than in Swann or the narrator. The sensuous richness is such that one half escapes the rigorous analytical truth, and then has to think again.

The sensuous richness sometimes obscures one of his greatest psychological gifts, which is his percipience about the future of a personality. He lets us see one of his people early on, and has absolute certainty as to how the person's future is already present within him. That is one of the greatest and rarest psychological gifts, impossible without immediate insight, but transcending insight. Think of Bloch, vulgar, exhibitionist, without taste, but with gigantic gusto; it is predetermined that he is going to make it. That isn't thrust upon us, but it sinks in and we see Bloch now and then over half a lifetime. Think of Madame Verdurin. She, too, is vulgar in her fashion, often absurd, but underneath she has great resources of character. Again, it isn't thrust upon us, but we ought to realize that she is a good judge of people and a better judge of talent. In a changing society she is not going to be possible to stop. Compare the Verdurin parties with those of the Veneerings in *Our Mutual Friend*. There are signs that Proust may have read *Our Mutual Friend*. Saniette has what may be more than a chance resemblance to Twemlow. The comparison gives us a sense of Proust's untiring subtlety about his people and, often half-concealed by the fun and the mimicry, his eye for the truth. He had more temptations to decorate, embellish, overromanticize the truth than most writers have, because he had so many other gifts, and gifts that sometimes cut across each other. But, when he was investigating his people, his conscience was as hard as a good scientist's, and that is why he tells us so much.

The present writer wishes to make a statement of his own. He has made some quibbles about *A la Recherche*. But, if he were asked to select one Western work of literature written in the twentieth century, there would not be any doubt. This would be the one.

EPILOGUE

WHAT conclusions can we draw from the lives and works of the great realistic masters? It isn't very helpful to discover that they were nearly all very short fat men, uncommonly bad at mathematics (exceptions—as to height, Galdós; as to mathematics, Stendhal).

After all, there have been plenty of short fat men, even including short fat men not good at mathematics, but not many have been splendid realistic writers. It may be slightly more useful to be reminded of one or two simple truths that emerge, I think, from the text. These were great writers; but great writers are also writers, and suffer from the occupational hazards and weaknesses of their profession. We have seen them behaving exactly like other writers, having to shape their work to fit the publishing needs of their time, often doing work they shouldn't have done because of need for money, and sometimes behaving with distinguished unscrupulousness.

Further, great writers, as well as being like other writers, are also like other men. None of these could be regarded as an exemplar for other human lives—certainly not Tolstoy, for all his striving after sanctity. It is probably more difficult for great writers to become moral exemplars than for most other men. Einstein used to say that he would rather have written *The Brothers Karamazov* than have achieved any other creative act, including his own. But, if he had done so, he wouldn't have been able to rid himself, as in his own life he did, of so many of the fallibilities of ordinary human beings. A great writer has to live with the worst side of his nature as well as the best. It doesn't make for an easy life, or often for a harmonious one. If learning about them teaches us nothing else, it ought to teach us that.

Finally, there is one question that is difficult to avoid. Would it be possible to write such realistic novels today? Will it be possible again? I am not sure that I feel able to give an optimistic answer. I have deliberately said nothing about realistic novels in our own time. We are not in a position to get recent literature in perspective, and it is one of the real morals of literary history that instant opinions are nearly always wrong. Any literary pundit should have a little placard above his desk reminding him that Sainte-Beuve lived at the same time as Stendhal, Balzac, Flaubert, and Baudelaire, and thought very little of any of them. As a provisional guess I should suggest that the social conditions of the advanced societies of the West aren't at all suitable for the writing of great realistic novels. From what we can deduce of the past and from the writers in this book, the best conditions appear to be an untidy but energetic social life around one; a public that may be quite small but is ready to respond, appreciate, and believe that such novels are really worth studying and cherishing; and, above all, hope, social and individual, somewhere in the future. Western societies, or at least some of them, possess the first of these conditions, but not the other two. I hope that I am wrong, but it seems to me that as a consequence the chances are against us. On the other hand, I am quite certain that the realistic novel is a wonderful form of art, and at its height has produced some of the richest literature so far known to man. In both depth and amplitude, it has been able to do things that no other literary art can touch. So I believe that, though it may be quiescent in the West, it is almost certain to rise again—in other societies at different stages of development from ours, maybe altered and refreshed by different cultural histories. I might take the risk of saying that I suspect there are already signs of this, but to justify that I should have to write another book.